Caffeine Ni

C000177119

White Lilies

RC Bridgestock

Published by Caffeine Nights Publishing 2013

Published in Great Britain by Caffeine Nights Publishing

www. caffeine-nights com

British Library Cataloguing in Publication Data.
A CIP catalogue record for this book is available from the British Library

ISBN: 978-1-907565-33-5

Cover design by
Mark (Wills) Williams

Everything else by
Default, Luck and Accident

Acknowledgements

Thank you to Emily & Maisy Murphy and to Kate Young & Matthew for your kind contributions to Jen's pregnancy story line and the subsequent birth storyline of Maisy Dylan.

Also to our publisher Darren Laws and Literary Agent Monika Luukkonen for their continued hard work, dedication and their belief in the Dylan series. Not forgetting Mark (Wills) Williams for once again producing the most excellent art work for the 'White Lilies' cover.

And last but not least for the support of our family & friends, the Wight Fair Writers Circle, the other authors in the stable at Caffeine Nights Publishing and Betty Jordan (Carol's Mum) for the tea, cakes, Sunday dinners and doing the odd load of ironing – we couldn't have done it without you.

Dedication

We dedicate this book to all our readers with our love, appreciation, and thanks for allowing us to be part of your lives. We hope that you will get to know a little more about one Senior Investigative Officer's real thoughts and feelings through reading the DI Dylan series of fictional tales.

And with love to our grandchildren Axel Maldini, Hermione Vegas Bridgestock and latest addition, Annabelle Rene Beckwith.

The D.I. Dylan Books

Deadly Focus
Consequences

White Lilies

Chapter 1

Today was one of mixed emotions for Grace Harvey as she sipped the Earl Grey from her china cup and admired the beautiful white lilies that sat on the corner of the dining table, where she'd left them after the florist's delivery a few moments earlier. Dancing above the floral arrangement was a helium balloon attached to a silver coloured ribbon. '80 Today', it read.

She wiped her hands upon her crisp linen napkin briskly before reaching for the small hand-written envelope nestling within the flowers. She opened it, placed the card on the table before her breakfast plate and put her glasses on the end of her nose to read the small writing thereon. 'From Brian', it said.

Staring beyond the card onto the front lawn, Grace swallowed the lump in her throat and sighed. With tears in her eyes, she put the card back in its envelope and her glasses on the linen tablecloth beside the condiments. When was she going to learn? Why did she let herself carry on hoping that one day her only child would remember such an important milestone? He was out of the country the last time they'd spoken and as usual he'd asked her for money. In fact between them, Donald and Brian were going through her savings like a dose of salts, as Alfred, her late husband, would have said.

'Well, I can't take it with me now can I?' she said out loud. 'One day it'll all be his anyway – and who knows, perhaps the money will make him happy for a while.' Brian, her friend and financial advisor, regularly said so, when he advised her to buy or top up her investment funds.

'Donald might ring later,' she said to Winston, her King Charles spaniel, who placed his head on her knee, knowingly. She smiled down at him. The arthritis in her spine wouldn't allow her to bend so easily to stroke his head, so she blew him a kiss. Seeing the acknowledgement of her action on his cute little face made her feel a bit brighter. The old dog cocked his head, looked at her lovingly, then closed his big brown eyes.

'What would I do without you?' she whispered.

Alfred had brought Winston home unexpectedly from his nightly constitutional, just before he died.

'What was I supposed to do, leave him tied to the tree?' she remembered him saying when she'd met him with a scowl. Alfred's baby blue eyes, framed with grey brows that flew out like wings, had been close to tears as he handed her a note that confirmed the puppy had been abandoned. He adored animals. She had always been unsure about having a dog, but Grace shuddered at the thought of her life without Winston now. Winston moaned contentedly and settled comfortingly on her foot.

'We miss them both don't we?' she said as she brushed away a tear that had fallen from the corner of her aged eye and onto her rosy weather-worn cheek.

Grace had lived in the same house in the quiet hamlet of Merton all her life. Yorkshire stone-built houses, just like hers, surrounded the village green, which was the centrepiece of this tranquil village community.

The Westminster clock that had been presented to Alfred on his retirement struck ten o'clock. She turned and read the inscription on the brass plaque that bore his name, pulled a hanky from her sleeve, leaned forward and gently dusted the metal until it shone brightly.

'Time for our walk,' she groaned, easing herself up from the chair. Winston instantly jumped at her words and, yapping persistently, he ran to the front door. She stood for a moment with her hand on the corner of the table until she felt a little steadier and put her hanky in her cardigan pocket.

Grace picked up her lipstick from the Welsh dresser in the hallway as she passed. Leaning forward on tiptoes to see her reflection in the mirror, she ran the pink gloss expertly around her lips. Smoothing her white wavy hair with the palm of her hand, she picked up her hat and popped it on her head. She collected her coat from behind the door, bent down for her smart black patent court shoes under the umbrella stand and picked up her gloves.

Winston's lead and the bag of bread she'd prepared earlier for the ducks were hanging on the door handle. Although it was summer there was a cool breeze she had noticed this morning whilst she'd stepped out to take the eggs from the milkman.

'Right little man, are we ready for off?' she said to Winston with gusto as she reached for the catch on the door. He didn't need asking twice as he darted ahead down the pathway, sat obediently at the wrought iron garden gate and waited patiently with a flurry of his wagging tail.

The locals had been known to say that you could set your watch by Grace and Winston's constitutional. Theirs was a slow stroll around the green, incorporating the mandatory stop at the pond before calling at the village shop for the daily paper. Grace did so look forward to doing the crossword with her elevenses. For her birthday present, Brian had booked a table for them both at a restaurant in the nearby town of Harrowfield.

'We'll give the ducks a bit extra bread today Winston, since it's a special day,' Grace said, chuckling as she struggled to break the bread with her bent and swollen fingers. Winston wagged his tail as he looked on from the grass banking at the side of the pond trying his best to intercept the bread between his owner's hand and the duck's beak. She laughed at his antics. He'd never caught a piece yet, but still he tried, bless him.

'Now,' she said putting the bread wrapper in the bin, 'it's time to visit Mr and Mrs Taylor at the store. I think I'll bake a cake,' she said as they stopped at the roadside. Grace looked right then left. Winston sat at her feet and waited patiently for her command. Grace tugged at his lead.

'Come on Winston,' she demanded as she stepped onto the road but he refused. 'What's up little man?' she asked. 'Don't be stubborn.' Grace plucked him up from the kerb and tucked him safely under her arm with a little effort. 'If you want some cake we'll have to get the ingredients,' she scolded, tapping his nose as she crossed the road.

Suddenly she heard music. She froze. The speeding vehicle didn't slow or swerve to avoid them. Grace and Winston were catapulted into the air and tossed into the gutter. The car disappeared as quickly as it had arrived. The noise that had spewed from it became inaudible in seconds.

Time seemed to stand still as Grace and Winston's crumpled bodies lay motionless on the tarmac. An eerie silence swelled across the green like a creeping mist. Villagers slowly started to emerge from their dwellings to see what the commotion had been. On seeing the bodies, some people ran to Grace's side. Others were too stunned, but there was nothing anyone could do. Mr Taylor shouted at his wife to bring blankets and call 999 as he bent over the bodies.

'Road Closed,' were the signs the young police constable and his mentor PC Tim Whitworth took from the boot of their marked police car.

PC Whitworth could see the villagers congregated in groups, watching. Some were being comforted by others. All had shock written across their faces.

'How could the car driver not have seen them?' he heard them say. 'The road's straight. There're warning signs in the village to Reduce Speed – Twenty's plenty.'

'Scenes of Crime Officers are on their way,' the younger officer said, hearing the whispers as he started the painstaking task of putting out traffic cones and the police incident tape to protect the scene.

But what could the witnesses tell the police? Very little; some heard music, others a thud. All of them heard the silence.

'A fatal road accident. Driver failed to stop. Sadly an everyday occurrence,' PC Whitworth told Mr Taylor, who brought the officer a hot, sweet drink.

'You don't happen to have a biscuit do you?' PC Whitworth asked as he took the mug from Mr Taylor.

'Err, I'm sure I can find one,' he said.

'Chocolate are my favourite,' the officer called to the retreating shopkeeper, as he stood slurping his tea and perusing the scene. The officer had already decided how this fatal accident was to be written up on the accident report and subsequently for the inquest.

OLD LADY STEPS INTO ROAD IN FRONT OF ONCOMING VEHICLE. DRIVER UNABLE TO AVOID COLLISION.

In his experience of traffic accidents, he would expect the driver to contact the police after a press appeal.

PC Tim Whitworth walked over to a bench and sat down. Scanning the village green with an expert eye, he'd just started to write up the scene notes in his pocket book when he heard footsteps approaching him and looked up.

'Ah, chocolate Hobnobs, my favourites,' the officer said, as Mr Taylor opened the packet.

'Would you care for one?' Mr Taylor said, offering him a biscuit.

'Too true,' PC Whitworth said with a grin as he took the packet. He removed one from the top, stuck it in his mouth and placed the rest in his overcoat pocket. Mr Taylor stood with his mouth open.

'Well, if I can be of any further assistance, I'll be in the shop,' he said huffily, and turned to leave the officer to his work.

'Just a minute.'

'Yes.'

'Another brew wouldn't go amiss,' said PC Whitworth as he drained his mug.

Mr Taylor grabbed the drinking vessel from the Officer's outstretched arm and, shaking his head, he walked at a pace back to the store. His old friend Grace and her dog Winston still lay in the road covered with nothing but a flimsy piece of plastic and PC Whitworth was acting as if he was on a picnic. What was the world coming to?

Detective Inspector Jack Dylan was sitting in his office unable to concentrate on his work. This was a rare occasion when Dylan pushed his work to the back of his mind as he thought about the future. He couldn't believe that he, of all people, was to become a member of the exclusive club of parenthood, although it hadn't been planned.

Dylan had promised Jen that her antenatal appointments were dates that work would definitely not interfere with. So far so good, but experience of life with Dylan told Jen not to hold her breath. Jen had never known when she said goodbye to him in the morning if she would see him again that day or even that week.

There was no reason for her to believe that being pregnant would change Dylan's attitude and dedication to the job he'd lived for, for the past twenty years. He'd spent long adrenalin-fuelled hours at incidents, some unforeseen, others pre-planned. Neither could he ascertain how long the enquiries to the incidents would take. Luckily for him, she understood that he was doing an important job, investigating serious crime and putting dangerous criminals behind bars. His job meant total commitment and she accepted that, because not only did she love him and it made him happy, but other people's lives depended on him.

However, she still got angry and lonely sometimes. After all, she was only human. She worried how she would feel when the baby came along.

Jen worked in the admin department at the police station, which is where they'd met. Being in situ she would hear when a job came in and Dylan would call into the office with regular updates, but once junior was on the scene she would be at home, away from it all, and alone. She missed her mum, but Jen had to be practical. Her mum and dad would have been on the Isle of Wight, three hundred and sixty miles, away even if her mum hadn't been killed last year.

She realised now that when you lost your mum, you joined a band of people that no one wants to belong to. Her mum would never see her grandchild and the baby would never know what it was like to have her granny's love. Jen ran her hand over her stomach and she felt a rhythmic twitch in her uterus. She giggled as tears pricked her eyes. Their baby had hiccupped.

Jen's phone bleeped and it brought her out of her reverie but she took a moment to remember how happy her mum would have wanted her to be and it stopped her tears flowing.

Missing you x, Dylan had texted.

Miss you more, she texted back.

Jen smiled broadly at DS Vicky Hardacre who was sat opposite her at the duty clerk's desk checking the CID rota. 'You look like the cat that's got the cream.'

'About as pleased as you when you found out you'd got the overtime to get your implants done,' she said with a chuckle.

Vicky grinned. 'Good God, that happy?' said the blonde haired detective who worked with Dylan.

'I had to go to Mothercare on my way to work to get a larger size bra today,' Jen whispered. 'My boobs have grown a cup size already. Look at the size of this.' Jen said throwing a plastic bag over the desk to Vicky.

'Oh, wow.' she said, pulling the nursing bra from within.

'Look, I can fit me whole face in one of the cups.'
The pair laughed out loud.

'Well, it's official. I'm getting fat,' Jen sighed.

'At least maternity gear now isn't frumpy. Middle-aged rags they used to be,' said Vicky. 'I'd even wear some of it. You gonna try hide your bump?'

'Bit late for that isn't it?' Jen said, looking down at her prominent bulge.

The Divisional Administrator's office door opened and Avril Summerfield-Preston stepped out.

Jen's laughter faded as she grabbed the bra and the bag and stuffed it under her desk.

Avril Summerfield-Preston was nicknamed 'Beaky' because of the size of her nose. She was an extremely prickly and unpredictable character with an alarming reputation, a caustic manner and looks that could sometimes curdle milk. Her partner was the Divisional Commander, Dylan's boss Hugo Watkins, which suited her perfectly. He was self-loving, vain and egotistic and the bane of Dylan's life. Having but a few years in the job, he thought he should be Chief Constable.

'Meeting of the Health and Safety Committee in ten minutes Jennifer and I want you to take the notes,' she ordered before tottering back into her office in her ill-fitting high-heeled shoes. 'We can't all be swanning off for the afternoon.'

Vicky burst out laughing.

'I'm sure she's a bloody witch,' she said, sticking her tongue out at the closing door.

'Shush … she'll hear you and then she won't let me go,' Jen said, grimacing at her friend.

'She's so far up her backside she'll get stuck one of these days if she's not careful,' Vicky said loudly.

Jen sniggered. 'Shhh.'

'Where you off to anyway?'

'The hospital for a check-up.'

'Sounds like fun, or not,' Vicky said, screwing up her nose.

'Last time we went the baby was a right little imp, it wouldn't move so the sonographer couldn't get his measurements. No amount of prodding, poking, moving around, emptying my bladder or eating sugary foods would get him to shift.'

'Lazy, must be a boy.'

'That's what we think,' Jen smiled contentedly.

'Is Dylan going with you?'

'He says so, work permitting but since last time the appointment took an hour instead of twenty minutes, it might have put him off,' Jen said, tutting as she raised her eyebrows at Avril's door opening once again.

'Jennifer …' she called.

Chapter 2

'She shouldn't be allowed out alone at her age. If it hadn't been for her we would have done the ton through Merton today,' Danny Denton yelled, throwing the full force of his six foot, lanky frame behind the kick to his front tyre.

'Look what she's fucking done.' he shrieked, rubbing his grimy hands over his skinhead. 'I'm going to have to get a new light casing now,' he said with a groan.

'Stupid bitch.'

Billy Greenwood, Danny's mate, passed him his roll-up. 'Have a drag. We'd better wash that shit off,' he said pointing to the blood on the wing.

'I thought the silly cow were gonna come through the bastard windscreen,' Danny said before drawing deeply on the cigarette. 'Good job she didn't, I'd have fucking killed her.'

Billy sniggered. 'You fucking moron. You probably did.'

'Oh yeah,' Danny said with a snort.

'Did you see her fly through the air, Danny?' Billy said in awe of their elderly victim's flexibility.

'Yeah,' he said with a swagger. 'We'd better get down the scrappers tonight though before the plods come sniffing round.' Danny added, clipping the back of Billy's head and handing him back his cigarette.

Danny fitted the light casing they'd acquired from the scrap yard next morning as Billy polished the car. Danny leaned in to turn on the radio. The news was on and instantly there was an appeal for witnesses to the fatal accident in Merton. He shouted Billy as he lunged forward to turn up the volume. 'Fuck,' he cried.

'How old?' Billy asked.

'Eighty, told you she shouldn't have been out on her own.'

Billy laughed so much his mop of blonde curly hair fell onto his face. He pushed it back with his tattoo-covered hand.

Their wheels back to normal; Danny drove the red Ford Fiesta with its sports tyres out of the garage and into the sunshine.

'Hey Danny, why don't we put a line on the wing like pilots used to do on their planes when they shot down the enemy?' Billy said eagerly, his eyes bright, dimples evident on his cheeky, fresh face.

Danny showed his yellow, nicotine-stained teeth in a grin. 'Let's make it two. We got the dog as well,' he laughed.

Billy picked up the tape from the bench and threw it to Danny. With his tongue between his teeth he concentrated hard as he applied it. Satisfied his masterpiece was well and truly stuck, they jumped into the car.

'Time for cruising Billy Boy,' Danny shouted as the turn of the car key brought the engine to life with a roar.

'Harrowfield High here we come,' shouted Billy above the rev of the engine.

Music thumped out into the afternoon sky as Danny steered the car up to the traffic lights. Pulling their hoods up to hide their identities, they laughed raucously. The pavement seemed to vibrate beneath the shop assistant's feet as she stood arranging flowers in buckets outside her shop. She looked over her glasses and stared at the car's occupants.

'Bloody lunatics,' was the mumblings of a young man wearing a wool hat, who grabbed a bunch out of her hand and ran off.

'Hey,' she called out, looking around for someone to help but the only thing in sight was the car, poised like a wild tiger about to pounce as the engine struggled to wait for a green light. Suddenly its tyres screeched and the smell of burning rubber filled the air. *What was the world coming to?* she thought as the smoke hit the back of her throat and she hurried back inside her shop with her hand over her mouth, coughing.

Danny drove a car as if he was playing a computer game, with no regard to safety. Their vehicle was legal, taxed and insured and although the police regularly stopped them, the boys were always confident they couldn't be touched. The local police knew their Modus Operandi was for thieving. They had been caught siphoning fuel from the villagers' cars, reported and charged for robbing houses, screwing garden sheds and selling the proceeds to car booters to raise quick cash. That and their hand-outs from the government was how they survived. Their young, free and single existence held no regard for man nor beast.

On school days they could usually be found hovering around the gates of the high school, like vultures. Today was no different. They would get some un-streetwise girl or impressionable boy to buy them chips from the van or con them out of cash for beer and cigarettes.

The young girls seemed to find them attractive and the boys thought they were exciting. To the youngsters, the pair seemed to have it all with their souped-up wheels. Forbidden fruit in this case was every parent's worst nightmare.

Chapter 3

'Welcome to the office and congratulations on making Detective Sergeant,' Dylan said as he realised his new DS was standing at his door. He had forgotten it was today she was starting work in the office.

'I'm so pleased I got sent to work with you,' she smiled flirtatiously at Dylan.

Taylor Spiers was a single 29-year-old woman who had been in the Police for nine years – and a Detective for four of them in a neighbouring town. She was doing well in comparison with some of her colleagues who continually threw their hat in the ring at the promotion boards.

Jack Dylan hadn't a great deal of knowledge about his new DS but he had heard she was a capable cop who loved the job. He'd heard rumours about her, but how much of that was true or pure fantasy by the men on the shift Dylan could only speculate. Looking at her now, he could see Taylor was definitely a stunner and he was in no doubt she would certainly brighten up the office.

Jack remembered telling Jen she was joining his team.

'Oh, Taylor Spiers, she'll eat you alive,' she'd chuckled, but wouldn't give any further explanation. Dylan was intrigued. He really should start listening to the girls' gossip instead of turning a deaf ear.

'I've got your first job here Taylor,' Dylan told her. 'If you fancy a run out, we'll give it the detective's overview together. What do you say?'

'Sounds good to me,' she replied with a smile.

'It's a hit and run fatal at Merton, happened yesterday. It'll give us chance to have chat about the office and the detectives on your team.'

'Great,' she said picking up her coat and designer bag. 'A measly hit and run?' she mumbled to herself, pulling a face as she walked away.

'Ten minutes, if you want to cast your eye over the police officer's report,' he called.

Within the hour they were walking by the side of Merton village green. Flowers and messages had been laid at the roadside at the spot where Grace and Winston had died.

'The accident investigators found some glass at the scene, but whether that was to do with the accident remains to be seen. Hopefully, we may get a make and model of the type of car involved; if so it would be a start,' said Dylan, as he crouched down to read some of the tributes.

'Do you want me to do an intelligence sheet for any stolen cars found abandoned with similar damage, or burnt out?' asked Taylor.

'Yeah, that'd be a good start – and let's put an early warning around local garages and scrapyards, should someone enquire about repairing a headlight or be looking to purchase a similar item.'

They strolled across to the little village grocery store where Dylan, like the gentleman he was, held the door open into the café for Taylor. Dylan was impressed that she had dressed to make an impression on her first day but looking her up and down he noticed how impractical her high-heeled shoes were as he followed her to the counter.

It reminded him of when he'd been a new Detective Inspector and been taken by his boss to view a body. It had been raining. The body had been found on moorland and he had been wearing his new light grey suit, which he could ill afford. Bought on credit; it had ended up ruined and so had his leather shoes. Returning to the office covered in mud, his boss had handed him a pair of Wellingtons with some advice.

'Always be prepared lad, unless you want to look stupid,' he'd said, smugly.

The bosses had been bastards in those days, Dylan thought smiling to himself. But it was a lesson he never forgot. As for his suit, thankfully it dry-cleaned okay.

'My golden rule Taylor; always visit the scene. See it for yourself, no matter how well you think you know the area.'

DS Spiers hung on his every word, nodding in agreement. Taking notes when appropriate.

'If the scene is outside, visit it at the same time of day that the incident occurred if you can, that way you'll get a better feel for it and see what usually happens at the time the incident took place.'

'I won't let you down boss,' she said eagerly.

'I know you won't Taylor. I'll make sure of that,' he said smiling at her young, sombre face.

'A bit more advice,' he continued.

'Yes boss,' she said, sitting up straight and leaning towards him with a serious expression on her face.

'Buy a practical pair of shoes to keep in the boot of your car,' he said looking down at her strappy high heels.

'Yes, sir,' she said with a blush spreading across her face as she uncrossed her bare legs and tucked them neatly under the table. The two waited for their drinks order to be brought to the table while Dylan went through the necessary lines of enquiry for the road death.

They looked over at the village green. 'What can the accident investigators tell us?' Then he stopped himself. 'Sorry, I'm teaching you how to suck eggs,' he smiled. 'But somebody was responsible for Grace's death and something I despise is when the perpetrator gets away or shows no remorse,' he sighed. 'But, Sarge, I'm sure you're quite capable of sorting this one.' Dylan said, leaning back in his chair.

Taylor grinned. She liked being called Sarge, but this case was hardly the gory, high-profile murder she hoped for. She looked at Dylan thoughtfully as they drove back in the direction of the nick and wondered if he fancied her. He was a bit old she thought but he wasn't that bad for his age.

'Right let's get back to it; you've a crime to detect and, who knows, it could be a murder.' Dylan said, turning to face her with his smiling eyes.

Yeah, he definitely liked her, she decided.

'I suppose so,' she replied sitting on her hands as she grinned up at him. 'But this one's a bit boring isn't it?' she said, screwing up her face.

'Boring,' screeched Dylan. 'Some poor old dear has been killed and you think the investigation is boring?'

'Well yeah, but who'd want to murder a little old lady and her dog?'

'If you investigate it properly who knows, maybe you'll find out.' he shook his head.

'Never assume anything, my girl. Always look for what the evidence tells you. Then, and only then, can you make an informed decision.'

Taylor sat pondering his words in silence for the rest of the journey. Was she going to like working under Dylan after all if he thought this was a meaty case?

Chapter 4

Pam Forrester was just thirteen, but like most of the girls her age she had the figure of a sixteen-year-old. Her mum, Stephanie, had been a model in her younger days, long before she'd married Pam's Dad, Bill, a dentist and she had to take on a more stable career of a florist. She would like nothing more than for her daughter to follow in her footsteps, which is why she worked so hard. 'The Flowerpot Emporium' would hopefully one day fund that dream.

Pam was the apple of her dad's eye. Like most daughters, she had the ability and the know-how to get what she wanted – and boy, did she milk it. Saying that, Pam was a good student, keen at most sports and loved horse riding. Her parents were rightly proud of her.

However, lately they had noticed that boys were becoming increasingly interesting to her and one boy in particular stood out from the crowd for Pam: his name was Danny Denton. Her crush on him was the first secret she'd ever kept from her mum.

Pam knew instinctively that her parents wouldn't approve. Daily she watched Danny pull up outside the school gates in his car and each time she saw him her heart would miss a beat, she'd become breathless and her legs would turn to jelly. Was that a sign of being in love, she wondered?

Pam saw older girls run out of school and climb into the back of his car and all she could do was watch and envy them. As far as she knew, Danny didn't know she was alive; but then why would he? She was just a kid.

Pam had thought long and hard of a plan to get herself noticed by him and started to put her ideas into action. She rolled up the waistband on her school skirt, which allowed everyone to see the shapely long legs that she confirmed to herself using the mirror in the girl's changing rooms. She decided to borrow her mum's expensive mascara and lip gloss from her make-up case. This didn't appear to be working, so, in desperation, she stepped out in front of his car. That got her noticed. Slamming on his brakes didn't appear to upset Danny and instead of screaming abuse at her like any 'normal' road rage driver, he simply smiled at her and waved her to the pavement.

He had a nice smile, she thought dreamily as she'd walked home that day. But Pam was impatient and wasn't content with a smile, she wanted more. She'd been an observer for far too long. Some of the students called the girls that got into Danny's car 'slags', but she knew they were only jealous.

Pam walked home sometimes with Leanne Gray. Leanne was in the sixth form and Pam only knew her because she worked at the flower shop for her mum on a Saturday. She hung around with a group of girls who talked to Danny and his friend and she couldn't miss the opportunity of discovering more about him. Whatever it took to get to know him she'd decided she would do, even if Leanne wasn't really her type.

Danny and his friend Billy screeched up alongside them one day causing a dust cloud. Pam's heart pounded and her head was in a spin. What would she say to him if he spoke to her?

'Ignore them,' Leanne said as she quickened her pace. She blanked Danny and Billy as the car crawled along beside them. Pam was transfixed as she trailed behind her companion. Danny leaned across the front of Billy and shouted through the open window. 'Legs, d'you want a ride?'

God, was he speaking to her? Well she wasn't being awful but there was no way they could say that to Leanne ... Yes, he had noticed her. Before she knew it, Danny had stopped the car some yards ahead. Billy had got out and was holding the door open inviting her to get in.

'Come on, don't take any notice,' Leanne told her as she walked on. 'They're nothing but trouble.'

But Pam didn't listen; in fact she couldn't believe her luck. Am I dreaming? She thought as she clambered into the backseat of the car in a trance like state?

'They're bad news,' Leanne shouted. She desperately banged on the window. Danny put his foot on the accelerator. Leanne's words were drowned by the noise and all Pam could see as she looked out of the car window was Leanne's wide-open mouth. She looked to be calling her name.

Pam had been waiting for this moment for so long. She smiled and a warm rush of adrenalin shot through her body. The only downside was there didn't appear to be a crowd watching; no one to envy her. She could feel her cheeks burning as Danny held her gaze in the rear view mirror. Her heart was hammering in her chest. This was what she dreamt of.

Danny steered the car expertly around tight bends as they drove at speed into the countryside. It caused her to roll from side to side on the backseat and she laughed out loud. It was like being on a waltzer at the funfair. She had no idea where they were going, but who cared? Nothing else mattered at this moment in time except she was in Danny's car having fun.

'What's your name, Legs?' said Billy, turning to look at her over his headrest.

'Pamela, err ... Pam,' she stuttered.

'How old are you?' Billy said, as Danny held her gaze for a few moments in the mirror.

'Sixteen,' she said not taking her eyes off Danny's. Her heart thumped in her chest. She held her breath.

'Thought you must be, with legs like them,' Danny quipped, turning to wink at his friend.

Pam could feel herself growing redder and redder. He believed her. Billy rolled a cigarette and lit it. There was a pungent smell.

'Want a drag?' he said, passing it back to her.

'Sure' she said, with a confidence she didn't feel. Never having smoked before, she puffed on the spliff, coughed and quickly handed it back. Its aroma made her feel nauseous. Suddenly she felt the car swerve and Danny pulled off the road and into a car park. The tyres crushed the layer of thick gravel and slowed the car down.

The car came to a halt and Pam looked at her surroundings. As far as the eye could see, there was nothing but moorland. No people, no cars, no houses. Danny switched off the engine and then the music. The silence rang in her ears. Why had he brought her here, she wondered?

'Isn't it lovely up here, eh Pam?' said Danny, staring out of the window as he tapped the steering wheel.

Pam nodded, not knowing what to say.

'It's really quiet ... nobody bothers you up here, do they Billy?' he said seriously.

'No,' said Billy, taking a drag of the spliff and handing it to Danny who did the same.

'It's our favourite spot, isn't it Billy?' Danny said turning to his mate, who nodded. He turned his head further round to look at Pam and she smiled at him nervously.

Billy turned to look at her too. 'It can be hours before you see anybody up here,' he said, his voice deep and his breathing heavy. His eyes had a fixed stare. Pam fumbled with the hem of her skirt and, tugging at it, she made a useless attempt to try to cover the top of her legs that Billy's eyes were glued to. She looked at Danny for support. Billy was scaring her. Danny stared at her with a silly lopsided smile on his face.

The reality of her situation began to sink in.

Chapter 5

'Grace Harvey might have been a nice old lady, boss, but her son sounds like a right tosser.' Taylor Spiers told Dylan as she walked into his office.

'What makes you say that?' he said, as he looked up from his computer screen. He relaxed back in his chair and with a sweep of his arm, invited Taylor to sit down.

'Donald arrived in Merton yesterday in readiness for her funeral,' she explained. 'And he's already making allegations that his mother's been fleeced. He's told us that he's come across documents that say the house doesn't belong to her any more and he knew nothing of her signing it over and he should have as he's the benefactor in her will. He's also suggesting that his mum's death wasn't an accident. I'm just off to see him.'

'I take it he was expecting to be a beneficiary to an inheritance he ain't gonna get?'

'Yep appears so. I'll see what proof he's got, if he stops shouting long enough to talk to me properly,' she said, grimacing.

'There weren't any problems at the opening of the inquest were there?'

'No, PC Tim Whitworth's evidence was pretty straightforward for a hit and run. He had hoped an appeal in the press might lead to tracing the offending vehicle and its driver but no one came forward admitting responsibility or providing any more information. There was very little evidence left at the scene, but Mr Harvey didn't attend.'

'Keep me updated,' Dylan said, picking up his pen thoughtfully and scribbling a few notes on his blotter.

'Winston will be buried with Grace, the Coroner's officer told me. Don't you think that's sweet?'

'Stop being soft and find out who mowed them down and why,' Dylan grunted as he turned his attention back to his computer screen.

Taylor shrugged her shoulders and left the office.

Dylan picked up his mobile phone when he heard the door close behind her. *Fancy meeting up for dinner? x,* he texted Jen.

Lovely, ☺ she texted back, with a smile on her face.

Will you get the food? My office at 12? X

I have to get the food as well? ☺

'Have they found the driver or the car yet?' Jen asked Dylan as she popped a cherry tomato in her mouth. Dylan, with his mouth full, could only shake his head. He took a sip of his coffee.

'How could anyone leave a person to die like that?' Jen said, taking a bite of her sandwich.

'You shouldn't judge people by your own standards,' he said. 'Whoever did it most likely would have panicked. They might be disqualified driver, a drink driver or drugged up to high heaven. We'll only know that when we trace him or her.'

'Talking of panic I'd better go,' she said, collecting the dirty plates. 'I only get 45 minutes, not like you. Some of us have to clock in and out, otherwise Beaky will have my guts for garters and I can't bear the thought of one of her moods this afternoon,' she said pulling a face.

'Okay love I'll see you later,' he said turning back to his computer screen as Jen stood to leave. He looked up at her. 'What about my kiss?' he asked. Jen leaned over the desk to kiss him.

'You'll get me the sack,' Dylan said with a groan.

'Good then we'll be able to spend all the time together,' she giggled.

He watched her walk to the door.

'Nice bum,' he growled.

She stopped at the doorway, turned and gave him a knowing smile.

'Get back to your work Mr and catch those criminals, otherwise we won't have any pennies to spend on the things we need for junior,' she said patting her stomach. Dylan smiled.

The death of a family member creates all sorts of upset. There are guilt trips. Should I have visited more often? Could I have done something for them? Dylan thought. Jen had coped extremely well since her mum's sudden death but every time there was a fatal accident such as Grace Harvey's he knew it brought it all back. Dylan would love nothing more than to be able to protect Jen from her thoughts but he knew it was impossible. He had to let her work through the grieving process like everyone else.

Vicky put her head around the office door. 'Ah. Nice to see you all loved-up boss,' she grinned at him.

'You don't get round me that easy, lady, what're you after?'

'Nothing, honest I'm just pleased I'm not on the new DS's team.'

'And what's wrong with Taylor Spiers?'

She pulled a face. 'Don't know but there's just sommat about her. Call it women's intuition, whatever, but I can't seem to bring myself to take to her,' she said thoughtfully.

'That's not like you Vicky,' Dylan said to his normally bubbly, friendly DC. 'Anyway, if you concentrated on passing your exams instead of working all hours to save up for your boob jobs, then it could have been you that was my new Sarge.'

'I might shock you one day boss,' she said grinning.

'You do now, regularly,' he laughed.

'Just watch your back, eh,' she said with a wink and nod.

Dylan's phone rang and his telephone manner suggested to Vicky that she should leave him be.

'Okay. I'll be there in about twenty minutes,' she heard him say. 'Keep things sterile, I don't want anything or anybody to cross the line. And when I say no one, I mean no one; do you hear?'

Chapter 6

Pam rummaged around inside her bag and grabbed her ringing phone just before it went onto the answer machine. She looked up into the big, round, staring eyes of a salivating Billy.

'Hi mum, no, no I hadn't forgotten. Yes, at your shop. Bye,' she said through teeth that chattered uncontrollably, she didn't quite know why. It wasn't cold – fear? 'Sorry, I've gotta go. I've got a riding lesson,' she said looking at Danny and then at her watch, 'like in the next fifteen minutes. I'm really sorry,' she grimaced.

Danny turned and started the car engine in silence.

Now he'd be mad with her and there was no chance she would ever be invited again, she conceded.

'Lucky horse,' sniggered Billy as he looked sideways at Danny.

'Where d'you want dropping?' asked Danny, his voice flat and expressionless.

'In the High Street, please.'

'What sort of shop's your mum got?' Danny said as he dragged the car's wheels round in the gravel.

'Flower shop,' she said, quietly.

They travelled in silence and Danny brought his car to a sudden halt in town. Billy appeared to be asleep.

'Thanks,' she said, lurching forward.

'No prob,' he said with a smile. 'I'll see you soon kid.'

Pam saw her mum emerge from the shop and look at her watch. Seeing her, Pam ducked down behind Billy's seat. Billy jumped. 'What,' he shouted as his friend poked him in the ribs.

Danny pointed towards Stephanie. 'Pam's mum,' he drawled.

'So that's where you get your looks from, eh?' said Billy, whistling long and low.

Pam felt her face turn red.

'What's your dad do?' asked Danny.

'He's got a dentist's down the road,' she said her head still tucked behind the seat.

'No way. Dentists freak me out.'

'She gone yet?'

'Yeah, coast clear. You can come out now.'

'Thanks,' she said. 'I've had a nice time.'

Billy stumbled out of the car and pulled the front seat forward for her to alight. He leaned heavily on the open door.

'Like I said, no prob,' Danny told her. 'We're a bit low on petrol; you don't happen to have any cash on you do you?' he said, as she put her foot forward to go.

'I've got a tenner if that's any good?' said Pam flopping unceremoniously back in her seat.

'That'd be good yeah,' he said smiling. 'I wouldn't normally ask but … I'll give it you back next time.'

'Next time?' asked Pam, her heart pumping.

'Yeah, we must do it again some time,' he said holding out his hand. She hesitated as she reached into her schoolbag. Handing Danny the ten-pound note meant their fingers touched, her heart skipped a beat at what felt like an electric current running from his hand to hers. She looked at his face but his eyes were on the money. She wondered if he'd felt it too, he pulled his hand back quickly, taking the ten pound note from her, and leaned forward. Was he going to kiss her? She closed her eyes briefly and leaned towards him.

'You getting out or what?' he said, as he stuffed the note into his pocket. How stupid she was. She got out of the car in a fluster.

'What's your mobile number?' Billy asked. Pam took out a pen and tore a piece of paper from a school book and wrote it down. She handed it to Danny.

'Come on, places to go people to see,' Danny said, tapping his foot slightly on the accelerator, which made the engine purr.

Pam stood back as Billy jumped in the car and Danny pulled away from the kerb with a screech. With a long, loud sounding of the car's horn they sped away, leaving her standing on the kerb watching them till they turned the corner out of her sight.

'No alarm,' Billy muttered.

'What?'

'There was no alarm on the shop.'

'Wonder how much float she keeps in the till, there's not much else to nick in there is there?' Danny said. 'Bet there's more in her dad's gaff.'

'Let's do a drive past,' Billy said, his eyes now wide and bright as he looked admiringly at his mate.

'I think we might have just found ourselves a little meal ticket there,' Danny said, as he turned to his friend. They both let out a squeal of delight.

'She's fit too,' Billy said, wiping his runny nose on his sleeve. 'I wouldn't mind giving her one.'

'Patience, Billy,' Danny laughed.

'It's you she likes,' Billy said, with a snivel. 'She fancies you summat rotten, I can tell.'

'Don't worry 'me old son, we share everything don't we?' Danny said, his grin widening as he noticed his friends downbeat look.

'Shall I text her? Find out where she lives?' Billy said, eagerly.

'Yeah, go on then.'

Pam replied immediately.

Danny laughed as his friend read out the address. 'How naive can you get?' he shook his head.

I were sad wen u ad to go but u cud sends me a pic l8ter to cheer me up. Billy spoke as he texted.

My hair looks such a mess when I've been out riding. She texted back. Billy read it out to his friend.

'Silly cow, as if we'd be looking at her face,' Billy roared.

'Ask her to meet us tomorrow at the same place,' Danny said. Billy concentrated hard to spell out the text.

Pam's phone beeped, loudly.

'Who's got their phone on?' shouted the riding instructor. 'Give it to me now, Pamela. You can have it back at the end of the lesson,' she said, taking the phone and putting it into her riding jacket pocket.

Pam put her foot in the stirrups and climbed up onto her horse, reluctantly.

Chapter 7

Grace Harvey's thatched cottage was just like a picture on the front of a chocolate box, Taylor thought, as she strolled along the country garden pathway that divided the magnificent display of flora. The wild flowers looked delicate to the touch but their scent was intoxicating.

Taylor knocked at the big, heavy wooden door. As she waited for an answer, she turned and surveyed the garden from her raised platform of the doorstop. Her gaze fell upon a lavender bush nearby and she leant across and squeezed the top of a pointed flower head. She put her fingertips to her nose and breathed in the scent, which was both soothing and calming. She closed her eyes and took a deep breath.

Taylor could smell chamomile and vanilla too, what a lovely combination. The fragrances were having a sobering effect on her until the creaking of the church like door opening jolted her back to the present with a start.

The giant of a man that stood before her wore gym shorts, a once white T-shirt and Wallabies without laces. His hair was wild and his beard straggly. If she had seen him on the street she would have presumed him homeless but his clothes weren't stained enough for a vagrant.

'Donald Harvey,' he announced with an unexpected gentleman-like voice and a white toothed smile as he offered her his hand.

'DS Taylor Spiers,' she said flashing her warrant card at him. Donald stepped aside and gallantly waved her into the house before him.

With a dramatic sweep of his arm, he cleared the dining room table of the papers. He took an old, battered suitcase off a chair, brushed the seat down and offered it for her to sit upon.

'I'm so glad you've come, Ma'am. I think my Mom has been taken for one hell of a ride,' he said picking up a handful of documents from the floor and shaking them before her eyes. 'I should have been here,' he said putting his free hand up to his brow as he leaned heavily on his elbow. 'Then, this would never have happened,' he sighed. Harvey's eyes looked up at Taylor as if emotionally wounded.

'The man is a vulture,' he suddenly cried. Taylor jumped. 'Mom cashed in the equity of this house but I can't trace a penny of money that she released,' he said with tears now visible in his eyes and a lump in his throat. 'I've rang him. But he tells me that everything he's done was her wish and all above board,' he swallowed hard. 'According to these papers it looks like she was about to lose the roof over her bloody head too Ma'am.'

DS Spiers raised her hand. 'Now let's take this slowly eh? Firstly, it's Taylor or Detective Sergeant Spiers. You don't need to call me Ma'am – you make me sound like Miss Marple,' she said, aghast.

'Whatever. I don't care, I just want you to find out what he's done with the money he's stolen. I want you to arrest him. '

'Mr Harvey, please, tell me precisely who you want me to arrest and for what reason? I can't detain anyone without evidence.'

Donald Harvey looked pale and tired and it was obvious to Taylor that his predicament had done nothing for his attitude. He sighed again. His breath stank of stale alcohol.

'My Mom, Grace Harvey, it appears has signed over her house to an equity release company,' he said pointing at a document on the table. 'Arranged by her financial advisor Brian Stevenson, and I can't trace any of the money that according to these papers has been released. Is that clear enough for you?' Donald said, picking up an old Harrowfield Building Society book that lay among the paperwork and throwing it in Taylor's direction. It landed on the table with a slap, but she didn't flinch.

'It's just not like her. She's always been so careful with her money. She's not stupid... was not stupid,' he said, coughing into the palm of his hand.

DS Spiers took out her pocket book and started making notes.

'Do you know this Brian Stevenson?' Taylor asked.

'No, do you?' said Donald. DS Spiers shook her head, holding his gaze.

'All I know about Brian Stevenson is that he was a friend of Dad's,' said Donald.

DS Spiers nodded and allowed him to continue.

'They worked together at one time and became friends. When Dad died, Mom relied on Brian to take care of her finances, probably because I wasn't around... I suppose she trusted him because he was Dad's friend. I've found some old pictures, look,' Donald said showing her a snap of a young guy with his arm round an older gentleman at a presentation ceremony. The older man was spitting image of the man sat in front of her but his hair was grey.

Donald appeared a little calmer now.

'Mom told me ages ago all about Brian Stevenson investing money for her, which I understood because she said it gave her a reasonable living,' he said. 'But from what I can see of her bank balance since Dad died, Mom has drawn money out and put nothing back. The receipts that she kept from Brian Stevenson show she was giving money to him on a regular basis, God knows what for, but it has made her almost destitute – which is why she obviously needed to draw upon the equity of this place.'

DS Spiers listened and took notes.

'I understood from Mom that he took her shopping, out for lunch, for hospital appointments. Look these flowers are from him for her birthday,' he said, pointing out the lilies on the dresser that were still in their wrapping. 'I thought he was looking after her, being a friend, a companion. A son she didn't have in me... I should have known that he wouldn't do all that for nothing. I should have come home sooner.'

'Mr Harvey, all I can do is promise I will look into your concerns. It would be very helpful if I could take away those documents,' she said, standing up. Donald gathered the paperwork into a pile and ungraciously stuffed it into the old battered case before fastening it and handing it to her. 'Well they're no good to me are they?' he said, looking defeated. 'But keep them safe won't you? The evidence against Brian Stevenson is in there, I can assure you.'

Saying her farewells at the gate, she noticed the car parked outside had recent damage to the front nearside wing. He sensed her interest in it.

'Damn deer bounded straight out in front of me on my way here,' he said, coming out of the gate after her. 'And it's a hire car.' He ran his hand over the paintwork. 'It shook me up, I can tell you,' he said, laughing half-heartedly.

'Have you reported it?'

'No, not yet, I didn't see the point. The bloody animal got up and legged it. Should I?' he said with a sigh at the look on her face.

DS Taylor Spiers eyed Donald Harvey with renewed interest as she watched him turn and walk back up the path with his hands in his pockets and his head down. She unlocked her car and got in. Sitting in the driving seat, she rang the police station and spoke with PC Tim Whitworth.

'DS Taylor Spiers, I've been tasked with looking into the hit and run in Merton village and I understand from the accident report that you dealt with it?'

'Y-e-s,' Tim said, in a drawl.

'Just a quick question; how sure are we that the glass found at the scene of the accident is from the offending vehicle and are we best-guessing what the vehicle's make is or was there sufficient debris to ensure there is no doubt?' she asked.

'Dunno yet.'

'Ah, it's just that I've just been with Grace Harvey's son and his car has recent damage to the front, near side light casing and wing. He says he hit a deer.'

'Not an old dear I hope,' he chortled.

'Not funny,' she sighed. 'Look into it for me will you. I need to know for certain,' she said, ending the call and throwing her mobile onto the passenger seat before starting the engine. Her mobile rang instantly. She sighed, leant over and picked it up.

'Taylor? Dylan, I'm on my way to a suspicious death at number eleven, Causeway Cottages. Can you meet me there?'

'Sure,' she said, with a renewed energy. 'But, you'll have to give me directions.'

'Row of houses on your left just up past the entrance of Harrowfield hospital, do you know it?'

'I'll find you.'

Dylan hung up.

A body. Now that was more like it, she thought, grinding her teeth together as she felt adrenalin starting to pump furiously around her body. She turned the radio on, clicked her seat belt, tossed her hair over her shoulder, looked in her rear view mirror and put her foot down hard on the accelerator.

Ten minutes later she arrived outside the house, which was easily identified on the street by the two uniformed officers guarding the scene. As she left her vehicle she could see Dylan in his scene suit, blowing air into his plastic gloves. She briefly wondered why that action made them go on the hand easier. As she walked towards him she could see he was deep in conversation with a smaller figure dressed like him, whom she presumed was the scenes of crime officer. Neither of them looked in her direction.

She noted that Dylan hadn't finished suiting up which she knew meant that they hadn't yet been inside the house. Good, she thought, as she approached them. She didn't want to miss a single moment at the scene of her first suspicious dead as a Detective Sergeant. Murder? She hoped so.

'DS Taylor Spiers,' Dylan introduced her to Jasmine, who eyed the high heeled, short-skirted beauty up and down with interest.

'Uniform got a call from a worried neighbour, to say that they hadn't seen the elderly lady that lives here for a few weeks and they'd become increasingly concerned.' Dylan told her.

'They thought at first she might've gone away or been admitted to hospital but when a vast amount of flies caught their attention at the upstairs window they knew something wasn't right,' he continued, pointing to the window in question. Taylor looked up. The glass was completely blacked out with the blowflies.

'Not only that, but as you probably noticed even from where we're standing there's a foul smell in the air. '

Dylan took the lead and walked towards the front door. DS Spiers followed him cautiously. Her nose tingled at the pungent aroma and she gagged involuntarily. She nipped her nose and covered her mouth to try and mask the stench.

'The house was secure. The uniformed officers had to force entry,' Dylan said, turning to her. 'We were lucky it was only on a Yale latch.

'You okay?' he asked as he noticed her pallor. She nodded. 'Horrendous isn't it, which is why I told them to leave the door open,' he grimaced. 'A quick look around by uniform brought to light a badly decomposed body on the main bedroom floor, which they believe is the body of the lady of the house, but since it's almost skeletal we'll have to wait for the post-mortem,' Dylan said as he stood at the front door.

DS Spiers eagerness had subsided like a thermometer put into ice. She looked up the stairs and remained standing close to her boss. This wasn't like it was supposed to be. Her stomach clenched.

'Get suited up quickly and get your mask on before we go in to see what delights await us,' Dylan instructed as Jasmine handed Taylor a scenes of crime suit to put over her clothing. DS Taylor Spiers, ever conscious of her appearance, looked at the suit with disdain. Dylan smiled at Jasmine whose eyes danced with delight.

'You want me to wear that?' she shrieked. 'I'll look like one of them *Teletubbies* off children's TV,' she said holding the suit at arm's length as Jasmine handed her the paper boots.

Suited and booted, Dylan led the women into the house. 'We'll go upstairs first since we know that's where the body is; get a few photographs in situ,' Dylan spoke his thoughts aloud and he could hear Jasmine behind him snap the cover from her camera lens.

He heard Taylor retch as they reached the landing of the upstairs and he turned. She nodded to him. Senses heightened the noise of the flies was surreal, the buzzing was irritatingly loud. They turned the corner of the bedroom door and Taylor trailed behind Dylan and Jasmine tentatively looking in at the scene around them. She could only describe it as something out of a horror movie. The blowflies blanketed everything in the room. The tiny decomposed body lay before them, feet towards the doorway.

'She's been here some weeks,' Dylan observed, as he bent down and looked at the skull of the body. The noise from the insects seemed to increase with his intrusion.

'Here look, there're maggots in her eye sockets Jasmine,' he pointed out.

Taylor's shoulders rose and fell as she breathed deeply. 'I need some air,' she gasped as she ran from the room, down the stairs and out into the garden where, leaning against the wall of the house, she threw up into a bush. 'Oh, my God,' she gulped, before throwing up again. This was not the impression she wanted to give Dylan.

'You okay?' Dylan called out after her while his eyes continued to scan the dead body.

'F-i-n-e,' she said in between swallowing hard to stop the bile rise in her throat again. She collapsed onto her knees. She just needed a minute, she thought, as she wiped the vomit from her mouth with her hand and took a few deep breaths.

Dylan turned to Jasmine, 'Nothing obvious. Just take a quick photo of her in situ will you, then we'll get her removed to the mortuary and see if we can find out what happened to her.'

Jasmine nodded and in silence did as she had been instructed without any fuss. Dylan reached up to open the bedroom window. Taylor looked up at the noise from above and she watched the swarm of insects being released from their breeding ground.

Dylan pushed the window wide open to try to clear the room. With the expertise of the man who had been to this sort of scene a hundred times before, he walked quickly around the rest of the house. His hands were firmly in his pockets, like he'd been shown as a young detective, so that he wasn't tempted to touch anything. Nothing else appeared untoward.

Stepping over the threshold of the front door he pulled his mask off and inhaled a lung full of clean air. Seeing Taylor sat on the grass leaning against the house wall, her head tilted towards sky he walked over.

'You okay?' he said.

'Yeah, I'm sorry – that smell .'

'Certainly not a pretty sight either is it? It won't be much better at the mortuary. Which we'll have to endure either tomorrow or the day after,' he said almost apologetically.

She took a huge intake of breath through her nose, counted to six and breathed out slowly between pouted lips to the count of six.

'One thing I detest is blow flies,' Dylan said flaying his arms at one that dared to come near his perspiration-covered forehead. He looked at his DS's pale face. 'It could have been worse,' he smiled, kindly.

'How come?'

'If you'd tried to stick it out you might have fainted on the body,' he chuckled.

'And is that supposed to make me feel better?' she said, leaning forward and burping loudly. 'Sorry,' she said, putting her head between her knees.

'Well you wouldn't have been the first and no doubt you'd wouldn't have been the last either,' said Dylan philosophically as he knelt down next to her and rubbed her back.

She turned to look up at him. 'Thanks,' she said with tears in her eyes.

Jasmine completed the task that Dylan had requested of her. He arranged for the body to be removed to the mortuary and he also told the uniformed officers present to have the house secured, before holding his hand out for DS Spiers to help her to her feet.

'Time to go, Ma'am,' he said, smiling at her.

'Not you an'all,' she said.

'Pardon?'

'Oh, nothing,' she replied. Dylan shrugged his shoulders.

'What do you think – natural causes?'

'I don't know,' she said nonchalantly. 'Probably.'

'Well, maybe not,' Dylan said. 'Can you get some detectives over here to start making house to house enquiries into her background, when she was last seen, who was the last person to see her alive, her doctor's name, next of kin, etcetera?'

'Yeah sure, I'll get straight on it,' she said weakly.

'I'm sure you will,' he smiled, knowing that by giving her a task it would give her a focus. Something to think about other than the smell and the sight she had just witnessed.

'We'll also need a recent picture of her if they can find one,' he said. 'A bit of advice Taylor, I always carry extra strong mints in my pocket,' he said, offering her one as they walked back to their cars. 'My way of coping with things is I try to concentrate on the job in hand,' he said. 'So, the name we've been given for the lady is a Mildred Sykes who we think is more than likely to be in her late seventies, eighty? Look, I've got to be elsewhere but you've got a good start and there are a lot of things to arrange, so I'll speak to you back at the nick later, eh?'

'Okay,' she replied. She wondered if he would tell them back at the office about what had happened to her.

Dylan had other things on his mind. Dawn Farren, his work colleague and long-standing Detective Sergeant, had been off work to have her baby and was suffering badly from postnatal depression. Dawn had become like a sister to Dylan over the years and he missed her jovial nature, their comfortable repartee, her larger than life figure and her loyalty. She was his safe pair of hands and he knew it.

He stopped en route to pick up some flowers and Jaffa cakes, her favourite biscuits, and before leaving the petrol station he sat and texted Jen, *Just been to see the smelliest body ever. I promised myself I'd get to see Dawn today so sorry if I'm late but coming straight home after for supper. Love you x*

Dawn and Ralph's home and restaurant 'Mawingo,' stood in three acres of parkland in the verdant valley of Sibden with the River Heddle meandering through it. It was a spectacular neo-gothic house, worlds apart from the hustle and bustle of modern-day life. Darkness was drawing in and Ralph was closing the curtains in their lounge when he saw Dylan's car approach and by the time Dylan reached the door Ralph was there to meet him.

'Come on in Jack,' Ralph said, holding out his hand.

Dylan took the hand he offered and shook it warmly, holding his gaze for a moment or two. He noticed Ralph's smile didn't quite reach his eyes.

'Dawn might be pleased to see you at least,' he said, raising his eyebrows. Ralph's voice sounded unusually flat and downcast to Dylan's ears. His normally ruddy complexion was pale and his face pinched.

'That bad?'

Ralph nodded his head and his eyes closed.

Dawn was sat by the window in semi-darkness. Violet lay contented in a crib beside her.

'Hiya,' he said in a whisper as he bent down to hand her flowers and biscuits as he kissed the cheek she offered. You look tired,' he said.

Dylan stood over the sleeping baby and touched her soft, peachy cheek. She stirred.

'She's gorgeous,' he cooed as he took a step back and sat in a chair opposite Dawn.

'That's very kind, isn't it love?' Ralph said, taking the flowers from Dawn who stared blankly at Dylan. 'I'll pop them in some water and put the kettle on, shall I?' he said nodding at the biscuits.

Dawn sat in silence as if she hadn't heard. She dropped her gaze to her hands in her lap with a nervousness he had never seen her display before. He hoped desperately that his face didn't show his shock at her appearance and he smiled the fixed smile of the professional police officer. Dawn had always been the life and soul of his enquiries. Her bright and bubbly character had been the comic to his scorn. The larger-than-life Dawn French lookalike that he had grown to love was wasting away before his very eyes.

'How're you coping?' Dylan asked and swallowed hard. He could feel his heart weighing heavy in his stomach as he scanned his friend's dishevelled hair and frumpy attire.

'Oh, you know,' she sighed, shrugging. Her eyes full of unshed tears as she looked directly into his eyes for the first time. He tried to speak but uncharacteristically found he didn't know what to say. He reached out for her hand and held it in his.

'Come on girl, I want you back, no I'll re-phrase that – I NEED you. Harrowfield nick needs you,' he said dramatically, and for the first time he saw a flicker of a faint smile flash across her face. 'Look, I've even bought you some Jaffas.'

'Oh God, it is bad,' he said, when she didn't take the bait of food.

'I'm trying,' she said with a little effort. 'And everybody's being so bloody nice, but I can't seem to...' She shook her head as if to clear the confusion within. 'It's like it crept over me after the birth, like black ink seeping over the scenery of my world. I'm in a black hole Dylan, looking up and I can't get out,' she added. Dylan listened. 'And the pills they give me make me feel so 'cloudy' and well, like a flaming zombie most of the time,' she said, pointing to the packets and bottles of tablets on the table beside her that was also littered with half empty glasses of water, cups of half drunk tea and the baby's bottle. 'Never mind walking through mud,

I feel like I'm sometimes being sucked into a bog. How can I expect anyone to understand? It's so bloody self-indulgent when I've got so much,' she sobbed.

Ralph stood at the door with the drinks. Dawn was talking at last. He stepped backwards, watched and listened.

Dylan squeezed Dawn's hand gently. 'Don't beat yourself up. You're just an emotionally sensitive person who strives for perfection, and I should know. Right now you're not in control but you'll get there. Just give yourself time. You can't keep a good Detective down, eh?' he smiled.

Ralph brought in the drinks but she didn't acknowledge him.

Her shoulders rose and then fell with a big sigh. 'I hear you've got a good-looking replacement,' she said, wiping away a tear that had escaped and run down her cheek. She looked at him, searching his face for a sign of his acknowledgement at her accusation.

'Not a replacement Dawn, cover – and believe me, she's not a patch.'

'Oh, yeah,' she said. Violet stirred and Dawn reached out for the little bundle of clothing. The effort seemed too much for her and Dylan stepped forward to take the now crying baby from her bed. He looked into Violet's little elfin face and smiled adoringly at her.

'She looks like you,' he said softly.

'Poor little sod. Look at the state of me,' Dawn quipped as she shuffled to a more comfortable position in her chair.

'You'll come through it love. How can you not when you look at this little one?' he said stroking Violet's soft mop of dark, poker straight hair.

'Why did my other babies die? What did I do wrong then? I feel so guilty,' she sobbed. 'I didn't see them. They haven't got a gravestone. No one understands how I feel.'

'Anyone who hasn't suffered like you have can't. But you've got to believe you did nothing wrong. The others weren't strong enough to live. You know that deep down. But, Violet is, and she needs her mum now,' he said handing the now screaming Violet over. 'I think someone needs changing,' he said, screwing up his nose.

Dawn smiled. 'Why are you always right. You're so bloody annoying, sometimes,' she snapped.

'No I'm not. You know me, I'm just a good bullshitter,' he said with a laugh. 'Look, if it helps buy a statue for the garden in remembrance. Somewhere close you can go and talk to them or think about them if you need to.' He saw Dawn's tears falling on Violet's head as she kissed her and held her tight. 'You look all in but I'll tell Jen to call in sometime soon, eh? And what about if I get you some help from Welfare?'

'Yeah,' she sighed. 'That would be a start wouldn't it? I hope I don't scare Jen to death though when she sees me like this with your little one on the way,' she laughed through her tears.

'Never,' he said, taking a last look over his shoulder at the nursing mother and baby as he left the lounge.

Ralph stood in the hallway, the tray still in his hands. 'I wasn't eavesdropping I just didn't want to disturb you.'

'She'll be okay, Ralph. She's very lucky to have you. Let me know if I can do anything to help, won't you?'

'Thank you,' he said, nodding his head.

Driving home, Dylan couldn't stop thinking about how Dawn had been changed by her pregnancy and the birth of Violet. Would Jen change too?

Most people who worked with Dylan thought him tough but fair. Little did they know how he covered his true emotions with the professional mask of the hard-faced detective.

Jen watched him closely as he left the supper table, silently, that night; she knew by his demeanour that he had things on his mind. He stopped briefly at her chair to lay his hands on her shoulders and kiss the top of her head. Max, their golden retriever followed his master into the lounge.

She boiled the kettle and took him a drink. He was fast asleep. Max lay over his slippered feet. Dylan had been visibly upset as he told her about Dawn's battle with her post-natal depression over dinner, and not for the first time she wondered how he coped with other people's sadness and the horrors he saw on a daily basis. She loved him for his tenacity but also for his sensitivity. Perhaps seeing the worst of man's inhumanity to man made him appreciate the good things in life more than most.

She placed his warm drink on the coffee table beside him and sat at his side. He didn't stir. She leaned over to plant a kiss on his cheek. He lifted his arm so she could snuggle beneath it and he smiled with a satisfying groan as she did so but he didn't open his eyes. The harsh reality of what life had thrown at Dawn and Ralph when they had waited so long to have a baby had made Dylan even surer that he wanted to spend as much time as he could with Jen and theirs.

'Perhaps I could go out walking with Dawn?' Jen said, thoughtfully. 'They say that physical activity lifts your mood better than anything else.'

'Mmm ... that's kind love,' he said raising his heavy eyelids for a second to look down at her. 'I'm sure she'd appreciate it and it might do you some good too,' he said pulling himself up from his slouched position. He patted her stomach and his hand lingered on hers, resting there. All of a sudden Jen felt the baby through her stomach for the first time – it was amazing to feel the hard lump that was an elbow or a heel perhaps, but a little freaky too.

'Did you feel that?' said Dylan, startled.

'Mmm ... it makes it all seem rather real, doesn't it?' she laughed. 'I wonder if Dawn has thought of trying herbal teas?' she asked.

'It's worth suggesting,' he said leaning forward to pick up his drink. He took a gulp. 'I'm going to enquire about getting her counselling. It might just unravel some of her issues and help her deal with what's going on in her mind,' he said lying back on the sofa and pulling Jen towards him.

'Can I do that for you?' she asked.

'Thanks,' he mumbled as he drifted back off to sleep, his head on her bump. Jen knew these were the moments that needed to be cherished and would be few and far between once the baby blessed them with his presence.

Chapter 8

Pam laid in her bed, wondering when she would hear from Danny. She stretched out lazily and yawned loudly. The sound of doors slamming had woken her. Slipping out from under her duvet, she tiptoed across to the bedroom window and pulled back the curtains. Her bedroom overlooked the driveway and, seeing both her mum and dad's cars gone, Pam ran on tiptoes into her mum's room and sat at her dressing table. She opened her make-up case and took out her lipstick and mascara. slipping them carefully into her dressing gown pocket.

A final check of her school apparel in the full-length mirror of her mum's wardrobe, half an hour later made her smile. She wondered if she needed a coat and walked to the bedroom window that overlooked the main road to check. 'Is that Danny's car?' she said, aghast. Her heart skipped a beat. It couldn't be, could it?

She ran onto the landing, grabbed hold of the banister and flew down the stairs. Picking up her satchel from the floor, she hurried out of the door, hearing it slam loudly behind her as she raced down the path. Standing at the bus stop, she stood on tiptoes as she scanned the road in both directions, desperate in her search to spot Danny's car heading her way.

Pam stood back quietly and let one bus go. She waited for the next. Oh, how she could just imagine the other girl's faces, green with envy if Danny Denton gave her a lift into school. She waited, giggling at her thoughts. The next bus drew up alongside her and although she was at the front of the queue she let the other passengers go ahead of her as she took one last glance. Pam looked at her watch. Disappointingly it told her in no uncertain terms that she'd better jump on board if she didn't want to be late for registration. She slouched next to the window and took her mobile phone out of her pocket. The bus was noisy. She willed the phone to ring. Thoughtfully, she requested the alert setting, selected vibrate, and slipped it back into her pocket. The last thing she wanted was to miss a call or text.

DS Taylor Spiers was on her way into the office. Her first job today was to look into the focus of Donald Harvey's complaint against Brian Stevenson to see if there was any weight behind Grace's son's allegations. Tomorrow was Grace's funeral, and although the event would be sad she would rather go there and avoid Mildred Sykes' post-mortem if she had the choice. Perhaps she could persuade Dylan that her presence at the funeral was more important than at the mortuary.

'Morning boss, can I get you a coffee?' said Taylor as she hung up her coat on the stand just outside Dylan's office door. 'You're in early today,' she called.

'White, half a sugar,' Dylan shouted back. She tilted her head trying to decipher by his tone if he was in a good mood as he chatted on the phone. No, she conceded she didn't know him well enough yet but she was confident she could wrap him round her little finger as she did with all men. It was only a matter of time until he succumbed to her charms.

'I thought I'd go see the financial advisor today to see what he has to say about Grace's finances,' she said, as she walked into his office.

Dylan nodded but didn't look up from his work.

'Her son was raging about him and his antics,' she added, standing in front of his desk, steaming mug of coffee cupped in her beautifully manicured hands. Dylan's head turned to his computer screen.

She walked round his desk and leaned over his shoulder to set the cup carefully in front of him, purposely brushing up against him as she did so and he turned as if in slow motion to watch her walk away from him and settle herself on the corner of his desk. He saw her cross her beautiful, long legs in front of him so that he could see her long brown pins in her new high-heeled black patent shoes.

To all intent and purpose she looked as if she was about to go on a night out in the town, he thought. The bright orange, low cut top clung to her voluptuous bosom as she leaned across him to pick up the printout of the Chief's Log, a resume of the major events in the Force area in the past twenty-four hours.

Dylan's eyes never faltered as they caught the twinkle of her long, dangly earrings.

'Yeah, who knows Taylor? People might take advantage of an old lady living on her own,' he said taking the mug by the handle and putting it to his lips. He studied a sheet on his desk.

'Don't forget, Mildred Sykes' post-mortem tomorrow,' he said.

Putting the Chief's Log back down, Taylor slid off his desk and headed for the door without speaking. She stopped and turned, leaning heavily on the frame. He could sense her waiting for him to look at her.

'Yes,' he drawled.

'Oh, tomorrow. Grace Harvey's funeral? I think I should go, don't you, to see who turns up? But, of course if you need me at the Mildred Sykes' PM?'

'Blast. I definitely need you at the funeral,' he said, thoughtfully.

Taylor quietly closed his office door behind her. 'Mission accomplished,' she whispered, smiling to herself as she sunk back into the chair at her desk and started to type Brian Stevenson's details into the intelligence systems.

'I wouldn't speak too soon,' said Dennis, who sat quietly at his desk.

'What would you know?' she said, casting a sly smile at the police officer who was on light duties with a hand injury.

She hadn't been at her workstation long when the phone rang.

'Taylor, Dylan.'

'Yes, sir,' she cooed, a broad smile crossing her lovely face as she tinkered with her earrings and lifted her head above her computer screen to see him through his office doorway as he talked to her.

'I've got them to put back Mildred's PM back to three o'clock, so it won't be a problem for you to attend both,' he said matter-of-factly and promptly hung up.

Dennis sniggered. Dylan was nobody's fool. Everybody tried to avoid post-mortems but thinking about what she'd said he deemed it was necessary that she attended.

'Er … great,' she said, her voice sounding flat even to her own ears as she flopped back down into her seat. She put the phone back on its cradle and laid her head in her hands on the desk, groaning.

The CID office door slammed signalling someone's arrival and she sat up quickly. Tomorrow was another day, she sighed, smiling sweetly at Karen the young, quiet, HOLMES indexer who had just clocked in to start her day. Taylor knew she had plenty of time to come up with something to avoid going to the mortuary. She didn't want her hair or her clothes smelling like rotting cabbage. What on earth would people think? After all she was a Sergeant now; she had the power to instruct other people to do the dirty work for her.

Try as she might, Taylor could find nothing on any of the intelligence systems for a Brian Stevenson but, having found a telephone number for him under financial services in the telephone directory, she made a call to see if he was available to speak to her – and within the hour was sat in a plush office having fresh coffee and oatmeal biscuits served to her by him.

He was tall and painfully thin with a hunched back, which made him look older than his years. His neck was long; reminding her of a swan's. However he had the smartest of haircuts, was clean-shaven and dressed in an expensive suit and silk tie. Most of all, he appeared polite and attentive.

'I've called to see you about Grace Harvey, Mr Stevenson,' she said, smiling.

'Call me Brian dear, please.'

Taylor nodded. 'Thank you,' she said.

'Ah, poor Grace. What an absolute shock it was to hear the news. She was a lovely lady and a dear friend of mine. Do you know the person responsible?'

'No not yet,' she said, catching a mischievous glint in his eye.

'I suppose you'll be checking cars for damage?'

'Well, yes,' she said taken aback by his question.

'The old Porsche is in the garage at the moment – had a collision with a bollard. The bollard won unfortunately,' he laughed, half-heartedly. 'Ah, well such is life,' he shrugged. 'Donald Harvey is concerned about his mother's finances I understand?' he continued. 'But believe me dear that's nothing unusual,' he said. 'Grace always needed to release capital to support his lifestyle.'

'And what lifestyle would that be Mr Stevenson?'

'He's taken to the fratty, vagrant way of life, as I understand it from Grace, after spending time in an American University. I believe he also has a yuppie lifestyle to match as well as doing a little gambling of late, Ms Spiers,' he replied, in a hushed tone.

'Is that why she had to release the equity in her home?'

'Yes. Oh, I advised her against it,' he said shaking his head.

'And?'

'I wasn't family Ms Spiers, just her friend and her financial advisor. Blood's thicker than water, so they say, and when it came to money she made that quite clear. Even though I protested quite emphatically, Grace instructed me to release monies as soon as possible.'

'And did you?'

'Of course.'

'What sort of amounts are we talking about?'

'One hundred thousand pounds,' he said.

Taylor pouted her lips and drew in a breath.

'Indeed. So now you can see why I was concerned.'

'That's one hell of a lot of money. When did this take place and what happened to the money?'

'Her finances have been slowly dwindling away for some time, but the equity release money was only finalised a few weeks ago. Then Donald has the audacity to ring me to threaten me about it.'

'Did you report the threat to the police?'

'No, I appreciate that he was upset about his mother's death and I expect he thought he would inherit more than he will now.'

DS Taylor Spiers had a conundrum. Who was telling her the truth? Within thirty minutes of talking with Brian Stevenson she found herself travelling through Harrowfield town centre.

She wondered about what Brian Stevenson had told her. No wonder Donald's appearance didn't appear to be 'normal' to her. He dressed intentionally like a vagrant, but a clean one. How bizarre. Was Donald Harvey disguising a gambling habit too? That did make sense. Grace sent him money and basically funded her grow-up son's chosen lifestyle. But, what didn't make sense was why Donald would then threaten Brian if Donald had had the money already.

Dylan was right about one thing; you never knew what you'd find out once you start asking questions. The hit and run incident was looking and sounding more appealing by the hour. Who the hell was telling the truth, she thought, as she stopped in a line of traffic in the high street and looked at herself in her rear view mirror. Rubbing her lips together she considered her main priority, which at the moment was getting out of the impending post-mortem. She liked the media side of her new posting. Her name and picture would be in the papers soon. Journalists would want to quote her.

She would work on Dylan to let her get involved with that side of things more. Who knows, she might get on TV? She smiled at her reflection in the mirror, licked her lips and considered seriously what she might wear for TV interviews. Perhaps she should go shopping for a new outfit while she was in town to that new little Italian designer shop, just in case.

Chapter 9

The school day was drawing to a close. Pam was downhearted. She hadn't heard from Danny all day, she must have blown it. Looking at her phone, she silently begged it to bleep a message arriving, as she walked along the long driveway leading from the school to the main road. Head down, she dragged her feet lethargically.

Suddenly she heard the distant, booming sound of loud music, but try as she might to see through the gaggle of pupils, staff and an array of backpacks in front of her, she couldn't see the car. A broad grin of anticipation grew on her face. She could hear the dull, repetitive thud from car speakers.

Pam turned to face the direction of the noise. Her pace quickened and her heart started to pump wildly. She stood on her tiptoes, eyes scouring the road above a sea of heads at the school gates. Friends shouted their goodbyes to her but she dismissed them with a wave of her hand.

The beat of the music was increasing in volume and then suddenly it was there, the red Ford Fiesta drew up on the opposite side of the road in front of her. Almost immediately a group of girls swarmed the car. Some bent down to the opening window and started chatting and laughing with the car's occupants. Pam stormed across the road, but as she neared, the girls started walking away, laughing raucously and her feelings of jealousy had subsided by the time she had reached it.

'Hi gorgeous, thought we'd come to give you a lift home?' Danny said leaning out of the car window. 'Jump in.'

'Did you come past our house this morning?' she said with a brilliant smile that showed her pearly white teeth. Billy stepped out of the car to let her in the back seat, as she walked around to the passenger door.

'We did. We were looking for you,' Danny said, his eyes glued to hers in the mirror. He smiled. Pam blushed.

'Don't worry. I'll be discreet,' Danny laughed. 'I won't drop you off outside. I know parents can be such a bore,'

'Oh, that's okay,' she said, confidently. 'My mum and dad work twenty-four seven, they won't be home for ages yet.'

The speed of the car pulling away from the kerb caused Pam to jolt backwards and roll over on the back seat.

'I think your legs get longer,' Billy said with a smirk as he put his head through the middle of the front seats and stared at them unashamedly.

Danny turned to see what Billy was looking at. There was a screech of brakes.

'Fucking idiot,' he screamed at the driver of the car that to swerve to avoid a collision. 'Fucking wanker,' he shouted at the top of his voice as he turned and made a one-fingered gesture. 'Just cos' he's got a fucking Porsche he thinks he owns the fucking road,' he raged. Danny rammed the car into first gear and yanked off the handbrake; revving the engine he swung the car around to follow the Porsche. The car had vanished.

'I think I know that guy. He lives there,' Pam said, pointing in the direction of a huge white house that stood in its own grounds at the bottom of the road where she lived.

'Number 42,' Danny remarked, nodding to Billy.

'He must be fucking loaded,' Billy said, giving a long low whistle.

'Whoever he is, he doesn't cut us up like that and get away with it,' Danny muttered.

Moments later they were outside Pam's home and Danny revved the engine once again. Pam stared out of the window at the neighbouring houses to see if she could see anyone watching. 'What're ya doing at weekend?' Danny asked.

She thought hard for something interesting to say. 'Nothing. I don't think,' she said instead.

'Good, I'll text you,' he said.

Pam got out of the car and stood on the pavement as Danny did a three-point turn. Without a glance from Danny she watched his car crawl down the street and stop outside number 42. She turned and ran up the path to her house.

Pam unlocked the front door behind her and dropped her bag at the foot of the stairs.

'Yes!' she yelled at the top of her voice. Punching the air, anyone watching would have thought she'd just scored the winning goal at Wembley. She'd got her first real date.

She took the stairs two at a time and launched herself into her bedroom, flinging open her wardrobe door. What on earth was she going to wear, she thought as she picked out her clothes one by one and discarded them on the bed? Tops, skirts, jumpers flew out of her drawers. She could feel panic rising. There were only a few days to decide. She stood at the foot of the bed and flopped backwards, sighing. Dreaming of Danny, she thought she'd burst with joy as she pulled her teddy off her pillow and hugged him tight. 'Teds,' she said. 'This is it. I'm all grown up now and I don't need you any more.' Teds flew up in the air and landed in the rubbish bin.

'We need to get Pam to invite us into her house,' Billy said.

'Not yet, we're gonna do that twat over that cut us up first,' said Danny, gazing at Number 42. He drummed his fingers on the steering wheel and Billy knew his friend was working out a plan of action. When Danny had his mind set, nothing Billy could say or do would change it.

'Whatever,' Billy said nodding his head to the beat of the music.

Chapter 10

The coffin bore a solitary arrangement of white lilies. Inside were the remains of Grace Harvey and Winston. Donald Harvey and her close friends inched their way up the slope towards All Saints Church, Merton which stood on a hill in the heart of the village, just a short walk away from the river Heddle itself and next to the village green.

Waiting for them at the top of the hill was a tight circle of Grace's neighbours and villagers. Taylor stood outside the entrance of the church and watched the tear-drenched face of a little girl break out in a nervous giggle as she walked the path between the gravestones. Overcome presumably by the stress of the funeral, she raised her trembling face, framed with a black Alice band, to an older lady at her side, as if in search of reassurance.

'So I won't weep any more, because you are now in a better place than you were before,' said the vicar with much heartfelt regret and resignation at his beloved parishioner's awful fate.

At the rear of the congregation Taylor stood looking up at the stained glass window designed by William Morris, the card next to her on a small lectern informed her. According to legend, said a mounted plaque above, the original foundations for the church were laid in a flat, easily accessible site but every morning were found transferred to the hill where the church exists today. Eventually the builders gave up building it in the planned flat location and built it on the hill.

The congregation stood in sombre fashion at the graveside. The sun was hot, there wasn't a breath of air, birds sang and the atmosphere was tranquil. There was no traffic noise and it seemed to Taylor that the whole of mankind had stopped for that moment in time as she stood on the periphery of the mourners, looking in.

It was her duty at the funeral to see what she could glean from people who attended. Already she had noticed that Donald Harvey didn't appear distressed, just agitated. He kept looking around him as though searching for someone in the crowd. Interestingly, there had been no words of anger from him or bitterness towards the party that did this to his mother. Only towards the man who he believed took her money. She needed to speak to him regarding her conversation with Brian Stevenson and she would when she could get him alone.

However, no sooner had Grace been lowered into the ground than she watched Donald Harvey sprint across the graveyard towards a solitary dark figure standing beneath a large oak tree. To the amazement of the mourners, within seconds he was raining blows on the man who he had firstly knocked to the ground.

Taylor hitched up her tight skirt and ran best she could across the grass in her stilettos, until her heel caught in the earth and she toppled face first to the ground. Picking herself up as fast and graciously as she could, she discarded her footwear and continued in bare feet.

'Pack it in! Have you no respect?' she yelled at the top of her voice.

The man lying flat on his back had blood covering his face and running profusely from his nose, along his cheek and down the side of his neck by the time she reached Donald Harvey's side. To her astonishment, it was Brian Stevenson who attempted to raise his head from the ground and wipe his face with the back of his hand. In between coughing he spat blood to the ground. Taylor knelt at his side.

'Are you okay?' she said.

Donald Harvey panted heavily. 'It's you who should be six foot in the under, you robbing bastard,' he said, spitting to the ground.

'Last warning Mr Harvey, otherwise I'll arrest you for assault,' Taylor warned.

'You're a dead man, Stevenson. You're a fucking dead man,' Donald Harvey called over his shoulder as he turned and walked away. Taylor offered her hand to help Mr Stevenson to his feet.

'I'm fine, fine... I didn't mean to cause trouble I just wanted to show my respects,' he said. 'I've known Grace a long time. I thought a lot about her even if her inheriting son doesn't think so,' he said, as he attempted to tidy himself up. He took a clean, neatly pressed handkerchief from his trouser pocket and sneezed before he could open it. Blood sprayed across the front of Taylor's white shirt and she jumped back with a squeal. She looked down at her new Jacques Vert jacket with horror.

'Sorry,' he said, sheepishly wiping his face.

'Do you want to make a complaint?' she asked with more composure than she felt. 'If you do, I'll go and arrest him.'

'No, I appreciate his emotions will be running high, which has to be understood,' he said. 'And, let's face it, he's got to blame somebody, so it might as well be me. I'll live,' he said gallantly.

Taylor attempted to blot the blood off her jacket with a tissue, only to find her fingers covered. 'The lack of closure is frustrating for some,' she said, impressed with his compassion.

'Please, let me pay for the cleaning.' Brian Stevenson said, reaching out to try wipe her jacket. Taylor jumped back.

'We'll see,' she snapped. 'If you're alright, I'll go after me laddo and let him know just how lucky he is that he isn't heading back to the police station with me in a pair of handcuffs.'

Taylor walked precariously around the gravestones on the grass to Grace Harvey's burial spot where Donald Harvey stood morosely looking in. She picked up her shoes along the way, only to find one of the heels hanging precariously by a thread. As she passed a bin she tossed them in, glancing back to the old oak tree; as she did so she saw that Brian Stevenson had disappeared. Donald Harvey looked across at her as she approached him. When she didn't speak he turned and walked away. She followed.

'Are you going to tell me what the hell that was all about?' she demanded, her face like thunder.

Donald's pace quickened down the hill towards the car park but he remained silent. She ran barefoot to keep up to his long, purposeful strides.

'You're very fortunate, you know, that Mr Stevenson doesn't want to press charges,' she said, hobbling behind him down the hill path. 'Shit,' she said under her breath as she trod on a sharp stone. Donald Harvey turned and saw her trying to balance on one leg as she as she rubbed her bleeding foot.

'Why're you shouting at me? It should be him you're reading the riot act to,' he said stepping forward and offering his hand to help her gain her balance. She took it gratefully and stared directly at his suited chest before looking up into his distraught face.

'This isn't over,' he said quietly. 'He's just lucky you were about, this time.'

Taylor looked into his deep-set, brown, hooded eyes and held his gaze for a moment or two. Unblinking, he turned and walked off to his car. She stood still and ran her dried blood-coated fingers through her hair in exasperation. 'What a bloody mess', she whispered.

'I don't understand,' she shouted after him. 'He says he only did what your mum wanted him to do so she could fund your lifestyle.'

He stopped in his tracks and turned. 'What?' he asked walking back towards her. 'What did you say? I didn't need her money,' he yelled, through gritted teeth. Taylor pulled herself up to stand as tall as she could.

'He says she took the equity out of her home for you.'

'Where's the money then? I certainly haven't seen it,' he said. 'And that pariah hasn't seen the last of me either,' he growled.

'Look, I'm the detective, not you. I'll get to the bottom of this. You stay away from him. Do you hear?' she called after Donald Harvey as he got into his car.

He slammed the car door shut. He drove towards her and, pulling alongside her, he opened his window.

'I need you to sign some authorities so that I can check into your mum's bank accounts,' she said.

You know where I am,' he replied. 'And tell Mr Stevenson if you see him he'd better keep looking over his shoulder because one day I'll catch up with him.'

As she saw Donald Harvey's car vanish through the village she could feel goosebumps rise on her arms and she shivered. 'Who was she to believe?' she thought as she stepped from the shade of the trees that lined the path to the church and into the warmth of the sun. She looked at her watch, there was no time to worry about that now, she needed to head for the mortuary to see what secrets Mildred Sykes post-mortem would reveal about her death. First though she must buy some 'practical' shoes, as Dylan would have said, on her way and drop her jacket off at the cleaners – her skirt and top would just have to do for the mortuary.

Chapter 11

'What a day,' said Taylor as she ran across the car park to the mortuary. It was obvious to her that the tarmac had just been laid and in the midday heat she could feel the heels of her new shoes sinking in. She dragged her brush through her hair briefly, glanced at herself in her hand mirror and ran a covering of gloss around her lips.

There was no time to fret further about her appearance she thought, kicking the door wide open; she'd have to do. She zipped up her bag, put it under her arm, tossed her hair over her shoulder and smoothed her skirt down with sweaty palms, as she stopped for a moment at the top of the steps.

Taylor took a deep breath before she entered the mortuary's office. This was the moment she had been dreading since she had seen the body of Mildred Sykes laying dead on the floor of her insect ridden bedroom. Watching some pathologist butcher any body was not her idea of fun, never mind a decomposed one. However, like Dylan said it was a necessary process she had to witness for the good of the investigation. She just hoped the pathologist wasn't Professor Bernard Stow, who thought he was a comedian. She opened the door and walked in. Professor Stow stood in the adjoining room. Her heart sank and she groaned.

'Good timing Taylor, do you want coffee or tea?' asked Dylan who was stood at the vending machine, waiting for his cup to be filled.

'Tea, strong and sweet please, preferably with a shot of brandy,' she replied sitting down with a thud on the only seat available in the mortuary attendant's office, which just happened to be the most uncomfortable old wooden ladder-backed chair with a flat piece of red material posing as a cushion.

'You remember Jasmine from SOCO who was at the scene don't you?' Dylan said ignoring her manner. Taylor nodded at the petite, pretty, dark haired, composed-looking young woman, who smiled at her from across the room as she tucked into a large bacon bap.

'I think you and I will stay in the police observation office area for this one, so we don't have to suffer the smell,' said Dylan.

'Thank you,' Taylor said, smiling briefly before looking heavenward with a sharp intake of breath. There was a God after all.

'Lucky you.' Jasmine drawled as she wiped her greasy hands on a napkin, put the remainder of her sandwich on a plate and picked up her camera to check its settings.

'Well at least the pathologist will be a laugh Jasmine, it's Professor Stow,' said Dylan.

Taylor closed her eyes briefly. 'Oh, joy...' she mumbled.

Dylan passed her a cup of tea and she reached out for it.

'Thanks.'

'You took my advice,' he said nodding at her sensible black pumps that had the smallest pointed heel.' She smiled, sarcastically. 'That's a nasty mark,' he said, pointing to her blouse. 'You been in a scrap?'

'Blood from this morning,' she said, standing up to show him the full extent of the damage to her clothing before she went on to explain the eventful morning she'd had.

'So who do you think's telling the truth?' Dylan asked.

Taylor shrugged her shoulders and tentatively took a sip of her drink. Looking down into her polystyrene cup, she noticed the blood and dirt that still clung to her fingernails. She grimaced and walked over to the sink to scrub her hands.

'Decisions Taylor, the jobs all about the consequences of the decisions you make,' Dylan said, beaming. 'And when you're a boss remember they're always the right ones 'coz there ain't no one above you to tell you you're wrong. Any luck in locating the hit and run vehicle yet?'

'No, and believe it or not, either one of the men could be involved yet too.'

Dylan raised his eyebrows.

'Both Donald Harvey and Brian Stevenson have recent damage to their cars by their own admission. I need the accident investigation branch to let me know that they are a hundred and ten per cent positive of the make of the car that we're looking for before I take it further.'

The door dramatically swung open and in walked the robust figure of Professor Stow.

'Good afternoon everyone. Cheer up,' Professor Stow trumpeted with a theatrical wave of his chubby hand in front of their solemn faces. 'Anyone would think someone has ... Ooops, they have,' he roared. 'Back in five minutes,' he said, talking very fast. His big fat red cheeks wobbled as he laughed. 'The old ones are always the best,' he chuckled as he took his coveralls from the peg. 'Got to smile once in a while' he continued, struggling to tie the green disposal plastic apron around his cumbersome frame.

'Well Dylan what have you got for me today?' he panted. 'Hello there Jasmine, Taylor isn't it?' he said, not waiting for either to answer before enthusiastically pulling plastic gloves out of a Kleenex style tissue box and shaking off the excess talcum powder. He commenced to blow them up like a balloon.

'Yes,' said Taylor bemused. She cringed as he slowly let the air out of the glove and it made a farting sound. He chuckled, shook each glove and fought to get them onto his huge hands. This accomplished, he rubbed his hands together and grinned, showing off crooked, yellow teeth.

'Thought so, never forget a good body,' he chortled eyeing her up and down. Her face was a picture. Dylan and Jasmine smiled knowingly at each other.

'Only joking,' he said looking seriously over his half rimmed glasses at her, 'so what have we got?' he said, turning to Dylan. Professor Stow's face mask hung round his neck waiting to be strung behind his ears as he entered the mortuary. He stood with hands on his hips as Dylan outlined in detail the discovery of Mildred Sykes' badly decomposed body.

'A bit of a rotter then?' quipped Professor Stow as he launched at the mortuary door elbows first to keep his gloves sterile. Jasmine managed to carry her equipment into the room behind him before the doors swung shut.

Dylan knew from experience that Professor Stow's post-mortems were quick and thorough. Insensitivity and bad jokes aside, he knew they wouldn't have to suffer him for long. Taylor was grateful to Dylan for allowing them to use the observation room. It was about time one of the bosses was concerned about people who had to attend mortuaries for post-mortems.

'A mint, Taylor?' said Dylan, offering her the sweets that said Extra Strong on its packaging.

'Tea and now mints, thank you sir,' said Taylor as she dragged an old battered grey, plastic chair from the pile situated in the corner of the room and positioned it as far away from the mortuary observation window as possible.

'What does a 75-year-old woman have between her breasts that a 25-year-old doesn't?' Professor Stow asked Jasmine. Jasmine shook her head. 'Her navel,' he laughed.

Although in a nauseous state and her heart leaping every so often into her mouth, Taylor found she couldn't take her eyes off the examination, gruesome as it was. At first she dare only look through her fingers as she had done as a child at horror movies but eventually the need to know what information the post-mortem could give them overrode her fear. Before long, she felt brave enough to stand behind Dylan and peer over his shoulder as he stood at the window, to see what was happening in the next room.

'She's got maggots big enough for my fishing box in here,' Professor Stow said, picking one up with a pair of tweezers and holding it up for all to see before dropping it unceremoniously in a plastic bowl on the trolley next to him. He continued to relay his thoughts and findings into his Dictaphone as he examined Mildred's body.

'Okay,' he said, at last with a big sigh. I reckon good old Mildred here's been dead for some...' he pondered, 'six weeks or thereabouts. There's some bruising to both her wrists, possibly as a result of being held and she has suffered a serious skull fracture, which I'll confirm shortly. Can opener please,' he said holding out his gloved right hand to his assistant.

The top of the skull, referred to as the 'cap', was removed. 'Yes, there is no doubt about it, it's a severe fracture to the skull,' he said looking up at Dylan over the mask. 'I know it's not what you wanted to hear and it's not consistent with falling either – much too severe. She was struck with a blunt instrument and with some force,' he said. 'Poor old dear,' he sighed. 'But it'd have been instant death, if that's any consolation.'

All the necessary samples were taken along with photographs and two hours later it was all over, much to Taylor's relief.

Professor Stow had nothing more to tell them in his debrief.

'Your first murder as a DS and a deputy SIO,' said Dylan to Taylor who walked down the steps with him.

'Yes boss,' she said with a smile.

'All you need to do now is find who did it,' he grinned. Her heart sunk. *Where did she start?* she thought as she looked at Dylan expectantly.

'Let's get Forensic to Mildred's house, the incident room up and running and do a press release,' Dylan said as if reading her thoughts as they walked towards the door. He stopped as the sun found his face and he took a large gulp of clean air into his lungs.

'Isn't it good to be alive, Taylor?' he said.

Taylor stood for a moment smiling. 'The Press' was all she'd heard him say after that everything else faded to oblivion. Taylor's excitement knew no bounds as the reality of what he had just said sunk in. There was going to be a press conference, which she was going to be part of.

Chapter 12

Pam couldn't wait for the weekend to come. What should she wear? Nothing in her wardrobe seemed to look grown up enough, she thought as she looked despairingly at the pile of discarded clothing on her bed and the empty wardrobe. Why did no one but Danny realise she was a young woman?

Meanwhile, Danny and Bill were planning their next move. Danny suggested he'd keep Pam occupied, ask about her family and gather information about their movements.

'Billy I want you to look in her bag and her pockets, in fact anywhere you think she might keep her keys. But before that you do remember that we have some unfinished business with the occupier of that house,' he said. The two observed the solitary property in its own grounds with a walled garden.

'It doesn't look like there's an alarm,' said Billy.

'No, and we can drive around the back of the house out of sight, by the looks of it,' Danny said as he peered in his rear view mirror, then spun the car around and drove through the open gates. Quickly they gained access via the rear patio doors by forcing them off the rails.

'Nice pad,' said Billy, as he strolled around the lounge.

'Look for cash and jewellery and then we'll think about the electrical stuff.' Danny called as he took the stairs two at a time. He peered over the banisters from the gallery landing. 'Don't forget before you touch anything to put ya socks on yer hands so you don't leave prints.'

'Yeah, yeah, yeah,' Billy said, sitting down on the tiger skin rug to take off his footwear and re site his socks. Dried mud fell from his trainers onto the cream carpet and he nonchalantly rubbed it into the deep pile.

'Five minutes, then we're out of here,' Danny said. Billy jumped to his feet and started pulling drawers out of the dresser, but disappointingly there was nothing to pocket. He flopped down on the sofa and opened the footstool. He eyes couldn't believe what they saw.

'Jackpot.' he screamed. 'I've found money – and lots of it.'

Danny hurtled down the stairs and grabbed the cash-filled holdall. 'Fucking hell, there must be a few grand here. Let's get out, we don't need ought else.' Danny said running towards the patio doors. He turned and stared at his friend who was struggling with a widescreen TV.

'Please Danny,' Billy begged. 'For the flat?'

'Come on, we've got to go. Go. Go.'

Billy staggered to the doors and, resting the TV on the kitchen worktop, he picked up a clock studded with gems that sparkled in the sunlight and stuffed it into his pocket.

Danny took one look at him.

'For fuck's sake Billy.' he said.

'I like it,' he said with a cheeky grin.

'You're soft in the bleedin' head,' Danny said to his mate as he opened the hatchback to put in their ill-gotten gains. The two opened their car doors in unison, casually took one last look around and jumped in. Danny turned the key in the ignition and as if they had just been a visitor to the house he steered the car carefully and calmly out of the drive and into the road.

Danny tipped the holdall upside down and the money rained down on their living room floor.

'Thirty-five grand.' Danny said, as he put the last fifty pound note on a pile.

'We're fucking rich.' Billy said, throwing the notes in the air. 'Let's go to
McDonald's and celebrate.'

'This is just the start. Nothing's going to stop us now,' Danny said, belching loudly, much to the disgust of a two young women with children at the next table. Danny smiled at them and, opening his mouth, he showed them his un-swallowed food. The children giggled. The women turned their heads, rose from the table and hurriedly prepared their children to leave.

Do you fancy going out? Billy texted Pam. 'If we get her house keys we might be able to double our money,' Danny scoffed. 'We could get a new car.'

'I'd be quite happy to just give her one,' he said grinning.

'Patience Billy, you've gotta have patience mate,' Danny said. The phone bleeped.

Sounds fab x

'Honestly Billy, they let kids have their mobiles on in school these days,' he said, shaking his head. 'What's the world coming to?' he sighed. 'Roll on the weekend – and in the meantime, let's have some fun,' he shouted as they headed for the car.

'Danny, blue and white to the right,' shouted Billy as they cruised the streets of Harrowfield.

'Showtime,' Danny yelled, excitement in his tone as he spun the steering wheel with the palm of his hand. Foot down, the wheels screeched and, as anticipated, it immediately attracted the police officer's attention. The blue lights and sirens of the police car were immediately behind them. The cat and mouse chase was on.

'Tenner says they don't catch us,' hollered Danny.

'You tight git.' yelled Billy, turning up the music. The police car was on their tail.

'Railway crossing ahead Billy, let's see who's chicken,' Danny shouted. Billy closed his eyes. The red lights were flashing. A train was due. The barrier jerked into action.

'It's coming down Billy, yee ha.' Danny shouted, as he pulled the car out past the stationary cars waiting at the level crossing. Billy felt the bumps of the railway lines beneath the car tyres as they were lifted from the tarmac and thrown through the air at speed. The barrier missed them by a cat's whisker and they avoided the vehicles at the other side by a hair's breadth. Even then, Danny continued to hold his foot down flat on the accelerator, excitement pumping feverishly through his veins. They would be long gone before the Police got across the level crossing, and he knew it.

'I think we better get rid of this as soon as,' Danny said, banging the steering wheel. 'We're gonna be the cops most wanted.'

'Can we afford it?' Billy asked seriously. Danny roared with laughter.

'Remember that black Subaru Impreza we saw in the garage in Tandem Bridge? We could afford that cash, mate.'

'No,' his friend said in awe. 'Come on then what're we waiting for?'

'Because we're gonna fire this on the moors, report it stolen and claim on the insurance too,' Danny rapped. 'Shake on it, mate,' he said, spitting into his hand and leaning over to shake Billy's.

Tandem Bridge Garage staff had moved the Impreza to a prime site at the front of the forecourt on a display turntable. Danny pulled alongside it for a closer look then, parking their car off the main road, they got out and walked admiringly around the prized vehicle. Pausing, they caressed the deep front and rear spoilers. Danny put his hand on the car door handle and instantly a burly salesman appeared from what seemed like fresh air.

'What can I do for you two?' he asked.

'Can we have a go? We might want to buy it, might'nt we?' said Danny, stuffing his hands into his pockets and cocking his head to one side.

'What with?'

'Dosh, what do you think mate?' Billy said.

'Cash, straight up?' he asked dubiously.

'Straight up, sir,' said Danny.

'I'll get the keys,' said the car salesman with a grin and a wink that said he didn't believe them. *What harm would it do to give the kids a look though*, he thought.

Minutes later, Danny sat in the driver's side, reaching for the large multifunctional display in front of him and fingering the touch panels on the steering wheel. The car smelt of adhesives and sealers. Billy turned on the radio. The salesman stood at the door, his frame stopping them from closing it and his hands in close proximity to the ignition key. There was no way these two scrotes were going to drive off in it without paying, that would be his wages gone for the rest of his life.

'How about a test drive?' Danny asked as he looked up from the racing seat.

'You're pushing it a bit now lads, anyway I can't at the moment,' said the salesman.

'But if you get out I'll start her up and give you a look under the bonnet.

Danny and Billy nodded at each other.

'Discount for cash?' asked Danny.

'No, we don't do discount. People who can afford these don't need discount or to ask the price in my experience,' he chortled. This was going nowhere.

'Car mats?' Billy enquired.

The salesman shook his head. 'They're extra.'

'Can I have one of the brollies with the Subaru logo on it?' Billy said as he pointed to a bunch of them in a stand.

'Yeah, if you like,' said the salesman, bemused.

'Deal, we'll be in for it tomorrow,' said Billy. Danny shook his head at his friend.

'Yeah, whatever mate,' said the salesman locking the car with the immobiliser fob.

'What are you going to do with a fucking golf umbrella?' Danny asked when they got back to their car.

'I dunno, but it's better than nought innit?' Billy said, grinning.

'I could have got some cash off of it if we'd haggled,' said Danny.

'Don't be tight. I've always wanted one of them big brollies,' Billy said, his smile falling into a frown.

'You're a fucking loony, do you know that?' Danny said to his friend. He sighed.

'Never mind we've got a new motor, courtesy of Mr Porsche,' Danny grinned. 'Now where we gonna to fire this baby, Billy?'

'Not too far away from the flat, I don't want to have to walk,' Billy said, yawning.

'How about we get a taxi to the garage tomorrow to pick it up?' said Danny.

'Can we?'

'No, we can't, you idle bastard.'

'I've never been in a taxi before, unless I nicked it,' said Billy.

They had travelled a few hundred yards from the garage when they heard the sound of a siren and Danny saw that blue lights were on their tail, in his rear view mirror.

'Shit. The sneaky bastards. I didn't see them sneaking up on us. Hold tight Billy, here we go again,' Danny said, slamming his foot to the floor.

'We're shagged Danny there's a red light ahead.'

'What red light? Fuck that. You think that's gonna stop me? Let's see how much bottle they've got.'

With the two cars in front braking and the cops almost on their bumper, Danny slowed down. He watched both policemen alight from their vehicle in his rear view mirror and immediately put his foot down hard on the accelerator. Yanking the steering wheel to the left, the car lurched up onto the pavement, past the stationary cars and into the bus lane towards the red lights at speed. A woman with a child in a pram was stepping onto the zebra crossing. It was instant, no time to swerve or brake, the mother and her child's pram were hit head on and catapulted over the bonnet.

Billy screamed.

'Fucking idiot,' Danny yelled. His foot was still to the floor as he headed for the moors, they needed to burn the car out as quickly as possible now.

Danny was visibly shaking but he didn't take his eyes off the road as the car gathered speed down 'Snake Pass' that led onto the moors. 'You okay Billy?' he said.

'Yeah, I'm fine,' he said.

'There was nothing I could do Billy. You know that don't you?'

'I know. Thank God we weren't in our new car,' he said swallowing hard.

They looked at each other and cracked up laughing. Fifteen minutes later Billy jammed a screwdriver into the ignition. Danny expertly siphoned petrol from it., poured the flammable liquid over the car and threw a match in the open window. Flames licked around on the inside and in no time at all it burst into an inferno.

The two stared at the billowing flames momentarily before running hell for leather down the hillside of coarse grasses and bracken. Danny and Billy thought their lungs were going to burst when they stopped for breath behind a stone wall and stared back across the heathland. Dropping to the ground on their knees, they laughed in between gasps. Tears ran down their grubby faces as they watched the black smoke heading skywards. The smell of burning rubber blew its way on the wind and filled their nostrils. They coughed and spluttered.

There was an explosion and they looked over the wall. The car was a fireball. The pair covered their heads as the debris flew and small particles rained down on them.

'It won't be long before the cops see that and come sniffing,' Danny said.

'You know what?'

'What?'

'The new car's wing'll have to have four stripes now,' Billy squealed before getting up and continuing to run.

'Better ring the cops and tell them the car's gone missing,' Danny shouted to his friend, as they stumbled together across the moor, sometimes hitting their shins on sharp stones, sometimes sinking to the tops of their trainers in swampy places.

From the safety of their flat, washed and discarded clothing in a plastic carrier bag ready for a neighbour's bin, Danny rang to report their Fiesta stolen. Must have happened overnight, he said.

'You'll have to come into the police station with your documents I'm afraid, Mr Denton and make the report in person,' said the lady on the switchboard.

The two set off walking.

'The tart didn't say it had been found. They'll want to know why we've waited to report it missing. We'll tell them that we've only just realised it has gone and thought it might be some toe rag on the estate who'd borrowed it. So we asked about first.'

'Yeah, there're some proper bastards around here, right Danny?' said Billy, laughing as they strolled into the police station.

Chapter 13

Bridey Tate, just twenty-one, was on a life support machine fighting for her life, as was her eight-week-old son, Toby. Mother and baby had been going out to spend the gift vouchers that her and her husband had received when Toby was born.

The buggy which the baby had been in now lay overturned on the pavement. Police and ambulances had arrived at the scene and, within minutes, others attended in numbers to seal off the area. The registered number of the offending vehicle had been circulated to all working police personnel by the officers in the car that had been in the traffic queue at the traffic lights. An independent police complaints commission investigation was started.

It wasn't long before a lorry driver reported that a car was on fire on the moors. The patrol car, which had been dispatched to the scene of the burning vehicle confirmed that it was the car probably responsible for what could prove to be a fatal accident and was expected to be the victim of an arson attack. Although the vehicle wasn't totally destroyed when the fire engines reached it, it wasn't far off being a blackened shell by the time they'd managed to put out the fire.

Meanwhile, Danny Denton and Billy Greenwood stood as bold as brass at the help desk counter of Harrowfield Police Station, on CCTV and in full view of all police personnel that were on duty. They smiled sweetly up into the camera in the foyer as if butter wouldn't melt in their mouths.

'Would you mind not leaning on the counter,' said the help desk assistant whose face was puffy, flushed and tight-lipped. 'We've got a major incident unfolding. What do you want?'

'I've just come to report my car stolen,' Danny said, sprawling his arms across the counter; the help-desk assistant tutted loudly. Billy stood behind Danny making rude gestures.

'Really?' said the hefty, white haired desk sergeant who rose from his chair at the back of the office.

'Yeah,' Billy replied, stepping forward to back up his friend.

The sergeant dismissed the help-desk assistant and took the relevant forms out of his grey metal filing cabinet drawer. With great care he took down details for the crime report.

'Sit down,' he ordered, pointing to a bench that was screwed to both the floor and the wall. The two did as they were told.

'No one's gonna nick this are they?' Billy laughed, touching the thick nut and bolt securing the piece of wood that emulated a seat.

'PC Whitworth'll be out to see you in a minute,' the sergeant called.

Inspector Jack Dylan walked through the foyer, glancing in their direction.

'What've you two been up to?' he asked the boys.

'Nothing sir, somebody nicked our car,' said Billy sheepishly.

Dylan laughed heartily. 'So now you know what it's like to have summat stolen don't you?'

Danny put one finger up behind Dylan's back as they watched him key in the security numbers to allow him to enter the station's offices.

'What're they playing at?' Danny whispered impatiently to his friend just as two police officers walked through the same door.

'I understand you've come to report your car stolen?' said the taller of the two.

'Yeah' said Danny, rising from the bench.

'That's convenient.' he said, looking straight into Danny's eyes.

'No, it ain't, we had to walk here,' Billy responded. The two officers looked at each other with furrowed brows.

'Who's the owner?' asked the smaller, fresh faced young officer who could have been the same age as them.

'Me, and before you ask, it's legit and I've got all the documents to prove it here,' Danny said, waving paperwork in front of his face.

'And who are you then?' the older officer said to Billy.

'I'm his best mate.'

The young officer pointed to a door.

'In there,' he said to Billy.

'And you come with me,' said the older of the two as he picked up the crime report from the desk sergeant and waved a finger at Danny that indicated he should follow him.

'So, Mr Denton, I'm PC Tim Whitworth. Now, when was this car of yours stolen then?' he said, pulling the chair out from beneath a small square melamine desk.

'We noticed it were gone from outside the flat this morning.'

'So let's get this straight. You're telling me you've walked round since this morning looking for your car, but since you've have no luck you've decided to report it to us, is that right?' The police officer said, staring deep into Danny's eyes.

Danny nodded.

'We believe your car has just knocked down a young mother and her child on a zebra crossing, both are on the critical list. If I find out you're lying to me I'll personally string you up and by God you'll wish you were dead,' he said leaning across the desk and grabbing Danny by the chin with a wrench-like grip.

'Argh,' said Danny, swallowing hard. 'It's wasn't me. I haven't done ought. Look, I brought my keys and my documents like I were told to on the phone. It weren't me. Come on, if I'd have done ought like that d'ya think I'd have been stupid enough to come anywhere near you? Let go of me,' he demanded through clenched teeth.

The officer squeezed harder then pushing Danny's head backwards he let go. 'God, if my daughter, our Sara, ever brought a lout like you home...' he started to say with a great in-drawing of breath. 'Stay here, I'll be back,' he said as he marched out of the door.

Danny sat looking around. The room was only about eight feet square. It had no windows and one door and it was unbearably warm. The walls were newly painted grey; he could still smell the solvents. Danny could hear the mumble of two officer's voices outside the door of the interview room.

It was strangely soothing. A camera was focused on him from the top right hand corner of the room and a strip of metal ran around the walls. He knew that was an alarm bell that the officer could use to summon his colleagues in case he was under attack. He smiled, he only knew that because they had had to use it when he had punched a copper in an interview room once.

PC Tim Whitworth threw the door back in a sudden, sharp movement, which made Danny jump as it slammed against the wall behind him.

'Your stories check out, so before I can think of something else to keep you in for, get out of my sight,' he spat, holding the door ajar.

'I need the crime number for the insurance, mate?' Danny said. He could feel the officer's anger and reluctantly PC Whitworth walked back into the room, leaned on the desk and wrote the number down on a piece of paper, and then threw it at him.

'Cheers,' Danny said, with a smile as he turned and reached out for the officer's hand. PC Whitworth grabbed his collar and standing up, he pinned Denton to the wall. 'Keep looking over your shoulder, mate,' he said, bringing his knee up into his crutch before throwing him out into the foyer.

'Hey you can't do that,' Billy shouted as he rose from the bench he'd been sitting on, loud enough for the desk sergeant to hear. The desk sergeant raised his eyebrows and craned his neck to look over the counter to see what the commotion was about and then carried on with what he was doing.

PC Whitworth glared at Billy. 'Fuck off,' he mouthed. Danny walked up to Billy and putting a hand on his shoulder turned him round to face the exit and pushed him towards it.

'He thinks he's hard in that uniform,' he whispered. 'But I know his name. We won't forget him,' he grimaced, rubbing in between his legs.

'Too true we won't, the bastard,' Billy said. PC Tim Whitworth stood at the exit of the police station and watched the two until they had walked under the subway tunnel towards the town and out of sight.

'We'd better ring the insurance company when we get home,' said Danny. 'And we need to give Pam that tenner back she lent us when we see her.'

'Why would we want to do that Danny?' asked Billy.

'Well, we wouldn't want her to think we're only after her for her money now would we?' he said with a grin.

'Oh, yeah,' Billy said.

'I'll text her.'

'Good plan.'

It wouldn't be long before news of Bridey Tate's fate and that of her son spread quickly.

The hospital and police were frantically trying to get hold of Bridey's husband and family.

The road remained closed and the police were interviewing the shocked witnesses. The mangled wreck of the pram remained in situ, battered and wretched and next to the police cordon was a growing memorial; a wall of flowers and soft toys.

CID was now at the scene.

This was an evil crime, a deliberate act. Why did the car need to get away from the police so badly?

PC Tim Whitworth took the call on his radio at the scene. 'The chassis number's been checked and the car is confirmed as belonging to a Danny Denton,' said the police officer from the control room.

Chapter 14

'I'm gonna be late tonight love. It looks like the old lady was murdered,' Dylan told Jen's answering machine. 'Catch up with you as soon as I can.' He put the phone down in haste and called out to anyone in the CID office within earshot.

'I need to get the incident room up and running, house to house enquiries urgently completed and forensic officers to the deceased's home please.'

The scene needed to be searched and the next of kin identified. Initial enquiries had suggested that Ms Sykes had no family.

'Who was the last person to see her alive, Taylor?' Dylan asked DS Taylor Spiers as he handed her a list of people to contact. She shrugged her shoulders, wide-eyed.

'Get the team together for a briefing as soon as possible will you, this bloody murderer has had one hell of a head start on us.'

He picked up the phone to ring the press office and give Liz a brief statement.

'*A murder enquiry is under way after the decomposed body of an elderly lady was found at her home address,*' he said. '*Number 11, Causeway Cottages. A post-mortem has shown that she died from a non-accidental head injury, which possibly occurred some six weeks ago. Police hope to name the lady later today but are appealing for witnesses.*' I know they'll want more, but I need to get things up and running and obtain more background information on the victim before I can give them anything,' he said to Liz at the press office.

No sooner had he put the phone down than it rang again and Dylan picked up straight away.

'Boss, John Benjamin, has anyone told you about the young mother and her son who've been mowed down on a zebra crossing by an alleged stolen car?' he said. Dylan leaned back in his chair.

'Go on, first I've heard of it,' he said, disgruntled.

'Twenty-one-year-old mum and her eight-week-old son are both on life support at Harrowfield hospital, it's looking like there is nothing that can be done – they've both got massive head injuries. I'm at the scene and we're urgently trying to trace next of kin.'

'What do we know about the car, John?'

'Been confirmed as a red Ford Fiesta that's owned by a local scrote; him and his mate apparently reported it stolen today.'

'I'll see you at the scene as soon as. By the way the PM on Mildred Sykes shows she was murdered by a fatal blow to the head. I'm trying to get that one up and running with Taylor.'

'No probs, see you soon.'

How accurate the saying is that *it never rains but it pours,* thought Dylan.

Quickly briefing Taylor of what he wanted her to do next, he excused himself to head towards the scene of the accident to ensure that no corners were cut and everything was done properly.

'My God, what sort of place have I come to work in?' Taylor said to Dennis. 'It's like that *Midsomer Murders.*'

'Arrange the debrief for five, Dennis, and in the meantime a photograph from the house of Ms Sykes would be helpful if you can arrange for someone to pick one up for me. Remember Taylor, I want SOCO and forensic at her address; I don't want anything leaving to chance. I'll give the team the update on this latest hit and run at the briefing and you can do the update on Grace Harvey's fatal so that they're all fully aware of what's going on.'

Taylor nodded.

'Right, I'll be back as soon as I can – and in the meantime I'm on the mobile, so ring me if you need to speak to me', he said as he picked up his coat and briefcase and flew out of the door.

Dylan could see DS John Benjamin's large frame stood in the doorway to Mothercare speaking to a uniformed officer.

He managed to drive to where the road was cordoned off then had to walk to where Bridey and Toby had been struck. John raised his hand in acknowledgement of his boss's presence.

People were already passing bouquets to the uniformed officers guarding the scene, who were in turn laying them neatly along the pavement's edge. The upturned pram was a stark reminder to Dylan of what had taken place. Local press were gathering in droves with their cameras. Vans with television station emblems were parked up with their masts aloft, their occupants frantically setting up filming equipment at the cordon. Tomorrow, the doom and gloom would be spread across the country in the national newspapers.

Dylan scanned the scene. He noticed the absence of skid marks on the dry road surface. There had been no attempt to avoid the pedestrians, so why such desperation by the driver?

'What's the story so far John?' asked Dylan.

'Earlier today police were in pursuit of a red Ford Fiesta which nearly caused an accident by going through a closing railway barrier towards Tandem in the chase and according to witnesses the train only missed the car by a split second. The police car had to stop and the car got away.

'Its details were circulated over the police radio and a short time later it was spotted on the high street, two up. A police car pulled up behind it and put its sirens and blue lights on to alert the Fiesta's driver to stop. Since it was stationary due to the traffic lights ahead changing to red, the police officers got out of the car and ran towards the Fiesta. Its occupants, presumably seeing them in pursuit, set off at speed, mounting the pavement to pass stationary cars and mowing down the young mum with her son who were just stepping onto the zebra crossing.

'It didn't stop, carried on at speed and was later found burnt out on the moors. The owner, along with his mate, reported the car stolen at the nick some time later – which undeniably stinks. The police officers have talked to them and the lads are singing from the same hymn sheet so they've had to let them go.

'It looks like the enquiry will have to be overseen by the independent complaints commission because of the police pursuit and that's about it in a nutshell,' concluded John.

'Thanks. Phew. Control have told me that professional standards are on their way, although by the sound of it I don't think it got as involved as a pursuit by the police, did it? We need to gather all the information from the scene and descriptions from witnesses of the occupants of the Fiesta. Even if they can only give us an indication as to what clothing they were wearing. And we also need to tie the burnt-out car to the scene to show it was the offending vehicle. Do we know if it's a total burn out?'

'Not completely, boss, so I'm told so we may be lucky.'

'Let's get it collected from the moors on a low-loader. We might have some impact debris on the part of the vehicle. Ave we checked near the car for footprints or anything that might have been discarded?'

'We're on with it, boss.'

'Just thinking aloud, we'll have to start a policy book. What's the update on the family?'

'I understand they're still trying to locate her parents. Graham, her husband is a brickie and he's out on a site. His boss has been made aware and was going over to collect him and take him to Harrowfield Hospital.

'I've arranged for a Family Liaison Officer to be turned out and I'm waiting for control to let me know who that is.'

'Good lad.' said Dylan.

'It's not looking good, I'm told, for either of the casualities.'

'The bastards eh?' Dylan said with venom.

'Yeah, exactly.'

'Look, I've got a briefing back at Harrowfield for the murder of the old lady from Causeway Cottages but I'll meet up with you afterwards at the nick and we'll speak more. I take it we don't think the car was stolen and the report was made after the incident?'

'PC Tim Whitworth and his partner say there was no proof to detain. I think it's an odd one but the only thing that concerns me is that there was a screwdriver stuck in the ignition according to our lads at the scene and the owner of the vehicle turned up at the nick with the keys. Would they have had time or the nous to think about staging it do you think?' John said, lines furrowing his brow.

'Let's just get all the information together before we make any assumptions. Never mind dangerous driving. Cars are weapons just like guns. They can and do kill. Make sure we get all the CCTV in the areas concerned – and that includes the information from the speed cameras if possible. See if we can nail 'em. Treat it as a murder. Oh, and if you...'

'Need to speak to you you're on your mobile,' John said. Dylan smiled.

Leaving John standing on the pavement by the scene, Dylan texted Jen.

I think the world's gone mad x.

And don't tell me. You're the only one who can put it right X, she texted back.

LOL Don't wait up. Love you X

Love you too X. Jen sighed. She had a sinking feeling that another meal for one beckoned her from the freezer.

Dylan felt bad as he drove back to the nick. He would never understand how Jen put up with him but he was grateful she did. She was his 'normal' and he loved her for it.

Dylan walked through the foyer of the police station eating a banana that Jen had packed in his briefcase earlier that morning. He wondered about the two lads he'd seen in there earlier. Was one of them the owner of the car that had been involved in the hit and run? Nah, if they were the owners of a stolen car, he pondered, they were far too calm. He tried desperately to put names to their faces but was distracted by the noise coming from the incident room as he walked along the corridor. He was late.

'Boss, the team are all ready for you. Shall I sit up front?' asked the pouting Taylor Spiers.

'Why not, I'll just pay a call and grab a coffee then I'll be with you.'

'Your coffee has been ordered, sir,' Taylor said, fluttering her long eyelashes at him.

DS Spiers sat facing the door when he walked in the briefing room, Dylan's coffee cup protectively held in her hands. She uncrossed her legs and stood up to greet him. The room fell silent at his entrance and he sat at her side, taking the cup from her.

'Good afternoon ladies and gentlemen. For those of you who haven't worked with me before I'm Detective Inspector Jack Dylan and I will be in charge of this murder investigation. My deputy will be Detective Sergeant Taylor Spiers.' Dylan said indicating the woman who sat facing him.

Taylor smiled and sat up straight with her head erect and looked straight at him. Her long black dangly earrings rested on shoulders tightly pressed against the back of the chair. Involuntarily her bust thrust forward and from where he was sat he could see straight down her cleavage.

Her black shift dress with long flowing sleeves clung to her slender frame. The long black ridiculously high thigh length black boots she was so fond of wearing with black fishnet tights, were crossed at the ankle and stretched out in front of her, she reminded him of a spider.

He looked at the eyes of the young men in the audience who were openly admiring her and smiled to himself. God, he wished Dawn was with him on this one. Better the devil you knew.

'Sir?'

'Yes, Vicky,' said Dylan.

'I've just heard Graham Tate has been collected and is en-route.'

'Thank you.'

Dylan couldn't help notice Vicky smiling sweetly at Taylor.

'Mildred Sykes,' he said with a cough. 'Excuse me, we now know was 78 years old and lived alone at number 11, Causeway Cottages. She hadn't been seen for some time and after neighbours raised concerns with the police, officers attended and decided to force entry. They found her fully clothed badly decomposed body in the front bedroom. From the post-mortem examination it looks like she has been dead for around six weeks.

'It is quite clear that the cause of death was a massive blow to the rear of her skull – that has been confirmed and could not have been caused by a fall. She has bruises to her wrists where she may have been held or bound. Why was this elderly lady brutally murdered? What was the motive? Only time will tell.

'At the moment we know very little about her and we will need to create a timeline to find out what she'd been up to in the last few days of her life. Who were her visitors? Who did she telephone? Who telephoned her? Is there anything missing from her home? So far we have failed to locate living relatives, so we're reliant on neighbours at the moment.

'It's not an easy one and the murderer or murderers have had approximately six weeks start on us, but I'm confident we'll catch up. Let's not forget, ninety per cent of the time a victim will have had contact or known their killer or killers. So let's find who did it. Any questions?'

'Do we know when she last cashed her pension boss? If we did, then it might give us some start on a timescale,' Vicky said.

'I don't think we do know at the moment do we Taylor?' Dylan said turning to his right hand woman.

'Er no, not yet,' Taylor answered as she glared at Vicky, Dylan noticed.

'Good point Vicky,' Dylan said. 'And just on that Taylor, see what dates are on the unopened post will you? Okay everyone, you'll get to know who you're working with and the enquiries that I want you to make will be allocated by the HOLMES team to the individuals as soon as possible. Ten o'clock finish tonight then briefing back here at eight am tomorrow.

'But before we close the briefing I just want to let you know about a hit and run today that because of the injuries sustained is likely to prove to be a double fatal. It maybe whilst you're out and about talking to people you hear something that's relevant. Bridey Tate and her baby son Toby were run over outside Mothercare. The car was a red Ford Fiesta and it has been found on the moors burnt out. The owner has reported it stolen.

'Bridey and her son are on life support. The hospital, we are told, can do nothing for them due to the severity of the head injuries. Sadly, it looks like we will have a double fatal on our hands when the machines are turned off. It is believed there were two people in the offending car according to a witness. Feelings are understandingly running high and as you heard DC Hardacre say, Bridey's husband is on his way to the hospital,' he said morosely.

He left the room while Taylor briefed the team regarding the Grace Harvey fatal.

Chapter 15

Graham Tate's heart pounded like a drum. He could feel the blood rushing through his veins and he felt sick to his stomach. In his heavy heart, he knew that after this his life would never be the same.

He tried to comprehend the sight before him. There wasn't a mark on his beautiful wife's pale grey, lifeless looking face as she lay upon the hospital bed. There were tubes everywhere and beeping monitors. A starched white sheet covered her. Graham tentatively stroked the soft, smooth fingers of her uncovered hand.

His eyes prickled and then tears sprung forth. His vision blurred and the floodgates opened letting them bubble over and flow silently down his cheeks. A river of his tears now dripped unashamedly upon the front of his coat. He tried to brush them away with the back of his hand. 'Why? Why? Why?' he whispered, looking heavenward as he caught his breath and sobbed.

Hearing someone enter the room, he let go of Bridey's hand, took a deep breath, put his chin to his chest and bit his lip to try control his display of emotion. Although he couldn't see who it was, he heard the distinct patter of footsteps on the hospital floor. He sat on the chair next to the trolley and gripped his head in his hands tightly, trying to make the pain go away.

A hand was laid on his arm. 'Can I get you anything? A drink perhaps?' the nurse asked soothingly. He shook his head, he didn't look at her; he couldn't speak for the knot in his throat which felt like it was about to choke him. If he tried to utter a word, he knew it would release the beast within him, which he was afraid he would not be able to control. Instead, he concentrated on his rough, shovel-like hands and he gently picked up Bridey's long dainty fingers in his once more.

'If you need anything, anything at all, I'm just outside at the desk,' the nurse said before she turned and walked quietly away. He wanted nothing, nothing but for this to be a bad dream.

'Wait,' he said. She stopped. He didn't turn to face her. 'Where's Toby?' he said. Closing his eyes and holding his breath, he waited for an answer.

'I'm sure the doctors will come and see you in a moment,' she said softly. 'Is there anyone else…?'

'No, no thank you,' he said, quietly. Graham stood over his wife for a brief moment and held both her hands in his before putting his face to hers. 'Please don't leave me, I love you so much,' he whispered kissing her lips.

Detective Sergeant John Benjamin was at the hospital with the Family Liaison Officer getting a brief resume from the paramedics and arranging with uniformed officers for statements to be taken. He was discreetly seizing Bridey's clothing and personal belongings from the hospital staff when his telephone rang. 'Excuse me,' he said to his companions as he stood aside to take Dylan's call.

'John, I'm going to have Danny Denton and Billy Greenwood's flat turned over,' he said. 'I've been speaking to PC Whitworth and he has confirmed to me that he wasn't happy with Denton but he had no evidence to keep him in.'

'Okay, boss,' John said.

'Keep me updated from the hospital will you, I'll have my mobile on.'

'Maybe sooner than you think boss, it looks like the doctor is heading towards the room where Graham Tate is.'

'Poor bugger, I wouldn't want to be in his shoes,' said Dylan.

'No, me neither,' said John.

Chapter 16

While some of Dylan's team were making enquiries into Mildred Sykes's murder, he took a handful of officers to lock up Danny Denton and Billy Greenwood and search their flat. The two youths needed to be placed in or out of the investigation once and for all and at the moment they were his prime suspects in the Bridey Tate hit and run enquiry.

Dylan stood looking up at the grey, sullen concrete monolithic block of council owned residences. What had once been deemed as ideal living for the masses was now nothing more than an urban eyesore of suffocating maisonettes piled on top of each other.

A man about Dylan's age came up behind him without him noticing, so deep was his concentration.

'I've been mugged twice,' said the man to Dylan as he looked down at his walking stick. 'Had my pelvis broken two years ago and it gets worse. I pay £53 a week for the privilege of having a flat with a two foot by four foot patch of soil outside my front door with a garden gnome and asthmatic rose bush,' he said sullenly. Dylan didn't know what to say so nodded instead.

'I see the comings and goings of all the shit round here you know, but I also look at the boarded up windows of the flat across the street that was petrol-bombed last week. You're not going to get anything out of folks round here mate, if that's what you're here for,' he said before shuffling on his way.

A call from Dylan's radio brought officers to his side from the nearby police cars. The assembled group climbed the stairs to the targeted flat. To be fair the flats were not the worst Dylan had seen. Some he had raided sported the metal grilles of a prison cell at the windows and doors.

However, the stairs and landing leading to Flat seven were dark, smelly and vermin infested. On seeing the half glass entrance door to the flat Dylan was tempted to instruct his officers to take it off its hinges, which he knew would bring about an element of surprise – but on reflection he decided he might get more co-operation from the inhabitants if he adopted the softly, softly approach; to start with anyway. He needed solid evidence to enhance what the investigation team knew already. He knocked at the door and got an instant response.

'What the fuck do you lot want?' said Danny with a swagger. 'You found out who nicked my car?' he said, putting his nose to Dylan's.

'You sure your car was stolen?' Dylan spat in reply. 'You're under arrest on suspicion of attempted murder,' Dylan said pushing him back against the wall with a hand that gripped his shoulder.

'What?' Danny screeched. Officers pushed past Dylan and Danny in a military fashion to seek out Billy. One stopped alongside Dylan to handcuff Danny and escort him out to the waiting marked police car. Dylan then walked through to the lounge and watched Billy Greenwood's jaw drop open as he was read his rights by a detective.

'Check their pockets for keys then take them away,' said Dylan to the officer as he walked Billy past him, leading the way with the cuffs. 'Let's search this shit hole.'

The flat screen TV in the corner of the room stood out to Dylan like a sore thumb and he ordered it to be seized immediately, along with anything else that looked out of place in the flat that resembled a doss house rather than a home. A scan with the ultraviolet light across the TV revealed a house number and a postcode.

'You see,' he said, smiling. 'It may not work very often but when it does it gives you a bloody good feeling, doesn't it?' he laughed. He knew further checks would tell them just who it belonged to.

The search team was thorough. They recovered an unexpectedly large amount of cash, tools and a key for a garage with a tag attached that read, No. 7, which would be their next point of call. Dylan held it smugly in his clenched fist. They also found a set of car keys, but for what car? Dylan pondered. They were on a new Subaru key fob. The car surely wouldn't be far away. The search of the garage didn't reveal much other than a few car parts, which were seized, bagged and tagged.

Now it was time to return to the nick and rattle the cages of Denton and Greenwood and see what dropped out of their interviews. Charging a person was complex. Although they had been arrested on suspicion of attempted murder, Dylan knew from experience that the charge was likely to be reduced to death by dangerous driving, even if it was proved they were in the car at the time of the hit and run accident. However before that the charge would be escalated to Murder if the accident proved fatal.

Next hurdle for them would be to prove which one of them was driving the car. Then, they had to show the passenger's involvement. Hopefully they would get the passenger charged for encouraging the driver to commit the crime. The team now had twenty four hours' detention of the men which wasn't a great deal of time to complete the necessary investigation, but Dylan would be moving the investigation forward all the time, and that was all he could hope for at this stage.

Chapter 17

Through his tears, Grahan saw the figures of two people in white coats walking down the corridor towards him, as if in slow motion. A nurse stood beside him and laid a hand on his shoulder as she settled him on a chair by the side of his wife. The surgeon bent down on his haunches in front of him. Graham held his wife's hand in his tightly and screwed up his eyes. 'Our son,' he said quietly.

'Mr Tate, I'm truly sor...' he said. Graham heard himself shriek like an animal in pain. The doctor reached out to him and, staring at Graham now wide-eyed, he gulped before he continued. 'Toby is being brought to you as we speak. I'm a procurement specialist; there is no easy way of saying this,' he inhaled. 'Your wife and child are clinically dead. They didn't suffer. Neither regained consciousness.'

The nurse bent down and put her arms around Graham's trembling body.

'No,' he wailed, flinging her to one side. 'I need to see him,' he begged. 'I want him here with us,' he sobbed, his hands shaking uncontrollably as he reached out into thin air.

'Of course, Mr Tate, he's on his way ...' the doctor said. 'This seems so inadequate but I really am truly sorry for your loss.'

What seemed like seconds later, Graham saw Toby's little lifeless body. He was swaddled in a white sheet. Graham's tears had stopped. He felt numb. There was nothing outside the tiny, quiet, dimly lit hospital room that mattered to him. He looked into Toby's face and gently kissed his tiny bow shaped pale lips that held a bluish tinge. He looked so peaceful, even though tubes and wires were attached to his little body.

'Somebody will pay for this if it's the last thing I do, I swear to you,' he said through gritted teeth. 'Don't worry, my precious.' Graham stroked his wife's cold cheek. 'I'll find you both again. We've so much yet to do together,' he sobbed. 'You know; like we'd planned,' he smiled. A sob caught in his throat. He inhaled deeply and brushed away his tears. The nurse knocked at the open door.

'A cup of strong tea,' she said, putting it down on the table. His wife and son were now side by side.

DS John Benjamin watched him from the corridor with tears in his own eyes. He couldn't help but think, what would he do if that had just happened to him? He shuddered at the thought and looking up to the ceiling he prayed silently that he would never know.

Fixing his mind to the job in hand he noted that Graham Tate was built like anyone would imagine a bricklayer to be; stocky, thick necked, rugged and muscular, but his deflated form portrayed a crumbled man with his strength sapped and his spirit gone.

A phone ringing at the nurse's station broke John's train of thought. 'Mr Tate, it's for you. I believe it's your wife's father. Do you want to take it? Graham stood robot like. Reluctantly he moved from Bridey's side to answer the call.

'Hello, is that you lad?' said the panic-stricken older male's voice at the other end of the phone.

'They're dead you know,' Graham managed to gasp.

'I know son they've told us. We'll get to you as soon as we can,' Ronnie said with a trembling voice.

Graham handed the phone back to the nurse, his face expressionless. There was nothing else to say. As if in a trance he walked past John and back into the room where his wife and child lay.

John saw Graham jump when the doctor pulled a chair up beside him. The man coughed before speaking.

'There is no easy way of asking but we've found a donor card in your wife's purse which signifies to us that it was her wish for her organs to be used in the event of her death. This is reinforced on her driving licence. I don't know how you feel about your son being a donor too.

'Time is a crucial factor in respect of some of the organs. They can save lives one person's death can help up to eight others. Let me assure you your wife and son are dead, the machines only keeping the blood circulating, preserving their organs but that's it.'

Graham stood; his face red and contorted as though he was about to burst. His fists clenched. 'Don't you dare. Do you hear me? Nobody touches them,' he shouted. John readied himself to go into the room.

'Mr Tate, please calm down,' John heard the doctor say in a gentle, soothing voice. It was obvious he had seen this reaction many times before. 'Let me assure you it was your wife's wishes, should she die, that her organs be used. Think about it, please.'

'Get out.' shouted Graham. 'Just leave us alone.'

'That I can't do Mr Tate. If we are to make use of your family's organs we need to act quickly to adhere to her wishes. I need an answer.'

Chapter 18

Graham knelt down at the side of Bridey; turned her hand over and kissed her palm, 'I don't know if I can do it,' he sobbed. 'The thought of someone taking away part of you and Toby,' he whispered. 'Please tell me what to do,' he begged.

Looking at her beautiful, tranquil expression, he sensed her answer. Suddenly, the image of the day she'd sat at the dining room table and filled in the donor card sprung to his mind. They'd been talking to a lady who had been running a stall for the Heart Foundation at a garden fete. Her name was Rita and she'd had a heart transplant six months before.

'I couldn't walk twenty yards without stopping for breath before, my love,' she had said. 'Couldn't play with my grandkids, or go shopping with my hubby, never mind go on holiday,' she said. 'And now look at me,' she'd giggled. 'We're off on a cruise in February,' she'd said as she hugged her husband tight.

Bridey had made her decision there and then. She had always said people were brave who donated their organs, but after meeting Rita she didn't have the slightest doubt that it was a wonderful gift to give to a fellow human being, the gift of another lifetime, to someone who deserved it like Rita had. He knew he would give his consent because she always knew the best thing to do.

He kissed Bridey's forehead, then Toby's chubby little cheek before he whispered. 'Remember I'll find you both again one day wherever you are. I love you.'

'I love you more coz I'm older,' she used to say back to him. Slowly, but without hesitation, he looked up at the doctor. 'Take them, but do it quickly before I change my mind,' he said as he sank into a nearby chair and put his head in his hands, weeping steadily.

'She would be very proud of you,' said the doctor.

Graham Tate's large hands easily cupped the mug of tea the nurse gave him and he squeezed the ceramic vessel tight as he stared into space.

'I'll go open the windows,' the nurse said putting her hand on Graham's shoulder.

'Why?' he asked.

'To let their spirits go free, together,' she said, simply.

Graham nodded. 'Thank you,' he whispered.

'Boss,' John said quietly into his mobile phone. 'Both mum and baby have been pronounced dead.'

Dylan couldn't find the words. He sighed deeply, instead. 'We've pulled Denton and Greenwood in, and their flat's being searched. Give me a call when you're leaving the hospital will you. I'd like you to be involved with the interviews.'

'It might be a while, I'm just going to try to speak to Mr Tate, but as you can imagine...'

'I know John. Just speak to me as and when you can mate.'

'Will do,' said John as he rang off.

DS Benjamin found himself in the room where Mr Tate sat, grasping the untouched mug of tea. 'Can I take that from you Graham and get you a fresh cup?' the nurse asked as she introduced John. 'This is Detective Sergeant Benjamin, who would like to talk to you.'

Without fuss or question Graham Tate handed the nurse the cup.

'Milk and sugar?' the nurse asked John who nodded.

Graham Tate's expression was blank.

'I'm really sorry about your wife and son,' John said. 'I thought you might like me to tell you what we know about the accident, unless it's too soon?'

Graham Tate shook his head. 'No, please. Are you married?' he asked, watching John who took a seat.

'Yeah.'

'Kids?'

'Two – and no, I can't begin to understand how you're feeling right now.'

Graham Tate closed his eyes and shook his head. 'They'd gone shopping you know, to Mothercare. Not a nightclub, nor a football match.' He sighed. 'A place you'd think they'd be safe. It's the first time she'd been out on her own since she'd given birth to Toby. Just a short walk round the block, she'd said; just a chance to try out the new pushchair, you know.

'I would have been with them if we'd not been behind on the house build. She'd rung me and left a message to say they were okay and they both loved me, listen' he said, holding his mobile phone tightly to John's ear. He pressed a button and played the message.

'Hi gorgeous daddy,' said a happy smiling girly voice. 'Toby wanted to let you know he's got lots of nice things,' she giggled. 'I know you'd be worried so I thought I'd ring you to let you know we're all safe and sound without you fussing over us. Just going back home now for a feed, aren't we son?' she said. 'We love you lots and see you soon.' The phone went dead.

Graham put the phone to his ear and played the message again. Tears ran down his face, his mouth wide with grief.

John's heart sank. The nurse carried in two mugs of tea and handed them to the men.

'Mr Tate, Graham, try drinking some, please? And let me tell you what we know.'

'Wait, let me show you their picture,' he said, taking photographs out of his wallet with trembling hands then touching the images fondly. He mopped his tears with a handkerchief.

'They're beautiful, Graham,' John said, looking closely at the young faces – so alive, so happy.

'I've just agreed to donate their organs you know,' Graham said. 'She'd signed up you see.' He looked to John for approval and John nodded. 'But it was the hardest thing ...' he said, gulping. 'And now I've got to live with it.' He looked up at John and he saw the panic rise in his eyes.

'How could I have agreed for my wife and son's body to be mutilated? How could I?' he said sobbing.

'Your wife and son will probably save more than one life, maybe even another mother and child who would have died without your bravery. Bridey was obviously a very sensitive and caring person. If she signed that donor card, she has trusted you to make sure those wishes are carried out,' John said.

Graham, deep in thought, took a sip of tea from his cup but didn't speak. However, obviously mulling John's words over, he looked calmer.

'The car involved in the accident was a Ford Fiesta. That car was found burnt out shortly after the accident but it was reported stolen,' John said. Graham turned his head to look at John with red, expectant eyes. 'Stolen?' he asked.

'Well, we're not certain it was actually stolen, although we did find a screwdriver jammed in the ignition. A police officer spoke to the registered owner of the vehicle and his friend when they reported the car missing. We're turning their house over at the moment and then we'll interview them.'

'Who are they?' Graham whispered. 'Tell me who they are?' he said his voice rising. 'I'll get the truth out of the bastards for you,' he said through clenched teeth.

'Listen Graham, earlier in the day we believe the pair failed to stop for a police car that was in pursuit of their car. They jumped a red light at the railway barrier, narrowly missing being wiped out by the Leeds train. At that point the police lost them. A few hours later, the car was seen again by a police patrol in the town centre as it was approaching traffic lights. The lights turned to red and the police driver pulled in behind them. The officers got out and as they went towards the car to speak to the two occupants, the driver set off at speed and went up onto the pavement, which is when they hit Bridey and Toby's pram. The officers cannot be sure who was driving the vehicle at the time though.'

'Who are they? Tell me?' Graham asked again.

John shook his head. 'I'm sorry, I can't give you the names. We've got to ascertain whether they were driving the car first.'

Graham Tate stared at the floor. 'And if it is them?'

'Then you'll be told.' John said, laying a hand on Graham's shoulder. Graham sat up straight and stared him in the eyes.

'Good, because once I know who did it they won't be safe even locked up.' he said, vehemently.

'Look, I'll arrange to speak to you and Mrs Tate's parents tomorrow with my boss, Detective Inspector Jack Dylan,' John said, standing up to leave.

'Come on mate give me their names. You can't tell me you wouldn't want to get hold of them if you were in my position,' Graham said, staring straight into John's eyes.

'You're understandably very angry at the moment, but I'm sure Bridey wouldn't want you to do anything stupid.'

'She won't know will she? She's not here to see.' he replied, shrugging his shoulders. 'So what does it matter?'

'If you need anything, here's my number.' John said, handing Graham Tate his card. 'The Coroner's Officer will be along to see you shortly and I'll see you tomorrow.'

'Come on, name them,' Graham shouted after him as he walked out of the room. John didn't look back. The door slowly began to close 'One father to another, I won't stop till I find them and then you'll have two more bodies,' he shouted. John heard a loud cry. The door banged shut.

John walked on not allowing the straight-faced mask of the detective to slip once, while inside, his heart ached for the young man who had lost everything.

Chapter 19

Danny Denton and Billy Greenwood signed their release from custody forms, agreeing to be bailed. Their black Subaru stood proudly in the back yard of the police station awaiting them. The officer dropped the key fob in Danny's outstretched hand. Danny examined the exterior carefully. The officer breathed deeply through his flared nostrils, turned and marched briskly across the parade square without a word passing his pursed lips.

'Best get ourselves a new phone Billy, it'll be ages before they give us ours back,' Danny said.

'And two more stripes for the wing.' Billy shouted, a cheeky grin crossing his face.

The officer stopped momentarily in his tracks, but thought better of retracing his steps and walked on into the police station.

The boys grinned. 'It's time we gave Pam a call to tell her we've been locked up and wrongly accused of sommat,' Danny said, sighing dramatically as he slid into the driver's seat. 'I wonder if that copper's kid Sara goes to her school? We should ask her.' Danny said with his eyebrow raised.

It was late. Pam's mobile phone vibrated.

'Hello' she said in a whisper as she answered the unknown number flashing on her phone, from under her duvet.

'Pam, Danny. We got pulled by the cops.'

'Oh my God,' Pam said.

'Don't panic, we've done nothing wrong. But they've took our mobiles off of us, so we've had to get a new one.'

'Are you alright?' she said.

'Yeah, course. Tell you all about it tomorrow,' he said, grinning over at Billy as he turned the wheel and revved the engine to take the next corner at top speed.

Pam sighed with contentment and plumped up her pillow. How awful she thought, snuggling down under her duvet, to be locked up for something you hadn't done. Why didn't the police leave Danny alone? She couldn't wait for tomorrow. She closed her eyes, turned over and willed herself to go to sleep, for the sooner that happened, the sooner it would be morning.

Before she knew it Pam heard the distant cries of her mum and dad calling her. In the transitional state between wakefulness and sleep she heard the front door slam and the house shake.

Pam yawned and stretched. Her eyelids shot open. She jumped out of bed and raced to the window to watch her parents drive away.

Outside, leaning against a black shiny new car, was Danny. She stood statue-like as she watched him look both ways up and down the road and then walk up the driveway, Billy in his wake. She heard Danny's knock at the front door. Flinching, she hid behind the bedroom curtain not sure what she should do. Her heart hammered in her chest. How long had he been there? The knocks got louder and followed by shouts of her name. She ran down the stairs, pulling her dressing gown over her shoulders. She'd have to answer the door before the pair drew attention to themselves.

'What're you doing here?' she said with a grin that spanned her flushed face. Danny stood leaning against the doorjamb, a cigarette hanging from his mouth.

'Thought you might want a lift to school in our new wheels.'

'That'd be great but I'm not dressed. Look, I won't be a minute. Come in before someone sees you,' she said pulling Danny in by his hoodie. She waved Billy in behind him and then popped her head around the door and glanced around to see if anyone was watching.

'Can I use your karsi?' asked Billy, as she shut the door.

Pam frowned.

'Your bog.' Danny said.

'Top of the stairs,' she said. Distractedly, she pulled her dressing gown tightly round her.

Danny and Pam watched him run up the stairs, two at a time.

'He's not the only one who's desperate,' Danny said with a grin as he reached out for her. He pulled her towards him. With two arms he held her tightly around the waist. 'But not for the...' Danny pulled her to him and kissed her roughly on the lips.

Pam's heart pounded. She could hardly breathe. This is how she had dreamt it would be to be loved by Danny Denton. He expertly untied the knot in the belt of her dressing gown and it fell open to reveal her pyjamas. He leaned forward and she dropped her head as he pulled the straps to one side and rained kisses on her neck. She closed her eyes. Her legs felt like jelly.

Billy searched quickly and quietly through the bedrooms, he pocketed the small amount of cash and jewellery that he came across. Inside the small drawer of the dressing table he could hardly believe his eyes, when staring up at him were keys tagged and labelled with the shop, surgery and house details. He put them in the breast pocket of his jacket and zipped it up, patting it gently. Grinning at his reflection in the mirror, he turned and headed for the door to the landing and shut it behind him with a bang.

Pam pushed Danny away. He moaned and tried to hold onto her by sucking hard on her neck. She heard the toilet flush, Billy's footsteps on the landing and then him running down the stairs.

'I'm gonna be late for school if I'm not careful,' she said, with a grimace as she released herself from Danny's hold and ran past Billy on the stairs. Billy winked at Danny.

'Pam stood before her dressing table mirror and inspected her blotchy neck. Damn it, she thought that always happened when she got excited. Then she saw the love bite. How on earth was she going to explain that to her mum and dad. 'Grrr...' she cried, grabbing a scarf from the door handle as she hurried out. Good job these things were in fashion, she thought. She was pleased with how organised she had been under the circumstances; that was what being grown up was all about, wasn't it?

Within minutes, they were in the car and on the way to school.

'The car is amazing Danny,' Pam said, admiringly stroking the leather seat.

'Special, int' it? Cost us a pretty penny didn't it Billy?'

'Sure did,' Billy said, turning around to wink at her.

'Ever thought of skiving off one day?' Danny asked as he made contact with her pale blue eyes in the rear view mirror.

'I've never had reason to,' she said shyly.

'Well, what if I asked you to? Good enough reason?'

'Yeah it is,' she grinned, shyly.

They were at the school gates and as she leaned forward to get out of the passenger side door Danny leaned over. 'I'll text you later, but think about what I said.'

Wow, she thought staggering up the school's driveway in a dreamlike state. 'What a morning.' The smile on her face reached from ear to ear. Now she sighed, the sigh of pure contentment.

In the classroom it mattered not what the lessons were, all she could think about was the impending day out and where they might take her. Dreams really did come true if you wanted them to, she sang in her head.

'Pamela, Pamela. Are you paying attention?' The teacher's voice broke her thoughts but only for a moment. 'You'll wish you'd listened to me one day, girl,' said her headmistress.

'Yep,' she replied, scrawling Pam Loves Danny on her notebook.

'Well, sit up and try to look as if you're listening. Sex education is important. even if you think you know it all at your age,' the angry teacher stressed.

Chapter 20

Danny stopped the car in the car park of the dam. Billy tore a can of lager from the four pack and handed it to Danny.

'So what did you get Billy?'

'A ring, a couple of watches and fifty quid,' he said, emptying his coat pockets onto his lap.

'That all?' exclaimed Danny, holding his hand out, palm up. Billy hit it with his before reaching into his breast pocket. Danny frowned.

'Ah, but there's more,' Billy said, as he pulled out a bunch of keys. To his friend's delight he read the tags. 'House, Shop and Surgery,' he read, beaming.

'You're a fucking star, you are,' Danny whooped with delight. 'Times are good.'

'How did you get on with her, get a feel did ya?' Billy asked with a sullen face as he pulled the ring-pull on his can. 'I would rather have been snogging her than thieving.' He took a long swig.

'Woh, she's really up for it. No doubt about that. She's hot.' Danny said, laughing. 'You'll get a go,' he said. 'Don't fret. Let's go for a drive, eh? Give the car a spin and see if we can sell that jewellery on over in Lancashire,' Danny said, pointing to the ring Billy had placed on his finger. Danny turned the key in the ignition and revved the engine. Music blared out, disrupting the quiet tranquillity of Dean Reservoir as he reversed back at speed, skidded and pulled the steering wheel to do a ninety-degree spin.

It was the morning that Dylan was due to meet with Graham Tate and Bridey's parents Ronnie and Rose Carter. He sat at his desk and tapped his teeth with his pen as he pondered over the meeting. He wished he had something positive to tell them, but all he could do was enlighten them as to what the investigation team knew so far, and assure them of their commitment to finding those responsible for the deaths of their daughter and grandson. He scratched his head and rubbed his eyes. A knock came at his office door and without preamble, in walked John Benjamin. 'I've offered to collect the Carters but they're gonna make their own way here. 'They should be with us in about ten minutes boss, you still okay?'

'Yeah, arrange some coffee will you and put the *Do Not Disturb* sign on the door. I was just sat here thinking about them.'

'It's difficult knowing what to say isn't it? Apart from the shock of the two deaths they've had to deal with their son-in-law agreeing to the organ donation.'

'Mm,' Dylan said, nodding his head.

The first to arrive was Graham Tate and John introduced him to Dylan. They shook hands. Graham had a fierce grip. His face was blotchy, his eyes puffy and he looked fatigued which was understandable under the circumstances, but he definitely hadn't lost his strength, Dylan noticed.

'Please take a seat,' Dylan said. 'We'll just wait for Bridey's parents to arrive before we begin. How did they take the news about the organ-donations?'

Graham put his hand to his brow before running his fingers through his hair. 'Not good,' he said taking a deep diaphragmatic breath. 'But it was Bridey's wish, not mine. What was I supposed to do?'

'I've got to tell you I've nothing but admiration for you,' said Dylan with feeling. 'It was not only a courageous decision but an unselfish one too, that'll no doubt save, or definitely dramatically improve the quality of a number of lives. Bridey would be very proud of you, I'm sure,' he smiled, reassuringly.

'So people keep saying,' Graham said with a wan smile back at him.

The sight of Ronnie and Rose Carter at his door stopped Dylan from saying more. John escorted them in. Graham and Dylan stood and John introduced Bridey's parents to Dylan.'

It was apparent the atmosphere between the relatives was cool as they nodded briefly in acknowledgment of each other's presence, but sat avoiding eye contact. Vicky brought in warm drinks on a tray and they sat with the mugs cupped tightly in their hands. Dylan started by telling them how sorry he was for their loss in such horrific and tragic circumstances. He outlined slowly and gently to them what had happened according to what the investigation had uncovered and what witnesses had told them.

'I want to reassure you that the paramedics did all they could at the scene but unfortunately they couldn't save Bridey, or Toby,' Dylan said, watching the numbed expression on their faces. 'I don't know if you were aware but your daughter carried an organ donor card and authority was given for her wishes to be carried very bravely by Graham at the hospital which must have caused him the most unimaginable grief,' he said with a sigh.

Dylan saw the tears well up in Rose's eyes and she turned to Graham, took his hand in hers, and smiled weakly at him. Dylan noted the gesture and decided to go on. 'That unselfish act in these terrible circumstances needs to be made instantly. The poor lad was put into a situation that, let's face it, no one would ever want to be in. Like I said to you earlier Graham, your courage at that time will no doubt have saved lives. And, you not only had to make that decision once, but twice.' I'm sure Mr and Mrs Carter you understand what a terrible predicament he was put in.'

Rose Carter sobbed into her handkerchief and looked across at her husband for support.

'We can't bear to think about it,' he said downhearted.

'That's understandable. And, I'm sure it was just the same for Graham when he had to make the decision to respect Bridey's wishes,' Dylan said.

Detective Sergeant John Benjamin watched and listened in silence with great admiration for Dylan as he carefully created the opportunity for them to discuss the situation with each other.

'It was Bridey's wish, not mine; I could never have...' Graham managed to blurt out as he struggled with the lump rising in his throat. 'It's what she... she said she wanted me to do if anything... I agreed at the time. I never thought anything would, and at first I said no to the doctor, quite categorically, no. I couldn't bear to think... But then I remembered why she had signed that donor card and I had to allow it to happen, for Bridey.'

'I'm sure she'd want you all to be together on this. It was her wish, like Graham said, no one else's,' Dylan added, gently. 'And I don't know if you're aware but no one has a legal right to veto Bridey's wish.'

'Thank you Inspector, we agree with Graham,' Rose Carter said with a stronger voice. 'Aren't we Ronnie? We're just in shock,' she sighed, looking at Graham who sat with disbelief written all over his face. 'Graham's like our own,' she said, turning back to Dylan as she reached out and squeezed Graham's hand.

'You did what you have to do lad. I can see that now. Let's concentrate on finding out who did this to her and Toby,' said Ronnie, nodding at Graham.

'I think you need to leave that to us, Mr Carter. When we know who did it we'll let you know,' said Dylan.

'Oh, don't you fret Ron. I'll find out who did it,' Graham said through gritted teeth, 'and when I do...' his face screwed up and he gulped back the tears.

'Look, at this moment in time you can't put the blame on the lad who owned the car because he had reported it stolen. I've explained that to you. Him and his friend are telling us the same story. We did find the car ablaze on the moors with a screwdriver stuck in the ignition and they still had the car keys in their possession, which at this moment in time convinced our officer of their innocence and he had to bail them. There may be some truth in their story,' said John. 'And until we can prove otherwise...'

'Never assume Mr Tate. That's one of the first rules of investigation,' Dylan said.

'Can you tell us who the owners of the car are then?' asked Ronnie.

John looked at Dylan.

'I don't think that would help, do you?'

'Come on, Inspector. We're upset and it'd be a comfort to us to know something, anything.'

'Okay,' Dylan said. 'It's a couple of lads from the Greenaway Estate called Danny Denton and Billy Greenwood. But let me warn you we'll know if you go anywhere near them. Look, let us do our job. If it was one of them driving the car we'll find out, I promise you,' said Dylan.

'The Inspector's right, Graham our Bridey would have been the first to tell you to let the police sort it out – you know, she would. Don't you go doing anything stupid now,' said Rose.

'I just feel so bloody helpless.' Graham said, flaying his arms. 'I've let them both down so badly,' he said breaking down once more.

Rose reached out to comfort him. She laid an arm protectively around his shoulders. 'Why, our Bridey and Toby? Why?' she said, shaking her head.

'I didn't think you'd name them boss,' John said, walking back into Dylan's office when he'd shown the visitors out of the building.

'I wasn't going to. Then I decided that some information, however small, would be a lifeline for them to clutch to, like Ronnie said.'

'You wouldn't want Graham as an enemy would you, boss?' John said, grimacing. 'I'm glad the doc didn't tell him he couldn't stop him taking their organs before Graham had come to his decision that would have been horrendous.'

'No,' Dylan smiled as he shook his head. 'I wouldn't like to think he had a grudge against me.'

Chapter 21

Outside school gates at 3? Danny texted.

Pam's phone beeped. 'Mum?' she mouthed, with a turn up of her nose and a frown.

Aunt Mona's ill. Off to France. Pick you up straight from school. Tell your teacher you'll be away till next Tuesday.

'Bummer.' she cried, stamping her foot.

As planned, Danny pulled up outside the school at three o'clock. Pam looked around cautiously for her dad's vehicle before she ran over to his car. She leaned in. 'What's up?' he said.

'Aunt bloody drama queen Mona is ill,' she said, kicking the toe of her shoe on the tarmac. 'We're off to France till Tuesday.

'Ah, never mind kid. Nought's spoiling, we'll arrange another time when you get back,' Danny said patting her hand. She took another look up and down the road.

'Dad'll be here any minute and if he sees me talking to you I'm dead meat,' she said with a grimace. 'I'd better go,' she said with a tut and a raise of her eyebrows.

'Hey, before you do, tell us, do you know a Sara Whitworth?' Danny said.

'Yeah. Why?' she asked with more than a hint of sulking in her protruding bottom lip.

'Is her dad a copper?' Danny went on.

'Yeah, I used to go round with her when I was a kid but she's a bit of a geek now to be honest,' she said pulling a face. Pam saw her dad's Audi creeping slowly past the stationary cars not fifty yards away.

'Text me, won't you,' she called as she ran holding her hand high in the air to catch her dad's attention.

Danny watched her go. 'I think we might need to visit the dentist this weekend Billy,' he said out of the corner of his mouth.

'And the flower shop,' Billy mumbled. Danny turned and sniggered at his friend.

Miss you already, hun. Danny texted Pam.

Pam snuggled down into the luxurious seats of her dad's car. As they cruised past Danny and Billy, Pam blew Danny a kiss and smiled to herself as she sighed with contentment, like *the cat that had got the cream,* as Aunt Mona would have said.

There was no sign of an alarm on the wall of the dentist surgery. Danny turned the key and pushed the door open with trepidation. It opened easily enough. He stood still, silencing his friend with a finger to his lips and listened. No bells, nothing. Billy followed Danny silently into a small, neat kitchenette.

Walking around the building, it became apparent that the pickings weren't that great from a dentist apart from a small amount of petty cash left in the open till.

'Danny, sit in the chair and let me look in y'gob,' Billy said, putting his arms into a white gown from an old coat stand in the corner of the surgery and picking up a face mask from the work units.

'Piss off. Grab the computers and stop arsing around.'

'We off to the flower shop next?' Billy said, grumpily.

'We'll go to the house first and see what they've got in the fridge, then I'll think about it if I can be bothered.'

Chapter 22

'Boss, Grace Harvey's fatal. Forensics just rang. The scientist, off the record, is certain some plastic from a light casing found at the scene of the accident is a match to an item taken from Denton and Greenwood's garage. She wants to do a further test before committing herself to paper but wanted us to know ASAP in case it fitted in with any ongoing enquiries,' Dennis said, with a glint in his eye.

'Wouldn't that be a great result? If it comes back a hundred per cent we'll have Denton and his mate in for one death by dangerous and they'd be on site to charge if we get the evidence for Bridey and Toby's murder. Do we know if Grace knew either scrote, or have we any intelligence as to why they might be in Merton on the day Grace died?'

'No, unfortunately we've no links between them and Mrs Harvey. They were probably just bombing through the village like bloody idiots.'

'If it turns out that the glass from the headlight that was seized with the car parts from their garage is a positive match, then we'll be able to drop it on Denton and Greenwood's toes in an interview and hopefully nail the little bastards there and then.'

'And on the Mildred Sykes murder boss, the only visitor seen going to the house recently is a man that matches the description of our Mr Stevenson. However, he doesn't deny going there and he's connected to her and Grace Harvey because of their financial affairs so that doesn't help us much, does it?' said Taylor.

'Are you happy with him? Have you got anything back from the financial investigation side?'

'No, is the answer to both your questions. It feels like there's a rabbit off there somewhere, but I just can't put my finger on it at the moment. Anyway, once I hear back from the Forensic Intelligence Unit I'll be having further words with him.'

'I'll come with you when you go and see him. So far he's the only person we've got with a connection to Ms Sykes, so we need to get his fingerprints and DNA to connect or eliminate him from the enquiry.

'Keep me posted Taylor, I'm going to call a meeting for everyone involved with Grace Harvey's death, Mildred Sykes's murder and Bridey and Toby Tate's murder to see if there's anything drops out by having all the teams together and also, to bring everyone up to speed. Let everyone have the chance to share their thoughts and information. Can you arrange, Dennis?'

Dennis nodded.

Taylor left the office and Dylan picked up the ringing phone. 'What are you eating?' he asked, with a smile.

'A strawberry cream tart,' Jen replied, giggling.' PC Whitworth just brought them in.'

'Very nice … What's he after?'

'Why do you always think people have an ulterior motive?' she said, laughing.

'I'm a suspicious kinda guy.'

'What's new at your end?'

'Not a lot, I'm waiting for forensics to come back to us and keeping my fingers crossed for their findings. Tell Brenda in your office she needs to reach for her prayer mat, again.'

'As bad as that is it?' Jen said.

'Yep, I'm afraid it is. It's good to hear your voice. I seem to have got myself so immersed in work again lately that I don't feel as if I've seen you much.'

'It won't be forever, will it? But, if you get your finger out in the meantime and solve a few crimes you can spend more time with me and other people won't have to keep treating me to cream cakes,' she said.

'You might well laugh. How does he know strawberries are your weakness anyway?'

'He doesn't. Now go solve some crimes and who knows, the next strawberries I have might even be with my fella.'

'Love you lots,' he sighed. 'I've had my fix now so I'd better get on with some work.'

'Let me know what time you're gonna be home and I'll have tea ready.'

'Okay love, bye for now,' Dylan said with a smile in his voice as he put the phone down. DS John Benjamin knocked at his office door and walked in carrying his coat.

'Boss, just to let you know I'm off to see a snout who's telling me someone is asking a lot of questions on the estate about Denton and Greenwood. '

'Graham Tate?'

'Don't know. I haven't used this snout before so I don't know how good he is. Do you need me to sign the forms for his money?'

'Yes, please and then I'll go up to admin. Looks like we might have to go and have a word with Mr Tate,' Dylan said, frowning as he scribed his name on the given supervisors place on the form.

'Get back to you as soon as,' John said, strutting out of Dylan's office with a purpose in his steps.

Lisa brought in a fax for Dylan's attention. The scenes of crime officers had lifted a number of fingerprints from Mildred Sykes' house. Of these; a duplicate was causing some interest as it appeared on her bedside cabinet and other drawers in her home.

They were satisfied that they were not Mildred's because they had checked them against the limited fingerprint impressions, that they had taken from the body at the mortuary. They were checking the marks found through the automated fingerprint identification system but they hadn't had any hits so far, meaning that the person who the fingerprints belonged to didn't have a criminal record. However, the information confirmed that someone had been searching the house, which would connect that person to the scene. What it wouldn't be able to tell him was if this occurred, during, or after her murder.

Impatient, Dylan picked up the phone to ring the forensic department. As he listened to their dialling tone he wondered if an update from them would continue in the same positive vain but the office manager told him they'd no results for him, as yet.

He sat doodling on his blotting paper pad, drawing lines down its brown leatherette corners. What could he tell the personnel at the meeting?

'Vicky, can you call a meeting for tomorrow morning in the incident room please?' Dylan called out.

'Yeah, and I'll stick a brush up my arse and sweep the floor while I'm at it if you like, sir,' she mumbled to herself.

Dylan sniggered to himself. 'Can you make a coffee at the same time, do you think?'

A pen flew through the air and landed in front of him.

'Missed.' he called out to her with a chortle.

Two hit and run fatalities in such close proximity. Could it just be coincidence? There could soon be a shout for a review team to look at on-going enquiries. What was he missing? The last thing he wanted was for this team to find fault with the investigation.

Got them strawberries in? I'm on my way home, he texted Jen.

Yep, but eaten them. Think I've found a craving, came her reply.

'What an excuse. Now I've heard everything,' he muttered.

Chapter 23

Holding the keys for the Forrester's home was far too tempting for Danny and Billy. The house, like the dentists and the florists, didn't appear to have an alarm, or at least not one that could be seen from the roadside. The boys drove up the drive and parked outside the house, letting themselves in without a backwards glance.

'I'm starving,' said Billy, heading straight for the kitchen. He opened the fridge door and shut it again almost instantly. 'Catch,' he shouted to Danny as a can of lager came whizzing through the air. He caught it – just.

'Bloody idiot,' scolded Danny. 'Let's not be too damned obvious. We don't want to upset Pam, not till we get our way, anyway,' he said grinning. Billy yanked the ring pull. Drinking the alcohol from the can didn't keep him still as he browsed around the room in between swigs, opening cupboard doors and shutting them again, without a care in the world. 'Kit Kat?' he said, offering Danny an unopened packet that he found.

'Just one and then put the rest back,' he said, opening the door into the lounge.

'Nice house, Billy,' Danny said, whistling as he walked slowly up the stairs. I wonder what they might not miss for a week or two?'

Careful not to disturb things, he opened and closed drawers and cupboards.

'God Danny, have you seen how neat everything is?' His face was a picture of wonderment. His friend laughed. 'You moron,' he said. 'Everyone ain't a scruffy bastard like you yer know.'

'We'll have this Billy,' Danny said holding up a gold chain he'd come across on the windowsill. 'It should be worth a few quid like the other stuff we sold.'

'Let's have a look in Pam's room,' Billy said. He was laid on her bed when Danny walked in.

'Oh, Danny,' Billy whined as he draped her nightie around his head. He cuddled and kissed her bear. 'I love you so much,' he said, in a high-pitched soft girly voice. Danny stood looking at his friend with amusement.

'This bed sure smells nice Danny. Come lay with me,' Billy said. 'Come on you prick. Stop pissing about and leave things straight,' Danny said, walking out of the room.

'Okay,' Billy shouted as he jumped off the bed. He knelt on the floor beside her dressing table drawers and opened the top one. 'Found them.' he shouted.

'What?' shouted Danny who was inspecting an old oil painting displayed on the wall on the landing.

'Knickers, knickers and more knickers,' he yelled throwing the garments into the air to Danny's amusement as he popped his head around the door.

'Control yourself man,' Danny warned him in a whispered tone.

'I'm gonna keep these,' he beamed, holding up a bright pink thong to his nose and inhaling the smell of it deeply. 'One day she might model them for me,' he grinned, stuffing them in his pocket. Danny shook his head. 'You're seriously sad,' he said.

'We've spent long enough here,' Danny said with a frown as he looked out of the window. 'Tell you what let's go up the road and do the rich bloke with the Porsche's house over again.'

Danny peered out of the front door and looked both ways before confidently walking out of the house. Billy slammed the door behind him and followed. They climbed in the car and drove up the road to number 42. The Porsche wasn't in the driveway and all was quiet.

'Idle Danny, bloody idle. Look, he hasn't even had the patio doors repaired yet. All that fucking money and he can't be bothered: serves him right if we go in again.'

'He might not have any money left now we've nicked his cash.' Danny chuckled. 'I wonder why they haven't pulled us about his telly. They knew it was his, the officer with the big tits told me.'

Billy put a crowbar in the boarded-up patio door and prised it open. Within a minute they were in the kitchen. Quickly and thoroughly they checked the rooms out. Within a matter of minutes they had grabbed a portable radio, DVD, camera, bags of sweets and small change. There was a pre-cooked chicken in the fridge.

'That'll do, Let's get out of here,' Danny called out.

They threw their spoils in the car, jumped in and threw their hoods up. As they pulled out of the driveway Brian Stevenson arrived home. Billy leaned forward and gave him a v sign.

'We can't outrun that car, Billy, you nob.' Danny scolded. Billy turned round to watch what the Porsche driver was doing.

Brian Stevenson had more to worry about than two-bit burglars.

'Bastards, absolute bastards,' he grunted through clenched teeth. 'They'll pay for this,' he whispered. He had already been told who they might be and seeing their car registration number had proved the money he'd paid to find out had been worth it. Now he'd seen their car for himself he didn't need to chase them, he knew exactly who they were and where they lived. Revenge would be sweet, but in his own time.

Danny and Billy laughed as they drove up onto the moors. Billy tore off a chicken leg and handed it to Danny.

'Text Pam.'

'Do it your bloody self, you lazy git,' Billy said.

'Doh, I'm driving…'

'What you want to say?' he asked, wiping his greasy fingers down the front of his jeans before picking up the mobile phone.

'When will you be home?' he said.

Billy took Pam's thong out of his pocket and wiped his greasy mouth on it.

The reply was instant, *'Tuesday,'* she replied, *'I miss you.'* Pam thought studiously. She was sure she had told Danny when she was home. *Wasn't he counting the days like she was?*

'Ah, she misses you,' Billy said, portraying his sad face to Danny. Danny screwed up his nose.

'Sad bitch,' he said.

Chapter 24

Dylan made his way to the incident room which was cram-packed with officers. The heat hit him. The smell of body odour was as intense and the lack of air was apparent. All heads turned at his entrance. Dylan fanned his face with his paperwork as he walked to the front of the room. He sat, leaned back in his chair and scanned the faces in the room. All was quiet and still. Anticipation hung heavy.

He introduced himself, DS John Benjamin and DS Taylor Spiers before he went on to outline the purpose of the meeting, which was to exchange and update the information on each of the three incidents he was currently dealing with. Whilst they were all being investigated independently, snippets of information suggested there might be a connection.

'In respect of the fatal, fail to stop accident that killed Grace and her dog, we recovered debris left at the scene,' said Dylan. 'We now know that she'd withdrawn a large amount of money from her investments recently and sold her home to an equity release company. Brian Stevenson was Grace Harvey's financial advisor and he was attacked by Donald Harvey, Grace Harvey's son, at her funeral. Donald Harvey accuses Brian Stevenson of swindling his mother out of her money. Brian Stevenson says Donald Harvey has had the money to help him maintain a certain lifestyle abroad. Donald Harvey denies the allegation.'

'Brian Stevenson was also the late Mildred Sykes's financial advisor,' added DS Taylor Spiers before shooting Dylan a toothy smile.

'PC Whitworth, boss,' said a uniform officer at the back of the room. 'Do you think the two whose car was involved in the double fatal outside Mothercare, might have ran over the old lady too?'

'Maybe, but we will need the evidence to prove it beyond doubt, as usual,' Dylan said.

'Boss, it maybe something or nothing but Stevenson was the name on the TV with a postcode that we seized from Denton and Greenwood's flat. I personally telephoned Mr Stevenson and although he said the TV was his he told me he'd sold it on,' said Vicky.

'But he was broken into,' said DS Taylor Spiers, defiance blazing in her eyes at Vicky. 'I've seen the damage to the patio doors.'

'Let's stay with him then. You will see I'm having passed around a picture of Mildred Sykes for the people who are not fully up to speed with that investigation. Was Stevenson the last person to see Mildred Sykes alive? We know he fits the description of a visitor to her home, and we have a re-occurring finger mark in her house that's yet to be identified. We do know that the fingerprint is definitely not Mildred Sykes's. We don't have Brian Stevenson's prints do we?'

DS Taylor Spiers shook her head.

'So, that's something we need to do as a priority,' Dylan snapped.

'Big mistake,' Dylan heard Vicky say to Taylor in a low murmur, but he let it go with a glare at the pair.

'We also seized a glitzy clock from Denton and Greenwood's flat that was obviously out of place and we're checking to see if we can find any marks on it to identify whose it is,' said Vicky, sitting up straight in her chair.

'Do we know if Stevenson, Denton and Greenwood know each other?' asked Dylan

'Sir, this picture of Mildred Sykes.'

'Yes Vicky.'

'The clock in the background is just like the one I've been trying to place.'

'Really?' Dylan said, feeling slightly excited at the revelation.

Vicky looked at the photo again. Her mouth opened and shut without her saying a word. She looked at Dylan. 'I don't believe it,' she said.

'There's no intelligence to suggest that they know each other but I don't know if that question has been put to any of them,' said Taylor.

'Okay, so, we've got on-going tests to prove Denton and Greenwood's car is involved in Grace Harvey's murder. Now, let's talk about the one involving Bridey Tate and her son Toby. You, PC Whitworth, dropped behind their car in stationary traffic at a red light on the high street didn't you?'

PC Whitworth nodded.

'You get out and proceed to approach the men inside when the car sets off at speed. Is that right?'

'Yes, sir.'

'But you don't identify them?'

'No, sir.'

'Then you see the occupants of that car mow down our young mother and baby who are stepping off the pavement at the time, shoot the red light and the car as we all know is then found burning a short time later on the moors. Our two suspects come into the station to report the very same car stolen with an alibi. So do we have anything new on this?'

'We're sifting through CCTV and speed cameras boss, to see if we can get a good enough picture to identify the driver and passenger of that vehicle. There are a few hours yet to be looked at to see if we can ID the vehicle and the occupants on their journey to the moors if it was them. At this moment in time we know there were two occupants in the car that was involved, but we can't get a picture that's good enough for the ID of Denton and Greenwood. It's apparent that the driver and his passenger have either their hoods up or hats on,' said John.

'Well, probably isn't going to be good enough for CPS. We need to ensure that we have the evidence to show there's no doubt,' Dylan snapped.

'And where did they get the Subaru from? Was it stolen?'

'No bought, cash, sir. I checked it out, it's legit,' said PC Whitworth.

Dylan shook his head. 'Well the cash must have been stolen or they've sold some stolen gear; any reports of a large amount of money going missing?' There was a sea of shaking heads before him. 'Come on, we're not talking peanuts here are we? I mean how much does a brand spanking new Subaru cost?' The room's occupants remained silent. Dylan sighed. 'I'm also hearing that there's someone asking about Denton and Greenwood on the Greenaway Estate. I thought it was Graham Tate, he makes no bones about the fact that he wants revenge, which is understandable but the description that John's snout has given us is definitely not him.'

'What about Stevenson?' asked Taylor, 'or Donald Harvey? He didn't hesitate in attacking Stevenson in broad daylight at his mother's funeral.'

'The answer my friends lies within a small group of people that are possibly connected, so we need to dig deep to find the evidence to connect them and prove who did what. If you're telling me we need more people looking at CCTV tapes then let's get on with it,' Dylan stressed.

The meeting ended with Dylan feeling frustrated. He walked down the corridor to his office like a man on a mission. He could hear Taylor's heels clicking on the lino as she followed him. The likelihood that Denton and Greenwood were responsible for the car incidents was looking good and Stevenson was looking more like a fraudster than a murderer; but what connected Stevenson to Denton and Greenwood?

'Taylor,' Dylan said without stopping or glancing back. 'Chase the financial investigation team up on Stevenson. Tell them I want a result in the next seventy-two hours and I don't want any excuses.'

'Sure, but you know what they're like,' she panted, as she tried to match his pace.

'Look, just do it, please, will you. Or do I have to do everything myself?' Dylan said stopping at Taylor's desk in the incident room. Taylor dropped into her chair. 'I'm on with it aren't I?' she said, raising her eyebrows at Vicky who sat sedately opposite her.

Dylan walked the few paces to his office.

'Want a coffee, sir?' shouted Vicky.

Dylan slammed his door shut.

'Guess that will be a no-thank-you then, Vicky,' she mumbled.

Dylan opened his door. 'Yes, please,' he said, in a softer voice, 'and about time too,' he smiled. It made him so angry when he knew who was responsible for a crime but he had to wait for the results of enquiries to come in. No singular person or department ever seemed to have any urgency unless they were being paid overtime. He wanted these incidents wrapped up – and he wanted them wrapped up now.

'Dylan,' he snapped, snatching up the ringing phone.

'Somebody sounds grumpy,' said Jen.

'I'm just busy, that's all,' he sighed.

'Shall I ring back?'

'No, no, I'm sorry Jen,' he sighed with his head in his hand. 'It just pisses me off. I just need that bit of concrete evidence to get these three jobs sorted. I can feel it in my bones that we're on the right track.'

'Jack you're letting things get to you and you know yourself it's making you grumpy. You're tired, it's not helping that you're not getting your sleep and people won't like you for it, you know.'

'Sorry, but I'm not here to be liked,' he said sulkily as he put down the phone.

Paperwork: Dylan looked at his in-tray in dismay. The pile must be at least eighteen inches high and he needed to clear it. With the mood he was in it seemed like a good time. Shredder at the ready, he took the first piece of paper off the top and stared at the subject matter.

'What? What the fuck is this?' he said out loud as Vicky walked in with his cup of coffee in her hand and two biscuits.

Chapter 25

'Boss, you ready to go?' asked John slightly unnerved by Dylan's tone. Dylan stood, took the cup off Vicky and gulped a mouthful of coffee before handing it back to her. He slid a biscuit off the plate she held and popped it into his mouth, collected his jacket from the back of his chair and headed towards the door, clipping on his black tie.

'Yeah, let's go,' he said.

The funeral procession for Bridey and Toby was about to commence when they arrived. Dylan stood alongside his colleague. A marked police vehicle shone in the afternoon sunshine at the front of the cortège. The streets were lined with townspeople for as far as Dylan could see. A camera was set on the procession.

Harrowfield Parish Church was at the heart of the town. Anglican worship drew the riches of the Christian tradition old and new. Dylan stood beneath its mighty towers and immediately realised these as the church's beacon to direct the faithful to the house of God.

There was a gathering of people in black. The footpath leading to the wooden porch was awash with bouquets, soft toys and photographs. Local media were there along with one or two Nationals who made themselves known to Dylan.

'Detective Inspector Dylan,' called a chirpy little voice, have you identified the driver yet?'

He looked sideways and saw Riley Shaw from the local paper.

'Not yet Riley, but we're making progress,' he called back. *Not quickly enough though,* he thought to himself.

The inside of the Church was full to bursting with mourners. Dylan felt a chill that sent a shiver down his spine, or a goose walking over his grave, as his old mum would have said. There was standing room only at the back, which is where John and he stood.

The music started. *I've Been Missing You* by Chris De Burgh echoed around the room and through the speakers to those stood outside. Dylan shuffled. He looked up at the stained glass window at the front of the church and clasped his hands in front of him.

Shuffling could be heard to his left and out of the corner of his eye he saw the first of the two coffins being carried down the aisle. The same aisle that Bridey and Graham had walked not long before, a gentleman whispered to his friend who stood in front of them. This time there was no smiling faces, no jubilation, and no wedding march. The coffins were adorned with brilliant white lilies, which Dylan thought created a heavenly light of their own, a halo and a tribute to the loves of Graham Tate's life.

The coffins were laid to rest at the end of the aisle in front of the altar, together side by side. The vicar read Psalm 23, *The Lord Is My Shepherd*; Dylan's favourite Psalm. Readings were read through the tears of loved ones and there was an address before *Jerusalem* rang out of the hearts of the congregation. Afterwards were prayers and Dylan prayed hard for the capture and conviction of the people who had done this terrible deed. Dylan watched Graham pick up Toby's tiny coffin and lovingly cradle it in his arms as he walked back up the aisle with it to Toby's final resting place with his mum, Bridey in the graveyard.

'Do not stand at my grave and weep, I am not there, I do not sleep. I am the thousand winds that blow. I am diamond glints in the snow. I am the sunlight on ripened grain. I am the gentle autumnal rain. When you waken in the morning hush, I am the soft uplifting rush of quiet birds in circled flight. I am the soft stars that shine in the night. Do not stand at my grave and cry. I am not there, I did not die,' said the vicar.

Dylan and John turned and left the family and friends of Bridey and Toby to their grief, tossing coins into the collection for the church roof fund as they passed.

'I need a drink,' said John, loosening his tie as he hurried his step to catch up with Dylan's long strides.

'Me too,' Dylan said, shaking his head. 'Tell you what; I'll stand you a brandy in a coffee, how's that?'

'Anything with a hint of alcohol sounds good to me,' John said, as they reached the car. 'Right or wrong boss I'd want revenge if that happened to me and mine.'

'It wouldn't bring 'um back.'

'No, but I'm sure it would make me feel a hell of a lot better. A few years in prison, which let's face it, is all the driver of the car will get, isn't sufficient for their lives.'

'I know but we don't make the law John, we only enforce it mate.'

'If Graham Tate gets hold of the people responsible for Bridey and Toby's death I can't imagine what state we'll find them in,' John said thoughtfully.

Chapter 26

It was that time of day. Billy and Danny were outside the school gates in their new car. Pam hesitated as she looked beyond the crowd and saw Danny. 'Wow,' she murmured.

'You look good,' said Danny to the excited teenager. Pam giggled and a blush crept up her cheeks. She stood coyly looking over at the group of girls who watched on. Throwing her hair over her shoulder she smiled at them like a cat that had got the cream.

'That's Sara you were asking about,' she said to Danny. A big grin spread across her face as she waved to a girl that stood at the opposite side of the road.

'Whitworth's daughter?'

'Yep, the ginger haired girl,' she said.

'She's not very old is she?' said Danny.

'She's my age,' said Pam, indignantly.

Billy stared at Sara Whitworth long and hard. 'Is she?' he said, with surprise.

'Enough about her. When you coming for a spin with us? 'What about tomorrow?'

'Yeah, that'd be great,' Pam said. She'd done her duty by going to France with the oldies, now it was her time and she'd do anything to spend some of it with Danny.

Billy was quiet as he watched the ginger haired girl cross the road. A car stopped in front of her and Billy thought she was about to get in but she walked around the back of it and made her way up the main road.

'Is he coming?' mouthed Pam.

Danny nodded. 'Don't worry, we'll get rid of him,' he whispered and she giggled once more. 'Pick you up from yours tomorrow morning.'

'The oldies will be gone by half-eight at the latest so see you after then. I've gotta go, I've got a riding lesson,' she said tucking her wayward hair behind her ear.

Pam's mind was all over the shop as she walked away from them with a grin so wide it made her nose wrinkle. What would she tell them at school? Would she need a note? What if her parents found out? If she didn't go Danny might not want to see her again.

Oh, it was a no brainer; she was going alright, what was she thinking of? How could she even contemplate missing out on a day out with Danny? It was a thrilling thought but scary too because she'd never done anything before that her parents didn't know about.

She shivered with excitement. What would she wear? She'd do her hair and nails tonight she planned. 'Whoopee.' she yelled flaying her arms in the air as she threw caution to the wind and ran down the grass banking in delight.

'Let's see where that copper's daughter goes Danny?' said Billy, pointing to the figure of a girl disappearing slowly out of their view.

'Why? What're you thinking?' Danny said suspiciously.

'Don't know yet, but I do know I'm looking forward to tomorrow,' he grinned showing off the big yellow stain on his two front teeth.

'Thought you weren't listening?'

'Well you know what thought did, don't you?' he said. 'Too right I was,' he said pulling the pink thong out of his pocket and sticking it under his nose as he sniffed it.

'She won't want to come out with us again after that then,' Danny snarled.

'So, we'd better make the best of it then hadn't we?' Billy said, with a glint in his eye. 'Why don't we give the copper's daughter a bit of a fright?'

Danny drove the car slowly. Just close enough to keep their prey in sight.

Sara Whitworth walked the well-worn route home, totally unaware she was being followed. She walked across the green and through the little park with the swings and slide that her mum and dad had taken her to often when she was little. She marched over the tarmac in the small car park where she had learnt to ride her bike. Next she came to the picnic area where they often had their tea outdoors and the onwards into the coppice that led to their back door. Although the traffic had been busy on the main road there weren't many people on foot, Billy noted.

'I've got an idea. Tomorrow if we've dumped Pam in time let's come back here and wait for her to walk home from school. I'll give her a message for her dad. I'll need a balaclava,' he said wistfully.

'You're a bad lad Billy Greenwood, a very bad lad,' Danny scoffed.

Chapter 27

It was a quarter to nine when Pam heard a car rolling along the driveway pebbles. She peeked out of her bedroom window to make sure it was them. She felt sick with exhilaration at the sight of the Subaru. She could feel the blood pumping through her veins. Was her heart going to burst she wondered as it beat madly in her chest.

She had tossed and turned all night with a knot of anxiety in her stomach. It felt like Christmas morning and the day held great expectation. At four o'clock she'd got up and poured herself a drink of juice, unable to stay in bed and walking back into her bedroom she had caught sight of the short denim skirt hung on her wardrobe door and the low cut bright pink lycra top, in the light from the hallway. She nervously giggled with the thought of wearing them.

She wished she knew where her pink thong had gone, but she could hardly ask her mum, could she? How could she explain she wanted a thong on a school day? Knowing her dad, he would have thrown the present her friend had bought her for her birthday straight in the bin. He had been very vocal in telling her she was far too young for such a thing.

A last look in the mirror and a spray of her mother's expensive perfume she ran out to the car, pulling the door with a bang behind her.

'Wow' Danny said. 'Look at you.' He held the door open wide. Billy poked his head between the front seats, grinning sleazily at her. She smiled back; the sooner they could lose him the better, she thought.

'You smell nice,' he said, his eyes willing her top to drop and allow him a glance at her breast.

'Thanks,' was all she could muster; she was feeling very self-conscious of Billy's roving eyes. She pulled her skirt down by the hem as far as she could and held her handbag tightly on her lap. Billy was weird, but Danny seemed to approve of him so that's all that mattered to her.

'What did you decide to tell the oldies?' asked Danny

'I haven't,' she said, shyly as their eyes met in the rear view mirror

'And school?'

'I'll tell them I was sick tomorrow.'

'I'm impressed,' he said with a nod of his head.

'Thought we'd go to the Country Park, it'll be nice and quiet there and there's that sandy stretch near the water where we can sunbathe.'

'Great,' she said. Her stomach did a flip.

'I'm going fishing, 'Billy said with a wink.

Even better, thought Pam; her eyes wide with glee.

'We'll call at the garage and get some sandwiches, drinks and that,' Danny said.

'Oh, I've got some money for...' Pam said, frantically scrambling in her bag for her purse.

'No, put your money away,' Danny said gallantly.

'Yeah, that's a first,' Billy said, chuckling.

Pam screwed up her nose. He was a sick pig and she couldn't wait to get rid of him.

Danny and Billy strolled into the garage and Pam took the opportunity to check herself in the mirror. She touched her cheeks, stroked her eyelashes and threw a smile that showed her even white teeth. She undid her bag and taking her lip gloss out she swiftly ran her index finger around her lips with the mint flavoured sheen. She'd seen her mum do it often when her dad was filling up with petrol. Was this how it was going to be from now on? A warm glow engulfed her.

Flipping the mirror up she watched the two friends saunter out of the store with carrier bags full to bursting. Danny opened the car door and passed a bag over the seats to Pam.

'Didn't know what sort of sarnies you liked so we got a selection,' Danny said with a big smile crossing his face. 'Pass a Snickers over will you.'

Pam delved into the bag. Beer, cider, sandwiches, crisps, more beer she noted as she groped around.

'You want a beer?' Billy said as he shook a can before pulling the ring tab. Foam and alcohol squirted all over the car much to the amusement of the pair.

Pam squealed, 'Oh, the lovely new ...' she said, trying desperately to mop up the spray that had landed all over her clothes. 'Later,' she said whilst blotting the rancid liquid from her skirt. The smell of beer and now the motion of the car made her feel nauseous. She had never been a good traveller and as she felt the familiar draining of colour in her face and shortness of breath, she prayed that they would soon be at their destination.

The Country Park was bathed in glorious sunshine. Meadow grass wafted in the warm breeze along the long winding path that led to the sculpture park. Pam breathed in the warm, clean air in big gulps as she stepped from the car. The views were magnificent for as far as the eye could see. Pam stretched her body to the sky. She lifted her face to the sun and was glad of its warmth. Swaying slightly, she found herself in Danny's arms and for an instant she felt like she was in heaven.

'Let's go down to the water's edge. Down there,' Danny pointed, as he gazed at her lustfully. Billy handed her bags to carry.

'Yeah, that looks like a good spot,' said Billy, heading for a shaded spot under a huge willow tree. There was a path down to the lake. Pam wished she had worn different shoes as she tottered behind the two tittering youths.

Turning round Billy grabbed the bags from her grip and ran ahead like an over-excited child. Danny held back and reached out for her hand. She sighed with contentment as she closed her eyes and wallowed in his closeness, confident as she was in his charge.

This must be what it's like to date an older, more experienced guy, she thought as Danny swung her round and kissed her roughly on the lips before laying a blanket on the ground. She would have liked to be alone with Danny but it was their first date and having Billy around would maybe stop him getting over-friendly, she thought. She wasn't ready to go all the way with him yet; after all she was only thirteen.

The water lapped a shingled path in front of them. They could have been at the seaside, she thought, as the boys discarded their tops and threw them in a pile on the ground under the tree. She reached out to fold them neatly, watching the boys playfully splashing around in the lake.

'Get the cans out. I'm thirsty,' Billy shouted as he got out of the water and began picking stones up and skidding them on the surface. Danny sat down next to her and threw a can of beer at Billy. It landed in the water and he waded out for it.

'Fancy a skinny dip Pam?' Danny asked.

'Oh, no thanks, it's too cold for me,' she said feeling very mature as she took a sip from the opened can of lager Danny offered her.

'Billy will do when he's had a few more. He's fucking mad.' he said rolling his eyes. For a split second she felt unnerved. She looked around. It was an isolated spot and all of a sudden she realised how little she knew of Danny Denton and Billy Greenwood. Danny put his hand on her leg just above her knee and stroked the inside of her leg gently without looking at her. She instinctively tensed.

'Here have some more lager, it'll help you relax,' he said, soothingly as he handed her a second can from which he had begun drinking. She took a long swig of the liquid and coughed.

'I don't usually...' Pam started to say, by way of an apology.

'Yeah, but today's special, so have a drink with me to celebrate, eh? '

She tilted the can and took a long drink. Danny held the bottom of the can in the palm of his hand and tilted it so that the liquid came faster into her mouth.

'Yeah, that's it, good girl – have a good drink.'

The liquid started to run down her chin and onto her chest as her throat tightened up. She knocked the can to the side and gasped for air and coughed uncontrollably. Danny patted her gently on the back, laughing hysterically.

'Come on, drink up, there's plenty more where that came from.'

'Let's open a bottle of cider each and see who can drink it the quickest,' Billy said joining them and instantly reaching into another carrier bag. 'Good game, good game,' chortled Billy as he stood shivering in his wet clothes.

'Perhaps we should have something to eat first,' said Pam, hoping that they might forget about the stupid game.

'Five minutes and there'll be a consequence for the person who finishes last,' Danny said.

'But ... but I'm not used to drinking so that's not fair,' said Pam, with a little cry. Her head was already starting to spin.

'It's not fair.' Billy mimicked the whine of her voice.

'No, Pam's right,' said Danny holding up his hand in protest. 'We won't start to drink ours till Pam is halfway down her bottle, Billy come on, don't be a dick.'

Pam smiled nervously and looked to Danny for reassurance.

'You'll be fine,' Danny said laughing at the look on her face as he pulled her backwards onto the grass and leaned across to kiss her full on the lips.

'Nice view,' Billy whistled. Pam knew he could see up her skirt.

She sat up as quickly as she could, 'Er, what's the consequence going to be if you lose?' Pam asked, taking a little sip of the cider.

'What d'you think it should be?' asked Danny.

'I dunno,' she said, quietly.

'The loser skinny dips,' Billy shouted.

'That's not a consequence for you, you do that anyway,' said Danny.

'Yeah, but I'm not gonna lose am I?' said Billy, with a squeal as he flopped backwards into the lake.

'But, I haven't got a towel.'

'Ah, never mind,' Danny said.

'Awh, just strip off, we don't mind,' Billy said, chortling.

Danny threw his empty can. Billy threw his further. Danny hurled a cider bottle.

'You shouldn't drink any more should you?' Pam said to Danny. 'You're driving.' Danny looked at her, eyes wide in disbelief. He sniggered. Billy laughed out loud.

'I think I need a slash,' Billy said, as he came to stand beside them. Stepping back he unzipped his fly and urinated on the grass.

Pam's heart jumped into her mouth. She felt the blood rush to her cheeks. It was the first time she had seen a man's penis except in pictures or on statues. She didn't know where to look. 'Like the look of it love?' he said laughing as he dangled his penis in front of them shaking the excess drips from its end.

'Quick,' Danny said, giggling like a little kid. 'He bloody means it,' he said pulling her up from the grass by her hand.

'You bloody moron. Put it away and go do some fishing or sommat for a bit,' Danny said nodding suggestively to his friend.

Without a fuss Billy snapped a twig from the tree, picked up his drink and winked at Pam. He sauntered down the side of the lake and out of sight behind the trees.

Danny and Pam sat in silence. Pam shivered and goosebumps rose on her arms.

'You cold?' Danny asked throwing his drunken arm around her shoulders. His breath smelt of beer as his mouth found hers and she gagged. 'Bet you're glad you skived off now,' he said putting a hand on her chest and guided her body onto the grass. Within seconds his body was on the top of hers. He started to fumble under her skirt.

'Stop, stop,' she cried.

'What the bloody hell's up with you?' he asked. 'Oh, no, don't tell me you're a prick-tease?' he said with eyes that looked dark and menacing to her.

'No, I ... I ... need the toilet,' she said, pushing his body off hers. He eyed her with displeasure and she could feel his anger.

'Well you'll have to go in the bush over there, there's nowhere else out here,' he said.

'Okay. I'll just be a minute,' she said, getting to her feet and brushing the grass off her skirt. Squatting behind the bush she heard the sound of a ring-pull being torn from a can and she knew Danny was opening another can of alcohol. She looked heavenward, what was she going to do?

The crack of a twig breaking close by made her jump. She stood hurriedly. Her heart raced. Staring at her she saw Billy watching her. She opened her mouth but nothing came out. Billy put his finger to his lips and grinned before casually walking away. Tears welled up in her eyes. She had a feeling telling Danny in his inebriated state might antagonise things so she decided to keep quiet and try and get him to take her home.

'Can we go home now, please?' she said as she sat down beside Danny who was laid on the ground pointing to the clouds in the sky and giggling to himself. He didn't reply but reached out towards her and pulled the back of her top with such force that she fell back to the ground. Instantly, he was on the top of her again, his hands up her skirt and inside the crotch of her knickers. Pam screamed and struggled to break free.

'Danny, please stop,' she squealed as tears sprung to her eyes. He pulled her hand away, looked at her as if he wasn't really seeing her and ignoring her plea he lifted up her top and tore it off. Pam cried out for help. He smiled at her. 'Nobody for miles around I'm afraid, sweetheart,' he breathed into her face. 'Come on now. Don't struggle, you know you want it as much as me,' he said in a calm, rich, dulcet tone.

Pam saw Billy's face hover over them.

'Need any help?' Billy asked. Pam sighed, a huge sigh of relief.

'Please Billy, please tell Danny to stop,' she begged.

'I didn't mean you,' he laughed, taking Pam's pink thong from his pocket and dangling it from his fingers above her.

'Hold her arms Billy,' Danny said, 'she's a right bloody wriggler this one.'

Pam screamed the loud shriek of a frightened animal. Danny put a hand over her mouth. Billy held her shoulders down so tightly that she had no chance of breaking free. Seconds later she was being raped. Pam whimpered for her mum, for her dad, for anyone who could help her, but her muffled screams fell unheard on the miles of countryside that surrounded them.

'I'm thirteen,' she sobbed, turning her head into the grass. She heard a groan and the weight of Danny fall upon her. He rolled off and she lifted her head and wretched to the side but before she had chance to get up Billy pushed her onto her onto her back and was raping her too.

'It's your own fucking fault,' Danny told her as he caught his breath. Billy bit her nipple hard and she screamed out in pain but once again a hand was put over her mouth. Billy quickly let out a moan and after a few seconds got off her. Pam turned and curled instinctively into a ball and held her stomach as if in excruciating pain.

From her place on the ground she saw Danny pick up a can of beer and throw it into the water. They both walked to the lakeside and sat drinking, talking and laughing as if nothing had happened.

She sobbed uncontrollably. Bile rose in her throat as she tried to heave herself onto her elbow. Her body ached, her stomach swirled and finally getting up onto all fours she was violently sick. Danny looked back, stood, walked towards her and picking up her clothes he hurled them at her.

'For God sake, you silly cow, get dressed. What did you expect? he shrieked. 'Get dressed.' Pam stood. Blood ran down her legs and she wiped it best she could with the thong.

'Dirty fucking bitch,' Billy sneered. 'Perhaps you should get a wash in the lake,' he cooed. 'Oh, but...' he said. 'We don't have a towel.'

'You, you raped me...' she sobbed. 'You raped me.' She screamed at them. 'How could you? I thought you liked me?'

Chapter 28

Dylan held the facsimile confirmation from the forensic science lab in his hand.

'The headlight found in Denton and Greenwood's garage is a match with the debris for that at the scene of the Harvey murder,' said the quiet, studious voice of the scientist. Dylan placed the phone down. He had it, he had the first positive link to Grace Harvey's fatality, but the connection was the car make and not the driver.

He picked up his phone, held it to his cheek and studied for a moment before dialling DS Spiers' extension. 'Come and see me in my office,' he said. Instantaneously Taylor breezed in.

'You wanted me, boss?' she said with a glint in her eye.

He tried to avert his eyes from her over-exposed cleavage, but she saw his interest and smiled.

'Have a seat,' he said. Taylor did as she was told. Sitting in the seat directly across from his desk, she slowly crossed and uncrossed her long brown legs. He knew exactly what she was doing, but like a rabbit in car headlights he was momentarily transfixed. Dylan coughed and resumed his conversation.

'The glass recovered from the scene of Grace's fatal.'

'Yes?' she said, leaning forward. 'Come on, don't you know it's rude to keep a girl waiting,' she said licking her bright pink lips as she played with the tips of her hair that was scraped back into a ponytail.

'They've got a match with a headlamp seized from Denton and Greenwood's garage,' he said shuffling the paper around on his desk.

'Fantastic, when're we gonna bring them in?'

'Don't get too excited, it's a match for the make of car Denton owned. There's a long way to go yet. I'm thinking about the day after tomorrow. That'll give us chance to plan the interviews and enable us to get stuck into their ribs,' Dylan replied. 'You never know, if they admit to Grace's death we might get them to roll over for Bridey and Toby's murder too,' he said, thoughtfully. 'The carriage clock that Vicky mentioned; have we got proof it was Mildred Sykes'?'

'Why would it be? The fingerprints at Mildred Sykes house are not theirs, we've checked.'

'Do we know if Denton and Greenwood knew Stevenson? Could they be on his payroll?'

'Dunno,' she said. 'Do you think they'll soften under pressure in interview?'

'Doubt it. On the advice of their solicitor it's more likely to be *no comment*. I'll give CPS a call and see what they'll go along with in respect of charging them. Probably, death by dangerous driving is as much as we can hope for, which is better than nothing. But we'll push for murder, manslaughter at the very least.'

'You must be feeling generous,' Taylor said, teasingly.

'Why?' he said, eyeing her quizzically.

'Day after tomorrow is Bank Holiday Monday, remember? Everybody will be on double time,' she said with a smile.

'Good God woman, it's a good job you told me. Headquarters would crucify me.'

'Ah but, the team would love you,' she said flicking her hair over her shoulder as she leant towards him.

'Make it Tuesday. Early start, you sort out the arrest teams,' he said as he dismissed her. She turned to leave.

'Oh, arrange for them to be taken to separate nicks. I want distance between those two once and for all. If Danny Denton's the driver then he's the man in control.'

'Billy Greenwood might grab a lifeline from us if it's offered,' she said as she stopped at the door and looked over her shoulder at him.

'And Greenwood might turn out to be the driving force of the pair?' he said, frowning.

'I'll speak to Stevenson again and get the samples off him that you want,' she said.

'Do it here, at the nick. Invite him in. I'll sit in with you. Let's see what vibes we get from him. It's about time I met him.'

'It'd be nice to find out what makes certain men tick,' she said looking at him quizzically.

Dylan looked to his computer screen. 'Try getting him in today and see if the financial unit's got anything to tell us about him before you do. The more ammunition we have the better,' he grunted.

Dylan watched her walk out into the CID office. She turned. Looked over her shoulder at him and smiled, just like Jen did. He felt guilty, he'd never once looked at another woman since he'd met Jen and there was nothing special about Taylor Spiers, she wasn't his type. What the hell was he thinking of?

He picked up his phone. He needed to speak to Jen. 'We've just got a breakthrough on the mowing down of the old lady and her dog,' he said excitedly.

'That's brilliant,' Jen said. She never asked him who the suspect was or what the breakthrough entailed, she knew if she asked he would tell her but if she didn't know then she couldn't accidentally mention anything to anyone else.

'It means an early start on Tuesday but the day after tomorrow I'm told is Bank Holiday so how you fixed for a lie-in?'

'Sounds wonderful, I'm shattered,' she said with a sigh as she rubbed her bulging stomach.

'I'll try to get a flyer today love, see you soon,' he whispered into the phone, 'I love you.'

'Me too,' she said, hanging up. Jen smiled to herself as she put her phone down and carried on reading her baby book. *At this stage of your baby's development*, she read, *you are probably feeling pretty tired and cumbersome. You may be feeling anxious or irritable and have mood swings.* Well at least she was normal. *You may also feel a heavy dragging feeling in your pelvis, as the weight of your baby bears down. You may be experiencing vivid and unsettling dreams, which is your mind's way of adapting to an approaching life change.* Her eyes closed slowly and she drifted off to sleep.

It was only since Dylan had met Jen that he had started to think he would rather be elsewhere than at his work. He picked up his phone and on impulse rang the pensions departments number to see what his finances would be if he decided to retire. He had an idea, but the figures he was given were better than he thought. Taking a moment to himself, he sat back in his old worn leather chair that he refused to have replaced by Avril Summerfield-Preston when she refurbished the offices. He scanned the walls of his office and took time to read the endless lists of detected murders and other crimes he had dealt with in the past two years along with the vast array of commendations for outstanding work.

The phone rang, bringing him back to the present. 'Boss, I've arranged for Stevenson to come in tonight at seven. It's the best I could do. Is that okay?'

'I suppose so. I'll let Jen know I'm gonna be late,' he sighed.' Taylor Spiers could see him over the screen of her computer; she winked at him as she put down the phone. Did she never give up?

Jen's phone bleeped and it woke her. Startled and sleepy she read the message. 'Another night alone Max,' she groaned as she reached out to stroke his head. She flopped dramatically back on the cushions. 'Flaming work,' she mumbled switching on the TV with the remote control.

Max settled on her handbag like a brindled suitcase – to be sure if she went out he wouldn't be forgotten. She picked up the newspaper but couldn't concentrate long enough to read it. She was tired and thirsty. She stood up and waddled to the kitchen to draw a glass of water from the tap. Making her way back to the settee she threw a cushion down first to support her bump then laid on her side to try and get comfortable. Within minutes she felt three large kicks from her baby. 'Oi, Buttons,' she said stroking her stomach and grinning to herself.

'Hormones,' she said out loud as tears rolled down her cheeks and she wiped them away with a tissue. Dylan was getting back into a routine of early starts and late nights and she was frightened he would make himself ill yet again.

'Awh, hurry home Jack,' she whined, and Max barked as if he agreed. She was never surer he understood everything she said as she stroked his strong, soft head to quieten him.

Chapter 29

Pam's sadness was reflected in her tear-filled eyes. She had fallen in love with the wrong kind of boy. How could she have been so stupid? She had turned a deaf ear to anyone who had badmouthed him. She'd truly thought he liked her.

The realisation that neither of the boys had worn any form of contraception made her blood run cold. What if...? 'Oh God no,' she moaned as her hand moved to her stomach and felt it contract. She started to shake uncontrollably.

'Come on,' Danny yelled. 'Move, otherwise we'll leave ya.'
Perhaps she would be better off left alone.

'If you don't move I'll give you some more of this,' Billy smirked, pulling his zip down. He rubbed his crutch, suggestively.

'No,' she said, sobbing, reaching for her clothes. Billy kicked them away just as her fingers touched the cloth.

'Let her have 'em Billy, we need to get going,' said Danny, his voice taking on a bored tone.

She felt stupid, dirty and ashamed as well as in pain. Again she reached out for her clothes, trying desperately to hide her nakedness with her free arm. Danny's phone clicked. She glared up at him.

'Just a couple of pictures of you crawling naked in the grass, just in case you decide to tell anyone about our picnic,' he said clicking the camera on the phone once again.

Her fingers were numb as she fumbled with the fastening on her bra. 'Shall I help you fasten that?' Billy said laughing.

'Don't... don't you dare touch me,' she said, staring angrily at him. 'Keep away,' she screamed.

139

Billy looked as though he was going to hit her. 'Leave her be Billy, she's not worth it. Let her scream all she wants nobody can hear her here.'

Silently, she followed them back to the car. As they neared their vehicle she saw an elderly man walking his dog in the distance. Danny turned to her as if reading her thoughts. 'Don't even think about it unless you want us to kill him,' he said flicking open a knife.

She froze. Danny sounded serious and she now knew only too well what they were capable of. If they attacked him what else would they do to her? They had her picture. Who'd believe that she wasn't involved? The man walked closer.

'She'll let you and the dog have a go for a tenner mister,' Billy shouted loudly.

The man put his head down and ambled on.

Pam looked ashamedly at the grass beneath her feet as she walked on. The man shouted his dog to heel and when she looked his way he had turned and had began walking in the opposite direction. Who could blame him?

Pam sat in the back of the car that was now strewn with cast-off food cartons, drink cans, pizza boxes and chip wrappers. She stared at the mess as if seeing it for the first time. She could taste vomit and smell alcohol and the stale cigarette smoke upon her. Hurting, she moaned. Quietly she closed her eyes and as she did so she was lulled by the motion of the car, which gave her a little comfort.

'I suppose you expect us to drop you off at home?' Danny said.

She nodded weakly, glancing up for one moment to see the stranger's eyes peering back at her from the car's rear view mirror.

'You'll be okay when you calm down. Remember what we said, say nothing and you'll be okay,' he said in a gentler tone.

Was this really the Danny she had fallen head over heels for?

'Yeah cross us and we'll show everybody your tits on the internet,' Billy said. 'Mind you, they're not bad,' he said.

Pam's lips were swollen and she could taste blood in her mouth. The journey home seemed to take forever but eventually she could see the familiar buildings on her street out of the window. The car came to an abrupt halt. Billy got out and opened the door. Reaching into the back he grabbed Pam's arm and unceremoniously bundled her out onto the pavement.

'Remember, say anything and there'll be trouble,' Danny called after her. He revved the engine ferociously three times. She stood at the gate looking dishevelled and forlorn. Danny drove off at speed, sounding the horn for everyone in the street to hear which spurred Pam into action. She ran into the house and locked the door behind her.

Pam held her breath and listened. Her mum and dad were still at work and she exhaled a sigh of relief. She ran straight upstairs and into the bathroom where she stripped off all her clothes. Feeling uncomfortable with her nakedness she grabbed her dressing gown and hurriedly set the shower running. Slowly she turned and caught her reflection in the mirror as she de-robed. Not only was her mouth red and bruised but there was a great welt on her arm. 'Oh God,' she said, gasping as she put her hand up to the tender flesh of her breasts that bore red, angry teeth marks.

She climbed into the shower and reached for the loofah. Scrubbing her skin until it felt sore, the feeling of nausea suddenly took over as she saw the river of dried blood on the inside of her thigh. She slid down the shower cubicle and sat on the floor of the stall, letting the water pelt down on her body like hailstones.

Suddenly, she twitched as if she had been falling into a semi-conscious sleep. The side of her face was squashed against the shower cubicle door. How long had she been there? The bathroom was full of steam. Fighting to stay lucid she managed to push the door open and claw herself up with the aid of the towel rail. She turned off the water. Wincing, she buffed herself dry with a big, soft towel. She wrapped a turban around her head and grabbed her toothbrush to brush her teeth until her gums bled. She swilled her mouth with cap after cap of mouthwash that burned, but it felt good.

As soon as she was dry she felt dirty again, dirty, used and stupid. She sobbed and sat in the corner of the bathroom on its cold tiled floor. She had no concept of time but slowly she gathered her clothes from the floor and, screwing them up, she threw them into the bin. She put on her Disney tracksuit and curled up on her bed. Her eyes closed, she cried hugging herself until she drifted to sleep.

'Pam. I'm home. Where are you darling?' Pam's mum's voice intruded into her dream and before she had fully woken her mum was through the bedroom door and at her side.

'What on earth?' she said, seeing her little girl's form curled up in a ball under the duvet. 'You ill? Did they send you home from school? You should have called me,' she said stroking, the top of her daughter's head. Her hand wandered under the covers to her brow where she let it linger to see if it were hot.

She sat beside Pam on the bed like she used to when she was little and reached out to cradle her in her arms. Pam couldn't look at her. 'What on earth has happened to your face?' she said, holding Pam's face by the chin and turning it this way and that. Pam's face screwed up and crying hysterically she held her mother tightly.

'Mum,' she whimpered.

'Darling, look at me, has someone hurt you? I need to know.'

Holding her daughter close quietened Pam but, she didn't speak. Linda stroked her daughter's head soothingly.

'I know some of my jewellery and money's gone missing. You've been bullied haven't you?' she said lifting Pam's face to look at her.

'Oh, sweetheart we can sort it, don't worry,' Linda said. 'I'm not cross with you.'

Linda pulled away slightly to get a look at Pam's face once again but Pam clung to her mum's jumper as if her life depended on it.

'You're safe now baby, you're safe. I told your dad there was something wrong. You were so... so quiet when we went to France. Tell mummy what it is,' Linda coaxed.

'I've been raped, mum.'

'What?' Linda yelled, as her heart stopped and she gasped for air.

Chapter 30

'She's never thirteen with tits like that,' Billy said as he looked at Pam's image on the phone's gallery.

'Nah, she were making it up so we wouldn't do her,' Danny said as he tapped his fingers on the steering wheel.

'Do you think she'll blag?'

'She can please herself Billy. As far as I'm concerned she was up for it. She was the one who gave us the come on; that's our story and we're sticking to it right? And she told us she was sixteen didn't she?' Danny said.

Billy looked confused, 'No, she told us she was thirteen.'

'She didn't, she told us she was sixteen,' Danny said, nodding his head and winking at his friend. Danny tutted, 'If you had a brain you'd be friggin dangerous man,' he laughed.

'She's fit though in't she,' Billy said, still studying her pictures.

'Delete the one where you can see her bawling,' said Danny.

'Oh, yeah, smart. Are we still gonna see if we can see that copper's daughter? I'm in the mood now.' Billy gave Danny a cheesy grin.

'Once you've been let loose there's no stopping you is there? Why not, I'm worried that you might be coming a bit of a cradle snatcher though,' he scoffed.

Danny pulled up outside the school entrance. Within minutes Billy had spotted Sara Whitworth running out of the gates and he signalled her appearance to Danny. Her run soon slowed to a walk.

When she was far enough up the road not to suspect them following her, Danny swung the car out of the lay-by and did a three-point turn in the road. Slowly and quietly the car crept close to the kerb behind her. At the very same point as the day before she crossed the road towards the green and they knew she would walk towards the swings. Danny steered the car past her and laid on its horn. Sara didn't give the car driver the satisfaction of a look as she put her nose in the air and walked on. Danny expertly steered the car at speed on the road leading to the children's playground.

'Drop me off at the car park near the picnic area,' said Billy.

'What you got in mind?' asked Danny. Billy put his finger to his nose. 'That's for me to know and you to find out,' he said.

'Moron,' said Danny.

Sara walked across the grass swinging her schoolbag in the air. It was a lovely day and she tipped her face to the sky to catch the warm afternoon sun. Being stuck in a classroom all day wasn't her idea of fun; she'd much rather be outside.

Billy squatted in the bushes, sniggering to himself. Seeing her pass he leapt from his haunches and grabbed her round the waist. Before she could scream he had his hand over her mouth.

'Tell your dad I'm repaying a debt. Tell him he doesn't bully me or my mate and get away with it, right?'

Sara gasped for air,

'Keep looking behind ya', coz next time. I plan to rape you,' he growled, rubbing his hand down her stomach towards her crutch. 'Go, run, as fast as you can to daddy,' Billy said menacingly as he released her from his grip. Laughing in a sinister manner he put a firm hand to her back and pushed her away from him.

At first she shuffled a few steps, and then, when she knew she was free, she ran like the wind – or at least as fast as her wobbly legs would carry her. Billy turned; ducked back into the bushes and out the other side. Looking both ways to make sure there was no one around, he ran quickly and jumped into the waiting black Subaru.

'Go, go, go Danny,' he yelled at the top of his voice. 'Maybe daddy might think twice about kneeing people in the bollocks now, eh?' he smirked, relaxing back in the passenger seat with a sigh of satisfaction. His friend shook his head.

'Thanks for that mate,' he said, throwing Billy an endearing look.

'Wassak,' he replied.

'Fancy a McDonald's?' Danny said, grinning.

'Yeah, think I deserve a Big Mac.'

'We'll be on CCTV there. Good alibi mate,' said Danny.

'You think of everything don't you?' Billy grinned.

It was reasonably quiet at McDonald's and they got served straight away.

'I think I'm in love,' Billy cooed as he threw his tray of food on a table. There was a young man sitting at a nearby table tightly holding a bunch of flowers.

'What's your fucking problem, nobhead?' Billy asked. The man stuck a middle finger in the air and resumed drinking his Coke through a straw.

'Weirdo,' Danny said screwing up his nose.

'I'm gonna have the fucking twat,' said Billy. 'Nobody does that to us and gets away with it, right Danny?' Billy rose from his chair and its legs scraped nosily on the tiled floor. The young man stared at Billy with deep-set dark eyes that were hidden under his woollen hat.

'Leave it,' Danny said, blocking his friend's path. 'Look, her, over there,' he pointed to a young waitress who was giving him the eye. 'I think she fancies me,' he whispered. The waitress winked and proceeded to clear the tables around them. Slowly but surely she got to theirs. She stood with her hand on the back of Danny's chair and holding a wet cloth with the other.

'Did you notice how dark it was last night Billy?' The waitress leaned over to pick up their used cartons, exposing a large cleavage.

'No, why?' asked Billy, screwing up his nose.

'Because this little angel must have fallen from heaven,' Danny said, smiling up at the waitress.

'Can I get you two any fink else?' she giggled. Billy was transfixed.

'When's your next day off?' Billy asked, speaking directly to the waitress's chest.

'You're cute,' she said. 'Tomorrow actually, why have you something in mind?'

'Well it could be your lucky day,' he grinned.

She reached over and pulled up Danny's sleeve. Taking a pen out of her top pocket she held his hand in hers as she wrote down her phone number on his forearm. 'Anytime after eleven,' she said, pulling the sleeve back down and releasing his hand slowly from hers.

'I'm Danny and this is my mate Billy,' he said.

'I'm Shaz, will you be coming?' she said, looking at Billy.

'I hope so,' he replied, swallowing hard.

'Well who knows it might just be your lucky day too little man,' she said over her shoulder as she winked at the boys and walked back to the counter.

'I'll call you. Can we have more Cokes over here, gorgeous,' Danny said.

'Large ones?' she called back.

Billy nodded as he watched their new-found friend. Neither spoke a word. As she walked back to the table, Billy noticed the man watching her and he glared at him with his chin jutted out towards him. Shaz put the drinks on the table and leaned heavily against Danny's arm.

'Who's that fucking weirdo?' Billy asked, nodding in the man's direction.

'Ah, he's harmless. Me mate Tracy says he's in love with me,' she said. 'Bless him, he comes in most days and sits there holding a bunch of flowers. Tracy finks that he's too shy to give them me, he always take them home with him,' Shaz whispered in Billy's ear as he drank his Coke through a straw. 'I'm glad he doesn't give them me; they're those ones that stink vile,' she laughed heartily.

'Fucking wanker,' Billy shouted out loud in his direction. 'He better leave our girl alone from now on.'

Shaz smiled as she walked back to the counter wiggling her large hips for their benefit.

'I am in love Danny,' Billy said, visibly swooning. 'Now that's what you call a woman.'

Danny laughed. 'You were in love with Pam two minutes ago. Make your bloody mind up.'

'Shaz what?' Danny asked as they passed the waitress to leave.

'McDonald,' she said pointing to the McDonald's sign. 'That's what they call me.'

Danny placed a ten pound note down her blouse. 'For you,' he whispered in her ear. 'Don't work too hard, it could be a tiring day tomorrow,' he said with a wink.

'Hey, Danny you don't think maybe we should have offered to wait and give her a lift home do you?' asked Billy, as they stepped outside. 'We don't want him to spoil our fun,' he said, throwing a backward glance at the man sat at the table near the window with the bunch of flowers still firmly in his grasp.

'Patience, Billy,' he laughed as he strutted down the precinct in front of his friend without looking back at McDonalds or the girls watching after them.

'I think I'm gonna dream about Shaz all night.' Billy pulled at the crutch of his trousers. 'I'm getting a stiffy.'

'Pam or Sara?' asked Danny.

'Nah, Shaz is the only girl for me now,' sighed Billy.

Chapter 31

'My God! Look at me Pam,' Linda said, tilting her daughter's face to her.

'When did it happen? Where? Your dad'll... The police, we must report it,' Linda cried. She sobbed as she rocked her daughter in her arms.

It wasn't long before two Police cars were gracing the driveway of the Forrester's home. Linda's call to her husband's receptionist had sounded frantic. Bill bounded into the house still in his dentist's scrubs.

'Where's Pam?' he asked as Linda flew into this arms.

'She's safe. She's upstairs with one of our female officers, sir,' the young uniformed officer answered as Bill held his wailing wife to him. He stroked her hair and made soothing sounds in an attempt to stem her tears.

'Can I see her? Is she okay?' he whispered, to the officer over the top of Linda's head. 'What's happened?'

An older looking lady, with kind eyes, walked down the steps towards them and stopped midway. 'I'm sorry Mr Forrester, you can't,' she said softly. 'Your daughter has been raped and we have to be ever so careful about contamination at this stage. Even though your daughter has had a shower, we want the best chance of obtaining any evidence that remains. We'll look after her, I promise you,' she said reassuringly.

Bill Forrester looked horror-struck. 'What?' he said with a lump in his throat that threatened tears.

'Once we've gone through the routine procedure here, we'll take her down to a specialist suite we have at the Child Protection Unit. She'll need to have a medical examination and make a statement,' the plain-clothes officer explained.

'If you could just give us ten minutes sir?'

Mr Forrester nodded, a numb expression on his ashen face.

'I'll put the kettle on,' Linda said, wiping a lone tear that tricked down her already mottled red, puffy, cheek. Bill smiled kindly at his wife but the smile didn't reach his eyes.

'That would be lovely, thank you,' said the officer.

Bill Forrester followed his wife into the kitchen. They could hear the uniformed police officer talking on the radio in the hallway. Appearing at the kitchen door, she made her apologies and left to attend another call.

'What's Pam said?' Bill asked his wife.

'Not a lot. Older boys who abused her naivety, and treated her badly from what I can gather. There isn't enough education in her world, Bill. She didn't say who they were, where it happened or when, all I know it's happened today. They could've killed her,' Linda cried. 'She's only a baby, my baby,'

Bill reached out to his wife and she went into his arms. He held her tight for a moment or two as she clung to him and sobbed as if she would never stop.

The whistling kettle pierced the tension of that moment and, on automatic pilot, Linda robotically pulled away from Bill's embrace and started to take cups out of the cupboard and place them on the work surface. How many did she need? She couldn't think straight. She placed four tea bags in the teapot and hoped that would suffice, filled a milk jug and slid the sugar bowl onto the wooden tray.

'Why do people always make tea in times of shock?' Linda said with a sniff as she wiped her nose with a tissue before stuffing it in her trouser pocket. Bill shook his head.

'I know I need something stronger than bloody tea,' he said, as he perched on a stool at breakfast station and put his head in his hands. 'When I find the bastard that did this to our Pam I swear I'll...' he cried, dragging his hands through his hair. 'Let's just say they won't get the chance to do it again,' Bill said grinding his teeth. Linda saw the hatred in his eyes and she knew he wasn't lying.

'I'll get you a brandy,' she said. Collecting a glass from the cabinet she headed for the drinks globe, poured a large Cognac and handed it to him. He took the bottle from her hand, drank from the glass and filled it again.

Linda took the tea upstairs with an assortment of biscuits on a plate. Pam's door was still closed and she paused awkwardly outside, not knowing what to do. Her hands occupied, she tapped the door with her foot and an officer opened it just enough to take the tray from her. The room with its curtains drawn was dark compared to the rest of the house and she couldn't see her daughter but could hear a mumbling of voices.

'We shouldn't be much longer now,' she whispered. 'Could I just remind you not to touch any of the clothes that Pam was wearing, please,' she said.

'No, no I won't. I've already been told to leave them. Me and her dad are downstairs in the kitchen if you want us.'

Linda and Bill sat in silence sipping their drinks as they stared into space. They waited for the sound of Pam's door opening, or a creak of a floorboard on the stairs that would indicate to them that someone was leaving her room.

'She didn't have a boyfriend did she?' asked Bill.

Linda shook her head. 'Not that I'm aware of, no.' The two looked at each other, a question was on their lips, but neither of them spoke.

'She only goes to the riding stable on her own, apart from school. Do you think it's someone she met there?' Linda said, putting her hand to her mouth to silence her gasp. Bill shrugged his shoulders.

A shuffling of feet upstairs warned them that someone was on the move. Bill jumped off his stool and Linda followed him out into the hall. A uniformed officer was coming down the stairs with a number of brown sealed bags in her hands. 'Pam's clothes,' she said, as if she needed to explain. Pam followed behind, her pallor grey. She looked longingly at her parents with sad puppy dog red eyes. Bill and Linda both smiled at her, eyes filled with tears.

'Mrs Forrester,' the plain-clothes officer said, breaking their reverie. 'We'll need you to come with us so that you can consent to the examination and to be the adult present for the interview, if you would?'

Linda nodded, smiling weakly. 'Of course,' she said softly. She reached out and grabbed her coat from a peg in the hallway, a force of habit as it wasn't cold.

'Is it alright if I come along?' asked Bill.

'Yes, of course Mr Forrester but I think it best if mum sits in on the interview,' she said.

'I understand. It's just... I want to be there.'

'That's not a problem. It's likely to take a few hours so be prepared for a wait. We'll have to take photographs and there will be a medical examination. Do you both want to follow us in your car?'

'Yes, whatever's best,' Bill said heading for the kitchen to pick his car keys from the breakfast bar where he'd left them.

'Should you be driving?' asked the uniformed officer as he passed her in the hallway. Bill handed his keys to his wife. 'Perhaps not,' he said wanly realising how much alcohol he had consumed.

Bill and Linda followed the police car that transported their daughter. 'Keep positive love. At least she's alive,' Bill said, trying to comfort her.

'I know,' she sighed. 'We have to think she's one of the lucky ones. She shouldn't be going through this. We should have been able to protect her.'

'Don't even go there,' he said, and she saw his jaw tighten.

'What if they've given her some horrible disease,' Linda said, with a sob that caught in the back of her throat and made her cough.

'She needs us to support her. We can't go thinking anything like that otherwise we'll go to pieces. We don't know exactly what's happened yet; so let's not let our imagination run wild yet, eh? One step at a time,' he said, with a glace in her direction as he patted her leg.

The building they were led to wasn't the police station as Bill and Linda expected, but a large detached stone dwelling that could have been someone's home. Bill was shown into a lounge area, while Linda went with Pam and the officers into what he was told was the medical room.

'The doctor should be here in the next half an hour. Can I get you a coffee or a cup of tea?' the clerical officer asked him.

'Thank you,' Bill said as he watched the lady go into the kitchenette. He heard her filling the kettle, saw her arm reach to a shelf for a mug and listened as she opened a drawer where no doubt she got out a spoon.

'Sugar?' she shouted.

'Yes please, two,' Bill said.

'Will this doctor be a man or a woman?' Bill asked as he stood up and started to read the posters that were pinned to the wall. 'Chlamydia' one read, another 'Vaginal Warts'. He shuddered and turned away.

'I'm sorry I don't know. It just depends who's the police surgeon on call, but don't worry, they're all really lovely,' she reassured as she studied him over her half moon glasses from the doorway.

Bill walked back to his seat and sat down, leaned forward and picked up a magazine from the low table in the centre of the room and prepared himself for the wait.

'I'm sorry, mum, for causing you all this trouble,' Pam said, as she sat on the examination table with her bare legs dangling over its side. She was draped in a dressing gown and looked so young and forlorn that all Linda wanted to do was cuddle her.

'You haven't caused us any trouble darling, you never have. Stop blaming yourself. We'll get through this together, don't worry, everything will be alright,' she sighed, patting the bed beside her daughter as she realised she couldn't touch her, just in time. Her hand rested on the bed. 'I'm just so glad you told me and didn't try to deal with this all by yourself.'

'Doc's here,' said the plain-clothes officer, rushing into the room. Seconds later the door opened with a creak and closed with a groan.

Doctor Lesley Lord proved to be sweet, gentle and kind, with the best of bedside manners.

'Pam, this is going to be a bit uncomfortable for you, but we need to take some samples. First of all I need some of your hair,' she said, combing Pam's locks with care. She collected the hair caught in the brush's bristles.

'This may seem insignificant to you, but it may give us anybody else's hair that may have become entangled with your own, on contact,' she said gently.

Pam shivered as the thought of her ordeal came back to haunt her.

'You cold?' Doctor Lord said.

'No,' said Pam.

'Next I'm going to have to cut a sample of your hair, but we'll do it from underneath so you won't be able to see. I'm no hairdresser, as my friends will tell you,' she smiled kindly at Pam. 'I once tried to cut my best friend's fringe and twenty years later she still hasn't forgiven me.

'The next sample is a bit more intimate I'm afraid. I'm going to have to take a sample of your pubic hair. Do you understand Pam? Is that okay?' Pam nodded her head as the doctor guided her down to lie on the bed.

The room was deathly quiet and the lighting was dimmed. Doctor Lord directed a spotlight onto Pam's body. Pam could hear the telephone ringing in the next room and a mumble of voices as she stared up at the ceiling, praying for the whole thing to come to an end. She felt a gloved hand run over her body.

'I'm examining your body for any bits, scratches or bruising Pam, then I'll take swabs and taping from your breasts and legs. This might help to pick up traces of semen or saliva that your attackers might have left behind.'

Pam swallowed hard as tears came into her eyes and rolled down the side of her head onto the pillow beneath.

'I'm sorry,' said Doctor Lord, 'but I am going to have to take some internal swabs from you in case they deny having sexual intercourse with you. Are you okay with that?'

Pam nodded once more but didn't take her eyes from the circle of light on the ceiling as she reached out for her mum's hand. The doctor nodded to Linda that contact was okay and she let her daughter squeeze her hand tight.

Chapter 32

Bill Forrester wasn't the only father in the neighbourhood rushing to his daughter's aid. PC Tim Whitworth switched on the sirens on his police vehicle and sped as fast he could to his home address when he got the call.

Braking hard, the car screeched to a skidding halt outside his house and he struggled, due to his size, to disembark in haste. Sara sat shaking in his wife's embrace as he walked through the door.

'This is your bloody fault,' Frances, his wife, said. 'Someone's attacked her because of you,' she spat out the words with pure venom.

'Be quiet woman,' he said.

Sitting down on the footstool in front of his daughter, he reached out and laid a caring hand on his daughter's knee. 'What's happened, love?' he asked, softly.

Sara looked at him with her big brown cow eyes that appeared sunken in her pale face. 'I was careful, like you always tell me to be walking home, dad,' she snivelled. 'But, he came from nowhere. I didn't hear, or see him before he...' she gulped. 'He grabbed me from behind and put a hand over my mouth,' she swallowed as she struggled to get the words out between sobs. '... then he told me to tell you to stop bullying people or next time he'd rape me,' she cried.

'And what happened then?' Tim asked.

'He pushed me and told me to run,' she sobbed. 'So I did, as fast as I could, and I didn't stop until I got home.'

'Did you see who it was?'

'No, I just remember the smell of alcohol and cigarettes and his stupid laugh,' she said, grimacing.

'For God's sake Tim, she told you he grabbed her from behind, what kind of a policeman are you?' Frances scowled at her husband. 'Don't you ever bloody listen?' she cried, laying her daughter's head to her bosom as she rocked her gently.

There was a knock at the open front door and uniformed officers walked in. Tim Whitworth nodded to his colleagues. The story was related to them and they began a search of the area where the offence had taken place.

CID were contacted and arrived along, with the scenes of crime officers. It was all a bit of a blur for Sara. They needed her coat, they explained, for possible fibre transfers; a sample of her hair to compare against any others they found and they needed a swab of her face to see if they could get DNA from the offender in case he hadn't been wearing gloves. The officers told her that anything at this stage was worth a try to identify the person responsible.

'This is all because of your flaming job,' Frances whispered to her husband as he followed her into the kitchen. She switched the kettle on and collected cups from the draining board. She could see her daughter speaking to an officer from where they stood. 'Don't you realise, she could have been killed. What if he'd have a knife? What if he had raped her?' she said, suppressing a cry. 'We've had a lucky escape this time but this isn't going to happen again. I want you to resign with immediate effect.'

'There you go again. It's always the bloody jobs' fault isn't it? The last thing Sara needs now is to hear us arguing,' Tim said in a hushed tone. He picked steaming cups of coffee from the worktop and marched into the lounge. Frances watched him hand them to the officers and walk back to her.

'This isn't just another one of your incidents,' she said handing him the milk and sugar bowl. He grabbed hold of them but she held on tight. 'This is our daughter's life we're talking about,' she said with her voice rising. He turned his back. She stood close behind him. 'Oh, it'll be the same tomorrow and the day after that. There is always going to be someone wanting revenge because of you, you arrogant bastard,' she said.

'It's only arrogance when you're wrong. I'm never wrong,' Tim Whitworth turned to answer his wife as he stepped forward. Reaching the coffee table, he slammed the milk and sugar down and flopped in his easy chair. His only ambition at that moment was to find out who had threatened his daughter – because once he had found out they wouldn't be able to ever threaten anyone again.

'If you won't do anything, I will,' Frances continued much to the other officer's surprise. 'I'm taking Sara to mum and dad's and we're not coming back till you catch him or you leave the Force, do you hear me?' she yelled grabbing Sara by the hand and pulling her up from the settee, she headed for the stairs. What did this say about him, them, their marriage? He wondered. Tim looked across at the two officers, who sipped their drinks in an embarrassed silence.

'Mum, I'm okay. Don't fuss,' he heard Sara cry. 'I'd rather go to school and be with my mates. Really, I'm alright now.'

'Just for a few days,' she said, as she pushed her daughter into her bedroom and slammed the door behind them.

Tim Whitworth raised his eyebrows to the ceiling at his colleagues who rose from their seats, shook his hand and wished him the best of luck as they left.

Tim climbed the stairs, knocked on Sara's bedroom door and opened it with trepidation. He found Frances throwing clothes into a holdall. Tim sat beside his daughter on the bed. She blew out a breath of exasperation before getting up and walking out of the door. Settling on the top step, she leaned heavily against the wall as tears ran freely down her face.

'I've got to ask you love,' he said. 'Did he touch you?' Tim said as he sat beside his daughter and handed her his handkerchief.

'He put his hand on my stomach and down towards my legs,' she whispered mimicking his actions. Tim closed his eyes and looked heavenward.

'But it was over my coat Dad. He didn't DO anything,' she said, her face turning mottled shades of red.

'Oh my God,' Frances screeched rushing out of the bedroom on hearing her daughter's admission. Tim laid a hand around his daughter's shoulders.

'And you're sure you don't know who it was?' she said, as she stood behind them, clothes hung over her shoulder and dangling from her arms.

'A lad from school perhaps, did you recognise the voice?' Tim asked.

'No Dad. If I knew who it was I would have said. Do I really have to go to Gran's with mum?' she said with a whine. 'I want to stay here with you,' she said, turning her head into his shoulder.

'It might be for the best, love,' Tim said, looking round at his wife. 'Just for a few days, to put your mum's mind at rest.' He squeezed her tight.

'Who've you been upsetting who knows our Sara?' Frances said.

'No one that I can think of,' he said.

'Trouble with your dad Sara is that he has lulled himself into a false sense of competence and for once in his life he needs to stop talking and get something done, because until he does we won't be coming back. Nobody in their right mind threatens a young girl just because their dad's given them a speeding ticket. So whatever he's done, it must be bad.'

'For God sake woman, I'm trying,' he yelled. 'But running away to your mum's is hardly gonna help is it?'

'Help who, you, the job, our daughter, or me? If you think I'm gonna sit around here waiting for our daughter to get raped, then you've another thing coming,' she said as she flew past them, bags in hand, down into the kitchen and two minutes later she stood waiting in the hallway with the car keys in her hand.

'I'll ring you to let you know we've arrived,' she said, beckoning her daughter. 'This needs sorting Tim, and quick,' she said, grabbing Sara's hand in one hand and the bags in the other before heading out of the front door.

'Bye Dad', Sara sobbed. 'I'm sorry.'

Tim ran after them; the door slammed and locked behind him. He looked back in despair.

'Think, did you see anything at all, anything that was out of the ordinary', he begged as Frances slammed the passenger side door, her daughter safely inside.

Sara wound down the window. 'No, I just left school as usual. There were crowds. There were cars. But the only one I remember was Pam Forrester's friend's car; he papped his horn as he went past,' she shrugged.

'Okay. If you remember anything else, let me know,' he said as their car pulled away. 'I'll sort it, I promise,' he called out after them.

He turned and secured the front door, retrieved the police car keys from his trouser pocket and got in. He turned the ignition on. Putting frighteners on a young girl could only be the trait of a coward. Who did he know who fitted that description?

Chapter 33

Brian Stevenson was late, and Dylan was just beginning to think he wasn't coming, when his office door was flung open.

'I'll take him straight into the front office, sir,' DS Spiers said, her hand still on the door handle.

'And I'll be with you in a few minutes if you want to get started taking down his details,' he said, as he put the top on his pen.

The door slammed behind her.

As she set eyes on Brian Stevenson in the foyer, Taylor Spiers immediately noted that he was smartly dressed in an expensive suit, complemented by a cashmere scarf. The undeniably strong bergamot aroma of his Vera Wang eau de toilette filled the small interview room. This wasn't a man who bought cheap, she knew, as the very same scent had put her back a good few pounds on many occasions.

'Now, how do you think I can help you, my dear?' he said, staring at her for a moment before cocking his head in a way that reminded her of a bird listening for worms in the ground.

He very slowly put his hands together on the table, which showed off gold cufflinks, and gave her a sickly smile. At their first meeting she had thought him quite attractive. Instinctively she now saw before her a smooth-talking serpent-like man who looked like nothing more than a snake in the grass.

'We need clarification on one or two issues, Mr Stevenson.' Taylor cleared her throat as she opened the file and pulled out several pieces of paper. 'Please bear with me until Inspector Dylan arrives,' she said with authority.

'Of course, sweetheart,' he said as he pulled his seat nearer the table. The sound of the chair's feet dragging on the tiles set her teeth on edge and she shuddered involuntarily.

'Did you happen to locate the relevant business documents I asked you about last time we spoke?' said Taylor.

Mr Stevenson opened his mouth as if to speak just as the interview room door opened and Dylan walked in. Taylor blew out a relieved breath.

'Can I introduce my boss, Detective Inspector Jack Dylan, to you Mr Stevenson,' she said politely and Dylan nodded in Brian Stevenson's direction.

'Please continue,' Dylan said.

'Where were we Inspector?' Stevenson asked Taylor, looking slightly confused.

'It's Detective Sergeant Spiers, Mr Stevenson, as I keep reminding you. Documents?' she said, tapping her pen impatiently on the table.

'My accountants assured me he'd send them to you,' he said with a surprised look upon his face.

'Well he hasn't. One thing I need to understand, and perhaps you can help me with in the meantime, is why you've had such large amounts of money deposited into your bank account this year.'

'Oh, I understand,' he laughed a smoke and whisky laugh. 'Money, you see my dear is paid into my account from several companies and then I pass this onto my clients. Business has been good.'

'Talking of your clients, Mr Stevenson, you told me previously that Mildred Sykes had released equity from her property. Can you tell me how much that was?' continued DS Spiers.

'Oh, quite a lot,' he mused. 'Several thousand pounds.'

Dylan sat quietly watching Brian Stevenson's body language as answered the questions put to him.

'I did warn her not to keep money in the house,' Brian Stevenson said, shaking his head.

'You mean you paid her in cash?' asked a wide eyed Taylor.

'Yes,' he said, nonplussed. Taylor appeared lost for words.

'So, what you're telling us, Mr Stevenson, is that there is no paper trail?' said Dylan.

'That's the way she wanted it. She was a cute old bird, Mildred was.'

'Obviously not cute enough,' mumbled Taylor under her breath. 'Do you have any idea why she wanted the money?' she asked.

'No. Mildred wasn't for small talk. Different as chalk and cheese were Grace Harvey and her. In fact she could be quite abrupt, to the point of being rude, at times,' he said, thoughtfully. 'Do you think she was killed for her money?'

'It's as good a motive as any, don't you think?' said Taylor.

'And you're sure she never hinted to you why she wanted the money?' said Dylan, with furrowed brows.

'No,' he said shaking his head.

'Your gain from this equity release transaction would be what, commission, a fee?'

'It depends. Most financial advisors charge a fee as well as receiving commission from the lender.'

'In Mildred's case?' Dylan asked.

'I managed to negotiate Mildred a free valuation survey. The lenders charged one per cent fee and they paid half of this to me. I also got her a solicitor whose fees she had to pay.'

'And what happens then?' Taylor said.

'The interest payment is rolled up until the house is sold either by her or her beneficiaries.'

'And the solicitor's fee is?'

'Usually between four and five hundred pounds.'

'She paid that, how?'

'I took her to the cash machine to draw the money.'

'When you visited Mildred, which rooms did you visit in her house?' Dylan enquired.

'The lounge, the kitchen and the bathroom, why?' he said, bottom lip protruding like a sulky child.

'How often did you visit?' Dylan went on.

'Depends.'

'Regularly?' Taylor said with a smile. 'No, doubt your elderly clients look forward to your visits?'

'Yes, I think they do,' he said, with a satisfied grin on his face. He glanced across at Dylan, who was watching him intently with a steely glare. Stevenson held his gaze and when it wasn't returned his smile faded.

'The flowers,' Taylor said. Brian Stevenson looked quickly back at her. 'When did you give her the flowers?'

'I can't remember when,' he said.

'Where did you get them from?'

'The Flower Pot Emporium, I always get flowers from Linda. Look, how long am I going to be here?'

'I'd like you to come with me so that I can take your fingerprints and DNA for elimination purposes, Mr Stevenson,' Taylor said, pushing her chair back and standing up.

'Oh,' he said, obviously taken aback. 'I hope it's painless,' he laughed waspishly as he stood.

'Sorry, just before you do, DS Spiers,' Dylan said. 'Mr Stevenson, I'll need a list of your current clients, please.'

'Er ... er yes,' he stammered.

'In fact, no, send me a list of your clients over the past five years and mark it for my urgent attention when you do.' Dylan said, thoughtfully as he rubbed the forming stubble on his face. 'I want them as a matter of urgency.'

'Yes, I'll see to it directly,' he said, sitting back down.

'Sooner rather than later, please,' Dylan said, waving him away to join Taylor. 'Just as a matter of interest,' Dylan said to the retreating Brian Stevenson, who stopped suddenly in his tracks. 'Are a large percentage of your clients elderly?'

Stevenson turned. 'Well, yes, they are. That's not a crime is it?'

'No, not that I know of,' Dylan said. 'But if you continue to lose them at this rate you're not going to have a business for long, are you?'

'Oh, of course. I see what you mean.' Brian Stevenson stepped in Taylor's direction and she opened the door.

'Have you had a burglary at your home lately?' Dylan said. Mr Stevenson didn't reply or turn around to face Dylan. 'Because DS Spiers tells me that she saw damage to your door when she visited but you told her there hadn't been a break-in. Then you told another officer there had, so which is it?'

Brian Stevenson pivoted around to face Dylan.

'I thought someone had caused a bit of damage to the door. Later I discovered someone had been inside,' he said.

'I understand you told my officer you'd reported it, but you haven't, have you? Why?' Dylan continued. He could see Brian Stevenson becoming agitated.

'I meant to, but...' he said, dropping his shoulders and letting out a tired sigh.

'So have you reported it now?' Dylan asked.

'Yes I … I telephoned the non-emergency number on the leaflet that was pushed through my letterbox and someone took details and gave me a number,' he said studying for a moment. 'A crime number. I think they said that I would need for insurance purposes.'

Dylan made a mental note to get his story checked out. 'So what did the thieves steal Mr Stevenson, anything?'

'Cash and a clock that was left to me.'

'Not a television?'

'No, your officers asked me about that, but I... I sold it. Look, do I need a solicitor?'

'Do you think you need a solicitor?'

'No.'

Dylan smiled. 'Then you're free to go when you've given DS Spiers your fingerprints and allowed her to take a buccal swab.'

Dylan followed them into the fingerprint room and stood leaning against the door jamb while Taylor opened drawers and extracted forms to be completed. Opening the fingerprint inkpad, she reached for Brian Stevenson's hand.

'Any idea who might've broken into your house?' Dylan asked. Brian Stevenson concentrated hard as Taylor Spiers rolled his fingers one by one on the fingerprint ink and then onto the designated places on the form. Without looking at Dylan he shook his head.

'Do you know, DS Spiers, I once knew someone who took the same fingerprint for each space on the form as the others were in plaster,' Dylan said. Brian Stevenson never flinched. 'Did you see anyone acting suspicious around your house, Mr Stevenson?' he asked.

Taylor Spiers handed Brian Stevenson a cloth to wipe his hands. 'Look,' he said, impatiently. 'I've got an appointment to keep, when can I go?

'In a minute, sir,' said Taylor as she extracted a cotton bud-like implement with cotton swab on the end of a longer reach from a DNA collection kit. 'Can I just check you have nothing in your mouth.'

Brian Stevenson opened his mouth wide. 'Now can you swallow for me and open again so I can buccal swab the inside of your cheek.'

Brian Stevenson did as he was told and Taylor inserted the swab. 'Just the same pressure as brushing your teeth, sir, it should only take about thirty seconds to scrap the inside of each cheek, lightly.'

'The term 'Buccal swab' derives from the Latin, Bucca, meaning cheek and a swab, therefore, refers to a DNA collection process involving cells taken from the cheek,' Dylan informed him.

Brian Stevenson swallowed and licked his lips. 'All done,' Taylor said, as she inserted the swab into a tube to keep it sterile and snapped the top shut.

'Now, can I go?'

'Yes, but before you do, can you just tell me about the clock that was stolen from your house. Was it identifiable?' asked Taylor.

'I'd definitely know it if I saw it again.'

'Good. Don't forget the documents. We don't want to have to get a warrant to search for them now do we?' Dylan said, as he reached out and took the fingerprint forms and the swab off the desk. DS Spiers silently guided Mr Stevenson out of the office.

'Nice job,' said Dylan to Taylor when she joined him. Taylor looked a little confused. 'The question you put to him about the clock?' She smiled at him knowingly.

'Do you think it is the one that's in the picture?'

DS Spiers shrugged her shoulders. 'Could well be,' she said.

'Get the photographic department to blow the shot of the clock up for us and let's see if he identifies it. I want to see the clock that was recovered from Denton and Greenwood's flat as soon as possible,' continued Dylan.

'Fancy a quick one Boss?' DS Spiers asked, as she collected her coat from the back of her chair in the CID office.

Dylan flashed her a wide-eyed glance.

'Drink?' she smiled.

'Okay, just the one,' he said, slightly flustered. 'I'll see you at the Kings Head in a minute.'

'Last one there pays,' she said, grabbing her bag as she hurried out. Dylan watched her out of his office window as she ran to her car.

Just calling for a drink on the way home. See you soon pretty lady x, Dylan texted Jen.

Dylan's mobile rang just as he placed a pint of beer and a glass of wine on the table in front of Taylor. She took the opportunity to shuffle on the seat closer to him as she removed her jacket.

'Somebody's popular,' she said grabbing his thigh with one hand as she picked her wine glass up with the other. She smiled at him with her perfectly painted red lips.

'What the hell are you doing?' he said, furiously wiping the beer he spilled down the front of his coat.

'Come on, all work and no play,' she said seductively. 'You could do with a relaxing massage.'

'Yeah, and I'm going home in a minute to the woman who knows just how I like it, so don't bother,' Dylan said.

Chapter 34

Bill Forrester paced up and down outside the video interview room. They waited and waited as the events of his daughter's ordeal were being disseminated piece-by-piece, minute by minute, in fine detail, so the officers could gain as full a picture as possible.

Inside the room Pam, was telling interviewers of her first crush on a boy called Danny Denton. How she'd lied to him about her age at the beginning of their friendship but how she'd told him and his friend Billy Greenwood the truth before they raped her. She told the officers that she was flattered an older boy had paid her attention and that she had thought he loved her. She wept, and Linda's heart went out to her.

'We need to start at the very beginning,' said the interviewing officer.

'But that's lies, all lies. I never agreed to… I told them how old I was… when I realised what they were after,' she said with pain and anguish in her eyes. 'I didn't want sex. I've never.' she sobbed as she wiped away her tears.

'I know, I know,' the officer said sympathetically. 'You're doing really well Pam.'

Bill Forrester was making plans. Once he had the names of who had done this to his daughter, it wouldn't take long to find out where they lived.

Pam talked. The officers took the statement. Linda had told the officers that both her shop and her husband's business premises had been broken into as well as their home over the weekend that they had been in France. They hadn't been able to figure out how the perpetrators had got in, as there had been no sign of a forced entry, but now it seemed possible that the intruders could have used a set of the Forresters' keys.

'Pam, you'll have to identify the exact location that the rape took place, so a search can be done to corroborate what you have told us.'

Pam nodded. Linda remembered when she had been upset as a child but this time was different; she couldn't put a plaster over a wound and kiss it better. The interview seemed to go on and on and all she wanted to do was hold her hand and give her daughter a cuddle.

Bill Forrester looked at his watch. Almost four hours had passed. One consolation was that they were together.

'What happens next?' asked Pam.

'The samples that have been taken from you will be sent to Forensics for examination, along with your clothing, and the two youths accused will be traced, arrested and interviewed as soon as possible,' said the interviewing officer.

Pam's face was now flushed with exhaustion.

'It isn't over yet though. You may have to go to court, but let's not worry about that at the moment,' said the officer kindly.

'I never want to see them again, not ever,' Pam sobbed.

'You did really, really well Pam. You've been very brave,' they said as Linda reached out to embrace her daughter in her arms.

PC Tim Whitworth sat in his local, thinking. He stared into the glass of beer stood on the bar, which looked a bit worse for wear. Frances always blamed his job. If the tea burned it was because he was home late from work. If his shift pattern didn't permit them to go somewhere it was the job that was at fault. If they had no money, she blamed his job. In fact the police force had a lot to bloody answer for in his marriage.

He was angry, frustrated and tired, not only with the person who had threatened Sara but also with Frances. It was a coward's approach to threaten his daughter instead of him though, so he decided he had the right to be angry as he downed his third pint.

'Little bastard,' he said out loud. It had to be Denton. It just had to be.

Dylan moved away from the saloon to hear the voice of the caller. He listened intently. Taylor sat looking up at him with puppy dog eyes.

'Drink up, time to go,' he said as he rang off and hurriedly picked up his coat.

'My place? I've got a nice bottle of Pinot Grigio in the fridge,' she said as she staggered around the table and followed his billowing coat out of the pub's swinging doors.

'No thanks, we've an early start tomorrow and you need to get people notified so that we can lock-up Denton and Greenwood earlier than planned. They've just been named in a rape.'

'It'll keep. I suppose,' she said flatly as she ran to keep up to him as he walked across the car park. What was wrong with him? He wasn't like the other guys she knew that would jump at the chance of being invited back to hers. 'I'll ring around the team leaders and get things organised for a meet at five in the morning then, shall I?' Taylor said.

'Yeah, see you then.' Dylan said jumping into his car and slamming the door shut in her face. Taylor stood alone, looking bemused, as he sped away.

'The good news is I'm home,' he told Jen. 'The bad news is that I have to be back for five in the morning.'

'Oh, Jack... how many times do I have to plead with you not to?'

Dylan gave her a tired look that told her he wasn't in the mood for an argument.

'I know, when the job's running,' she sighed. There was no point in trying to discuss it. 'Go up and put something comfy on; I've got something warm in the oven.'

'Thanks,' he said with a wan smile before reaching out to cuddle her. He buried his head into her shoulder and, hugging her tight, he moaned with fatigue.

Max laid across Dylan's feet in the lounge. For now, the dog was going to make sure he wasn't going anywhere.

'I suppose it'll be a long day tomorrow too?' Jen said as she put a plate of stew and dumplings in front of him. Dylan screwed up his nose. Jen laughed. 'You are funny. Stew's good for you.'

'But I like pies and chips and crisps and...' he wailed at the tray balanced precariously on his knee.

'And I'd like you to be around to see our baby and not in an early grave, thank you mister. Now eat that veg and then you can fall asleep,' she scolded, sitting down on the settee next to him with his drink in her hand.

'If I can get these two put away then things will quieten down, I'm sure,' he said, shovelling a mouthful of dumpling into his mouth; his dislike of vegetables soon forgotten in his haste to tell her of his day. 'I want to disturb them before they wake, if I can, tomorrow morning, which is why we're in so early.'

'Until the next murder you'll rest then, eh?' she said reaching over to stroke his brow.

He didn't reply.

'I only nag because I love you,' she whispered, kissing the top of his head as she stood to take away his plate and fix him rhubarb crumble and custard.

Chapter 35

There was an almighty crash.

'Billy. Coppers.' screamed Danny. His eyes were blinded by the torchlight. Blood beat within his temple. Fear gripped his entire body.

Billy pulled the duvet over his head, curled up in a tight ball and braced himself.

Danny saw the outline of a dark figure before he felt a blow to his head and heard his nose crack. His legs buckled and he fell heavily to the floor. A strong hand grabbed him by the hair and yanked his head backwards. There was a jab at his throat and the intruder drew a sharp knife expertly across his neck.

Billy could hear a tussle and waited for them to come for him. He knew it was only a matter of time.

Due to the carotid arteries being severed and the lack of oxygenated blood to the brain, Danny passed out almost immediately. Blood pumped from the gaping wound and the intruder stepping over Danny left him to drown in his own blood.

As suddenly as the noise started it stopped. Billy dared to raise his head from under his bedcover to hear nothing. The weight of a body thrust upon him took his breath away. Suddenly, he felt a sharp stabbing pain. He screamed. His attacker pressed the pillow in his face. Billy gagged for air.

Another flurry of stabs rained upon him and he tried in desperation to prevent the blade from penetrating his torso. But, it was no use. The knife was piercing his body in the frenzied attack. In a dazed, death-like state, he realised the attack had ceased. He groaned. Everything was still. Then with no warning his attacker jumped on him again, as he screamed like a banshee.

Dylan and the arrest team made a silent approach to the target's flat. Eight shadowy figures crept up the stairwell. A rat scurried in front of them making headway to an overflowing bin. Dylan stopped in his tracks and shuddered. The stench of the landing was gut-wrenching.

Bemused by the open, smashed door at the abode of Denton and Greenwood, he turned to face his colleagues and shrugged. He put a finger to his lips and signalled to them to stand flat against the wall. The council flat was in darkness. Dylan reached inside and fumbled for a light switch. He found one just inside the doorway. Only then did he start to take the lonely walk of an SIO into the flat, unaware of the horrific sight that awaited him.

A corpse lay at the end of the hallway. He stood over it and noticed the resemblance to the man he knew to be Danny Denton. Gingerly he stepped to the side of a two-foot square patch of thick bright red blood so that he could check the rest of the flat, mindful that the murderer might still be there. It wouldn't be the first time he had caught someone at the scene shortly after they had committed a crime. He cautiously looked around him as he stopped frequently to listen for the tell-tale sounds of the killer.

He pushed open wide a door, which led into a bedroom. Again, he reached for the light switch inside. This time the bulb was out. Using the light from the hallway, he could make out bedcovering in a heap on a mattress laid on the floor. Examining it as much as the darkness would allow, he could make out cuts in the cloth that appeared to be consistent with it being slashed. Carefully he lifted one edge of the duvet and beneath it saw the motionless body of another male that Dylan automatically presumed was Billy Greenwood.

Multiple stab wounds were now visible as his eyes became accustomed to the light and he bent down further. Greenwood was motionless. Dylan assumed he was dead too until he did something that he had never needed to do before in his career, he felt Greenwood's neck for a pulse. Was it wishful thinking, or could he really feel a faint throb beneath his fingers?

'Get paramedics here quickly,' Dylan shouted. 'And arrange for the scenes of crime supervisors. We've one dead male and another with multiple stab wounds. I think I might have a pulse.'

He noted the body was still warm to his touch, so he knew the attacks had happened just a short time ago. There was very little first aid he could do and even if he tried which wound did he try to stop the bleeding from first?

He felt helpless. The injuries were beyond any training Dylan or any members of his team had ever had, he was sure of that. If they'd come to the flat an hour earlier? He should have come to arrest them last night. They had the relevant evidence. His thoughts quickly moved to suspects as he stood above the dying man.

Who was enraged enough by these two to commit these premeditated brutal murders? In his experience he didn't give Greenwood a cat in hell's chance of survival. Where should he start?

Careful not to disturb any evidence, Dylan retraced his steps, best he could towards the entrance of the flat.

'Where's SOCO?' he asked, impatiently. 'I need footplates and I need them now.'

He tiptoed past the body of Danny Denton and for the first time noticed flowers strewn on the floor. What on earth were flowers doing in Denton and Greenwood's flat?

DS Spiers stood in the doorway. 'Boss, maybe I can help. 'I'm first aid trained.'

'So am I, but what we've been trained to do would be futile,' Dylan replied.

'But at least I'd have tried,' she pleaded.

'When I say no, Taylor I mean no,' he said firmly. 'Billy Greenwood may be dying but his best chance of survival is with the paramedics when they arrive.'

'But, you're just letting him die.'

'Taylor, go back to the nick and start calling staff in will you, please.'

If looks could kill, Dylan thought, he would have fallen on the spot. He stood with the team outside on the landing. Scenes of crime personnel arrived.

The sirens of the ambulance could be heard getting closer. As always it was a comforting sound.

'Get the footplates down. They'll want to go in,' Dylan said, pointing his finger at the ground.

As DS Taylor Spiers left, the green suited paramedics arrived in the car park.

'Danny Denton's been almost beheaded,' Dylan told SOCO. 'It appears that he was disturbed from his sleep when the door was put through and was the first to meet the prowler. The reason I say that is that there's another person, who I presume is his flatmate Billy Greenwood, who's still under a duvet in the bedroom. He's got numerous stab wounds but I think he may still be alive,' he said, nodding towards the approaching green suited paramedics. SOCO officers moved into the scene.

'There is one body in the hallway – that's obviously dead.' Dylan told the paramedics. 'There's another person who's got numerous stab wounds, but I found a faint pulse. Can you confirm life extinct for me on the first and be as careful as you can there's lots of blood and we're trying to protect as much of the scene as possible.

'We need to get this entrance secured and then searched along with the flat. DS Benjamin, can you make a call and arrange for uniform to do the necessary with the scene to keep it sterile,' he added. 'We'll let SOCO do their stuff while we all re-group at the nick. We need to plan our lines of enquiry, the management of this scene, mortuary and maybe the hospital if Greenwood is alive. We also need to select arrest and search teams for the suspects we identify. He or they are likely to be covered in blood. Time's important. Any questions?'

It seemed like only minutes later the paramedics came out of the scene with Billy Greenwood on a stretcher, an oxygen mask clasped tightly to his face.

'Very week pulse and vital signs aren't good,' commented the paramedic at the rear of the stretcher as they passed Dylan. 'We can confirm the other's dead so we've left his body in situ for you.'

'Vicky, go in the ambulance with Greenwood for continuity,' Dylan said. 'Don't forget about dying declarations. You never know, he might come round briefly and talk.'

'Okay boss,' she said, nodding to Dylan before running after the paramedics who he could see carrying the stretcher out of the stairwell and into the car park towards the waiting ambulance.

Dylan watched the scenes of crime officers taking photographs of Danny Denton's body from a distance. Once this was done, he could arrange for it to be taken to the mortuary. At this stage he had to consider calling Forensics but he would discuss that with SOCO. Dylan knew he would be back at the scene booted and suited in his protective clothing to take a more detailed look but for now he would put scene guards on the entrance, go back to the nick to get the incident rooms established and create direct enquiries for immediate suspects.

There was no time to waste – they needed to move fast.

Chapter 36

Detective Sergeant John Benjamin sat straight-backed in the chair opposite Dylan. 'My money's on Graham Tate. He's got the strength and the motive,' he said, stabbing the lead of his pencil into a page of his notebook.

'He's got to be a prime suspect with an abundance of reasons but I don't know, is he our killer? At the scene there were white lilies, strewn on the floor near Danny Denton's body. Do you think that's the kind of modus operandi a man like him would use?' Dylan said, screwing up his face.

'He arranged for a bouquet of white lilies to lie on Bridey's coffin,' John said, raising an eyebrow. 'Who knows how your mind works when someone has just killed your wife? Maybe, in planning the murder of the killer, in his eyes, it was something he just visualised.'

'They were also the flowers on Grace Harvey's coffin. So does that put her son Donald in the frame too?' asked DS Taylor Spiers. Her voice held a note of sarcasm.

'Has Donald had any contact with Denton and Greenwood that you know of?'

'No, but... well, what about Brian Stevenson? He sent Grace and Mildred flowers and Grace's flowers we know were lilies,' she said.

'Did Denton and Greenwood know Stevenson? I suppose if it was them that burgled his house and he'd found out,' Dylan said, thoughtfully.

'You'd better put Bridey's dad on the list to be eliminated too, he did threaten to kill them,' John said. 'And let's not forget the recent events. These two were accused of raping Pam Forrester, which is why we were going to arrest them. We need to eliminate her parents and relatives too.'

'Her mum owns a flower shop,' Vicky mumbled sleepily. Her head rested in the crook of her arm on the desk.

'Brian Stevenson uses her shop for his flowers,' said Taylor.

'That's enough, for now,' said Dylan.

'I'd like to start with Brian Stevenson, sir,' said Taylor.

'Okay, you start there with your team. John you take the others for Graham Tate. Let's see how we go with them two for the time being. Then, due to limited resources we'll have to have a rolling programme, to trace and eliminate each and every suspect, as soon as possible. I also need a team to deal with the latest scene, which I'll take charge of,' said Dylan. 'Vicky, you stick with me on that one, will you?'

'Nowhere else I'd rather be boss but your right-hand woman,' she yawned, with a distinct smile as she rested her chin in her hands and looked at him with puppy dog eyes.

Taylor glared in her direction. 'You're so bloody obvious,' she whispered with a sneer.

Vicky tilted her head and blinked her long eyelashes at Taylor as she smiled broadly. 'And I suppose you aren't?' she replied.

'Remember everyone; it's our first chance to secure evidence against the suspects, maybe our only chance. We need concrete alibis for the full night in question from these people, and I want their co-operation. Any issues, I'll be at the end of the phone – so don't hesitate to call me if you need to.'

'I think it's worth a mention, boss, that PC Tim Whitworth's daughter was stopped on her way home from school and threatened with rape. His wife has taken their daughter to her mother's and he was out drinking on the town last night I'm told, drowning his sorrows.

'He hasn't turned in as yet for his shift. He had involvement with Denton and Greenwood after the Tate fatalities if you remember. I'm not saying for a minute he is capable of such an act, but I thought I should mention it,' said the uniformed duty Sergeant.

'Sorry I don't know your name. You are?'

'Sergeant Palmer, sir.'

'Thanks for that. Let's see if we can locate him as soon as possible.'

'If I know Whitworth, he's probably got a massive hangover and he'll still be asleep,' said Vicky.

'But, he'll still need an alibi like any other suspect. Could you follow that one up for me Sarge please? Also no doubt there's a welfare issue that needs monitoring too,' Dylan said considerately.

'Yes for sure. No, I wasn't pointing the finger, sir,' said Sergeant Palmer looking slightly flushed.

'You never knw. History, as we are all aware, tells us policemen can turn into murderers too. We have to consider all possibilities. Right, so that's everybody occupied then, I think,' Dylan said with a deep sigh. 'We'll have to leave Bill Forrester until a team comes free. He too, like you said, has one hell of a motive, Denton and Greenwood raped his daughter.' Dylan told the assembled team of officers. 'Okay everybody, let's get out there and be professional. Don't forget the reporters will be sniffing around, and remember keep me updated with any developments. The slightest of problems, anything you need to discuss, well you know where I am. If the press ask questions refer them to Liz at the press office. I'll put out a brief statement. Debrief at five. Let's do it,' Dylan roared.

The room emptied with a noisy buzz. Everyone was eager; all had a mission. Dylan wondered about Sergeant Palmer's reason for throwing Tim Whitworth into the pot as a suspect for murder. Did he know more than he was sharing with them?

Everyone slept in from time to time. Dylan remembered one occasion when he had slept in as a rookie. He should have been ready to parade at 05.45 for the six o'clock shift. He got there at 07.30. He'd thought about telephoning in sick when he'd woke late after working over until midnight the previous day, but hadn't wanted to let his team down.

He'd dreaded what his Sergeant would say. His supervisor at the time was a stocky bull necked ex-military man who spoke with his fists, then asked questions. He wasn't known for patience in waiting for answers. Dylan recalled sheepishly sneaking in the back door of the nick that morning as if it was yesterday. The sergeant had been ready to lift him off his feet by his collar and pin him up against the wall, as Dylan feared.

'The shift Inspector doesn't know that one of his men is missing yet,' he had said through gritted teeth. Dylan smirked as he remembered vividly trembling in his boots – all nine and a half stone of him, at the time. 'And it'll stay that way...' he sniggered, putting Dylan's feet back down on the ground. 'Now get yourself some coffee and toast before you get out there, otherwise you'll be useless to me. MOVE,' he'd hollered. Dylan had scarpered so fast he was sure he'd created sparks on the wooden floor with his toecaps.

'It'll never happen again. Will it PC Dylan? The sergeant had shouted after him.

'Not on your life sir,' Dylan had hollered back.

Dylan remembered taking off his helmet and mopping his brow in front of the mirror in the gent's toilets. In those early days supervisors didn't stand for any messing about – and the strategy worked, Jack Dylan had never been late for a shift again.

Dylan was concerned that he didn't have an obvious front-runner for Denton and Greenwood's demise, someone who stood out from the rest of the pack who would have viciously attacked the pair. He didn't even have a strong feeling towards any one of the suspects. It could be any of them or then again, none. They had angered, upset and annoyed so many people.

He knew the death of a loved one affected people differently but rarely to the extent of making them murderers too. There was no love lost for these two by the investigating teams either. Denton and Greenwood to all intent and purpose had got what they deserved, summary justice, were the whispers around the room even at this early hour of the investigation. Dylan wasn't naïve. It was a bad on bad murder. Who really cared if gang members or drug dealers killed each other, as long as innocent people weren't hurt? He knew it was his job to motivate the team to gain results.

It certainly wouldn't be an easy investigation unless they got an early break. Some of his counterparts seemed to fall on the domestic murders or the ones that didn't need a lot of investigation. Dylan always seemed to land what the police force deemed 'the runners'.

He absentmindedly wrote on his notebook, *Ring to see how Dawn is* ... he kept intending to, but hadn't got around to it.

He picked up the phone to call Jen to let her know that their plans for a quiet Bank Holiday were out of the window. He knew he was giving her information she didn't want to hear yet again and his heart sank.

'It's only me,' he said trying to put a smile in his voice.

Jen knew by his tone what he was going to say. Dylan always started the same way when he was about to give her disappointing news, she dreaded the *'It's only me,'* phone calls.

'The lock-up never happened. Someone got there before us,' he said with a sigh. 'It's gonna be a long day. One's been murdered in the flat and the other's critical in hospital.'

'Oh no, you owe me big time Mr, leaving me to spend the Bank Holiday alone.' Jen tried to sound cheerful but she had a heavy heart.

'I'll make it up to you, I promise,' he said. Jen put the phone down and rubbed her stomach lovingly, once again the job had won. Yes, she knew she was being selfish but didn't she deserve the time with her man that others took for granted? He'd bring the smell of mortuary home with him again tonight and no doubt wake her up but, she smiled, she knew she could cope with anything as long as he came home.

Chapter 37

John Benjamin was confident that his target was the murderer. In fact, he was so confident he would have bet his salary. The pain and anger Graham Tate must be suffering was beyond anything he could imagine. And he was just as confident that once he locked him up he'd confess. Why wouldn't he want to tell the whole world about his revenge on the men he believed to be the murderers of his young wife and child?

In a few minutes John would know if his gut instinct was right, as two cars containing his team of eight police officers drew up outside the Tate family home. The curtains were closed and a car was in the driveway, which intimated to John that Graham was inside.

Three officers were directed quickly and quietly to guard the back of the house with a dog handler. John could only hope and pray that the dog would be quiet as he watched the handler open the van's doors.

Satan was a huge black Alsatian with fierce, staring red eyes. As he was unleashed from his cage he lurched from the vehicle and standing by his master he started barking with excitement and John cringed. Everyone moved rapidly into position.

John walked up the garden path and banged with gusto on the front door. There was no response; tilting his head he listened intently for noises within. The sound of him knocking again echoed down the street. Still there was no response. He stepped back and looked up at the windows before hammering again and this time he peered through the letterbox.

He wondered whether Graham might be dead. It wasn't unknown for people to commit a murder and then commit suicide. But, on the other hand he could just be refusing to answer the door to them. A hell of lot of people did, in DS John Benjamin's experience. They often thought that the police would go away, but they soon learnt that they were wrong to assume.

Again, he beat his fist against the door. The noise was beginning to raise interest from the neighbouring houses as curtains were drawn back and doors opened. People stood in their gardens now and at their gates. John was left to make the decision. Did he go away and come back later or did he force entry? Graham Tate could be inside injured. Should he ring Dylan? What would Dylan do in his position? He closed his eyes, prayed he was making the right decision and gave his colleagues the order to smash their way in. At the third attempt the door gave way to the battering ram and the front officer was catapulted inside.

Shouts of *POLICE* rang out from his team members as an organised search of the house commenced. There were pots in the sink, empty beer cans and take away food containers littered about the kitchen worktops. Photographs of Bridey and their son Toby were scattered over the sofa. John could feel the deep sadness in the darkened lounge. The scent of the room smelt familiar; musty like a muddy river, the air thick in some way. Where was Graham Tate, he wondered?

'Arrange to have the door boarded up,' he told the team, despondently.

John stood in the garden of the house watching daylight rapidly bringing sunlight to the street as he keyed in Dylan's mobile number. He took a deep breath.

'Boss, there's no one home,' he said, his head hung low.

'What do the neighbours say?' asked Dylan.

'We're just going to start house to house. I have had the door put through.'

'You've put the door through before asking neighbours if they know where he is?' Dylan shouted down the phone. Vicky put her hands over her ears. 'Why did you need to get in there so quickly? What if he's totally innocent? After everything that's happened to the poor guy and then we go and smash his bloody door down. Great.' Dylan said with a moan as he held his head in his hands.

'But I thought he might've attempted to take his own life or...'

'You're assuming a hell of a lot weren't you?' Dylan yelled. 'Look, stick with the fact that you were concerned about his welfare and you thought he was inside requiring medical assistance. I presumed you thought you saw the curtain move or heard a noise from within?'

'Err, if you say so, boss.'

'What a bloody mess,' Dylan groaned.

'I'm sorry, sir.'

'In future, just have a bit of patience, eh?' Dylan sighed. Dylan broke the silence. 'Look, don't worry, we'll find him. And by the way I'd have probably done the same mate, speak to you later,' Dylan said. He knew how John felt and he knew he'd done the same thing over the years and it soon brought you down to earth when the target wasn't where you thought he should be.

He knew young John Benjamin would learn from his mistake and Graham Tate would be incensed by it, but nonetheless it – was and always would be – an everyday occurrence in policing, that he knew for a fact. Unfortunately, in that situation, as the man in charge were damned if you did and damned if you didn't.

'At least it was the right address,' Dylan said out loud. Vicky smiled, but her face held a grimace. 'Oh, yes. I've known officers raiding the wrong houses. Now, that's embarrassing not only for the officers but petrifying for the innocent occupiers.'

'I'll go and make us some strong coffee, shall I?' Vicky said.

Dylan was worried. He was feeling negative. He was in charge of enquiries into three road deaths, a rape, an assault, a murder, and an attempted murder that could turn at any minute into a murder. None of the aforementioned looked like being solved and all eyes were upon him. The public wanted people locked up. Headquarters, hierarchy were on the warpath. The performance figures for violent crime were no longer on a downward spiral, because of these crimes. All, his fault of course, or that's how it felt when his bosses contacted him for answers. In spite of his predicament he smiled. Isn't that why he loved the job; the challenge? His office door opened, bringing him out of his moment of self-pity.

'Billy Greenwood's in theatre. News is that they don't think he's gonna make it,' said Lisa. 'He's not regained consciousness and the officer guarding him just told me he's got at least thirty-five stab wounds.'

'Thanks for that,' he sighed. 'We have his DNA and fingerprints on file but it would be helpful if we could get a sample of his blood for comparison purposes. Liaise with the incident room staff, will you. We need to arrange to keep him under constant supervision, that's if he survives theatre. If he recovers consciousness, no matter how briefly, he might be able to tell us something about his attacker and we've a duty of care, even for scumbags like him.'

'Will do boss. Do you want a coffee, you two?'

'That would great,' yawned Vicky.

'Looks like you'd better make it another strong one,' he laughed.

'You know I don't do early mornings and late nights,' she scowled.

No sooner had Lisa closed the door, the phone rang.

'Ignore it,' Dylan said to Vicky as she reached out to pick it up. 'It's time we went back to the flat. Danny Denton's body is still in situ.'

Suited and booted in protective clothing, they re-entered the scene for a closer look, accompanied by the scenes of crime officer.

'The flowers need collecting as an exhibit,' he instructed. To Dylan they were just flowers but who knew what they could reveal? There was no murder weapon to be found inside the flat, he was told by SOCO, and searches were on going of the immediate area outside, including the drains as he'd instructed.

Although he talked of the murderer being one person, there was a possibility that he couldn't ignore that there may have been more than one attacker.

'I hate bloody lilies,' Vicky said, screwing up her nose. 'They stink,' she said as she picked them up with a gloved hand and put them in an exhibits bag. 'I'd rather have daffs if you ever feel the need to buy me any.'

Dylan couldn't help but smile. 'And the likelihood of that is?'

'If the murderer did bring them with him, what's he trying to tell us?' she said with a puzzled look on her face. 'Time will tell, as you say boss,' added a distracted Vicky as she leaned over the body on the floor. 'It's a bloody massive wound that, in't it? The killer certainly wanted to make sure Danny Denton was a dead man.

'On the positive, we shouldn't have any problem proving intent and pre-meditation,' Dylan said. 'He nearly took his flaming head right off.

'Mmm that's true.'

The scene itself revealed nothing else but Dylan decided to keep it sealed just in case they needed to return. His phone rang as he left the flat.

'Taylor sir, Stevenson's not at home. His Porsche has gone and neighbours tell us they last saw him leaving the house with a suitcase yesterday evening.'

'Do we have his car registration to circulate?'

'Already done, boss. I'll take my team onto Donald Harvey's, shall I?'

'Yeah, if you're sure Stevenson's not there you might as well.'

'Oh, I'm sure,' she said, climbing into her car.

'You haven't forced entry have you?' he asked with baited breath.

'No, why would I?' she snapped.

Dylan exhaled. 'Just wondered: we've got Stevenson's DNA on recorded. Let's hope he gets stopped quickly,' he said.

'Yeah, I'll be in touch,' DS Taylor Spiers said, as she rang off and tossed her phone into her handbag.

'No suspects in custody yet,' he sighed to Vicky.

Brian Stevenson was becoming more and more interesting to Dylan. There were no apparent friends of his that had come to light. Dylan had taken an instant dislike to him. But then again there were quite a few people he didn't like but that didn't mean they were criminals.

'What you got to smile about?' Vicky asked.

'Ah, nothing,' he said. 'Why doesn't Taylor like you? Is there some history between you two that I should know about?'

'I don't know do I? You know me I'd tell you if there was. But, I'll let you into a secret. I don't like her much either,' she whispered. 'So, it makes no odds to me whether she likes me or not,' she said, shrugging her shoulders.

'Women. You're about as clear as mud, Vicky,' he laughed. 'But, if she causes you any problems then let me know.'

'She doesn't frighten me boss, I'd deck her and then ask questions later,' she said with a belly laugh.

'Yeah, I know and that's what frightens me,' he said. It was nice to hear someone's laughter amid the sadness. What did they say 'If you didn't laugh, you'd cry sometimes?'

Chapter 38

Danny Denton's body was as pale as the mortuary slab he was laid on. The fatal wound now cleaned, Dylan could see how close he had really been to being beheaded. It wasn't a sight for the faint-hearted. A body in a mortuary seemed more clinical to Dylan, whereas at the scene it looked like something out of a macabre horror film.

'Guess where I am?' he said to Jen as she answered his phone call.

'Too easy,' she said. 'About now, I guess you'll be in the mortuary. How's it going?' she asked.

'Slowly, very slowly,' he said, taking a seat as he waited for the pathologist. 'Our two main suspects weren't at home,' he said groaning, as he stifled a yawn.

'You sound a bit flat,' she said.

'I am. I was looking forward to a day off with you just as much as you were.'

'Then I guess I'm lucky, because you miss me just as much as I miss you,' she said.

Dylan grimaced. 'I treasure our time together too, you know. When something happens like this there is no warning, is there? We lose weeks out of our lives. But more than that.' 'I know, but I'm fine, honestly.'

'Just to hear your voice lifts me,' he said with a disappearing smile.

'And just knowing that you feel like that, believe it or not, makes it bearable,' she said.

'So will you be okay?'

'Course I'll be okay,' she smiled, rubbing her aching back. 'Keep in touch.'

'Yeah, gotta go, it looks like we're about to start the lovely process,' said Dylan sarcastically.

'Love you,' she whispered as she replaced the phone. She loved the way he cared about her. It made her feel warm, safe and content. She listened to the other girls at work and their turbulent relationships. Dylan and her rarely had a cross word. If they did, it was through their disappointment because they had to cancel something they were looking forward to, because of work, always work.

The post mortem began and Dylan's attention was immediately brought to the fading numbers written on Danny's arm. Vicky was writing down the digits on her notepad. From their position, it looked as if they had been written by a third party. The sound of a click from the camera held at the arm told Dylan it was being photographed.

'Vicky, do the necessary will you and see what enquiries you can make of them,' Dylan whispered.

The rest of the examination was quick, clean and straightforward, with necessary samples taken and cause of death given as loss of blood due to the throat being cut which had severed the jugular vein. Two hours had passed and Dylan was pleased that the home office pathologist had been available for it to be done immediately. The formal ID would have to be done later by family, if any could be traced, or by his fingerprints held at the station.

Back in the tranquillity of his office Dylan sat quietly tucking into his fish, battered sausage, chips and curry sauce, followed by a can of diet coke. Not a healthy diet, he conceded as he burped loudly, but it tasted mighty good. He wiped his greasy hands on his handkerchief and gave a satisfied sigh as Vicky walked into the office with a cup of steaming coffee.

'Have the search team come across a mobile phone at Denton and Greenwood's flat, do you know?' Dylan asked.

'No, sir not as far as I'm aware, but they haven't searched their car yet,' she said, stifling a yawn. 'How the hell can you eat all that after seeing that disgusting sight?'

'It's called hunger,' he replied. 'I suppose they haven't found a weapon either?

'Any luck with the phone number written on Danny Denton's arm?'

Vicky shook her head. 'No, it's a mobile and it's either switched off or the battery's gone,' she said, turning to leave the room.

'Come on,' he muttered tapping his fingers rhythmically on his desk as he booted up his computer to check for messages. He wanted some answers and he wanted them now, not tomorrow. Dylan snatched up his ringing phone.

'Boss, John. It appears Graham Tate set off to Scotland for a couple of days fishing in the early hours according to his father-in-law. Mrs Carter confirms Mr Carter was at home all evening.'

'Who's he gone with?'

'A couple of lads from the building site where he works, seemingly, Mr Carter doesn't know their names but he thinks they'll be doing more drinking than fishing. Graham has apparently turned to alcohol for comfort since the accident. I've got a mobile number for him but I'm not getting a response.'

'Okay John, get your people back here and we'll have an update, re-group and see where we're going next. There are still others to eliminate.'

Taylor had had no joy with Donald Harvey either; she told Dylan as she slumped into his office and threw her exhausted body in his visitor's chair. 'He's not at his mum's address and no one has seen him in the village since the funeral,' she said, despondently.

Dylan had experienced days like this before.

'For some strange reason we always seem to expect people to be home when we call and surprised to find they aren't. It's bloody frustrating I know, but once everyone's back we'll have a debrief to see exactly where each enquiry has got to.

'We need to let everyone know what's happening, who's been traced, and who hasn't, and what lines of enquiry are available. We need to keep the ball rolling.'

The team pulled up chairs and leaned on desks and filing cabinets for the de- brief. The CID room was full and noisy.

'We got a relatively recent picture of Mildred Sykes now which I'll circulate. I know you'll have seen the scene photographs and those of the post-mortem, but it is nice to put a face to the lady's name isn't it?'

Lisa stood and passed the pictures round.

'Now we know that we've positively identified debris recovered from Denton and Greenwood's garage as being from the offending vehicle at Grace Harvey's incident so it's highly likely it was them that mowed her down. White lilies were sent to her by Brian Stevenson for her birthday and were also laid upon her coffin at her funeral by her son.

'Mildred Sykes's decomposed body was found at her home. She was murdered by way of a violent head injury. Brian Stevenson was both Grace and Mildred's financial advisor and a visitor to both their homes. We know by his own admission that he sent flowers to Mildred Sykes by way of a thank you for her business. The lady at the florist from where they were purchased has confirmed now that they were white lilies.

'The clock that was seized in Denton and Greenwood's flat; have we had a close look yet? If not, make it a priority.' Dylan said going back to his notes.

'Then we have Bridey and her young son Toby, killed outside Mothercare, Denton and Greenwood's car is involved we know but they alleged that it was stolen beforehand but only after it was found burnt out. Flowers at their funeral were white lilies.

'Denton and Greenwood also feature again in a rape allegation of the thirteen-year-old girl named Pam Forrester whose mother owns the florists where Brian Stevenson purchases flowers; also possibility of access to white lilies for Bill Forrester too. Have we located Tim Whitworth?' asked Dylan.

'Yes sir,' said Sergeant Palmer.

'Thank God we've been able to find someone,' Dylan said sarcastically.

'Let's just say he's nursing a very painful hangover, sir.' he said. 'He turned up at home this morning and we hope to verify his whereabouts last night, later today,' Sergeant Palmer continued. Vicky nodded knowingly.

A wave of laughter went around the room.

'Okay everyone, quiet,' Dylan said taking a deep breath. 'Let's keep at it. John, Taylor, a quick word, please before you disappear,' he said. The officers and civilian staff filed out of the room as Dylan took Taylor and John to one side. 'It may be that Pam Forrester can tell us a lot more than she has about Denton and Greenwood and their movements and acquaintances etcetera. I'd like a timeline created so we can show when they were seen and who they spoke to.'

'I'll talk to Pam,' said Taylor.

'Good, Taylor; Denton and Greenwood's phone number would be helpful from her phone and we need her mobile if we haven't already seized it. The technical boys could get on with tracking their movements and calls for us if we get them.'

'We're on with it boss,' they said in unison.

'I really appreciate your efforts even if I don't show it sometimes,' he said, smiling wanly.

Dylan knew he had to get his head down and catch up with the policy logs and ensure all the actions on the enquiries were recorded for the incident room. There was no doubt about it; the recurring theme with all these deaths was Denton, Greenwood and white lilies.

Chapter 39

Jen was fast asleep, her head neatly tucked under the duvet. It made Dylan smile as he looked upon her lovingly; goodness knew how she slept comfortably in that position. Due to her ever-increasing waistline, she had taken to putting a pillow under her knee and her stomach as she rested on her side.

She was right, he frowned. He did smell when he'd been to the mortuary, he thought, as he caught the pungent aroma that emanated from his jacket as he hung it on the plinth above the wardrobe. Although he felt weary, he headed for the shower. The lukewarm water's deeply penetrating force roused him and, stepping out of the shower, he felt refreshed.

He towelled himself dry then, quietly turning out the light, he walked the few steps to the bed in the darkness and lifted the duvet before climbing into bed. He slid across the mattress and cuddled up close to Jen, she felt lovely and warm and he moaned with pleasure as he nuzzled in close to her. Kissing her shoulder he closed his eyes. His hand rested on her stomach and for a moment he was sure he felt the stirrings of the baby.

'Get used to this little one,' he whispered. 'Your daddy comes home from work at very strange hours of night and day.' Jen didn't wake, but stirred momentarily.

He sighed with contentment as he lay quietly in the darkness. His mind raced through all the information it had stored throughout the day. Vicky had retrieved Danny Denton's mobile phone number eventually so Taylor could get started with that enquiry tomorrow.

John Benjamin had been unable to speak to Bill Forrester as he had left the family home for a golf tournament the night before. Genuine excuse and a pre-planned holiday, he contemplated? Only time and enquiries would tell. As for Billy Greenwood, he was out of theatre they had been told and in an induced coma; a state the doctor said they would leave him in for seventy-two hours. He needed a police guard, which meant more expense, he turned over onto his back to try to get comfortable and stared up at the ceiling. Sleep would not come. Forensics, fingerprints, and process, he chanted in his head, as he felt himself falling into oblivion.

The bright morning sun shone through the yellow bedroom curtains and lit up the whole room. Jen nibbled Dylan's ear, playfully. He screwed up his sleepy face. 'Stop it Max,' he moaned, keeping his eyes tightly closed. Jen squeezed him round his midriff, giggling.

'What time did you get in? I sort of half-heard you, but couldn't for the life of me wake up.'

Dylan turned on his back and he lifted his arm so she could lay her head on his chest. 'I wasn't too late but you were snoring your head off,' he smiled. She lifted her head and looked at him with a furrowed brow.

'I do not snore,' she said indignantly.

He kissed her forehead. 'You so do.' he exclaimed. She tapped him lovingly on his chest.

'I left my clothes in the washing basket, so if it reeks of formaldehyde you know why.'

'You smell nice now,' she said, snuggling her face into his upper body.

'And you feel nice,' he replied with a groan as he squeezed her buttocks.

'You rushing off this morning?' Jen murmured.

'Not now I'm not,' he said, smiling down at her upturned face as he pulled the bedcovers over their heads.

Dylan felt more relaxed as he entered the police station than he had done when he'd left. The incident room was buzzing and as he walked towards his open office door he saw Sergeant Palmer sat waiting for him inside.

'Sir,' he said, with a cough as he stood when Dylan entered. Dylan nodded and motioned for him to sit. 'I've spoken to a woman who was drinking with Tim Whitworth last night.'

'And?' Dylan said with a puzzled look on his face. He threw his briefcase on the floor beside his desk and took off his jacket that he placed around the back of his chair.

'It appears Tim spent the night with her after he accompanied her home from work. She wasn't very complimentary about him, in fact she said she thought he was a pathetic loser, who moaned about his wife until he collapsed, drunk, on her kitchen floor and that's where she found him when she woke this morning. So I think it's safe to say we can probably eliminate him.' Sergeant Palmer nodded.

'You'd better contact the welfare department as a matter of urgency.' Dylan said pulling out his chair to sit behind his desk.

'Ah, she'll have looked after him,' he said. Vicky knocked on the door and walked in.

'He's had a lucky escape then,' Dylan said, taking his morning mail from Vicky's outstretched hand.

'Oh, yeah he was lucky alright, there's a lot worse than her about,' said Sergeant Palmer.

'Worse than who?' asked Vicky.

'Some woman that Whitworth spent the night with, that's all. Sergeant Palmer's dealing,' Dylan said absentmindedly as he pressed the button to boot up his computer.

'Get a statement did you?' Dylan asked Sergeant Palmer.

'She was working sir, so I've arranged to see her later at her home address,' Sergeant Palmer mumbled.

'Okay, Sergeant Palmer let me have it for the file ASAP, please.'

Sergeant Palmer coughed, again. 'I will, sir,' he said getting to his feet and walking to the door. Holding the door handle, he turned. 'Oh, by the way she did say his shirt was covered in blood when he turned up at the restaurant where she works, sir.'

'What?' Dylan shouted, looking up from his work wide eyed. 'How'd that happen?'

'Don't know yet,' he said with a shrug.

'Oh, for Christ's sake. We'll need his clothes to eliminate him and that means whether he's washed them or not – and I want a statement from him regarding his movements on the night in question under caution, if he can remember, that is. Everything needs to be covered. Belt and braces, do you understand?'

'Of course sir, leave it to me,' Sergeant Palmer said as he quickly turned and walked out of the door. Dylan shook his head.

'The phone number written on Denton's arm is a girl's named Sharon McDonald, sir,' she said. 'I've spoken to her on the phone.'

Vicky had Dylan's full attention. 'She's just told me Danny Denton and Billy Greenwood were in McDonalds yesterday and she was due to be meeting them today. I'm just off to get the CCTV tape, I'll get it copied then go see her again,' she said with a smile.

'Great, keep me posted,' said Dylan with a sigh and a shake of his head.

'Sure boss,' she said sweeping out of the office.

'Oh, Vicky.' he called. But he had a feeling his voice fell on deaf ears, as there were more than one phone ringing in the incident room.

'You want something?' Taylor asked as she walked passed his open office door.

Dylan shook his head. 'Nah, it doesn't matter,' he said.

'Well, something's brought a smile to your face this morning,' she said flashing her eyelashes at him.

'Contrary to what you think, Taylor, I do smile occasionally,' he said. 'Now have we sorted out Pam Forrester's mobile so we can plot our pair's movements and contacts?'

'No, not yet but I'm on with it.'

'Good, as soon as, then eh?' he said returning to his paperwork.

'I told the Liz in the press office last night I'd update her today.'

'Oh, you did, did you? Does Denton or Greenwood have next of kin that we know of?'

'No. Shall I make you a coffee?' she asked.

'Yes, thanks,' he said.

Taylor wiggled hips that barely fitted into her tight blue skirt at Dylan as she left the office. Looking over her shoulder to see if he was watching, she gave him a smile.

Dylan texted Jen, *Thinking of you*, he wrote.

Taylor returned carrying both cups precariously in one hand as she finished a call on her mobile.

'Ah,' she winced as she put Dylan's steaming coffee cup on his desk in front of him. She sat down opposite and crossed her legs. 'Motorway have just stopped Stevenson's Porsche on the M1, one male inside. I'm just waiting for an officer to call me back to confirm the driver's details.'

'Excellent. At last one of our suspects in the net.'

Taylor's phone rang and on answering it she listened intently. Dylan stared into the blank expression on her face. She ended the call. 'Bad news,' she said. 'It's not him.'

Dylan ran his fingers through his hair and sighed. 'Who the hell is it?'

'An Asian businessman who checks out. He bought the car yesterday.'

'Stevenson is circulated. All ports mind. We need to speak to him and fast. Make sure he's flagged up on PNC as wanted in connection to Mildred Sykes murder.'

'On with it, boss,' she said as she leapt up from her chair and glided out of the office.

His telephone rang, 'Jack Dylan,' he snapped.

'CPS Inspector Dylan, Case Progression. I'm just confirming the date for R V Harold Wilkinson Little, your double child murderer at Sheffield Crown Court, a four-week space has been allocated.'

Dylan scrawled the date on his blotter.

'The necessary notifications will be sent out to you shortly but I thought you'd appreciate the early call.'

'Thank you, forewarned is forearmed as they say. I'll let them know to diary it for relevant witnesses.'

The evidence was overwhelming and the sentence wouldn't be much different either way, so there was only one conclusion to come to – that Little was making the families of the victims suffer still. He wanted to see for himself the pain on their faces in court and the distress he had caused them. Was his need for revenge so deep-rooted? Or was he just pure evil?

Now that Dylan had a date he would contact Dawn. He felt guilty that he hadn't been in touch with her lately, but every time he reached for the phone he wondered what he was going to say to her. 'How are you?' He knew how she was. She was having treatment for postnatal depression. He felt sad, inadequate – there was nothing he could do or say to change her situation so he'd done what he always did when he didn't know what to do and worked his socks off to blot it out.

John made him jump; he was deep in thought as he rushed into Dylan's office. 'Had a call from Graham Tate's neighbour; he's back. She's keeping an eye out for us till we get there.'

'Get round there at once,' he ordered. 'And invite him in for questioning. If he refuses, arrest him.'

Chapter 40

Dylan sat patiently listening to the ringing tone that in turn went onto the answering machine. Leaving a message, he wondered if Dawn would be well enough to attend court. Of course she would, he told himself. What was he thinking? She wouldn't miss this court case for the world.

'Just got confirmation that Stevenson's profile's been circulated to all ports, sir,' Lisa told him as she walked in his office. He took the paperwork she held out for him.

'If he was intending to leave the country, we might just get lucky,' he said, hopefully.

Taylor headed for the Forrester's home. The priority was to question Bill Forrester and Graham Tate about their whereabouts at the time of Denton's murder. It was highly likely these two had lots of enemies, but, as ever, Dylan would follow the detective's golden rule and clear the ground beneath his feet before he went on to do anything else. Graham Tate had two good reasons to want to see them dead; the Forresters, too.

Dylan closed his door. While the officers were out and about making their enquiries, he decided to sit quietly and grab the chance to review the investigation into Mildred Sykes's death. He needed to satisfy himself that they had left no stone unturned.

If she had opted for equity release like Stevenson had said, where was the flaming money? Was Donald Harvey's accusation right? Where was Grace Harvey's money? Striking similarities of the two crimes were too close for comfort, thought Dylan. Did Denton and Greenwood do Stevenson's dirty work for him?

Found in their possession was a silver carriage clock, which was obviously stolen property. There couldn't be anything more out of place in their bachelor pad than that bejewelled ornament. Dylan opened the envelope that contained the blown-up photograph of Mildred and stared at it. The clock seized from the flat that Vicky had shown him was most definitely like the one in the picture. He was certain that the clock was not still on the mantelshelf at Mildred's house when he had walked around after her murder.

'Vicky,' he called.

'Yep,' she said opening his door.

'That clock seized from Denton and Greenwood's flat. Has it been checked out yet?'

'Not that I'm aware of.'

'Get me it out of the property store will you? And be careful, I don't want any unnecessary fingerprints on it.'

Vicky nodded and slowly turned. 'Yes, boss,' she drawled.

'Vicky, like yesterday please. Oh, Vicky,' he hollered.

'Yes?' she said, stopping in her tracks and retracing her steps.

'Coffee,' he gestured with the cup in his hand.

She smiled. 'Lisa,' she called as she across the office. 'Boss wants a coffee.'

Dylan smiled.

The clock, of course, would need to be thoroughly examined inside and out and fingerprinted. With vigour he set about writing a list of actionable enquiries for the HOLMES team to put onto the database, to be allocated to ensure no duplicate actions were undertaken. He needed evidence to prove beyond doubt it was Mildred's. If it was, had they stolen it from her or from Brian Stevenson? He needed to prove a sequence of events.

Had Stevenson been systematically robbing his elderly customers of personal property and their savings? His head was buzzing. He searched his desk drawer for his Paracetamols. Popping two in his mouth he chomped on them, swilled his mouth with cold coffee and swallowed them, grimacing at the taste they left.

It was evident Stevenson hadn't liked all the attention he was getting from the police, and Dylan was sure they were only scratching the surface of his unscrupulous dealings with his clients. Picking up his phone, he dialled the number of the coroner's officer to see if he could get a list faxed to him of elderly people and their cause of death, registered in Harrowfield within the past two or maybe three years.

Stevenson's trade may have been that of an accountant/financial advisor – but was that just his cover? He had money, but was that because he'd stolen it? Had they stumbled on a serial killer, a wolf in sheep's clothing who had charmed and fleeced his victims? As soon as Dylan obtained the list, he would put the names in the system for them to be checked against Stevenson's clients.

Had they got the list of clients from him yet? The documentation from his account – where was it? Had Grace Harvey's death just been a coincidence, a little too close for comfort for Stevenson? He wanted the financial investigation unit to prioritise enquiries into Stevenson to see what it revealed and he'd also get a warrant for his home address to get it searched, make use of the time before he was detained, before the Police and Criminal Evidence custody time limit clock started running.

In some circumstances, he may have been the only visitor to these lonely people. Would anyone be surprised or shocked if an elderly person with a bad heart had fallen at home and died? After all it was a daily occurrence. Had he found himself a profitable niche for a man with no scruples?

Dylan was satisfied with where the investigation was going. He now needed to find Stevenson – and the evidence to nail him.

He moved onto Denton and Greenwood. Dylan had no doubt their car had killed Grace Harvey and they had raped Pam Forrester. He urgently wanted evidence to prove beyond doubt that this pair had callously knocked down Bridey and Toby. But, who'd killed Denton? Was Greenwood going to survive? If so, would he talk to them? The dilemma laid heavily on Dylan's mind.

Dylan walked through the incident room with a wedge of paper enquiries he had written for the HOLMES team to process. He was conscious that the team were spread thin. They were all working independently, which he deemed the right approach in this situation.

'Boss, I think I better make that coffee a strong espresso,' said Lisa, looking up from her computer screen at him.

'I'm flagging,' he said, gratefully. 'And it'll soon be time for the debrief.'

'Hey, I might even be able to find some choccy biscuits too,' she grinned as she stood and headed for the kitchen.

'You're a treasure,' he said looking at his watch. Was it that time already? The teams would be back in soon, but at least he'd had some time to mull over the recent incidents without interruption.

'Two biscuits,' he remarked a few minutes later as Lisa handed him a plate across his desk.

Lisa smiled.

'Thank you,' he said. The HOLMES team were the lifeblood for this SIO. They were a constant source of support and he really appreciated them, which was why he always ensured that they were included in everything to do with the enquiry.

Dylan's phone vibrated in his trouser pocket and he jumped, spilling his drink. Lisa laughed. 'I put it on vibrate so it wouldn't ring in debrief,' he said. 'I'll never get used to it doing that.' Dylan's face flushed as he pressed the buttons to read the message.

Hiya, been baby clothes shopping with Dawn. She sends her love. All okay, said the text from Jen. Dylan closed his eyes. Bless her. She knew how busy he was but also how concerned he was about Dawn so she'd gone to see her. Now he knew Dawn was okay he didn't need to worry about ringing her any more.

Thank you, love. You're a star x he replied.

Jen grimaced as she felt the baby kick her under her ribs.

Dylan dunked his biscuit in his drink and thought instantly of Dawn. How often had he seen her do that and lose half of it? He smiled as he popped the soggy biscuit in his mouth remembering how she would chase the remnants around her cup with a spoon. His phone vibrated again.

Just opened a letter from the hospital. They want to give me another scan – think you can make it, he read.

Try keep me away x

Jen knew he meant every word but she also knew she could be quite easily going alone.

Vicky knocked at his door and, seeing him put down his mobile, she entered his office and closed the door behind her.

'You'll never guess what?' she said sitting down opposite him, a look of bewilderment on her face.

'What?' said Dylan?

'Guess who was there when I called on Sharon McDonald?' she whispered.

Dylan smirked. 'A uniformed sergeant by any chance?'

Vicky looked disappointed. 'You knew he'd be there? Thanks a bunch,' she said, throwing the piece of paper she was carrying with her on the desk. 'I've never been more embarrassed in my life.'

'You embarrassed?' he laughed. 'Now that is something I'd like to see,' he scoffed.

'I'm jealous though,' she said dreamily.

'What? I can arrange for you to spend more time with Sergeant Palmer if you like?' he said, amused.

'No silly, she's got the proudest looking tits you've ever seen... and they're not...' she grabbed her own bought and paid for large bosoms in both hands, 'even implants, I might add,' she said looking down her own top.

'She, being the cat's mother or Ms McDonald?' Dylan asked, taking a sip of his coffee.

Vicky ignored him. 'She is the cat's mother. Sharon opened the door in the shortest skirt; I swear she looked like she was going to a gypsy wedding. Well, she may as well have been bloody topless, and,' she continued aghast, 'not only that; she was wearing red high heeled shoes too. Well you know what they say about red shoes don't you, boss?' she added, leaning towards him, arms crossed and wide eyed.

Dylan laughed.

'Enough to give you a bloody thrombosis, I'll tell you.' she cried.

Dylan laughed a hearty laugh.

'Anyhow, there're way too big for me actually,' she said screwing up her nose. 'I'm quite happy with my babies, thank you,' she quipped.

'You are a drama queen,' Dylan said, shaking his head.

'I'm so not.' she said. 'That bloody Sergeant had his tie off.'

Dylan sat grinning. 'It's warm, there is nothing wrong with an open necked shirt.'

'Well, straight up I got the distinct impression he'd been there for a while, especially when she asked him if he wanted another top up or something stronger,' she said.

Dylan laughed out loud.

'You'll see boss, he'll still have a glow about him when he gets back for the debrief. That's if he makes it.'

'More importantly did you get the statement from her?'

'It's not funny. I had to sit there asking her questions and she was nearly sat on his bloody lap.'

'Vicky, did you get a statement?'

'Yes, but I think I'm suffering from shock.' she cried, hand to her brow.

'I'll send you for counselling afterwards, damn it, but what did she say,' he said.

'I'd rather have a lager and black,' she grinned.

'The statement, Vicky?' Dylan growled.

'The boys were in McDonalds. Denton chatted her up and she agreed to meet them, so she wrote her phone number on his arm – end of. She's a nympho, boss, I swear.'

Dylan was still grinning, 'Did you get all her details?'

'Didn't need to, did I? I'm sure Purvy Palmer got them down and yes, I mean her details. I wouldn't bother going there boss, you'd get fed up waiting in the queue. She's a very popular girl is our Shaz McDonald, so they tell me. I hope sweaty Palmer doesn't catch something. She's known on the street as Big Mac.'

'One shouldn't make assumptions Vicky. He is there on police business. He's Tim Whitworth's Sergeant and PC Whitworth allegedly spent the night there in a drunken state with her on the night Denton got killed, so he's every right to take his time taking a thorough statement.'

'She's well known on the shift you know. McDonalds' a coffee spot for officers. There'll be trouble there in the future, mark my words, unless they want to be in the Sunday Sport. I can see the headline now. 'Big Mac's Bobbies.''

'And what do you know about the Sunday Sport?' asked Dylan.

'Long story, about a red-blooded rugby player I dated for a while – what a bloody loser he turned out to be. Always had a copy in his van. Yuk.' Vicky's face fell. 'Why do I always attract them eh? What I need is a nice decent, honest guy,' she sulked. 'You ain't got a younger brother boss, have you?' she said seriously.

'No, sorry,' he chuckled. 'But thanks for the vote of confidence in this situation. And you don't need to worry, if I have to go anywhere near her or McDonalds I'll take you with me for protection. How'z about that?'

Dylan heard the girls in the office laugh out loud a few minutes after Vicky had left his office. He shook his head and smiled.

'I wish the criminal grapevine was as good.' he yelled and looked up from his work to see a sea of raised eyebrows and broad smiles.

'Oh, you wouldn't begrudge us a bit of gossip would you, sir?' Lisa said.

Dylan, smiled and shook his head before turning to face his calendar on the wall. If he didn't get a breakthrough soon on the Mildred Sykes murder he knew he would have a review team breathing down his neck; as if he didn't have enough pressure, he sighed.

Twenty minutes later, the debriefing began.

Chapter 41

It wasn't long before Taylor returned from the Forresters' home, just in time for the debrief.

'Pam's mobile has already been seized by the Child Protection Unit, I've been told, and Danny Denton's number was stored along with text messages from him. It looks as though the love-struck teenager has kept them all.'

'Her clothing and relevant samples have been sent to Forensics so the rape investigation is well underway, but Bill Forrester hasn't returned home from his golfing trip which means he can't be eliminated from the enquiry into Denton's murder and Greenwood's attempted murder, yet,' she said.

'Because Mrs Forrester and Pam haven't seen him since Denton was killed I didn't think it was right to tell them about the murder or that Billy Greenwood's life is on the line,' said Taylor. 'Have you spoken to the press? I told them I'd update them, sir.'

'Taylor, don't worry about press. I don't want anyone to speak to them just yet,' snapped Dylan. 'What's up with you woman? You're obsessed with the press.'

Taylor bit her lip and her face flushed with embarrassment.

Just then there was a tap at the door and Sergeant Palmer slunk quietly into the room to a few sniggers. Vicky nudged Lisa. She was right, he did have a glow about his face. Vicky stared knowingly at Dylan. He cleared his throat and carried on.

'Nice of you to join us Sergeant. Have you anything you want to share with us?'

'Sir, sorry I'm late,' he said, bristling. 'I ... I've been having an interesting chat with Sharon McDonald,' he said. The

Sergeant had everyone's undivided attention. 'She confirms that PC Whitworth was blind drunk when he came into the restaurant, er... McDonalds where she works, which is why she took him back to hers where he crashed out for the night.'

'When she says crashed out?' asked Dylan.

'Ah, he was so drunk he could hardly stand, sir. Apparently he collapsed on her kitchen floor and that's where he stayed till this morning. She tells me his T-shirt was covered in blood. She thought he'd been in a fight but she says he could quite easily have fallen in the state he was in. She believed the blood had come from his nose.'

'And his clothing, has it been washed?'

'No, I've got it here bagged and tagged for Forensics and he has confirmed to me that it is his. I just took notes of what she can tell us at this moment so I could get back for this meeting. I've arranged for her to be seen again for a detailed statement because she says Tim Whitworth was mumbling about Denton followed his daughter home from school and threatening her.'

'Is this the same lady you saw earlier today?' Dylan said.

'Yes, It is, sir,' Vicky said, looking Dylan straight in the eye. 'Basically, two lads, who told her their names were Danny and Billy, came into McDonalds where she works. It was quiet, they got chatting and she arranged to see them again. I've seized the CCTV tape from McDonalds and it is being copied as we speak. The original will be retained as the master. Then we can view it. She says nothing untoward happened and she confirmed she wrote her phone number on his arm because she wanted to see them again.'

'Is there anything else you need from her that I could get for you when I go back?' Sergeant Palmer asked Vicky.

Vicky looked at Dylan and then to Sergeant Palmer. 'Oh, I think you've got your hands full with your own enquiries, thanks Sarge,' she said politely. 'But, I'll let you know if anything comes up.'

'Thank you Vicky. At least that accounts for the phone number written on Denton's arm – and thanks Sarge for getting stuck in... in respect of PC Whitworth's movements, that is,' he said.

Vicky held her mobile in the air, signalling that she had to take the call.

Dylan continued. 'Okay, I've arranged for a warrant to be obtained from the duty magistrates for the search of Stevenson's house. Let's see what's in the property including documents referring to any of his clients. I've also asked for a list from the Coroner of elderly people who have died in Harrowfield lately to see if there is any connection, plus we are still awaiting the financial investigation result. Does our Mr Stevenson prey on the elderly? We'll do the searches tomorrow morning.'

Vicky re-entered the room. 'Boss, Billy Greenwood's been taken back into theatre, he's got internal bleeding,' she said. 'It doesn't sound good.'

'Bloody hell.' said Dylan. 'Has he said anything?' he asked, anxiously.

She shrugged her shoulders. 'Not that I know of, sir.'

'It sounds like it's highly likely he's not going to be able to help us now.'

Dylan rang Jen as he left the building, 'Setting off now love, what's for tea? Please don't tell me it's McDonalds?' he laughed.

'As if. I'll give you McDonalds. Get yourself home'.

'On my way, boss.'

'Shall we discuss baby's names? Dylan asked, as he yawned loudly.

'Let's wait to see if your eyes are still open when I've finished washing the pots first,' Jen said, rolling her eyes as she handed him his coffee cup.

'Yeah, good plan,' he said. Stretching, he yawned yet again as he stood on his tiptoes and touched the kitchen ceiling.

'If I've got my eyes closed when you come in I might be just having two minutes,' he smiled as he rubbed his tired eyes.

Jen unpacked the bags of clothes that she had bought and folding them lovingly, she laid them out in the drawers of the nursery. She touched the border that they had bought as the basis for the rest of the decor and a warm feeling ran through her body. It was a good thing that they'd had a decorator in to paint the walls, if she'd waited for Dylan she knew she would have waited forever.

Perhaps this could be her 'happy place' in which she could take herself mentally during the birth. It was hard to believe that before her next birthday, before Christmas, she would be 'mummy'.

The clock struck ten. Jen woke Dylan.

'Bedtime, sleepy head,' she whispered as she shook his arm so they could go to bed. 'I think we'll just call the baby Buttons for now shall we?'

'Suits me,' he grinned, sheepishly.

Chapter 42

Dylan's priority today was no different from yesterday's; to trace, interview and eliminate the main suspects.

'Boss, you know we've spoken before about the significance of white lilies?'

'Yes, Vicky.'

'I've been thinking.' Dylan raised an inquisitive eyebrow.

'There's nothing unusual for lilies to be sent in bouquets or to funerals is there, but left beside the body at the scene of a murder, that's sick isn't it?' Do you think the white lilies are the murderer's MO? There are lots of lilies, aren't there? And these might be bought in by a particular florist or supermarket.'

Dylan looked thoughtful.

'We got pictures of the flowers, I know, but did we get samples? Could they be one and the same type?'

'Yes, I put them in an evidence bag myself at the scene, don't you remember?'

'Yeah, You hate the smell, right? Anything's possible. It might just be the missing link we're looking for. I'll have that line of enquiry allocated to you. We'll make an SIO out of you yet,' he smiled. Vicky smiled sweetly at Taylor. Taylor scowled. Why hadn't Vicky told her about her stupid thought – or better still kept it to herself, she wondered?

'I'll have to speak to one of those horticut, horticult … oh, you know what I mean, them there flower experts,' Vicky said, with renewed vigour in her voice.

'Yeah, you do that,' said Dylan.

'Why don't you see what Linda Forrester can tell you about white lilies? Unless you've already done that, of course Taylor?'

'No,' Taylor's mutterings were barely audible.

'No worries sir, I'll do it,' Vicky said with a gleaming smile.

Dylan checked his watch. 'Okay you lot. Let's see what today brings. Keep in touch and we'll debrief at five.'

Dylan checked for himself that scenes of crime had photographed the white lilies found in Denton and Greenwood's flat and swabbed them for a pollen sample. He also made sure enquiries were initiated to ascertain where the lilies for Grace and Winston's funeral were purchased from and what type they were.

Stevenson bought the flowers for Mildred and Grace — they already knew that, so on his admission they would have come from Linda Forrester's stock. Just how many types of white lily were there? They'd have to locate the source of the white lilies at Bridey and Toby's funeral too, if possible. It was obvious the Forresters had a connection with white lilies through their florist. He'd leave nothing to chance. Vicky's suggestions had stimulated his mind.

Dylan strolled down the corridor of the first floor of the police station to attend the uniform briefing. Catching the officers at the start of their shift meant he could update them about the investigations himself.

He knew uniform appreciated the time the SIO took on an enquiry to brief them first hand to keep them in the loop, and as far as he was concerned they were the eyes and ears of the police force at street level, for the next eight hours at least.

'Although there are lots of lines of enquiry, I want you to bring me hard and fast evidence,' he told his attentive audience. 'Then it's our job in CID to meticulously sift through that evidence to make sure we haven't missed or overlooked anything.'

The shift personnel hung on his every word. 'Billy Greenwood's out of surgery and back on ICU so I'll need one of you on guard at his bedside today,' he said, as he watched their eyes turn from his gaze and fall on their pocket books. No one wanted to guard a prisoner in hospital.

'You never know,' he added. 'Greenwood might just wake up and give you the information to nail the killer.' With that, a few hopeful faces lifted their heads to look at him and he saw a spark of interest in their eyes for the job in hand. 'If, he talks, you will simply need to record what he's saying. Remember, no questions though. He's not under caution.'

Dylan picked up his ringing phone the moment he got back to his desk.

'Hello. Ralph, is that you?' he asked, leaning heavily on his desk. Lisa walked in his office with a drink and he took hold of the mug.

'Yeah Jack, how are you?'

'Fine, and Dawn and baby Violet?' he said, switching on his computer, absentmindedly.

'Baby's great. Dawn's still tired, the pills make her feel weary.'

'And how're you bearing up?'

'Oh, coping, you know,' he said with a sigh. 'But what I'm ringing for is the doctor has given her another month's sick note so I wondered if I should send it to HQ?'

'Has welfare been in touch?'

'Yeah, but to be honest her day out with Jen shopping for baby clothes did her more good. They mean well but...'

'Yeah, I know.'

'The doctors say the anti-depressants will kick in and the Diazepam does help her feel less anxious but it makes her feel numb too. As for the court case Jack, she says she wouldn't miss it for the world, so that's optimistic.'

Dylan heard the lump in his throat and imagined him holding back the tears.

Putting the phone down, Dylan felt useless. In this situation there wasn't a thing he could do to help his old friend and colleague. Fancy, after trying so long for a child, the IVF and now this. Sometimes life just didn't seem fair.

Dylan needed a distraction. It was all too easy to get sucked into the sadness of others. He had been ignoring Liz in the press office and there seemed like no better time than the present to take the bull by the horns as he picked up his phone and called her.

The full facts spewed from his mouth of the two young men being subjected to a ferocious and callous knife attack in their own home. He released their names and he told Liz that Danny Denton had died at the scene, while disclosing that his friend Billy Greenwood was critically ill in hospital after receiving multiple stab wounds in the frenzied attack. He appealed for witnesses and, to reduce the public's fear, he told them this was an isolated, targeted attack. As usual he gave out the incident room telephone number and

Crimestoppers contact number for any information that the public felt they could share.

Another day had quickly passed without success. Stillno suspects were traced or eliminated – and now it was time for the daily debrief.

'I've spoken to Mrs Forrester and made an appointment to see Bill Forrester tomorrow when he arrives home,' said Taylor Spiers.

'Good, at least that's two suspects traced,' said Dylan.

'Actually three, sir. Donald Harvey contacted me, and he's travelling north tomorrow to see me,' Taylor smiled.

'Great. Was there anything that Linda Forrester could enlighten you with regarding the white lilies?'

'No, she says they're a common flower and used daily at funerals. Hers are bought in from a local wholesaler that also supplies the supermarket, so there's not much chance of that action coming to anything,' she said. Taylor raised her brows from the paper she was reading and cocked her head at Vicky as she threw her a smug grin. Dylan couldn't help but notice.

'But' she continued. 'I've also learned quite a lot today from the horticulturist. Even how to pronounce their name,' she said.

Taylor rolled her eyes, 'Oh, please,' she muttered.

'I didn't know this floral malarkey was so interesting,' she said. 'The experts are telling me that there are quite a few common species of the *Lilium Candidum*, bulbs and flowers of the lily plant are used for therapeutic purposes. Stargazer lilies are an ideal way to convey your condolences, and the modern funeral tributes, peace lilies, or *Spathiphyllum,* are very popular for that. Mind you, Lily of the Valley, also known as Mayflower, is poisonous.'

'You sound like Alan Titchmarsh,' Taylor said, snidely.

'But seriously,' Vicky continued, ignoring the DS's comment. 'They were fairly sure if the same lily had been used in all the incidents and because we have pictures and, even better, swabs of the pollen, we will be able to track down the source for them,' she said with a nod at Taylor.

'Hold your hands out,' said Dylan.

'What?' Why?' Vicky said holding her palms upwards for him; her brow furrowed and quizzical look.

'Just checking in case you've got green fingers,' he said, checking the tips of her fingers. 'I think that perhaps you're the best person to see if there is anything of credence in respect of the lilies that might take us forward in that line of the enquiry,' he said, slapping her palms. 'Well done Vicky.'

'Thank you sir,' she said, as her cheeks flushed high.

'Okay, flower power or elbow grease, I'm not bothered – whatever it takes, as long as we find the people responsible. Another day tomorrow to chase our suspects,' he said with a sigh. 'Let's make tomorrow the day, everyone.'

There were still a lot of unanswered questions and tomorrow Dylan would go back and look at each incident in isolation. He was always conscious that something may have been inadvertently overlooked.

I'm on my way, he texted Jen, as promised. He knew better than anyone that there were no quick fixes to any enquiry. And he knew that every hour that passed meant less chance of recovering evidence. Where the hell was Graham Tate?

Chapter 43

The day started on the positive note that two of the people sought would be seen.

Dylan was scheduled to go to Brian Stevenson's home and a nominated team was to execute the warrant that had been sworn out for them at the local Magistrate's home by the evening divisional detective, DS John Benjamin. DS Taylor Spiers would start the search with the rest of the team, however Dylan couldn't assign them specific tasks as he needed them to be available to go see Bill Forrester and Donald Harvey as soon as they got word they were back in the area. The three also needed to be ready and able to respond in the event Brian Stevenson was detained or Graham Tate returned home. Dylan was also mindful to ensure that none of the tasks were rushed due to the deployment

'I want a thorough search,' Dylan told the team as he stood on a box so he could be seen and heard at the short briefing in the void of the police station, before they set off in convoy. 'Carpets rolled back, furniture and drawers pulled out. If anything is hidden, we need to make sure we find it.'

The nominated exhibits officer made the dining room table his temporary desk at Stevenson's home – a central point where people could bring him the items they had seized to be recorded with details of where they were found, by whom, the time, date and the said exhibit numbered for easy retrieval. Should a court case develop against anyone, then all the collated items would have to be disclosed to the relevant parties.

'Make sure his rubbish bins inside and out are emptied and checked,' he told Taylor. 'Find me all his bank details if you can, John,' Dylan shouted as Benjamin turned to climb the stairs. Dylan looked at his retreating figure, a fixed and alert expression on his determined face.

'There's a secured filing cabinet in his office, boss,' he called down within minutes. Dylan took the stairs two at a time.

'Break the lock if you have to,' he called ahead.

Once items had been seized and recorded, there would be a careful sifting of the relevant items. This didn't stop the officers from noting details to make immediate enquiries if they felt it necessary. The search was now in full flow and Dylan watched his officers working quietly and diligently to accomplish their actions. Taylor's mobile rang.

'Bill Forrester's arrived home,' Taylor yelled to Dylan.

Bill, Linda and Pam Forrester sat waiting for the officers on the sofa in the middle of their large antique-cluttered lounge. A suitcase on wheels stood in the corner with a set of golf clubs on a trolley next to it, Taylor noted.

Pam clutched one hand to her chest, the other to her belly and her mouth gaped when DS Taylor Spiers broke the news of Danny's murder.

'Oh, my God,' she simply said, turning to her mother. Linda followed her daughter as she ran out of the room. Pam's footsteps could be heard running up the stairs and Linda's close behind. A door slammed shut.

'I'm sorry Mr Forrester, but there is no easy way of imparting news of a murder,' said John.

'I'd have hoped she'd be jumping up and down after what they put her through,' said Bill, his face pinched but his complexion ruddy. 'Pity whoever did it didn't do it earlier, they could have saved us a lot of heartache.'

'I'm sorry to have to ask you this,' Taylor said, tentatively. 'But we need to verify your movements for the past forty-eight hours, for obvious reasons.'

'Of course,' he said. He glanced down at his hands, clasped in his lap, and shook his head. 'I'm sorry,' he said. There was a moment when no one breathed. 'I wish I had the guts to do it, but I haven't; not even for my daughter. What kind of a man does that make me?'

'We can't find Denton's mobile. It may be the murderer took it,' John said.

'Oh no,' Bill Forrester groaned, his face in his hands. 'The pictures they took of Pam; they might still be on there? If they are put in the public domain who knows who might see them? This could push her over the edge.'

'Well we presume it's the same phone, we don't know of him having another,' said John.

'As if the attack on Pam wasn't bad enough, the thought that someone out there has those pictures of her naked is too painful to think about,' Forrester said, with tears in his eyes. 'Hasn't she, haven't we all been through enough?' he said, searching the officers' dour faces.

'We are doing our best to trace whoever is responsible. There doesn't seem any logical explanation why anyone would take the phone – unless,' Taylor said.

'Unless what?' Bill Forrester stared at Taylor and tried to read her face, it looked stressed. He stared into her eyes and froze for a good few seconds. 'Hold on a minute, you think I might have killed him don't you? Let me tell you, I'd do anything for my daughter – and I mean anything,' he said, his eyes bulging in their sockets. 'And to be honest I can't honestly tell you...' he said, gulping for air, 'how I'd react if I'd come across them. In fact,' he added, rising from his chair. 'I'd even go as far as to say I'd shake the person's bloody hand that did it.' He ran his hand through his hair and paced the room. John Benjamin held his hand up.

'We can understand, Mr Forrester, how upset you are,' John said. 'But we're just doing our best to catch the killer and we have to eliminate anyone with a motive,' he emphasised.

'Not if she thinks I did it you aren't. Can you even begin to imagine how we feel at the moment? Do you have a daughter that's been raped? Do you?' he said with venom. Taylor physically flinched at the emotion in his words.

'Everybody is a suspect Mr Forrester until we find out who did it, and we will. Remember, we've spent years dealing with victims of crime so we do know how badly people feel. We really aren't immune to it all,' said John.

'Of course,' Bill Forrester said, taking a seat once more. 'I'm sorry. It's just the thought of naked pictures of my daughter being out there. Will you let me tell Linda and we'll explain to Pam. She's very distressed as you can see – and who knows what this will do to her?'

'Of course,' said John.

Together they sat and painstakingly went through Mr Forrester's movements over the past few days. John looked at Taylor's face. There was no doubt in his mind that they would be able to confirm his account of events as being true. Linda and Pam entered the room once more; the mother's arm around the daughter's shoulders protectively. Quietly, and without a fuss they sat back down on the sofa.

'Do you know a Brian Stevenson who lives at the bottom of your road?' Taylor asked.

'Yes, he's a customer of mine,' said Linda, looking surprised.

'You don't think?' said Bill.

'We have many people, who are subjects of enquiries at this stage,' John said.

'Do you know if Denton and Greenwood knew him, Pam?' asked Taylor.

'Not, really.' she whispered, glancing up at her mother. All was silent. The adults' eyes were upon her as she regained her composure and recalled a memory. 'They asked me about him once,' she said, wiping her tear-stained face with the back of her hand. 'I can't tell you anything else.'

'Can't or won't?' asked Taylor.

'No,' she sobbed. 'Really, I don't know any more.'

'Tell me what you do know,' John said in a softer tone.

'I was in the car with them one day. They'd given me a lift home from school. He cut them up or we cut him up at the junction. I can't remember which.'

'Go on,' said John.

'I said I knew who the driver was, or at least where he lived.'

'And?'

'And when they dropped me off outside our house, I watched them drive to his and stop outside.'

'And when was this?'

'I don't know,' she cried, as she turned to her mother for comfort.

Taylor's mobile rang and made them all jump. She stood up, excused herself and walked towards the door to take the call.

'Donald Harvey is at Harrowfield nick,' she said to John as she popped her head around the living room door. He nodded and rose to his feet. 'I'm sorry, we are going to have to go. Thank you for your time.'

Taylor opened the passenger car door. 'What a nob,' she said.

'Who?'

'Forrester.'

'He seems pretty genuine to me,' said John.

'Typical man.' she said, flicking her hair back over her shoulder.

John inhaled deeply.

Dylan was also on the move. Leaving his team industriously searching through Stevenson's home and personal belongings, he drove in the sunshine to Harrowfield Police Station.

His first stop was the Imaging Department. They had Danny Denton's mobile number, so he knew that there was a good chance they could get the service provider. Dylan had to know if it was switched on, being used, and if so where? A location would be a godsend at this moment in time. He desperately wanted to move forward with the investigation.

He wondered how Billy Greenwood was. No one had contacted him so he presumed he was still alive. Passing the hospital he had a sudden urge to go and see for himself and speak to Greenwood's medical team. He still didn't know much about the weapon that had been used to stab him other than it had been a knife. Was it double edged? What length was it?

The surgeon who stitched him up might be able to help, he thought, as he parked the car. Maybe if he went in on spec to introduce himself, he could have a quick word without having to make an appointment.

Chapter 44

Donald Harvey had been on the south coast, visiting friends to update them on the death of his mother, he told Taylor and John. He seemed genuinely shocked when they informed him about the attack on Denton and Greenwood.

'I'm sorry, if you want me to feel sympathy though mate, I can't. What goes around comes around, as my mother used to say. Have you locked Stevenson up yet?' he asked.

'We're actually trying to locate his whereabouts at the moment. Any ideas?' asked John.

Donald Harvey shook his head. 'He's absconded? He's done a runner, hasn't he?' he said, straightening up and looking into Taylor's eyes with an expression – as much as to say *I told you so*.

Taylor nodded. 'We'll find him.'

'Well doesn't that just say it all?' he said. 'And when you do, let's hope it's not too late to save another poor biddy – and you recover some of my mother's money too.'

Dylan's arrival at the door of the ward where Greenwood was put a smile on the face of the uniform officer guarding him.

'You okay?' Dylan said, putting a hand on the officer's shoulder as he stood to greet him.

'Yeah, it's alright here, sir. I'm being well looked after by the nurses,' he grinned.

'I bet you are.' Dylan smiled. Any change?' he said, tilting his head in Greenwood's direction.

No sooner had he spoken than he heard a man's deep voice calling down the corridor from the nurse's station.

'Would your friend like a cuppa tea?'

'Hey Gus,' the uniformed officer called. 'Come and meet my Inspector, who's in charge of the investigation.' Dylan's face must have said it all. A male nurse was the last thing he expected after the officers comment.

'Thrilled to meet you,' said the nurse, smoothing the blue plastic apron that protected his uniform as he walked down the corridor towards them. Dylan offered his hand.

'White coffee, one sugar would be nice. Is the staff nurse about?' Dylan asked.

'Yeah, I'll get her for you. You want a top-up?' he asked the officer as he took his empty cup.

'No thanks mate,' he grinned. 'I'll be peeing all day. But thanks for the offer.'

Never assume, Dylan thought to himself as he smiled at the male nurse. What did he always tell others? His golden rule, assume nothing.'

'See what I mean, sir.'

'Mmm ... I'd prefer women myself,' he grinned.

The staff nurse appeared and Gus left to make the drink. She was a buxom woman with kindly eyes. 'Staff Nurse O'Grady, Inspector. Now how can I be helping you?' she said in a strong Irish accent as he held her soft, chubby hand in his.

'Jack Dylan, I wonder if we can have a chat about Greenwood and his injuries?'

'Dr Thomas is on his rounds but if you'd like to come along to my office?' she said throwing an infectious smile in Dylan's direction. 'We can have a little chat over that cuppa and I'll see if I can find a biscuit.'

'I'll follow you then,' he said, gesturing for her to lead the way.

Staff Nurse O'Grady flopped onto a chunky, low, cushioned seat in the staff room.

'Blessed chairs, once I get into these buggers I've one hell of a job getting out,' she said. The telephone rang and, apologising to him, she leaned over the back of the chair to lift the receiver. The male nurse brought in Dylan's coffee and at the same time a young-looking female nurse came to the doorway with something in her hand. Seeing Staff Nurse O'Grady on the phone she waited, patiently. Dylan looked at her and smiled.

'They used to say in my younger days that if you wanted to look busy you should walk around with a piece of paper in your hand,' Dylan said in a hushed tone. She giggled.

'Everything needs a signature,' she said, as a rosy glow crossed her elfin face.

'Protocol eh? How much more time would we have if we didn't have to fill in all the damn forms?'

She nodded in agreement. From where Dylan was seated he could see the hustle and bustle of the nurse's station beyond and it reminded him of the police enquiry office. The staff members were obviously busy going about their own personal duties and yet there was no panic. The overall atmosphere of the place exuded an ambience of peace and relaxation.

He had had occasion to investigate rogue nurses, and likewise rogue policemen. There was always one bad apple; the proverbial black sheep, but they were few and far between, he conceded. Staff Nurse O'Grady interrupted his thoughts as she beckoned the nurse over and signed the paperwork. She took a package from her hand. The nurse left with a backward glance and a smile.

'Dr Thomas won't be long now... in fact.' Staff Nurse O'Grady cupped her ear and they both stopped and listened. Dylan could hear the heavy sound of a man's step walking towards the room, '... that's him now. Metal segs in his shoes, always gives him away.'

Dylan had expected a stooped, grey haired older man with half-moon spectacles on the end of his nose. How wrong could he be? Dr Thomas was a tall robust young man with a curly mop of blonde hair and ruddy cheeks. In fact Dr Thomas looked like a surfer. His handshake was such that Dylan thought he was about to dislocate his shoulder.

'Mr Greenwood's nurse tells me you want to know about his injuries,' he said, perching on Staff Nurse O'Grady chair arm.

'Yes please, if you've got the time,' said Dylan, taking his notebook out of his jacket pocket.

'Well,' he said, thoughtfully, 'some injuries were superficial due to the fact that they hadn't penetrated deeply into the young man's body and those luckily missed vital organs and major arteries. However, others slipped through the rib cage and deflated his left lung. One caught the edge of his liver and spleen, which caused a vast amount of blood loss and pretty much a blood bath internally as well as externally.' He sighed.

Dylan looked up from his notes.

'One injury went through his calf muscle right to the bone where we recovered a fragment of metal.'

Dylan's eyes lit up. 'Really?'

'Really.'

'From the weapon used?'

'I would have thought so. Do you have the weapon he was attacked with?'

'Not yet, but when we do that'll prove to be an excellent piece of evidence for us,' Dylan said with gusto. 'What state is he in at the moment?'

'His vital signs are good. We've placed him on a life support machine to allow his body to deal with the injuries and the shock. He should survive however, he's likely to be left with some disabilities and what they'll be, we don't know as yet. He's still on our critical list and at this moment in time his life is in the lap of his God – if he has one.'

Staff Nurse O'Grady crossed herself, got her rosary beads out of her pocket and kissed them. Dr Thomas smiled at her.

'We all pray,' he said with a smile.

'I know you'll think I'm being impatient and downright insensitive,' Dylan said. 'But what sort of timescales are we looking at before you take him off the machine, to see if he can hold his own?'

Dr Thomas screwed his face up in thought. 'Mmm ...'

'He may have seen his attacker or have an idea who it was, you see,' said Dylan.

'I understand your frustration, but I'm afraid it's likely to be another fourteen days at least.'

Dylan's face grew glum. 'We also want to speak to him about a serious sexual assault and a couple of road deaths too, so when and if he pulls through he'll be arrested and taken from the hospital to the police cells. Until then, we'll have to guard him.'

Dr Thomas and Staff Nurse O'Grady looked at each other.

'His future's not good whichever way you look at it, is it?' said Dr Thomas. 'But let us do our bit and if, or as soon as he's able, we'll gladly release him into your hands. Believe me, we need the beds, don't we Staff Nurse?' he said, standing up and offering his hand to Dylan. 'If that's all, I must be going. I've a clinic in a few minutes.'

'Of course, thank you for your time Dr Thomas and Staff Nurse O'Grady,' Dylan said, handing Nurse O'Grady his cup that she placed on the table beside her.

'Come on old girl,' grinned the doctor as he offered Staff Nurse O'Grady the use of his hand to help pull her out of the chair.

'It'll come to you both one-day,' she groaned, as she took the hand gratefully.

'Inspector,' she called out to Dylan as he headed out of the staff room. He took the few paces back down the corridor and put his head round the doorframe.

'You'll be wanting this?' she said, handing him the package the nurse had brought her. Dylan frowned.

'The piece of metal we found in Billy Greenwood's leg.'

'Marvellous.' said Dylan with a smile. 'We'll need a statement. I'll get an officer here to take it.'

Staff Nurse O'Grady smiled. 'It's already done, here,' she said. 'See how efficient we are.'

Dylan walked out into the fresh air. As he did so he saw the directional sign for the maternity department.

Guess where I am? He texted Jen.

The mortuary? ☹

Nope, he smiled. *Give up?*

Yes.

The maternity unit.

You're a bit early for that love. ☺

Passing the main entrance, Dylan caught sight of two women who looked as though they were about to give birth any moment, in their dressing gowns, sharing a cigarette. Not a good advert for rearing children, but who was he to condemn them. If that's the drug they needed to cope with their life, he wouldn't be the man to point the finger. How could he, a reformed smoker himself?

He reflected for a moment as he started the engine of his car. In his youth, when smoking was in fashion, it was advertised as much as chocolate. Every household had an ashtray or two and the ones in the CID offices were always overflowing with cigarette butts. The ring marks from coffee cups marked each and every wood-grained desktop that had scorch marks along the edge where cigarettes had been left to burn out. Ashtrays in the police cars were always full and everyone and everything smelt of smoke now he thought about it, but he hadn't noticed that they had until he'd stopped smoking himself, how strange.

Cigarettes were more available than biscuits in the office in the past and everyone always had a light, be it a lighter for the well-off or a match. Personally, he always used to smoke a cigarette last thing at night and one first thing in a morning. When the pressure was on at work the total of his nicotine fix could rise to sixty a day. He smiled as he remembered one of the greatest teachers he had ever had at Detective training school would smoke throughout his lesson. None of the students were allowed, mind, and by the end of the day the overhead projector resembled a birthday cake with a hundred candles of tab ends stood upon it.

Dylan was always reminiscing these days; it must mean he was getting old, he pondered. But what he didn't regret was kicking the habit, especially now they had a little one on the way.

He looked at the package on the seat next to him, put the gear stick into reverse and manoeuvred the car out of the parking space. His next job was to see this fragment of metal that could link the murder weapon to its owner, and he couldn't wait to get back to the nick.

His telephone rang. He cursed it as he pulled into a side road and stopped to answer it. 'Jack Dylan,' he growled.

'Boss, John; Graham Tate's arrived back at his home. Our information tells us that he's drunk.'

Dylan grunted. 'Well, that was expected I suppose. Least we know where he is.'

'I'm getting a team together to go and see him.'

'I'm on my way to the nick. Keep me updated,' Dylan said, as he hung up.

Chapter 45

In the privacy of his office, Dylan sat at his desk holding the small plastic tube and stared at the coveted minute piece of metal recovered from Billy Greenwood's body. He could see very little. The fragment couldn't have been much bigger than a pinhead. Forensics would put this under the microscope to examine and photograph it. A blown up version of that picture would hopefully give him the start to a puzzle.

He could hear voices from the adjoining office and it didn't take long before the banter between Vicky and Lisa became a loud exchange.

'How's it going, you two? Anything startling come from Stevenson's house?'

The room before long resembled a makeshift store of Stevenson's property in clear and brown bags of all shapes and sizes. Some looked full to bursting, others contained a single document.

'There's been a lot of shredding going on,' Vicky said. 'And,' she said, coming into his office, leaning over his desk and looking into Dylan's eyes. 'He hasn't got a hamster that he needed bedding for.'

'There's a lot of post that we brought with us and we're just gonna start to sift through it all,' said Lisa with a big sigh, as Dylan saw her empty a black bin liner full of unopened mail onto her desk.

'What do you think he's shredded? Give me an example, Vicky?'

'Well, in a pile next to the shredder were forms for investments, equity release papers, cheques. No cash though.'

'He'll have taken that with him.'

Dylan's phone rang and he stopped her with the raising of his hand, to pick it up.

'Boss, Graham Tate has barricaded the front door. We're now at the back of the house. The door is slightly open and it leads into the kitchen. We can see him through the gap and we're at a stand-off. He says he's turned the gas ring on and is threatening to strike a match.'

'Put them down or I'll force entry and use the CS Spray,' Dylan heard a female shout.

'Who the hell's that threatening him?'

'Taylor,' said John.

'Tell her to back off at once and get everybody away from the door as a matter of urgency.'

'Taylor.' John shouted, so loud that Dylan thought the noise would burst his eardrum. 'The boss says out. That means now,' he screamed at the top of his voice. Taylor glared at her colleague but moved reluctantly.

'What's the situation now?' Dylan asked, calmly.

'Taylor's in the back garden and I've got uniform at the front stopping anyone coming near.'

'Okay, let's get everyone away from the house – and that includes you. Get the road blocked at both ends.'

'Taylor,' shouted John. 'Tell the people up-front to block the road.'

'Where are you?'

'I'm moving out of back garden now, but I could see him clearly through the partially open glass door from where I was stood. He's in the kitchen, leaning against the worktop, drinking from a bottle. He's definitely pissed.'

'Okay, I'm on my way. In the meantime, make sure everybody keeps at a safe distance from the house. If he strikes a match or puts a light on you'll have an almighty explosion that might take more than his house. Get Control to get the uniform Inspector down there to evacuate nearby houses and get the fire brigade, ambulance and the gas board there too. Let's see if we can turn the bloody gas off in the street and hope he goes unconscious with enough of whatever he's drinking before he kills himself or anyone else. Be with you shortly,' Dylan said.

A major incident was well and truly lying at Dylan's feet, thrown at him from afar like a hand-grenade minus its pin. He knew the press would love it and the TV would be there before him if they got wind of it. Driving at speed, Dylan was soon at the scene. All the emergency services were at the designated 'safe place' of a rendezvous point. He was relieved to see the gas board van.

Inspector Mark Baggs greeted Dylan. 'Jack, I've briefed ambulance and fire teams. They are happy to stand by should they be required. The gas board have been to the front of the house and turned the gas supply off, so hopefully, with his kitchen door open – which it still is I am told from an observation point – the gas should disperse quickly. The people we've evacuated are making their way to the community centre. They're not pleased, but are they ever?' he grimaced. 'At least they're safe.'

'Good, thanks Mark. It's nice to know the scene is under control. It feels like a promotion board scenario doesn't it?' he smiled at the uniformed officer.

'Your female DS is over there with the press and TV,' Mark Baggs said pointing towards Taylor.

Dylan glanced in her direction and shook his head. 'That woman should be in the PR department, not CID,' he said. 'No matter, I haven't got time to deal with her now, I'll have to see if my negotiating skills can get through to Tate first.'

'The gas board personnel tell me they're not getting any strong readings of gas outside. He's all yours Jack. Good luck,' said Mark.

Dylan walked under the blue and white police taped cordon and he set off down the street. The smell of gas lingered.

'I suggested she wait for you, boss,' John said, as he nodded in Taylor's direction. 'Can I come with you?'

Dylan nodded. 'There was no way Taylor is listening to me today,' he said, exasperation clear in his voice. 'She's been off on one all day. Like a dog on heat.'

'Do you know what she's told them?' Dylan asked as the men reached the path together.

'No, I heard her mention the recent murder and that's when I created some distance between us. I thought if she was digging her way into a hole then there was only room for one.'

'Sensible chap. Okay, let's go and survey the situation.'

The two walked down the side of the house in silence.

Taylor stood with her back to Dylan, preening, as she busily fed the hungry press. Dylan left her to it. He couldn't do anything to save her now. If she'd said anything untoward she would have to learn the hard way. He had a more pressing engagement with a suicidal, drunken man who might have already killed one person and seriously injured another.

John followed Dylan. The kitchen door was still open, but the blind on the windows to the right of the door was down. They stood for a moment and listened. No sound came from within. With bated breath, Dylan peered carefully inside. He could see Graham Tate slumped on the kitchen floor with his back against the kitchen units. He looked unconscious. Near him, an empty bottle lay on its side.

Dylan pushed the door slightly with his fingertips; it opened easily, giving him a clearer view. Dylan thought he could make out what looked like a cigarette lighter hanging limply from Tate's right hand. The smell of gas seemed stronger in the room. Graham Tate wasn't moving, but a sudden jerk of alertness and he could strike the lighter.

'Have you got some handcuffs with you John?' Dylan whispered.

'Yeah, what're you thinking?'

'Well, I can't negotiate with someone who's out cold. I'll go in quietly and try to grab that lighter from his hand. You follow me and try to cuff him at the same time.'

'Sounds good to me.'

'Only if it works,' Dylan grimaced as he inhaled deeply. 'Here goes.' On tiptoes and with bated breath, the two walked towards the drunken man. One flick of the lighter and they could all go up.

Everything was deathly quiet. The floor was lino and the soles of Dylan's shoes could be heard squeakily peeling themselves off and on it as he walked toe to heel. He stopped and scowled. He looked down at his shoelaces; there wasn't time to take his shoes off.

With one leap, Dylan launched himself forward and grabbed the lighter. Tate stirred and mumbled something incoherently. John swung the handcuffs from his pocket and used every ounce of bodily strength to put Graham Tate on the floor and cuff him.

The two men glanced at each other, relief evident in their faces. Sweat was visible on the brows. Graham Tate was truly out of it as he lay face-down on the lino, his mouth open wide.

'Perhaps, it's not just drink John. He might have taken something else. Get the ambulance crew here, will you?' Dylan said as he reached out to turn the knobs back to their off position on the cooker. His head was pounding and the palms of his hands were slick with sweat.

The paramedics were quickly in the house, their blaze of green suits a welcome sight. An out of breath Taylor Spiers appeared at the kitchen door. Putting her hand around the doorjamb she reached for the light switch.

'STOP,' Dylan screamed reaching out to slap Taylor's hand away. John and the paramedics, who were down on their haunches, froze.

'I was only going to put the light on so you could see better,' Taylor said. Her bottom lip trembled as she rubbed her pained hand vigorously.

'Don't you realise that a little spark from that switch could still blow us all to smithereens? You stupid woman. Can't you still smell the gas? Open the blinds and the windows,' Dylan shouted, his heart still in his mouth.

Taylor's hands were shaking as she pulled open the blinds. She would never, ever forgive Dylan for his embarrassing outburst.

'I'm pretty sure it's probably just alcohol,' said the Paramedic. 'We'll take him to the hospital to run some tests though, just to be sure.'

Dylan nodded. 'Shall I go with him boss, for continuity?' asked John.

'Yeah, do that. There are some nice nurses up there,' Dylan said with the ghost of a smile on his blanched face.

'Really?' John said, 'very accommodating?'

'Really,' Dylan nodded.

Dylan put his hand on the worktop to steady himself. There beneath his fingers was a note that read: *I HAD TO DO IT. THERE IS NOTHING LEFT FOR ME IN THIS WORLD.*

Dylan quickly pulled his hand back and pointed to the scrap of paper, 'Just be aware and seize it will you Taylor.'

Following the ambulance staff John turned and looked at Dylan. 'The press are still outside, sir.'

'Taylor, what did you tell them?' Dylan asked.

'I just tried to keep them satisfied, sir, that's all,' she said.

'I didn't ask you that. I said, what did you tell them?'

'Just that we were investigating the murder of Danny Denton and we needed to speak to Mr Tate to eliminate him.'

Dylan let out his held breath. 'And that's all?'

Taylor nodded her head.

'For a moment there...' he dropped his head to his chest. 'Okay,' he said looking up, 'while we're in the house, let's get a team here and search to see if there's anything to connect Graham Tate to Denton or Greenwood. I'll see you back at the debrief.

'Taylor, I've had to deal with the aftermath of someone simply switching the lights on, which caused a massive explosion and serious injury to one of my colleagues. My outburst was instinctive.'

Walking back up the street he saw the local reporters with their cameras in tow.

'What's the update Dylan?' called one.

'Give us the story,' called another.

'There isn't a story, yet,' he smiled, stopping to speak to them.

'Alright, look, you're aware of the accident outside Mothercare a few weeks ago?'

The men and women of the press stood quietly.

'That was Graham Tate's wife and son.' The observers nodded in unison. Their expectant faces reminded him of vultures waiting at a dying animal's side.

'The car that killed them was reported stolen and the registered owner was found murdered a few days ago.'

Their eager faces were frozen in anticipation. 'Well, Mr Tate is understandably depressed and we just needed to eliminate him from our enquiries, which is why we came here today. On arrival, we found him unconscious.' A wave of moans waved through the crowd.

'Let's face it,' Dylan grimaced. 'It's only one line of enquiry that's ongoing and there's no more to tell you at this moment in time. I honestly wish there was,' Dylan reiterated to their disappointed faces.

Striding purposefully towards his car, he dialled Jen's number.

'Today's briefing may go on longer than usual, love,' he said, which she instinctively knew meant yet another long and   lonely   night.

Chapter 46

Dylan updated the team in debrief regarding Billy Greenwood's injuries, the prognosis of his recovery and the securing of the piece of metal from one of his wounds. Although the piece of evidence was minute, he told them it was highly significant as it was more than likely part of the tip of the blade, which he knew would be an invaluable piece of evidence if the murder weapon was found.

He also updated everyone in respect of the suicide attempt after tracing Graham Tate, and John told the assembled group that the hospital staff had confirmed that he had taken a cocktail of drinks and drugs. He was still in ICU and as yet had not regained consciousness, which meant that he remained under constant watch due to his present state of mind. A suicide note was also recovered.

'Is he in the same ICU as Billy Greenwood, John?' asked Dylan.

'Yeah, but I've made uniform staff aware of who they both are and their history and they are making arrangements for him to be relocated to Leeds.'

'Well, they're hardly likely to cause any trouble judging by the state of their health,' Taylor said, sarcastically. 'It would appear Bill Forrester can be eliminated from our enquiry too, sir, although I don't care for the man.'

'Oh, come off it,' John snapped, 'the man only said he didn't feel any sympathy for the two who had just subjected his daughter to a violent rape attack.'

Taylor glanced at John with a look that said it all. 'We also saw Duncan Harvey, whose whereabouts will also be verified I'm sure,' she continued.

'Just for your info boss, a lady phoned in to the incident room this morning after your press release to say that someone had stolen the lilies she had fastened to the railings on the road about half a mile from Denton and Greenwood's flat.

'Her son died at the spot some years ago and she always leaves white lilies there to mark the anniversary of his death, which happened to be the day before our two were attacked. She didn't know if it was relevant,' said Lisa.

'I want her seen as soon as possible and a statement obtained. Find out where she bought them from. It could give us a source for lilies if nothing else.'

Vicky read out a list of items seized from Stevenson's house.

Dylan concluded the debrief by thanking everyone for their efforts. It was time for home; tomorrow would be another day to move the enquiries forward.

Jen was nervous. The fact her bump had measured 34.5 cm when it had measured 34 cm the week before, had concerned her midwife enough to schedule the imminent scan. Jen was pleased that Dylan was able to go with her. He'd told the office staff he wouldn't be in until after lunch. As they waited at the hospital, Jen squeezed his arm.

'Thanks for being here with me. I'm so scared,' she said, as she slipped her hand into his. He noticed that her palm was a little sweaty, so he squeezed her hand tight.

'Nervous? I'm excited,' Dylan said with gusto. 'Just think we wouldn't be having another scan if the Button wasn't measuring small. We're lucky to get to see him again before he's born.'

'He?'

'Whatever,' Dylan laughed. 'I don't care if Button is a he or a she as long as he or she are okay,' he grinned like a Cheshire cat.

'I know and at thirty-seven weeks I've been really lucky haven't I, not to have had any problems?' she said. She licked her lips and stretched her back. 'It'll be okay. It's probably because his head is engaged or I was laid on the bed last week when she measured me and this week I was laid on the sofa.'

'Exactly,' said Dylan. 'So enjoy the experience,' he smiled.

'My mouth is so dry. Can you believe that when I've had so much water to drink?' Jen fidgeted in the uncomfortable hard hospital chair as she tried to get comfy with a full bladder. 'If they don't hurry up I'm going to pee my pants,' she whispered.

Dylan put his arm around her shoulders and squeezed her tight. 'We were fortunate not to have had to go through the dilemma of 'should we or shouldn't we' at our age, weren't we?' he mused.

'And if we had, we'd have doubted whether we could afford to raise one?'

'Best decision I didn't make,' Dylan chuckled as he patted Jen's bump.

'He'll be fine. Just lazy like his old dad,' he chuckled.

Jen looked up at the clock as the door opened and a Radiographer stepped out, calling her name.

The lighting was subdued in the room where the scan was to take place. Jen was told to lie on the bed. She kicked off her shoes and sat on the side of the bed before raising her legs. She lifted her top up above her bump and her trousers below before eagerly looking towards the screen.

Jen lay perfectly still and Dylan sat beside her holding her hand tightly. He too scrutinised the blank monitor in anticipation before looking back at Jen and grinning.

The Radiographer chatted amiably as she squeezed clear gel out of a tube and into the palm of her gloved hand then she put more on the end of the probe before rubbing it onto Jen's tummy. They always warned her: 'This might be cold.'

Jen flinched as the ice cold jelly hit her stomach.

'There's your baby,' she said, with glee as she rolled the ball like probe around Jen's stomach indicating with her spare hand its movements on the monitor.

Jen and Dylan looked at each other in amazement as every time they saw Buttons he seemed to have grown. Dylan's eyes unexpectedly filled with tears and he reached in his pocket for his handkerchief. The scan wasn't as clear as it had been previously but this time the baby did turn his face towards the camera. They saw him gulp whilst taking a drink. Jen and Dylan could have stayed there all day listening and watching their baby.

'The images aren't as clear as there is a lot of tissue on the baby now,' explained the Radiographer. 'Do you want to hear the heartbeat?'

Dylan and Jen nodded together.

'Would you like to know whether the baby is a girl or a boy?' The Radiographer asked.

Jen looked at Jack, 'Yes, please,' she grinned. 'We've resisted till now, but if it's okay with you Jack, I'd like to know.'

Dylan nodded with a smile.

'You have yourselves a little girl,' she said. 'According to my notes and from what I can see.

'But it can't be. She's a he,' said Jen, in amazement.

'Dylan rose from his seat and hugged Jen to him. Jen let out a huge sigh of relief and tears ran down the side of her face and onto the pillow below. Dylan laughed at her with tears in his eyes.

'Oh, that often happens.'

'They said the baby was small.'

'Don't worry, babies have spurts of growing. She's just fine.'

The Radiographer reeled tissue from a roll and wiped the gel off Jen's taut skin on her bulging stomach.

'Not long now, eh?' the Radiographer said.

'I don't want to go back to work,' Dylan said as he walked out into the warm sunshine. He turned his face to the sky.

'Me neither,' Jen said, cuddling up to him.

Jen put her seat belt around her but couldn't look at Dylan – the flaming job always got in the way of everything.

Having dropped Jen off, he walked through the yard at the police station he took the treasured photograph of his little girl out of his pocket and placed it inside his wallet. He headed for the incident room while Jen walked to the admin block. He switched his mobile phone on. It beeped incessantly.

'Boss,' he heard Taylor shout. The spell was broken.

'Let me get in first,' Dylan shouted as he opened his office door and put the lights on. The fluorescent lamp juddered once or twice and then lit up the room. John and Taylor followed close behind him vying for his attention.

'Stevenson's been traced to a Travelodge near Heathrow Airport,' John said.

'He's booked in till tomorrow, so it's likely he's arranged an early flight,' Taylor added.

'It's a single room, so presumably he's on his own and keeping a low profile,' said John.

'Why the hell are we sat here talking? Have you informed the local nick? We need to get a team down there and I want the local lads to be aware,' said Dylan.

'It's all arranged, sir. We're going in, in the early hours of tomorrow morning unless he tries to make a move first. We've got him under surveillance till then,' said John.

'Good. You two happy to go down there with an exhibits officer and two uniform to do the arrest?' Dylan asked.

'Two uniform?' Taylor asked with a furrowed brow.

'They can cuff him and set off straight back here with him. I don't want anyone accusing us of trying to interview him en route. You can stay and do the search and the exhibits officer can register and bag the property.'

'Sounds good to me,' said John.

'Okay,' Taylor said.

'So you'd better think about getting off home then. Get your head down for a few hours and I'll arrange with uniform for a plain car from the night shift to be here at twenty-two hundred hours. When you get there, arrange for the night porter to let you into Stevenson's room and that way you can surprise him. Remember he might be our murderer though, so leave nothing to chance.'

'Okay boss, we'll keep you updated.'

'Not too early though eh?' he laughed.

At one time Dylan would have worked till late arranging the details of the arrest himself, dashed home to pack a bag, lead the team south and brought the prisoner back to interview him himself. But not tonight, tonight he wanted to spend time with Jen.

Experience had taught him he would be a lot fresher to deal with a prisoner when others had brought him in. It would be lunchtime tomorrow before he was safely ensconced in a cell in Harrowfield police station – and even then, Dylan knew Stevenson would no doubt want the eight hours' sleep that the Police and Criminal Evidence Act dictated he was entitled to. Of course it was wrong to interview someone when they were tired, he thought, tongue-in-cheek.

Jen couldn't believe he hadn't headed south with the team – her spirits rose.

Chapter 47

Stevenson's arrested without any problems. Uniform are on their way back with him. Just starting the search of his room – will speak before we set off back, came the text from Taylor.

'That's a good start, Jen,' Dylan said, as he put his mobile phone on the kitchen table and sunk his teeth into a thick slice of toast and honey. 'Mildred's murderer is well and truly locked up.'

Jen looked at him with a wide-eyed smile as she picked up his empty porridge dish. 'I didn't know you knew who'd done it?'

'Proving he did it, is well, mere detail,' he grinned, sheepishly as he rose from his chair and leaned towards her for a kiss. 'If only that was true.' She walked to the sink and dropped the dish into the soap suds.

'So, it'll be another long day, then?' she said reaching for the fruit bowl. 'I'll put extra bananas in your jock box and make sure you eat them,' she said, wagging a finger at him.

Dylan grimaced.

'Bananas are a good source of energy. Slow release of natural sugars. A lot better than pies – or even worse, a bag of crisps that has no nutritional value at all,' she said, mocking his vigorous dislike of anything good for him.

'Speak when I can love, as usual,' he said, taking the sandwich box from her outstretched hand and placing it on the top of his overflowing briefcase.

Jen sighed as she watched him leave.

Forty-five minutes later, Dylan was in the incident room telling his staff that Stevenson had been arrested and John and Taylor were searching the hotel room he had been using.

'That for me, Dennis?' Dylan asked, seeing the detective that was on light duties, who resembled The Hulk, walking across the room with a cup of tea in his good hand.

'Just getting yours, boss, white with one sweetener isn't it?' he said, swivelling on one foot and retracing his steps back to the kettle.

'Well done Dennis, I'm impressed.'

'Yeah, you might well be,' he laughed, 'I'm still only just managing to negotiate the coffee powder on the teaspoon and into the cup without too much of a mess on the table, with this heavily bandaged hand.'

'Hey, Bandit, mine and Lisa's are both white with one sugar, and you owe a quid for the tea fund,' Vicky called from where she sat at her desk.

'A quid?' Dennis shrieked.

'Yeah, and that's cheap. Tight arse,' she called. 'If you can't manage to get a quid out of your pocket I'll help?' Vicky laughed.

'She's not joking either, mate,' Dylan said.

'I can tell that by the look on her face,' Dennis said, fumbling in his pocket for a coin. 'This is victimisation of the afflicted,' he muttered.

'All I can say is it's a good job Sgt Finch took the job at HQ training,' Dylan responded.

'And I'm sure you had nothing at all to do with that eh, boss?'

'Development Vicky, the man needed developing when it came to working in CID,' he chortled.

'Ah, I miss Finchy though,' said Vicky. 'Even if he had to be bloody 'PC' about everything.'

'Yeah, note to myself. Always ask around about people that I haven't worked with before, before agreeing to supervise them,' groaned Dylan.

'His heart was in the right place,' said Lisa.

'Yeah, till he produced a document listing all the unacceptable comments made by officers during the investigation we were on.'

'Not the best way to win friends and influence people, I don't suppose,' said Dennis as he concentrated on getting the drinks-filled tray to the group without mishap.

Dylan's phone rang in his office. He hurried to pick it up.

'Taylor.' he said, immediately as he held the phone to his ear.

'Morning boss,' she yelled in order to be heard over the noise of the traffic. 'One alleged financial advisor nearly crapped himself this morning when we awoke him but he's not talking to us.'

'He's probably still in shock.' Dylan found himself shouting back, needlessly. The office personnel stopped to listen and expectant faces stared at him from the incident room.

'What did you say?' Taylor yelled.

'Never mind, did you find anything on him?'

'He had a large amount of cash and about two dozen gold rings in his belongings. There's also a few sets of keys and a Lloyds TSB debit card and credit card in the name of a Brian Stewart.'

'A new ID?' Dylan pondered. 'Why would he have that? We'll give it straight to the financial team when you get back. With their contacts, they might get a quicker result than us.'

'Can't hear a thing, sir. Look, we've done all we can here, so we're going to get some breakfast and then make our way back'.

'Okay. Drive carefully,' he said, but the phone line was dead.

A new identity? Rings? Brian Stevenson was becoming interesting. He strolled out into the CID office. 'We've got Brian Stevenson on his way and I want him to be under constant supervision when he gets here,' Dylan informed the office staff before shutting his office door. Dylan sat at his desk in the quiet; thinking. He picked up his phone.

'Can you let me know when Brian Stevenson's in?' Dylan asked the Custody Sergeant.

Vicky burst into Dylan's office.

'Boss, CID are being requested to attend a stabbing on the shopping precinct.'

'What do we know?' he asked, putting the phone down with a degree of urgency.

'Young lad has been stabbed in the back by a bloke. No apparent motive, according to witnesses. The bloke's legged it and the lad's being taken by ambulance to hospital.'

'Get your coat, I'll come with you,' said Dylan grabbing his jacket. 'Dennis.' Dylan called. 'You're in charge of the office. Just answer the phones and keep scouring the McDonalds CCTV tapes,' he said, sweeping past him towards the door.

'Okay, boss,' he said.

Dylan stared at the scene of the stabbing on the precinct for several minutes before entering the cordon. A crowd had gathered. Vicky spoke to uniform, who told her that the police had saturated the area, but so far the attacker hadn't been traced. Dylan lifted the police tape and walked into the inner cordon.

'Do you want a suit sir?' a SOCO officer enquired, handing him a packet containing a disposable SOCO suit coverall and overboots.

'Yes, let's not take any chances,' he nodded to Vicky who took one too.

Suited up, Dylan padded over to the spot where the incident had taken place. He could see suited SOCO officers stooped on their haunches, carefully taking swabs of marks on the flagstones. Others dusted the window of the Next store nearby, but as far as Dylan could see there was nothing to suggest that anything sinister had taken place.

'Get the CCTV tape seized. At least it should be on camera,' Dylan said to Vicky pointing to the camera above. 'Please God, let it have a tape in,' Dylan groaned.

'Sir,' shouted a uniformed sergeant running towards the cordon, his hat under his arm. Dylan walked towards him. 'I have an officer in Union Street, who has found a bloodstained knife dumped in a waist bin,' he panted. 'Apparently a witness saw a man disposing of it. I've called for SOCO. And just to let you know I have a unit at A & E who will update me as soon as they've any information from the doctors regarding the victim.

'A witness has told us that the man he saw had two knives on him. Seemingly the bloke just ran up behind the kid, stabbed him and ran off. Officers are getting statements from anyone who can tell us anything.'

'Thanks Sarge, we'll just have a walk round to Union Street for a quick look at the weapon and then nip over to the hospital,' said Dylan.

'Mmm. He's rather switched on isn't he?' Vicky said, thoughtfully.

'He's certainly got everything covered,' Dylan said looking at Vicky with approval. 'But he's done nothing that you wouldn't have done.' Vicky screwed up her nose and pulled a face at Dylan. 'I know, I know, same old, same old. I should take my exams, don't go on,' she whined as they walked to the scene where the knife was discovered.

Dylan studied the implement carefully. It was rather like the knives butchers use, he observed. He'd get a closer all-round look at it once scenes of crime had photographed and placed it in the protective clear view 'sharps' tube.

At the hospital, the boy was being prepared for theatre, Dylan was updated via his radio. He and Vicky were on their way. Initial examinations showed that he had one stab wound to his back. The concern was how deep it was and if it had affected any major organs. The boy had been identified and his family contacted.

'So Vicky, we've now got a stranger attack on a young lad and Billy Greenwood with a serious wounding that could have easily been a murder. Seize the boy's clothes when we get to the hospital and arrange for another detective to meet us there so that they can stay when we leave, for continuity.'

'Sure,' she said, keying the CID's office number into her mobile.

'Oh, and Vicky?'

'Yes,' she said, as she ran after him up the path of the hospital entrance.

'Take charge of the CCTV and get it copied as soon as, so we can view it.' Dylan said as got his mobile phone out of his jacket pocket and put it to his ear.

'Brush and arse comes to mind.'

'What?' he scowled in Vicky's direction. 'Dennis,' he said, turning his head to get the reception to hear his detective back at the office. 'Can you make some calls for me and find out who we've got in the hostels around here and who's been released back into the community recently. The stabbing of this young lad appears to be random. Have we got a name or description of the victim?' he went on.

'No, but we will have once the statements are in,' said Dennis.

Dylan threw a look at Vicky as he held the hospital door open. 'Give Liz at the press office brief details of the incident and ask her to appeal for witnesses will you? I'll see you on the ward.'

Dylan stood at the nurse's station. Vicky joined him. 'The cells rang to let you know that Brian Stevenson has arrived and they're booking him in at the custody suite. He's still not speaking to us.'

'Not even to confirm his name?'

'Nope, he just nodded when they asked if he wanted the duty solicitor.'

Vicky walked over to the drink dispenser and held a cup under the machine. She sipped the cold water tentatively.

'He's not going to roll over easy is he?' said Dylan.

'When are murderers agreeable?' she said. 'Look at poor Dennis, who'd have thought he'd be attacked by a machete in Blackpool by an uncooperative child murderer.'

'I'm just happy we've plenty to put to him when it comes to the interviews, which reminds me to get Dennis to chase up the identification of the silver carriage clock for me. I still want to know if the one in Mildred's photograph is the one recovered from Denton and Greenwood's flat and the very same one that Brian Stevenson says he had taken from his house. It's doin' my head in. I never want a flaming carriage clock.'

'Detective Inspector Dylan?' said the nurse, hurrying towards them down the corridor.

'Yes.'

'I'm sorry to say that the young man just brought in with a stab wound has had an adverse reaction to the anaesthetic. He's now classed as critical. I'll keep you updated on his progress.'

Dylan looked up at the ceiling. 'That's all we bloody need,' he muttered.

Chapter 48

Dylan's phone flashed DS John Benjamin's name. Technology was bloody good these days. To know who was ringing before you picked the phone up was a godsend – sometimes. 'John,' he said on answering it.

'We've broken down. We're on the hard shoulder off the M1 about eighty miles away from home,' John shouted.

Dylan could hear the high-pitched screech of a woman's voice in the distance amongst the whoosh of traffic, then he heard a door slam. It was quieter – John must have got into the car.

'Taylor's onto Vehicle Fleet Management playing hell. The car's just been serviced according to the log book but I think it's the fan belt that's gone.'

'Can't you use a flaming stocking,' yelled Dylan in exasperation.

'A what?' John looked down at Taylor's trouser covered legs. 'I don't think.'

'Oh, never mind,' said Dylan as he put his hand to his brow. 'Look, give me your exact location and I'll get a garage out to you.'

'I've already arranged for the motorway cops to ferry us to the end of the motorway. Our lads are picking us up there as per Dennis.'

'Good man. Make sure you get out and wait on the banking for them. Motorways are dangerous places,' Dylan said involuntarily shuddering as he remembered a job he'd once dealt with where a whole family had been killed by a heavy goods vehicle while waiting on the hard shoulder in their car after they'd broken down on a motorway.

'Now you sound like my dad,' he said.

241

'Mmm ... thanks,' Dylan mumbled. 'But you wouldn't say that if you'd seen the carnage I'd seen.'

'Yes, boss, sorry,' John said, in a more sombre tone.

'Let me know when your arrival's imminent. I've gotta go mate, we've got a young lad been stabbed in the precinct and it's not looking good'.

'Gang related?'

'No, first reports suggest it's one man.'

'Known to him?'

'Initial enquiries seem to suggest it's a stranger.'

'Gotta be a nutter then, surely?'

'Time'll tell,' Dylan said. 'Never assume.'

'See you soon, boss,' John said.

Dylan inhaled deeply as he walked back into the CID office.

'How're you doing with the recent releases and the return to the care of the community, Dennis?' he asked.

'Still compiling a list boss and then I've gotta run the names through the system. I thought there'd only be one or two but there are bloody loads.'

John was right, Dylan conceded. It probably was somebody with mental problems who was out roaming the streets of Harrowfield. That's all Dylan needed, and if his victims were being chosen at random, God knew where he'd strike next?

'Message for you, boss.'

Dylan looked up from his writing; pen in his hand.

'Cells say the duty solicitor is from Perfect and Best who have been contacted and to let them know when you're ready to start interviewing,' said Vicky.

'Have you heard from John?'

Vicky shook her head.

'They've broken down. '

'Shame,' she said, shrugging her shoulders.

'Vicky,' Dylan growled. Vicky looked sheepish.

'Just a thought boss,' she said, changing the subject before he gave her a lecture on how capable Taylor was as a DS. 'On the stabbing incident, if the young lad dies and I hope to God he doesn't, but if he does and it was due to the adverse reaction to something the hospital staff did, would it still be murder?'

'It would be about causation. If he hadn't been stabbed he wouldn't be in the hospital. If he hadn't been taken to hospital then would he have died because of blood loss as a direct result of the stabbing?'

'Probably,' she said with a frown.

'So, you've got your answer then.'

'We'd charge murder,' she said. Dylan nodded.

'And the defence would have all the relevant case law out about causation to defend their client, but the bottom line in my book is, did the attacker, when he stabbed him, intend to kill him, and did he die as a result?'

Vicky nodded. 'Guilty, but hopefully the young lad won't die, eh?'

Dylan cocked his head and smiled wanly at his DC. The phone rang in the CID office.

'Call for you boss. It's Sergeant Wilson from the hospital,' Dennis shouted. 'I'll put him through.'

'I'll come in there,' Dylan said, rising from his desk and walking the few yards to the desk Dennis was sitting at. Dylan took the phone from him. His face looked serious. He sat down.

'Sir, a few updates for you, first and foremost the young lad's stable.'

Dylan heard himself sighing with relief and his heart lifted.

'The wound, they tell me, is about three inches deep but fortunately it's missed his vital organs and they've managed to stem the bleeding. His parents are here and are obviously distraught, but I've explained best I can what's happened. They tell me that their son had gone into town to the florist to collect flowers for his sister's birthday.'

'And his name?'

'Oh, yes, James Drinkwater, and he's fourteen.'

'And his parents?' Dylan asked, pen poised as he grabbed a piece of scrap paper and sat down at a desk.

'His parents are a Julia and George Drinkwater.'

'His clothing?'

'It's here,' Vicky whispered, pointing to evidence bags at her feet.

'Vicky Hardacre has them, sir, I understand.'

'Yes, she's just informed me,' said Dylan.

'I've some statements for you so I'll drop them into your office within the hour.'

'Brilliant, thanks for your efforts and see you soon,' Dylan said.

'Sounds like I'd better get my lippy on if that gorgeous Sarge's coming,' said Vicky raising her eyebrow in an impish fashion. She winked at him and tottered towards the ladies. He shook his head and Dennis smiled at him knowingly. What was he to do with her?

'Hey, never mind lippy where's the copy of the CCTV?' Dylan shouted, after her.

'It'll be with you anytime now,' Vicky called over her shoulder.

Jasmine glided through the door. As she saw Dylan her brown eyes lit up and her thin face broke into a smile. The petite SOCO supervisor's long brown hair was tied in a high ponytail, which made her look younger than she normally did.

'Boss, did you want to see the knife from the precinct incident?' she asked.

'Please,' Dylan said, walking into his office. She followed close behind.

Dylan sat at his desk expectantly and she passed the sealed protective tube with the knife inside to him. Dylan looked at the prized object laid on his desk with interest.

'I've swabbed it but surprisingly it doesn't appear to have any blood on it; the lab will confirm that for you though.'

Dylan picked up the tube and held it in the air, studying it intently.

'Oh my God are your eyes that bad?' said Vicky, who had returned and was standing at his door. Her hair was brushed, her glossy lips puckered like she had just eaten something sour.

'Cheeky mare,' Dylan said, glancing towards her.

'Well, you know what they say you should've listened to them when they told you it would make you blind,' she chuckled. Jasmine blushed.

Dylan laughed. 'My sight might not be brilliant lady, but if I'm not mistaken the very tiny tip of this blade just happens to be missing. Jasmine?'

'You don't miss much do you?' she said, 'and I'm convinced it's the knife that was used on Greenwood and killed Denton.'

'No.' Vicky said, hurriedly walking towards Dylan to look for herself. Hearing the commotion, Dennis walked into the office doorway.

'Ooh, wait on, I might have something that may help,' Vicky said, turning quickly and running into Dennis in her rush to get the magnifying glass out of her drawer.

'I knew this useless Christmas present from my Nan would come in handy one day,' she said, fumbling around in her drawer.

Gathering around Dylan's desk, they all stared in amazement at the picture of the tip Jasmine produced.

'Coincidence or what?' Vicky said, peering through the looking glass.

'Well, fingers crossed that it can be proven later today?' Dylan asked, Jasmine who nodded in the affirmative. 'Let's stay on the positive and assume it is 'the' knife', but right now we need to find out who it belongs to before our man attacks anyone else. Let's prioritise anyone returned to the care of the community and early releases – and let's get that bloody CCTV Vicky pronto and see what this man looks like.'

'Knife to the lab ASAP?'

'Yeah, on its way now, sir,' Jasmine smiled, as she disappeared through the doorway.

Dylan looked out of his window. Avril Summerfield-Preston, the Divisional Administrator, was getting into her car, parcel in hand.

'She's just going to visit Jen, she told me when I saw her just now in the loo,' said Vicky. Dylan grunted.

'For goodness sake, can't the woman leave her alone she's supposed to be resting,'

'Welfare check.'

'Welfare my arse, she'll only go and upset her. Does Jen know she's going?'

Vicky shrugged her shoulders.

'I better ring her to warn her,' Dylan said, picking up his mobile. The battery was dead. He took his charger out of his briefcase and was just about to plug it in when Dennis came charging into his office.

'Boss, you might wanna have a look at this guy who has come back into the community recently,' Dennis said, going back to his chair in the office and turning his computer screen around towards his audience. 'Released on life licence at the beginning of last month,' he read.

'Frederick Gladwin Wainstall, twenty-nine years old who was sentenced to life imprisonment at the age of eighteen for murdering his parents, who died from multiple stab wounds,' read Vicky.

'He only served nine years. Nine bloody years and released on life licence which was revoked after wounding a stranger within weeks.' Dennis read out his voice getting louder and louder with ever spoken word. 'The weapon used; a knife.' Dennis looked up into the faces of those who had gathered round him. 'He's back out.'

Dylan continued read to about Wainstall feverishly over Dennis's shoulder. 'No wonder the incident doesn't ring any bells; it happened in Brighton,' he said.

'I don't believe this, his parents were found with white lilies next to their bodies,' Vicky said quietly.

'Okay we need to pull out all the stops. Let's get everyone looking for him. I want you to get hold of probation, prison, social services. We need an up-to-date photograph of him. What address have we got for him?

'It looks like we have a madman on the loose who may just be looking for his next victim – and I for one don't want that to happen,' said Dylan.

It was like lighting a blue touch paper. There needed to be a sense of urgency throughout the building, in the town and villages surrounding Harrowfield. Dylan looked as a recent image of Wainstall sent by email from the prison. He printed it and carefully soaked up the man's features. He had a shaven head, clean-shaven face except for what looked like a small goatee beard on his chin. His deep-set dark staring eyes looked vacantly back at him.

'Brian Stevenson's custody clock is running away with us, sir,' said the officer from the cells who burst into the CID office, only to be met by a group of silent people crowded around the photograph.

'Yes, yes. DS Benjamin and DS Spiers will be with you shortly,' Dylan snapped.

The officer retreated out of the door leaving it swinging in his path.

'Only trying to help,' he mumbled. 'If we don't tell them they shout at us. If we tell them they shout... Can't do right for doing wrong,' he grumbled as he made his way back to the custody suite.

'Did we get a statement off the woman who rang in about the flowers being taken off the railings?' asked Dylan. Vicky and Dennis looked blank. 'Check. If not, let's get that done.'

Vicky nodded.

'The McDonalds' CCTV, have you viewed that yet for around the time when Denton and Greenwood were in there?' Dylan asked Dennis.

'No, not yet you told me to concentrate on prison releases,' Dennis said.

Dennis took the envelope from his tray with the CCTV video enclosed and slotted it in the machine. He looked at the monitor then back at Dylan with a startled expression upon his face.

'Look, that's him; sat in the corner, the man in the wool hat holding the flowers,' he said

'Let's get the video to Imaging and get it enhanced,' said Dylan, with more than a hint of urgency in his voice.

'Traffic'll get it there at speed, Vicky.'

'Traffic'll do what?' asked Sergeant Wilson.

'My hero,' said Vicky.

'What?' he asked, with a puzzled look on his face.

'Oh, nothing, ignore her,' Dylan said. 'Get this to HQ will you mate ASAP. And take Hardacre with you. She's about as useless as a glass hammer to me at the moment,' he said quietly, winking at Sergeant Wilson. 'And she'll be able to fill you in on the way,' said Dylan.

'Sure,' Sergeant Wilson smiled at Vicky.

'That okay with you?' asked Dylan.

'Is it ever.' she said grabbing her bag and rushing after Sergeant Wilson as he headed for the door with the CCTV footage in his hand.

'And see if you can persuade her to take her bloody Sergeant's exams while you're at it.' Dylan called after them.

Sergeant Wilson raised his hand as he looked over his shoulder at Dylan.

Within the hour Dylan had viewed the CCT seized from the town centre precinct. It showed a man running around the corner onto the precinct. He stops, looks around. James Drinkwater emerges from the florist with a bunch of flowers in his hand. Suddenly, for no apparent reason the man begins to run after him, pulling two knives out of his coat pockets. He stabs James in the back with one, turns, and runs away.

'He's wearing a wool hat,' said Dennis.

'The witnesses got that right. But look at his footwear,' Dylan said pointing to the brilliant white training shoes the man was wearing on the screen.

They let the tape run, but it didn't show the attacker's face. With fumbling hands Dennis quickly swapped the tape for the CCTV tape recovered from Union Street where the knife had been found.

'It doesn't get much better than that,' Dylan said, with a smile, as they viewed a clear picture of a man dropping a knife in the bin from where the officer had recovered it. He looked up directly into the camera. The man didn't quite have a goatee beard but what looked like a bad case of acne and unshaven hair on his chin.

'It's Wainstall.' came the chorus of voices.

'That's for sure,' said Dennis.

'Let's get his picture printed off and get him found. Remind people he's dangerous and is likely to be in possession of a knife that he won't hesitate to use. We don't want any more stabbings'

The incident room telephone rang. Lisa answered it and listened intently. She put the phone down as if in slow motion.

'Yes?' said Dylan.

'The hospital, sir,' she said. All eyes were on Lisa's grave face. 'Billy Greenwood lost his fight for life a few minutes ago'.

Chapter 49

Dylan hadn't heard from Jen. His phone charged enough to have a signal, he turned it back on. It beeped a message. He didn't recognise the number. Taylor stumbled into Dylan's office door and dropped the evidence bags she'd been carrying.

'Shit.' Dylan heard her cry.

'More haste, less speed, don't they say?' said Dylan as he rose from his chair behind the desk. John opened the door and guided an unsteady Taylor inside.

'You okay? Come in,' he said.

'Flaming heels, they'll be the death of me,' she said, standing on one leg as she removed the offending broken shoe. Her concern only fuelled the cruel sting of embarrassment.

'Am I glad to see you two,' Dylan said, with a sigh of relief as he looked at his dirty and exhausted DSs. Taylor dumped the bags of property seized from Brian Stevenson's hotel room on Dylan's desk, then fell unceremoniously into a chair.

'You look just about all in.'

'Nothing that a strong cup of coffee won't put right,' said John. 'You should have seen the hotel room, boss. It was like a haul from a jeweller's, plus sixty grand we reckon, in cash.'

'How do you two feel about going into interview?' Dylan asked tentatively.

'You're joking, aren't you? I can't wait to see what Stevenson's got to say for himself,' said Taylor. Her face was flushed and her eyes lit up with anticipation.

'Me too, there's a lot for him to explain away,' added John. Dylan saw the bags that had formed under his eyes in the past few weeks and he knew he was feeling the strain of the enquiry.

'I'm told it's Lin Perfect from Perfect and Best that's awaiting your call to attend to represent her client – so let's get cracking, shall we? Remember keep an open mind and don't accept the first thing that he tells you.'

Dylan intently watched the live stream footage of the interview on the monitor in his office. He could hear his heart beating with anticipation but as a higher tier trained interviewer he missed the face-to-face confrontation and psychological battle on a regular basis.

The two detective sergeants appeared before him on the screen and Dylan shuffled in his seat. He leaned closer to the screen. He saw Brian Stevenson sitting alongside his solicitor.

'For the purpose of the tape,' John said. 'Please can you give me your name?'

In unfaltering, clear voices, the financial advisor and solicitor spoke their names clearly. The interview commenced. Dylan shook his head; he would never understand the reason for the caution. Why would anyone but the British put a suspect in an interview room, wanting them to admit to an offence and then spend time telling them that they don't have to say anything?

Firstly, John went over Brian Stevenson's background before asking him to explain where he was going when they had found him in his hotel room and account for the large amount of money he had with him along with the numerous bejewelled rings.

Stevenson didn't answer any of the questions put to him. He stared at them, never blinking, never taking his eyes off them, never showing an ounce of emotion.

Taylor was to play the friendly cop to encourage cooperation by Stevenson in building his trust in her as opposed to John, the aggressor. John pushed the issue of the murder of Mildred Sykes and the silver carriage clock.

It was obvious to Dylan that Stevenson didn't like the way John put things to him in a manner that he was made to face the facts. The response was still the same. The two detectives now knew that Lin Perfect had advised Stevenson not to answer questions put to him as he 'no commented' repeatedly. They were prepared however to ask everything that Dylan had planned for them to ask, giving him the opportunity to answer. If not, at a later stage, the solicitor could argue that her client would have replied if the questions had been put to him.

They meticulously asked every question. Dylan was pleased. Some questions that were put to Stevenson provoked a flicker of something in his eyes. Every now and then Stevenson ran his hand distractedly through his hair.

For the forty-five minutes duration of the tape, Stevenson managed to remain silent while under extreme pressure, which Dylan knew wasn't an easy thing to do. He didn't appear unduly fazed. They would take a thirty-minute break.

From the confines of his office, Dylan saw Sergeant Wilson arrive in the incident room. He knocked at the door, Dylan bid him entry and he took a seat after placing the paperwork and exhibits from the hospital on Dylan's desk. Within seconds, Vicky entered with coffee for the men.

'He deserves this, boss. He's been working ever so hard,' she said. Dylan smiled. Sergeant Wilson blushed.

'Oh, have you got it bad girl?' Dylan laughed when Sergeant Wilson excused himself to go to the rest room.

In typical Vicky fashion, she brushed her long blonde hair over her shoulders with a flick of her hand and looked at Dylan through her fringe, smiling. On his return, Dylan gave them the update on Wainstall and a copy of his mugshot.

'I'll get his description circulated on a bulletin on the intranet to all relevant areas for PCs and PCSOs to look out for him, boss. He shouldn't be that difficult to find if he's still out and about,' said Sergeant Wilson, looking at Vicky and smiling as he spoke.

'We haven't found him yet though,' Dylan said.

'Do you know, I think that CCTV footage is one of the saddest things I've ever seen,' said Vicky, emotionally charged. 'How could anyone stab a kid like that for nothing?' she said.

'Looking at the tape, it's apparent he had two knives. One we've recovered, but the other? The likelihood is that he still has one with him, so be sure to remind everyone how bloody dangerous he is,' Dylan said.

Sergeant Wilson got up to leave. 'I'm on with it sir.'

'Be seeing you soon, Sarge,' said Vicky. Sergeant Wilson nodded at Dylan and smiled fondly at Vicky.

'Bit too obvious, mate,' whispered Dylan.

'You think so?' she cringed, as she sat on the chair facing Dylan, swinging her legs. She sprung up, smiled and glided out of the office.

Dylan shook his head.

To give John a break and allow him to nip home and see the family, Dylan agreed to stand in for him on the second interview with Stevenson. A different face might get a different response from him, occasionally he knew it did. On impulse, Dylan grabbed the crucial exhibits recovered from the hotel room to take in with him.

Taylor opened up the interviews after the usual caution. Stevenson once again sat staring at the detectives and didn't respond to the change of personnel.

Dylan sat quietly watching every twitch on Stevenson's face.

'You were the last person to see Mildred Sykes alive according to her neighbours and on your own admission.

You took her a bunch of white lilies, didn't you?' said Taylor.

Stevenson didn't respond.

'Mr Stevenson, the purpose of an interview is to ascertain the truth. If you have nothing to hide, I can't understand why you refuse to answer our questions,' she continued.

Two blank faces looked at Dylan and Taylor from the other side of the table. Lin Perfect made a note in her book. 'Inspector, it is my client's right to remain silent if he so wishes,' she said, raising her eyes to look at him.

Dylan cleared his throat. 'I understand that, and you will understand that it is my duty to put the allegations in order to him to give him the opportunity to respond,' he said. He turned his head to address Stevenson. 'So, do you agree you saw Mildred Sykes?' said Dylan. Stevenson stared directly into his eyes. 'Well?' said Dylan, raising his voice. The pair jumped. Taylor suppressed a smile.

'You know I did,' said Stevenson, quietly hanging his head. Dylan was pleased he'd spoke, but hoped he would continue to do so.

'According to reports handed to your solicitor,' Dylan said nodding in Lin Perfect's direction. 'It was about that time that she died. We know of no other visitors after you left. Your fingerprints are all over the house. Can you tell me why?'

Dylan said eagerly. Brian Stevenson brought his hands up to his face and rubbed it vigorously.

'What were you looking for?'

It was now or never.

'We have paper evidence that tells us you'd already taken large amounts of money from her. Does the jewellery that's been recovered – for the purpose of the tape, DS Spiers is showing Brian Stevenson the rings they recovered from the hotel room Mr Stevenson was arrested in earlier today – belong to her?'

Stevenson glanced at the rings on the desk in the plastic bags.

'Well, does it?' Dylan said impatiently.

'Multiple questions, Inspector,' Lin Perfect interrupted.

'Feel free to answer any of them, Mr Stevenson,' Dylan fired back. 'Start with your prints on her bedside drawers, eh?'

'I helped her look for things,' Stevenson stammered.

'What things?'

'All sorts of things,' he said obviously agitated.

'Like what?'

'Look, I was just about her only visitor, her only friend, so if she needed anything, I'd help.' Stevenson said.

'Friend? Is that what you call yourself?' Dylan stopped and checked himself before resuming the mask of the hardened detective. 'So, how did she get her head injury?' Dylan said in a quieter fashion.

Brian Stevenson shrugged his shoulders.

'Don't you see that's why you're sitting where you are? I think you should think very carefull about your situation, Brian.'

The room went silent. Dylan knew that neither Taylor nor he would break that silence. A minute passed. Dylan could almost see Brian Stevenson's brain working, considering his options. Stevenson looked sideways at Lin Perfect. She stared at him long and hard. It was the look of a parent to a child to behave, or else. She opened her mouth to speak and Dylan held his hand up to stop her. Stevenson turned to Dylan.

'When I called to see her, she had already fallen and hurt her head. She refused to let me get any medical attention for her. She was a stubborn old thing, just like my mother used to be,' he said with tears in his eyes. 'I went back to see her the next day to make sure she was alright and took her the flowers to cheer her up but she was already dead. I was shocked, shaken,' he swallowed, 'afraid I would get the blame. That's why I haven't said anything before. I was frightened, old people die in their homes all the time don't they? So I thought it was best to let her be found by someone else other than me.' Stevenson said. He stopped talking momentarily. 'There was nothing I could have done for her.'

Dylan and DS Taylor Spiers remained silent. The tape purred on. By remaining quiet and listening, Dylan hoped Stevenson would continue.

'She was undeniably dead. I was sure she was, otherwise I would have called for an ambulance,' he said, tears now rolling down his cheeks.

'Do you know where she'd fallen?' asked Dylan.

'I think she had fallen down the stairs,' he said, thinking aloud as he looked up at the ceiling and inhaled deeply. 'Yes,' he sniffed. 'I think that's what she said.'

'And you didn't push her?' Dylan said.

'No,' Stevenson said. 'No, I didn't push her.'

'You understand we've got to ask the question.'

'Yes, but I didn't,' Stevenson got a handkerchief out of his pocket and wiped his tearstained face.

'Okay, then. Now, do you remember the silver carriage clock that we asked you about earlier?' For a minute Brian Stevenson looked bewildered by the question. He physically shook himself. 'Yes, yes I do. It was stolen from my house. That clock was the reason I knew my house had been burgled.'

'If that's the case, why do we have a photograph of Mildred Sykes with that same clock behind her on her mantlepiece?'

Stevenson stared once more through the detectives and made no reply.

'And can you explain why Mildred Sykes's fingerprints are on that clock?'

Stevenson's face blanched, but he made no reply.

'Well?'

Dylan waited for a reply that never came. 'You robbed an old lady of her savings, her personal belongings and when you had bled her dry you battered her to death, didn't you?

Her injuries were not as a result of a fall, as you would have us believe, but as a direct result of being hit over the head with a ferocious blow by you. It was the same system you'd used on Grace Harvey and I wonder how many more old people? It was unfortunate for you, wasn't it, that Grace's death was around the same time that Mildred was found, so you had to think of getting away and had obtained another name.'

Brian Stevenson fidgeted for a moment, swivelled round on his chair and turned to face the other way.

'You can turn your back. You can remain silent. What you can't do is change the facts, which are that you befriended, robbed and beat to death a defenceless old lady. You're nothing but a greedy, evil man,' Dylan spat.

Suddenly Stevenson turned and opened his mouth, his eyes wide, his face contorted. Lin Perfect jumped up from her seat and moved quickly to DS Spiers' side. Stevenson threw his arms in the air. 'You know, nothing. They were nasty, bossy women, just like my mother and they expected everything from me, everything. Do you hear me?' His outburst stopped as suddenly as it had started and he sat down once, more facing the wall.

'I think we need to have a break, Inspector, please,' Lin Perfect said, holding up her notepad in a shaking hand. She stood at the door like a caged animal hoping to be let out of the room, quickly.

The interview was terminated.

'Donald Harvey was telling the truth,' Taylor said thoughtfully as she hurried behind Dylan on the corridor. 'I think I owe him one hell of an apology.'

That was the last thing on Dylan's mind as he went over what Stevenson had said – and, more importantly, what he hadn't said.

Chapter 50

Flashing blue lights could be seen and sirens heard as he arrived back in his office. A note was pinned to his desk. *Jen rang, can you ring her back,* it said. Dylan brushed it aside and picked up his mobile phone. There was a message.

☺ *Avril Summerfield-Preston left her calling card. I was out walking with Dawn and Violet trying to get little Button to make her appearance. Aren't I the lucky one? ☺ Speak soon. X.*

'Oh, I'm sure she'll catch up with you sooner or later, love,' he mumbled, as he tucked his phone in his pocket and smiled to himself.

'Lisa,' Dylan called. 'I need a team briefing and I need it ASAP.' Lisa pattered into the office with a pad and a pen in her hand. 'We need to discuss the results of the interview with Stevenson and speak about need for the extensive work that will have to be done now, in respect of other elderly women that have died or any that are still alive and on his books, with a view to linking them to him.'

Lisa nodded in agreement as she took the notes in shorthand.

'I need to identify the owners of the rings – and the only way to do that is if the relatives of the deceased, or his female clients who are lucky enough to still be alive, are able to help us. We'll need to find out the cause of death of any of his clients that have died.'

'That's not going to be easy, sir.'

'Not impossible though. The easiest way of course would be if he'd speak to us but that's unlikely based on his present behaviour and responses.'

Dylan stood before his team the next day. He was satisfied that Brian Stevenson had murdered Mildred Sykes after systematically stealing from her. He told them Stevenson had admitted being at her house, stating that he knew she was dead.

'The fingertip marks inside the silver carriage clock casing along with Mildred's are his, fingerprints have confirmed it,' Vicky said.

'Fantastic. We'll have another interview with him and then we'll charge him and get him remanded for Mildred's murder, which will allow us to continue our enquiries. Find out how his own mother died will you, Dennis?'

'I'm waiting for you to get stuck into him again, boss,' said Taylor. 'Shall I arrange for the solicitor to be ready in half an hour?' she said looking at her watch.

'Yeah,' said Dylan. John had arrived, looking suitably refreshed. Dylan put an arm around his shoulder and led him into his office, closing the door before Taylor could enter behind them.

'Going well then boss?' said John. Dylan nodded.

'At least we're going to be in a position to charge, whether he continues to speak to us or not. So far so good,' he sighed. 'But it would be nice if he bared his soul.'

There was a knock at the door. 'Ten minutes for the solicitor boss, I'm ready when you are,' Taylor said with a smile.

'In that case Taylor, any chance of some coffee?' he asked.

'I hope that won't spoil a celebratory drink later, sir,' she said.

John pored over the notes that Dylan had given him. Updating him as to what needed to be talked about in interview was important at this stage. The time was ticking away on Stevenson's custody clock and they needed as much information from Stevenson as possible before they charged him.

When she came back with the coffee, Dylan told Taylor that he had fully updated John, who would resume interviewing with her.

'Oh, okay,' Taylor said with disdain.

Dylan was trying not to dislike her. Visually the woman was attractive, but unfortunately her personality didn't match her looks. She was moody, he already knew that, but he didn't like the way she thought that men couldn't or wouldn't be able to resist her. She had a lot to learn if she was going to continue working with Dylan because at the moment she didn't know him at all.

He texted the only woman in his life. *Things going okay will be charging later so it could be a late one, don't wait up.*

'Boss, the blue lights, a short while ago,' said Vicky. 'They were speeding off to St Thomas' – a woman called on three nines about a bloke acting suspiciously in the graveyard. She'd been to put some flowers on her late husband's grave when she saw him taking flowers from the others.'

'And,' Dylan said.

'He had a knife in his hand.'

'She obviously got away.'

'Yes, but the description she gave our boys sounds like Wainstall.'

'I wonder if the flowers were white lilies?' said Vicky. 'God, a goose has just walked over my grave,' she continued, rubbing her arms. 'How weird is he, eh? Helicopter has been scrambled; dogs have been called for, but nothing yet.'

'He's one of the evil ones, Vicky, who needs to be back behind bars sooner rather than later.'

'The lady wasn't wrong; the town centre CCTV control room have informed Control they had sighted a man fitting Wainstall's description carrying a bunch of flowers and heading towards the subway from Crown Street which leads under the ring road to the Midland Road area. Units have been deployed.' Vicky said.

'There are four exits from that one, aren't there Vicky? One that takes you towards Pellon Lane as well as Gibbet Street, Crown Street and Silver Street?'

'You're probably right. I wouldn't know the street names.'

'Get us a radio switched on and we'll listen in to see what's happening.'

Vicky and Dylan sat quietly together in the CID office listening for developments. All units were in place with each exit covered, helicopter overhead and according to CCTV control he was still in there.'

'Like a rat in a drainpipe boss. They must have him, they must,' said Vicky

'What worries me Vicky is who else might be in there with him. He could have attacked someone or be attacking someone – and we have no way of knowing,' Dylan said, tapping his fingers on the desk. 'Come on, come on.' He picked up the phone. 'Control room, DI Dylan, regarding the incident in the subway. Can we get double crews to enter each entrance with care at the same time. I'm concerned that our suspect may have cornered someone in there.'

'Affirmative,' the officer replied.

'Vicky, get some car keys and grab that radio; we need to get down there.'

The phone rang. 'Boss, it's for you,' said Dennis covering the mouthpiece.

'I'm not here,' he replied.

'Do you want me with you boss? ' asked Taylor.

'No, crack on with Stevenson – we need him sorting. Hopefully it will be over by the time we get there.' Vicky appeared with a pickaxe handle from behind her desk.

'What the hell?' Dylan said.

'I know we've got CS spray and that boss, but I don't want Edward Scissorhands cutting me, especially across the bloody chest. My stab proof vest doesn't fit me anymore.'

Dylan tutted. 'Come on let's go.'

'But boss, Avril Summerfield-Preston wants to speak to you ...' Dennis mouthed the words to him so she couldn't overhear.

'If it's her, I'm long gone,' Dylan shouted as he strutted towards the door with Vicky in his wake.

Dylan's right hand was placed expertly on the steering wheel, while his left grasped the top of the pickaxe handle. 'Put that bloody pickaxe handle on the back seat will you before you take my eye out?' he said. She moaned.

Dylan looked at Vicky and they knew they shared the same thought. 'Hold on tight,' he said.

The nearest access for them was Pellon Lane.

'Stand off situation, sir,' said the uniformed officer as they alighted from the car. 'Our man has a lady at knifepoint and is threatening to slit her throat.

'I knew it. Don't take his threats lightly, he'll do what he says,' said Dylan, gravely.

As Dylan and Vicky strode down the subway, all Dylan could hear were their own footsteps and the echo of a dog barking which seemed to him as if it was bouncing off the cold, damp, tiled walls.

Chapter 51

'You still got that pickaxe handle, Vicky?'

'Right here boss, up my sleeve,' Vicky said.

Dylan smiled despite the dire situation. He could see before him a large black Alsatian straining at the end of a leash held by a dog handler as they turned the corner of the underground tunnel.

'You better get the handle out. It might give the dog something to chew on,' Dylan grimaced.

'Thought you liked dogs?' she whispered out of the corner of her mouth as she let the wood slip down the sleeve of her coat and into her hand.

'I do, but not attached to my leg.'

A group of officers stood in their line of sight. Shouting could be heard.

'Let her go now. Do it now. Let her go!'

Dylan could see the backs of the uniformed personnel who wore stab-proof vests and slash-proof gloves. They were standing in an arch, each about ten yards from Wainstall. A couple of the officers brandished their batons were holding CS spray in their outstretched hands, but Dylan's attention was drawn to the terrified look on the lady's face.

It was apparent that Wainstall was holding her up by her hair in his left hand and Dylan could see he had a large bladed knife in his right hand, pointed at her throat. His eyes were dark and dead, like a shark's eyes. He towered over his hostage who was ashen-faced and gasping for breath. Wainstall didn't look like a man who had an ounce of compassion in him as he taunted the police with all the arrogance of the victor.

'Come on,' he growled, brandishing his muscles. His lips curled tightly over his clenched teeth. 'Come on then. Come near me copper and I'll cut her fucking throat.'

'My God,' Vicky said, her lip trembling and her voice shaking. The reality of the situation hit home with a force she hadn't felt before.

Dylan realised at that moment that he was the most senior police officer present and therefore in charge of the scene. The officers in attendance would expect him to take control.

'I need a firearms unit immediately,' he told a uniformed officer.

'At least then there'll be an option of taking him out if he makes a move to use the weapon on her,' he whispered to Vicky. 'Get me an ambulance on standby. The poor woman will already be in shock – and who knows who else will need it yet,' he said. Vicky nodded her head.

'Step further away and to try silence that dog will you,' Dylan told the dog handler in a hushed tone. 'Take a few paces back, lower your batons and put your CS gas away,' he told the officers with a calm, controlled and quiet voice.

'Give me two full-length riot shields,' he ordered. Now everything was urgent and Dylan was pleased his commands were being obeyed immediately and without question. Wainstall, Dylan knew, enjoyed using the knife and Dylan was aware that he could do so again, at any moment.

Fortunately, the shields were in the police transit van at the mouth of the subway. Dylan breathed a sigh of relief at the sight of the officer carrying them down the tunnel towards him. He didn't know how long he could hold Wainstall's attention.

Taking the two officers with the shields to one side, he told them of his plan, which he tried to keep as near to a well-rehearsed public order training exercise as he could.

'Flatten the armed man against the wall with the shields,' he said. 'Ensure the arm holding the weapon is outside the shields so he can be disarmed.'

'Vicky, I want you to look after the victim once we've got her released. I'm going to try to negotiate the release of the lady, then you'll have a chance with the shields to try and contain him – and if that doesn't work, well we'll have to use the firearms,' he said. 'It's a life and death situation. Try to stay calm at all times.'

Dylan moved forward, between the two shielded officers, to within a couple of yards of Wainstall and his captive and with his outstretched hand he grabbed the wooden pickaxe handle Vicky was holding.

'How the hell do you negotiate with someone hell-bent on killing?' he mumbled giving her a fleeting look. He needed to try, quickly, for the sake of the poor hostage.

'Frederick, Frederick Wainstall what're you doing? Let her go immediately,' Dylan shouted with an authority that he believed Wainstall would be used to responding to.

Wainstall had a fixed smile upon his face as he looked towards Dylan.

'What're you doing? You don't know this lady, do you? Let go of her now,' Dylan continued. Wainstall didn't move, just gripped the knife tighter and raised his arm as though to stab, as opposed to slash, his prey. There was an intake of breath and the woman appeared to moan and flop to the floor. Wainstall's arm jolted – and if he hadn't been holding her up by the hair before, he definitely was now.

Dylan could hear the sound of running footsteps behind him, which he knew would be the instant response firearms team. He knew Vicky would brief them and they would get themselves into a position to be able to fire, if required.

It wasn't long before Dylan saw the red dot of the laser sight from a firearm on Wainstall's forehead. Dylan exhaled – that reassured him. They were not only in position, but he and the other two officers were not blocking their view.

'Wainstall.' Dylan shouted again, with vigour. 'Stop this at once. Can I call you Frederick, or would you rather I call you Fred?' he tried a different approach. At least while he was listening to Dylan, he wasn't using the knife.

'You can call me Mr Fred,' he said, to Dylan's surprise.

'Mr Fred, could you please let the lady go? You don't need to hurt her. Look how frightened she is. The poor woman has fainted,' Dylan said.

'No way. You'll beat me. When I've got a knife nobody beats me or makes fun of me. Nobody,' he shouted, his voice rising into a scream.

'But the lady hasn't made fun of you or beat you, has she?'

'No, but she looks like my aunt – and she did,' he snarled, pulling her head back so he could see her face. 'She always beat me, till I got a knife.'

'What about the boy in the street, Mr Fred? He didn't.'

'Kids do. All kids. They make fun of me, but not when I have a knife,' he snarled.

'I'm worried. He's agitated. Be ready to react,' Dylan whispered to the officers by his side. 'Pass it back to the firearms team to keep flashing the red dot in his eye. Here goes.'

'Do I make you angry Frederick?' Dylan said. Purposely, he didn't call him Mr Fred, the name he had elected to be called. He could see the red laser dot flashing across Wainstall's eye and he knew it was annoying him, much to Dylan's delight.

'It's Mr Fred to you,' Wainstall screeched.

'But, I don't want to call you Mr Fred,' Dylan said.

'You're fucking annoying me,' Wainstall shouted, lifting his right arm with the knife above his head once more in a threatening manner.

'I don't make you angry, you're just an angry man,' Dylan shouted back.

Wainstall's hair fell over his face and he tossed his head back. He let go of his victim's hair momentarily to rub his left eye and she fell on her knees to the floor. Wainstall went to grab her.

'Now.' shouted Dylan at the top of his voice as he surged forward with the two officers who held the shields. Vicky threw herself across the tiled floor to snatch the old lady, dragging her sideways and shielding her as best she could with her body.

Wainstall was squashed against the subway wall with the shields like a pressed flower. Dylan's reach with the pickaxe handle landed straight on top of Wainstall's head. The knife fell from his hand. The push behind the front three officers made their advance feel like Dylan was in a rugby scrum. Wainstall had been well and truly taken by surprise.

The knife was picked up off the floor, out of Wainstall's reach. Dylan stepped back to take a breath as the officers with the riot shields grappled with him on the floor. Wainstall kicked out like a mule, but he was outnumbered. His wrists were handcuffed and his legs bound. He wriggled with all the strength he could muster, trying to bite the officers who carried him out of the subway.

His piercing, sadistic laughter echoed through the tunnel and up and out of each exit with the breeze that emanated from the underground. As he was carried up the steps and into the sunlight Dylan could hear his voice and that of the officer shouting at him fading away.

All that was left in the tunnel were the whimpering sounds of the poor soul he had petrified. Dylan saw the elderly lady sat with her head bent as far as she could between her knees. Tears streamed down her face and she gasped silent sobs. Her back was safely against the subway wall, the contents of the handbag strewn across the floor.

'Are you okay?' Dylan said gently as he bent down to her. She shook her head and her moan filled the air as she leaned her head back against the cold tiled wall. Vicky sat alongside her and held her tightly.

'Just shocked, I think boss,' she said reassuringly. 'That was a close call.' Vicky let out a huge sigh and moved her hand to rub the lady's back reassuringly as she leaned forward once more. The paramedics arrived and lifted her to her feet. Slowly and reassuringly they walked her to the waiting ambulance. Around them, officers scurried quietly and efficiently collecting the contents of the lady's shopping bag.

'Could someone go with her?' Dylan asked. 'Ensure her family are contacted will you and arrange to take a statement from her,' he said.

A paramedic lifted Dylan's hand. Blood dripped from his fingers.

'Ouch,' he said as he pulled it away.

'Nothing broke,' she smiled as she wiggled his fingers, 'but it's a nasty cut ...' she said. 'If it still hurts when the swelling's gone down,' she told him, 'then it might need an x-ray.'

'You'll never hear the end of it from Dennis, boss,' Vicky said with a relieved laugh.

'You've obviously recovered from the shock of it all,' Dylan said wincing as the paramedic tied on the bandage.

The local press had been at the subway's mouth taking pictures of Wainstall as he was carried out. They waited patiently to speak to Dylan.

'He's an extremely violent man who didn't want to be arrested. I'll update you later,' he said. 'Yes, before you go to print,' he promised.

Dylan walked towards the team who were gathered beside the marked cars. 'Thank you,' he said, to the staff who had held the shields for him, and the firearms team.

There was a female stood at the fore that looked too young to be a police officer, let alone carrying a firearm. He was getting old, he conceded for the umpteenth time lately. He had nothing but respect for them. The intense training they did, their individual and team restraint they showed in life threatening situations such as this was admirable.

Dylan considered himself quite a calm individual but with a firearm in his hand he could think of many occasions in his career when he would have used it.

'Vicky,' he shouted. She looked toward him as she stood at the open ambulance doors. 'Back to the nick please. I think we deserve a strong cup of coffee,' Dylan said as he climbed into his car.

'If he'd gone to stab her, boss, do you think firearms would have shot him?' asked Vicky as she unceremoniously hurled herself into the passenger seat. 'Hey, you okay to drive?' she continued, without waiting for an answer.

Dylan shook his head. 'Of course. That's what they're there for Vicky, and I wouldn't have expected much of his head left if they have done.'

'Urgh,' she shuddered. 'That's gross. Can't you just take me on a nice quiet enquiry next time,' she asked.

'In this job?' he said raising his voice. He was quiet as they drove into the station yard.

'Tell you what,' Vicky said. Dylan looked across at his passenger with a raised eyebrow. 'It's gonna be fun interviewing him though in't it?' she said.

'I hadn't thought about that,' said Dylan.

'Well you better have. He's like Mr Evil, never mind Mr Fred,' she said. 'He puts the willies up me.'

Dylan looked at her with both eyebrows raised this time as he put the car into reverse and negotiated his way into his parking space.

'You know what I mean,' she chuckled, slapping his arm playfully.

'Hey, look out – I'm injured,' he wailed.

'Serves you right.'

'What? I never said anything?' he said.

'Maybe not, but all you blokes are all alike. I know what you're thinking.'

'We're not all the same – far from it? Look at Mr Fred'.

'Yeah, but he's sorted now.'

'Not quite, but think how many lives as he's ruined in his life, so far? And fortunately the subway arrest worked out well, otherwise we could have had more bodies to deal with,' Dylan said.

'Not with you in charge, boss,' she smiled.

'It doesn't matter who's in charge, Vicky. When the negotiation technique works everything is fine, however when it doesn't the proverbial shit hits the fan, no matter what.'

'I can think of some bosses who would still be considering whether or not to send anyone into the subway. Believe me, there's nothing worse than being stood around in a group waiting for a decision to be made,' said Vicky.

'If you don't like it, you know what to do.'

'I know, take my bloody sergeant's exam.'

'Yes, and then you can make those decisions. You don't have to be in uniform long before you can come back into CID.'

'You're right boss, as usual.'

A knock came at the window. Dylan wound it down. 'John and Taylor are in interview with Stevenson, sir,' said Lisa. 'The monitor in your office is on for you to watch.'

'Be right with you.' Dylan said, hurriedly getting out of the car.

Chapter 52

Dylan headed straight to his office; if he'd still been a smoker then the trail he'd have left in his wake would have resembled a smoking chimney. As it was, he had to be satisfied with a mouthful of chewing gum.

He knew how fortunate the woman in the tunnel had been. He didn't know how he would have felt if Wainstall had slashed her throat or the firearms team had taken off his head. Would he have felt like a failure? Would an investigation into the events have blamed him? Would the scenario be used as an example at training schools nationwide of how not to negotiate with a man with a knife? He shook his head to clear the paranoid, spiralling thoughts.

Stevenson sat in the interview room with his back to his interviewers.

Dylan could tell by DS Taylor Spiers and DS John Benjamin's faces that they weren't fazed by Brian Stevenson's actions, and after the formal introductions, they followed the structured interview plan. Systematically, they went through each item they had seized from his hotel room. This needed to be done to show the court at a later date that they had given him every opportunity to give an explanation as to how the jewellery had come into his possession.

'Is one or more of these rings Mildred's?' asked Taylor.

Stevenson stared at the blank wall.

'Is that why she wasn't wearing any rings when her body was found?' asked John.

Stevenson looked mannequin like as he sat perfectly still and made no comment.

'Was she sat with her back to you when you smashed her skull in? Is that what you do when the people you prey on no longer have anything to give?' John said.

Stevenson made no comment but his shoulders rose and then dropped as he sighed, as if he was bored.

'Are you sat with your back to us as a protest against the interviews or is it simply that you don't like to face up to what you've done?' Taylor said, with venom in her voice.

Stevenson swiftly turned, which made Taylor flinch. His eyes were bright and Dylan saw he took confidence from her reaction to his movement.

'If you've got all the answers, why don't you charge me?' he said with a sneer.

'Hardly the response of an innocent man, is it?' John said.

He turned away from them very slowly and was silent.

'Damn,' Dylan said through gritted teeth.

'Never been married have you?' said Taylor.

He didn't respond. Dylan could see the muscles in his neck tense. She continued the line of questioning.

'Do you have some sort of fetish for elderly women, Mr Stevenson?'

Stevenson took a deep breath. Dylan saw Taylor steel herself for a reaction that never came.

'Well, I don't see many men's names on the list of your clients. Neither are there any men's rings in this hoard of jewellery. Is there a sexual motive to your crimes? Is the theft of property to hide a more deviant side of your nature, Mr Stevenson?'

The room was quiet. Neither interviewer spoke for at least a minute.

'I'm sure an innocent man would be protesting,' John said at last.

Dylan could see Stevenson hunch his shoulders and it reminded him of a cat that was ready to pounce.

'Steady now, steady... wait for his reaction,' Dylan mumbled.

'Was Mildred's murder sexual, Mr Stevenson?' Taylor said swiftly.

The questions were like darts piercing Stevenson's back and Dylan could tell he was feeling every single one. He turned to face the officers. 'One last time, she fell. She just fell. How many times do I have to tell you?'

'Right, she fell,' said John.

There was another pause, 'I admit I stole some bits from her, but I found her dead at the bottom of the stairs. I never touched her.'

Dylan's skin tingled and he could feel his blood pumping through his veins. It was the breakthrough they were waiting for. The detectives never once let their professional mask slip.

'You know that's not true Mr Stevenson. Her injuries are not consistent with a fall. Why are you avoiding the question of sex?' Taylor said, pushing the boundaries.

'I have to challenge your line of questioning, officer. There has been no disclosure of any sexual assault or any suggestion of such to me,' said his solicitor, Lin Perfect.

'Yes you're right. I'm simply trying to understand why the majority of Mr Stevenson's clients are female and elderly,' responded Taylor contritely.

'Don't make me out to be a pervert,' Brian Stevenson said. 'You have no proof of that and I have nothing else to say,' he said with a new-found authority in his voice.

Taylor and John tried to question him further but it was obvious that he was not going to speak to them anymore. Dylan ran a hand through his hair, sat back in his chair and forced the expelling air out of his lungs. The interview was terminated and Brian Stevenson could be seen on Dylan's monitor being escorted out of the interview room on his way back to the custody suite to be charged. He made no comment.

'There's no way he's gonna make our job easy is there?' John mumbled to Taylor as they walked into Dylan's office.

'No, and I'm sure Mildred isn't his only victim,' Dylan said.

'At least we have him in custody, we just need to prove the charge now and focus on the file for the murder of Mildred Sykes to get him convicted and sentenced to life. He can always be brought back before the court if there were other charges proved afterwards.'

The incident room was buzzing. It was late. 'We off for a drink?' Taylor asked.

Lisa picked up the ringing phone. Her already tired face paled. 'Stevenson slashed his wrists in his cell, there's an ambulance en route,' she said.

'What?' John said. 'I thought he was being watched? The boss is gonna go ape,' he said as he turned towards Dylan's office, where he could see his boss in animated discussions with someone on the phone.

'The wanker. That'll cause an internal investigation, overseen by the independent body, which will be more of a priority than the bloody murder,' John groaned into his hands.

'He may have just realised that he was looking at life inside,' she said. 'How serious is it? Do we know?' Taylor asked Lisa.

'No,' she said, biting her lip.

'It's ironic isn't it; the amount of people that will be scrambling to save a murderer's life now,' Vicky said.

'And they'll probably save him? Only the good die young, don't they say?' Taylor added.

'We'll be alright then,' Vicky said, looking at Taylor in a different light. 'I'm going to the cells. I want to know what's happening. You coming?'

'They won't tell you anything,' said Taylor.

'No, but I want to know if the bastard's going to live or die.'

'I'd better go break the news to the boss,' John grimaced.

Chapter 53

'Coffee, Boss?'

Dylan lifted his head from within his arms on the desk as John walked into his office, his hand wrapped round a mug of coffee. 'You're gonna need this,' he said, pulling a face as he placed the drink in front of him.

'Now what's happened?' Dylan groaned. He could hear Vicky's loud raucous voice outside. He smiled weakly. You should be like the cats that got the cream.'

'We were.'

'Were? What's the bloody problem, it can't be that bad, surely?' he said, the smile on his face fading.

Taylor knocked at the door, opened it and rushed in. Her face was flushed. 'He slashed his wrists,' she said, flopping down in the only vacant chair in the office.

'What, how?' Dylan demanded. 'With what; I thought he was on suicide watch?' Dylan's face paled at the look on her face. 'How bad is he?' he continued.

Dylan and John looked at Taylor for the answers.

'With a paper clip, believe it or not, the cells think he might have taken it from his solicitor's paperwork'.

'So has he been treated and is he back in the cells?'

'Yes. The wounds are superficial. Although there was a lot of blood it was a half-hearted attempt according to the staff downstairs.'

'So what's up then?'

'We thought,' John said, meekly ' you'd be fuming that a potential serial killer might have taken his secrets to the grave with him.'

'Fate and luck always play a part in this game, you should know that by now. Come on you two,' he smiled at their serious faces and his normal pallor returned. 'I think we all deserve a drink, don't you?' The pair smiled, tiredly. 'Let's just find out what's happening to Wainstall first.'

The sight of relief on their faces told Dylan how much the case meant to them. At one time he would have gone mad, they were right to be concerned about telling him. Was he going soft in his old age?

Dylan picked up the phone and spoke to the Custody Sergeant regarding Frederick Wainstall.

'Boss, he's loopy if you want my opinion,' he said. 'He's like a bloody animal. So much so, that I've had to call in the doctor to confirm that he's fit to detain and check his fitness to interview. For the time being I'm keeping him handcuffed.'

'Safest way,' Dylan grinned. 'That'll keep you on your toes for a few hours. He's been deemed fit on both counts previously, but he's no stranger to being locked up so he might just be playing the game. Let's hope this time he's locked up once and for all.'

'We'll see what the doc says.'

'I'm going to arrange for him to be interviewed tomorrow morning. Give me a call will you, when the doctor's been?'

'Will do boss. By the way before you go; he had a mobile phone on him and some bits of paper, and flowers, of all things, stuffed in his pockets. DC Hardacre has just been down for them and taken them away.'

'Thanks Sarge,' he said as he heard Vicky's dulcet tones in the CID office outside.

'Whose mobile is it then? Let me guess Denton's?' Dylan called out.

'Well it's a Nokia sir, like Denton's,' she said. 'How good would that be if it was? Battery's flat,' she said, screwing up her face.

'Handle it with kid gloves and get it checked for fingerprints on the inside, battery, sim card. The database should confirm it for us one way or another,' said Dylan.

Vicky stood by Dylan's open door.

'Take it to the technical unit. By early tomorrow morning we should get a result.'

Vicky turned to obey his instructions. 'On second thoughts, get a motorcyclist from traffic to do it. You look all in.'

'Yes, sir.' she said.

'Right enough,' he said as he stretched. 'Give me half an hour to get the policy logs and reports done and I'll meet you in the bar for a swift one, eh?'

The office emptied as, one by one, the team headed for the pub. He noticed the jaded look on their faces when he caught up with them. They'd had two good lock ups – but the journey was far from over and they knew it. Dylan ordered a drink from the bar and when he turned, Taylor was behind him.

'How many have you had?' he asked her. She stumbled towards him and into a table. He pulled her to her feet and steadied her. She leaned against him.

'I've still got that bottle of wine in my fridge with your name on it, sir,' she said. 'If you want to take me home, sir?' she slurred.

Dylan sat her down on a chair, brushed the front of his suit jacket and looked around him.

'Oh, don't be such a prude,' she said, her arms flying high above her head. 'You'll weaken. They all do eventually,' she whispered, in her drunken state.

Dylan leaned down to her. 'Taylor, let me assure you, I won't,' he said.

'Oh, yes you will,' she said, raising her voice. 'You really will,' she giggled putting a finger to her lips.

Dylan leaned towards her and she leaned forward to hear him, her eyes glazed. 'Taylor, once and for all fuck off and pester someone else will you. It's never going to happen,' he said.

She jumped away. 'Assault,' she shouted, at the top of her voice. 'Just because you're a boss,' she slurred, 'doesn't give you the right to grope me,' she said, slamming her glass on the table and leaning heavily on the wall she made her way out of the bar.

'Take her home Vicky, will you?' he said.

All was quiet. Dylan looked around him. He could feel a hot flush rising in his body and his hands felt clammy and warm around his cool glass. He would expect an apology from her tomorrow and he would deal with her outburst then. He put his drink down on the table and walked from the room. Things were going well for him. The last thing he wanted now was an immature female alleging he had assaulted her. Neither he, nor his team, needed the diversion.

He headed home. He was too tired to celebrate and needed the comfort of Jen's arms around him. Lying in bed next to her he told her about the day's events. As expected she told him off for going near a madman and advised him to make sure he dealt with Taylor properly. There was no room for trust with the woman, in her eyes.

'Why would she do that?' Dylan asked.

Jen shook her head. Dylan was really naive where women were concerned.

'Women's intuition,' she smiled. 'You'll ignore my advice at your peril,' she warned.

Dylan was asleep but Jen laid next to him awake for long into the night wondering how someone like Taylor Spiers would do such a thing. She knew that Jack Dylan was far from the type of man to grope a woman.

She was angry and her anger made her restless. Her legs involuntarily jumped and she pushed them out from under the covers. She couldn't lie on her back any more because of the size of her stomach and it was even becoming uncomfortable to lie on her side even with a pillow beneath the bump and in between her knees. No matter how much she was enjoying pregnancy, she now wanted it over. Eventually she dropped into a deep sleep.

Chapter 54

Dylan shared an early breakfast with Jen. It was warm and the air humid. The sun hadn't burnt through the morning mist but it was certain to be a hot day. He kissed Jen goodbye, patted her stomach lovingly, picked up his briefcase and walked towards the front door. Max followed.

'Not this time fella,' Jen heard him say and she knew Max understood he was going without him. Jen stood at the sink watching the bamboo fountain. It had such a calming effect on her and she couldn't wait to sit out on the patio with Buttons in her pram.

All of a sudden she felt a stabbing pain in the region of her bladder. Not an unfamiliar pain when Buttons was feet down but now she knew the baby's head was engaged it alarmed her. She turned and headed to the bathroom. One thing she wouldn't miss when Buttons was born was nipping to the loo so often, she sighed, using the handrail as she dragged herself up the stairs.

'These steps get steeper every day, I swear,' she groaned to Max. As she reached the top a cramp hit her and she clenched her stomach. Water started trickling down her legs. She turned to grab a towel from the airing cupboard – and as she leaned backwards to open the door she fell backwards with a crash.

The hot, humid air hit Dylan as he opened the car door and he stood still for a moment. He took off his jacket and threw it over to the back seat and glanced at the lounge window before he got inside. He opened the car windows and mopped his brow with his hanky before he turned the engine on.

Avril Summerfield-Preston's car stopped to allow Dylan to enter the police yard. 'Where's that interfering old bat going so early in the morning,' he muttered to himself. He didn't bother to wave.

The CID office was quiet and he switched on the lights and unlocked his office door, leaving it open to allow air to circulate.

Picking up his phone immediately he sat down behind his desk, he called the cells to find that Frederick Wainstall had been deemed fit to be detained by the force medical officer and had settled down to sleep through the night in his air-conditioned cell. Lucky bugger, Dylan thought as he tugged at his tie and opened the top button of his shirt.

'He's been a model prisoner,' the detention officer said. It never ceased to amaze Dylan that when some aggressive offenders were finally imprisoned they were calm and rational, but Dylan imagined that being institutionalised meant normality to some people.

'The prisoner has also been deemed fit to be interviewed, as long as a responsible adult is present along with his solicitor, sir,' the detention officer continued.

Dylan looked up from the paperwork on his desk and saw Taylor standing before him. He pointed to the chair opposite, inviting her to sit while he finished his phone call. From the glance he'd given her he couldn't read the expression on her face.

He could hear the team beginning to arrive in the CID office outside his own and he was pleased that she'd left the door ajar. Dylan put down the phone purposely slowly and brought his hands together on the desk before looking across at her.

'Your outburst in the bar last night was uncalled for and totally unacceptable,' Dylan said in a calm, controlled voice. 'Do I make myself clear?' He continued, his voice rising. Taylor sat with her head bowed, which reminded Dylan of a naughty schoolgirl.

'I'm sorry, sir it won't happen again,' Taylor mumbled into her chest.

'You can be sure it won't. And if it does, I'll take it further. Do you hear?'

'Yes,' she said in her strangled girly voice.

'Right, get round to the court this morning with John and make sure the remand for Stevenson goes smoothly,' he said shuffling his paperwork. 'Any problems, ring me.' Dylan didn't look up but dismissed her as he picked up his pen and continued with the work set out before him.

'Yes, sir,' she whispered and walked out of the room. It was important to Dylan that the team moved forward without distraction. Banter he could accept; lies he wouldn't.

'Coffee for our hero?' Lisa hollered from his doorway. She still had her cardigan and handbag thrown over her arm. Dylan fleetingly looked into her open smiling face.

'Love one, thanks,' he said gratefully.

'We could do with you in every subway,' she laughed as she turned, pulled out her chair from under her desk and unlocked her drawer. 'The Council thinks they're great those subways but nobody dare use the bloody things, they daren't,' she said, talking to him over her shoulder. 'Toast anyone?' she asked.

Dylan stood up and got a five-pound note out of his pocket. 'Here, get toast for the office out of this and keep the rest for the tea fund,' he said.

'Thank you, sir,' she said walking into his office briefly to collect the money from his desk. 'You sure?'

'Certain, coffee and toast might just about get me through the day,' he said with a smile that didn't reach his eyes.

'That bad eh?' Vicky said, as she passed Lisa on the way out. 'I hope Taylor apologised.'

'Yeah, she did,' he sighed, as he picked a piece of paper out of the fax machine that was on his desk and scanned the text with his eyes.

'It is Denton's mobile,' she said, taking a seat.

Dylan's face lit up and his eyes found hers. 'Yeah?'

'Yeah, and it still has pictures of Pam Forrester on it.'

'Tremendous.' Dylan said, bowing his head into his hands as if to pray. 'We now want some forensics on Wainstall's clothing. His shoes must be a favourite. We need just enough to nail him. Get the interview arranged for as soon as possible. Probation are sending someone over to act as the responsible adult,' Dylan said, lifting the fax that told him so.

'Top man,' she grinned.

'Sergeant Wilson?'

'Yeah,' she grinned.

'I'll ask Wainstall about the most recent events first. It'll make it easier for him to follow, hopefully.'

'Okey, doke.' she said as she walked from the room. She stopped and turned. 'Guess what?' she said.

'What?'

'I've got a date.'

'The Sarge?'

'Yes,' she smiled.

Avril Summerfield-Preston knocked at the brightly painted red door. There was no reply. Jen's car was in the driveway and the dog was barking so she must be home, she thought. She stood for a while and listened. There was no movement from within other than a constant yelp from the dog. Perhaps he was trapped?

She walked to the gate at the side of the house and tried the handle. It was locked from the other side. She reached over the top of the panels and her fingers traversed the wood. She stopped. There was a bolt. She hesitated. No, the last thing she wanted was an angry Dylan at her door – she'd been at the sharp end of his tongue before.

She walked away from the house and opened her car door. She saw the dog jumping up at the lounge window furiously leaping on the furniture within. He wasn't trapped then. But where was Jen?

Wainstall sat smiling at Dylan in his white, cotton, prisoner issue coverall in between his probation officer and solicitor. The interview room was for once a pleasant place to be as the air conditioning blew down on Dylan's face and he felt more comfortable than he had done all morning.

He and Vicky had spoken to Wainstall's solicitor and probation officer prior to coming into the room and they in turn had spoken to Wainstall so the charge didn't come as a surprise in the interview due to his delicate state of mind. After formal introductions and ensuring Wainstall's understood the charge, Dylan began.

'Apart from being arrested for kidnap, threats to kill, possessing an offensive weapon and wounding; you are also under arrest for the murders of two young men, namely a Danny Denton and a Billy Greenwood. Yesterday, you held a woman at knife-point in the subway didn't you?'

'Yes, I'd collected flowers,' he smiled around at them all.

'Were you going to hurt the lady?' asked Dylan slowly and clearly.

'Yes, and you hit me, didn't you?'

'I did, but not with a knife.'

'I like knives,' he replied. Yvonne Best, his solicitor, looked at him wide eyed. His probation officer didn't flinch.

'Were you going to hurt the lady with the knife? Were you going to stab her?' Dylan asked.

'Yes, and when she died I could give her the flowers.'

Vicky remained quiet.

'There was a boy in town. You stabbed him in the back too, do you remember?'

Wainstall looked thoughtful but didn't answer.

'Why? What had he done to you?'

'Boys are bad, they laugh at me,' Wainstall scowled.

'When you were arrested and brought here, you had a mobile telephone in your pocket that wasn't yours. It belonged to a man who was killed in his flat and his friend was stabbed there too when he was in bed. Do you understand what I'm telling you?' asked Dylan.

'I took their phone after I'd stabbed them, and stabbed them, and stabbed them,' Wainstall said. His arm rose and fell as though he was carrying out the act. 'Dead, they can have flowers, lots of flowers,' he said.

'What's your favourite flower?'

'White lilies,' he said in a song-like fashion.

'Why white lilies?'

'Because you give people them when they die, my mother told me,' he said matter of factly. 'Death. That's what they mean, so that's what I do.' Wainstall started laughing. His laugh became frenzied and Dylan decided that he would have to end the interview. Wainstall was taken back to his cell.

'Mrs Best, Mr Hirst,' Dylan spoke across the table inside the interview room. 'Do you really think that your client is fit to interview?'

'According to the medical practitioner he is,' said Yvonne Best. 'Don't be fooled by his actions, Mr Dylan,' she said with a shake of her head. 'I've known this man a long time, and believe me, he is good at playing the dunce when he wants to. I'm satisfied he's fit to interview.'

Avril walked back to the gate and took the bolt off. The gate opened easily and she pushed it open wide enough to pass through. This side of the house was free from the sun and the flagged area was dark and cold. She stopped at the end of the path and listened. As she entered the back garden she walked into a different world and the warm sunlight gave her a renewed confidence. The back door was open and she could hear the washing machine spinning merrily away. Breakfast hadn't been cleared away she noticed and the tea towel Jen had been using was lying on the floor by the door into the hallway.

'Jen?' she called. The dog yelped. 'Jen' she called again as she went into the hallway. The noise from the dog was coming from upstairs. With trepidation she walked to the foot of the stairs. At the top she saw the dog standing, yelping. His tailed wagged furiously but he didn't attempt to come down.

'Jen,' she called once more. She stopped to listen. Should she go? She tiptoed up one step then two. Max hopped from foot to foot but still he made no attempt to come towards her. Then she saw it. Jen's blonde hair was draped on the floor of the landing and flowed onto the top step. Avril rushed up the stairs. Jen moaned and tried to move.

'Oh, my God,' Avril said as her hand flew to her mouth.

Trembling from head to foot, she reached out to Jen's pale face. She was warm to her touch.

'My waters,' Jen said in a laboured voice, without opening her eyes. Avril was already dialling for an ambulance.

The monitor showed that the baby was fine but Jen wasn't having contractions of note. 'I suppose a water birth is out of the question now?' Jen said to Avril who was smiling down at her. She'd never seen Avril so at ease before as she held her hand. She was pretty when she smiled.

'I think because of the risk of infection that is most definitely not on the cards now,' the doctor said kindly. 'We'll start you off with a hormone pessary to soften the cervix but you can only have one because your waters have broken – as you will probably have guessed.'

'Am I in labour?' Jen asked.

'Yes dear, you won't be going home now until after the birth,' he said, patting her arm tenderly. 'I want to put a hormone drip into your arm in a while, so you're going to be wired up and you'll have to stay in bed then.' He walked from the room.

Jen turned to Avril. 'Jack? Please will you try to get hold of Jack for me?'

'Of course,' she said, reassuringly. 'If he answers my calls, that is,' she said.

'I know you two don't get on, but Avril, thank you,' said Jen. 'I don't know what I would have done without you.'

Avril shook her head, and Jen could see that she was embarrassed.

'Why did you come out to see me this morning?'

'Oh, nothing for you to worry about, just a personnel check and to bring you a gift for the baby,' she said. 'Look, let me get Jack for you.'

'Avril?'

'I can't have children Jen. I know you think I'm a cranky old thing,' she smiled, nervously. 'But my work is all I've got. I'll never have what you and Jack have.'

'But Hugo?'

'Hugo only thinks about himself, Jen. He is far too selfish to want children,' she sighed. 'But at least he won't leave me.'

'Well, I can never thank you enough – and, believe me, Jack will be just as grateful.'

Avril raised an eyebrow.

Jen smiled. 'You should get to know each other, you're both as stubborn as each other.' she said. 'Oh Lord I think that's another contraction.'

Questions were being put to Frederick Wainstall thick and fast in the second interview but he didn't tell them any more than they already knew and Dylan knew the interviews were going nowhere. With a heavy heart and a banging headache Dylan reached into his pocket for his handkerchief. His phone vibrated. Damn, he should have turned it off and he did so immediately with an apologetic nod.

Dylan reached for the paracetamol as soon as they got back to the office. Vicky slumped in her chair in the CID office, both were exhausted.

Lisa took the call that came into the office. 'Wainstall's shoes have tested positive for blood and the wooden handle knife recovered from the bin did too,' she said. Dylan breathed a sigh of relief. Forensics would in due course identify whose blood it was. 'Another positive indication sir, is that the initial comparisons showed the piece of metal recovered from Greenwood's body appeared to match the knife blade in a perfect fit.'

'You're required at the hospital, sir,' shouted Vicky. 'Jen's gone into labour.'

Dylan's head was in a spin. Did he have time to charge? No, there was too much paperwork remaining to do.

'Get a pen, Vicky. I want you to charge him for me. Nothing is going to stop me from seeing Buttons born,' he grinned, his face aglow.

'Buttons?' she said.

'Oh, yeah, the baby's name we've given her, you know,' he said with a flush to his cheeks.

'You, big old softie,' she teased.

'Just charge him, will you. Attempted murder, murder, threats to kill and then charge him with the double murders in a week's time if I'm not back.' Dylan grabbed his keys and ran to his car. Vicky followed him.

Grace and Winston had been knocked down and a catalogue of events had followed in which Denton and Greenwood had been the catalyst – but right now he was going to see the start of a life for a change.

Jen was in agony and Avril Summerfield-Preston was right by her side.

'What the hell are you doing here?' Dylan asked.

'Jack, don't. If it hadn't been for Avril I would still be laying on the floor at home. She got an ambulance… please. Argh,' she cried out.

'But why?'

'I bought you a present for the baby. Is that okay?' Avril said, with tears in her eyes. 'And further to your belief that I don't earn my salary I do follow my job description to your annoyance to the letter and Jen was due a visit.'

Jen squeezed Jack's hand tightly and started panting furiously. 'Oh, no, another … argh,' she screamed again.

'I think my job here is done and I wish you both well,' she said.

'She's six centimetres dilated,' the nurse told the doctor.

Jen shook uncontrollably. 'I'm freezing,' she said to Dylan through chattering teeth.

'Her temperature's shot up to 39.8,' the nurse continued in her assessment as she wrote on the chart hung at the bottom of Jen's bed.

'Infection,' the doctor said looking at Dylan in a serious manner. Dylan caught a glimpse of himself in the mirror over the doctor's shoulder and saw the eyes of his victim's families looking back at him. Is this what it felt like for them when they waited for every word to come out of his mouth to update them on their loved ones?

'Take the drip down and wrap her in ice packs, nurse,' the doctor demanded.

Dylan didn't have time to think, as a sponge and a bowl of cold water was thrust in his hand to mop Jen's brow. He could hear Buttons' heart racing on the monitor.

'It's just hit 190 beats per minute,' Dylan said in amazement.

'I want a caesarean section, please,' Jen begged. 'I just want the baby out, now,' she screamed.

'The baby is safe enough and it is so much better for you if you can avoid having a major operation. Look,' the doctor took Jen's hand in his and sat beside her on the bed as a contraction subsided. 'Trust me, please. We'll try to proceed as we planned and I'll give you an epidural.'

Dylan stood next to Jen mopping her brow when she allowed him. She tossed and turned her head on the pillow rubbing her cheeks that now looked red and sore. The nurse gave her the gas and air apparatus for pain relief, but she was too weak to hold it. The doctor could see she felt everything as he internally examined her. By the early hours of the morning Jen was ten centimetres dilated and started to push.

The doctor tried desperately to get the ventouse on the baby's head because it was lying slightly skew-whiff, but it proved impossible.

'Prepare her for theatre, nurse,' said the doctor much to Dylan's disbelief. Dylan's heart was in his mouth and he prayed. He prayed so hard. He thanked God for what he had and begged him not to take it away from him. He even promised to be nice to Avril from now on.

'Jack, don't worry,' Jen told him in her drug-induced state. 'I'm not ... I just want to see Buttons now.'

Dylan kissed her forehead and held as her best he could in his arms.

The spinal injection seemed to take ages to take effect from the mid-chest down. Then there was a cry and Buttons was out in the big wide world. Boy did the baby howl.

'You've got a beautiful little girl,' the nurse said as she handed Buttons to Dylan. Jens eye's filled with tears as she saw her two favourite people in the world together for the first time.

'This is what matters, darling. Nothing else,' Dylan said through his sobs.

Jen started laughing through her tears. 'Until the next murder,' she said.

'And Jack, make sure you send Avril an update and flowers from me. No...from us all.'

Jack nodded. 'Hello, little Maisy,' he said to his daughter with tears spilling down his cheeks.

Lightning Source UK Ltd.
Milton Keynes UK
UKOW05f1014290614

234246UK00001B/24/P